fifty shades
of
decay

zombie erotica
edited by stacey turner

First published by
Angelic Knight Press 2013
ISBN-13:978-1482580846
ISBN-10:1482580845

ANGELIC KNIGHT PRESS

Cover Design by atrtink.com
Photography Courtesy of Depositphotos.com

Table of Contents

Foreword

Funny story. Picture Danielle Day and I hanging out at the Angelic Knight Press vendor table at KillerCon in Las Vegas in September of 2012. We're discussing with Tim Marquitz, Benjamin Kane Ethridge, and a few other authors how hard it is to make a living from writing, or even from publishing. And I add, as a joke, "I think I'm just going to give in and write some zombie porn. It's got to be good for some quick cash, right?"

And we laughed. But only for a few minutes. Then we started kicking the idea around. Well, it wouldn't be porn, of course, but what about erotica? Had anyone even done that yet? And looking at the popularity of *50 Shades of Gray*, the reading public is obviously in need of more erotica. And wouldn't there be a challenge in coming up with an erotic story using a sub-genre that is usually gory at best and disgusting at worst? Could it even be done?

Then, Ben came up with our title, *50 Shades of Decay*. After that, well, it was a done deal. We were doing this. And the idea caught on. We continued to talk about the project for the rest of the convention. I decided I'd rather edit the anthology than write a story for it. Many of the authors present at the con decided they'd write stories. And those authors delivered. You'll find stories by Mandy DeGeit, Tim Marquitz, Benjamin Kane Ethridge, Erik Williams, John Palisano, and Mike D. McCarty, all present at the convention where the idea was born.

But I wanted more (because I'm greedy like that), so we put out a sub call. And we didn't just keep it in our sandbox. I wanted horror to play with erotica, a good mix of both. So in these pages you'll find stories heavy on the horror, stories heavy on the erotica, and stories that marry both. But each

i

story is original. It literally blows my mind how some of the authors took this idea and ran with it.

I wanted 50 stories to tie in with the title, but I found a submission in the spam file after the due date, I couldn't pass up. So there are 51 stories in this anthology. 51 tales of sex and zombies, a match I doubt I could have conceived anywhere but Vegas. I think this book's beginnings more than match its finished work. It's been interesting putting it together and I hope you enjoy reading it as much as I enjoyed working on it.

I have to say thank you to all of the staff at Angelic Knight Press for their help; to all of the authors for being such good sports and writing such weird, wild, and titillating stories; and to my family for putting up with me chaining myself to my desk and editing for two weeks straight. It was a labor of love. I never dreamed in the beginning, I'd come to be so fond of this book. But that's what happened. And so, I present to you Dear Reader, 50 (plus one) shades of desire in the time of zombies ...

Stacey Turner
February 14, 2013

Rabbits

Guy Anthony De Marco

She's back again. Guilt claws at my stomach, but I had hoped she would've been killed by now. Jill was always a stubborn bitch, back when she had most of her brain intact.

We all joked about the zombie apocalypse, until one day we woke up to people turning feral. They weren't quite undead, just brain-dead from a new form of Creutzfeldt-Jakob, the human version of mad cow disease caused by genetically modified crops. The megacorps bought their way into the government so they didn't have to actually do much testing before foisting their shit on the populace. The only survivors left are those who raised organic heirloom crops. Lucky for me, my fiancée made her living by selling at farmer's markets across New York. I miss Lisa. She died two days after the population turned into packs of roving animals, killing and eating whatever moved. I saw her getting ripped to pieces by a crowd, and I ran like a fucking coward, my eyes leaking tears of terror and my bladder soaking my pants.

I thought my old apartment in Brooklyn would be the best place to hang out and wait until I got rescued or I made a decision on whether to continue this existence. The old brownstone had a massive cistern, and the roof had a decent potted garden and cages filled with rabbits thanks to the kids who had lived next door. I could survive, probably for as long as I wanted to.

I spent my time watching for survivors with my binoculars. All of the doors of the building had wrought-iron bars, thick as thumbs and embedded in the stonework. My fire escape provided me with an exit and a spot to sit and watch civilization erode around me. I thought I was the only one who could operate the ladder that went from the second floor to the filthy alley.

I had just exited the bathroom, scratching my nuts through my boxers, when I saw her. Jill, my old girlfriend, standing in the middle of the dining room, breathing heavy as though she had finished a marathon. They all breathe like that, I don't know why. Panting like overheated dogs, salivating over anything they can fit into their mouths.

I knew I was about to die. In this case, perhaps I deserved it.

I hooked up with Jill when she dated my best friend. I was drunk, but that's no excuse. We were all in Central Park, hanging out and enjoying the Perseid meteor shower. I staggered off to take a leak, and Jill followed. She watched me unzip and water a bush while she squatted a few feet away. The next thing I knew, she had me on my back and was riding me like a mad cowgirl.

From that day forward, she would climb up my fire escape ladder at random times to push me down and be her meat dildo. She never said a word. She used my willing cock as she pleased, and then she was off to be with her boyfriend. I didn't give a shit for almost a year. I was getting laid by a nympho with a surprisingly flexible body and a massive mane of auburn hair.

Jill didn't care how my day went, nor how much money I didn't have. She took what she wanted, and I was her fuck toy. The one time I tried to say something besides grunting noises, she slapped me across the face, jabbed one of her French-manicured nails into my chest enough to make it bleed, and said, "Don't."

The blood turned her on. She smeared it on her breasts and pounded herself down on my dick so hard my balls ached for the rest of the night after she left. It freaked me out, and I locked the fire escape ladder. No goodbye, no "thanks for one year of the best fucking I will ever be lucky enough to get." Just a piss-stinking alley and an out-of-sight dismissal. I heard her swearing, threatening, and finally nothing. I thought she was gone for good.

Jill launched herself across the room, knocking me over. I froze, wide-eyed with fear, like the rabbits I picked up and killed for dinner. At least the wait would be over, and someone else was making the decision for me.

She straddled me, baring her teeth at my throat. I closed my eyes, until she began to sniff my head. I stared at her face, still youthful but full of small scratches, her hair a reddish bush studded with leaves and twigs. She looked like a homeless bag-lady version of herself, until I locked on to her eyes. They were hard and cruel, and she showed her teeth until I glanced away in submission.

Her shirt and bra were missing. The only clothing left was a leather mini skirt. Her heavy breasts stirred up memories of getting wildly fucked, and my cock stirred. She felt it, and she began to sniff my body, picking up pheromones. She tore my boxers away and buried her nose in my crotch, began licking my hard shaft. I almost came right in her face, something she used to hate.

Like old times, she straddled my torso and lowered herself onto her favorite fuck toy. I lay perfectly still while she thrashed around and squeezed herself so tight around me she milked every drop of cum that I could muster. She kept on gyrating and slamming herself onto my prick; I didn't have any time to get flaccid in between filling her with my seed. Nothing leaked out, her tight pussy held everything in as though dining on sperm and it was the last meal it would have in months.

I came six times in that four-hour fucking marathon.

Jill finally let my cock go, nuzzling it and licking the balls a few times. I swear that she seemed to purr, and then she was out the window, down the fire escape, and gone from sight.

She's been back two or three times a week since her first appearance. I'm still her fuck toy. Her meat dildo. Something to be used. I understand how she must've felt when I rejected her and went after Lisa. I still feel like shit when she's done with me.

One day she'll end up killing me or getting killed herself. Until then, I sit naked, waiting in the apartment for her to arrive, sympathizing with the rabbits on the roof.

Fucking and dying, in a cage with a view. That's all life is for me and my bunnies.

Dead Things Don't Rise

Mandy DeGeit

David tripped over his own feet, staggering in his haze of intoxication, and nearly fell face first to the ground. He managed to keep his balance by grabbing the wrought iron fence that ran along beside him. His hand wrapped around the rough, flaking post as he caught his breath and squinted in an attempt to adjust his blurry vision.

"Fucking drop shots." David said as he swayed in place, a hiccup punctuating his obvious and extreme intoxication. To anyone passing by, David's slurred words may have sounded more along the lines of "Fargy lop shitz." The hiccup added the perfect drunken emphasis to the entire garbled mess.

"Home." David gazed longingly off into the dark distance towards his house. The lights along the line of trees danced like lightning bugs through his haze of booze.

David leaned against the gate and took a deep breath, straining his eyes in an attempt to regain focus. The world blurred to a fuzzy mess as the massive amounts of ingested alcohol wreaked havoc on his gastrointestinal system.

"Urk." David fought back his gorge as it threatened to rise. The acidic burn of the bile stung as it pushed its way up to the back of his throat. He swallowed hard and took a deeper breath, filling his lungs with cool night air. He loosened his grip on the fence as the world spun and swam before him. Straight as a board, David fell back to the moist ground. The air was knocked out of his lungs upon impact, and whatever little bit of control he had, over the turmoil in his stomach, was lost. A jet of rank vomit spewed from his lips, fountaining in the air above him.

Gravity took over and the stream arched, splattering down on him and saturating him in partially digested street meat, rancid alcohol and bile.

The heady smell of his own vomit caused him to gag multiple times as he fought himself into a seated position. Finally, everything left in his stomach was expelled in his lap as he vomited with his head down and chin tucked to his chest. He wrinkled his nose at the offensive liquid that had permeated his clothing.

David attempted to wipe away the chunks that clung to his shirt and pants, but as he touched the still warm, slimy pieces of what he had eaten, he felt ill again. He wiped his hands on the wet ground in an attempt to clean them and swore to himself as he tried to push himself up to his feet.

After a few moments of struggling, David was right back where he started. Holding onto the wrought iron fencing for balance, staring off in the distance and wishing he were already home.

He took a tottering step forward and slowly inched his way along the length of the fence towards the entrance of the cemetery.

The short cut home would be faster than staying on the main road, but the amount of booze in his system was a huge hindrance as David staggered and shuffled past the tombstones. As he neared the middle of the cemetery, he paused for a moment, leaning on a large cross in a poor attempt to catch his breath and compose himself.

Through the darkness of the night, he heard something off to his left. He turned his head and tried to focus on whatever was making the noise.

What is that? David wondered as he squinted off into the night. He rubbed his eyes in an attempt to clear the blurriness from his vision, momentarily forgetting about his gore-covered hands. The bile stung, tinting the whites of his eyes a deep crimson red.

"Farrrrghhhhh." David groaned, blinking as he vacated the newly formed tears down his cheeks.

"Uhhhhhh." Whatever was moving off in the distance answered David's pained grunt.

David staggered off the cemetery path and onto the grass, making his way over to the where the sound came from. As he approached the figure, he noticed it was a girl, a pretty girl at that. Her bright red hair hung to her shoulders and swayed with every drunken step she took. Her clothes and skin were dirty and disheveled and both her shoes missing. She staggered bare-footed towards David, limping slightly. She seemed to favor her right side. David assumed she must have fallen, since she seemed to be in the same state as he was. He ran a hand through his hair, in an attempt to fix his vomit-covered 'do as he trudged closer to her.

"Heyalabee" David's words were unintelligible as the booze coursing through his blood stream stole his coherence. He attempted to offer a quick wave, but nearly lost his balance. He grabbed onto the nearest tombstone for support.

"Ughablah." She said softly as she titled her head, watching him as he struggled to regain his balance.

David took a deep breath and wiped his hands down his shirt. A cold chunk of something was dislodged from his sweater and fell to the ground unnoticed. He swayed as he made his way closer to her.

"Agg." She missed a step, her legs crumpling beneath her as she fell to the ground with a throaty cry.

David reached out to catch her, his hand narrowly missing hers as she tumbled to the ground. He watched her crawl into a kneeling position and reached down to help her up. Instead of grabbing his hand, she tucked her hand between his legs, stroking his cock through his pants with a slender hand.

"Mmmm." David closed his eyes, relishing in the sensations that stemmed from her touch. His cock stiffened from within his jeans, longing for release. Instead of helping her up, David dropped to his knees in front of her.

David grabbed her by the shoulders and pulled her lithe body to his.

He kissed her, his lips meeting hers with a clumsy, drunken voracity.

She was so cold. David wondered how long she's been outside without shoes or a jacket, but the thought quickly left his mind as she slid her tongue in his mouth to meet his. David nearly gagged as her breath was unbelievably bad, but remembered he was also covered in his own vomit, so he kept his comments to himself.

He fumbled at his zipper in order to free his hardened cock for her roving hands.

David pushed her back onto the cool grass and started to undo the buttons on her shirt. Focus became a fleeting thing, as the world blurred around him. He pushed her shirt aside, revealing her pale, sunken breasts.

Beggars can't be choosers. David thought as he bent to take her nipple between his lips.

"Ughhhhhh." She moaned from beneath him as David's tongue and teeth tried to coax her nipple into a hardened state. While he worked at her flaccid breasts with his mouth, he slipped her panties down from beneath her tiny skirt with his free hand. David tossed her panties off to the side, and spread her legs as he positioned himself between them.

"Urgonna." —David's slurred words were ignored as the girl reached out and pushed David's head down to her pussy. David's tongue delved into the cool recesses of her vagina. Never once had he encountered a cunt so cold. Again the thought of how long she'd been outside crossed his mind, but only for a moment. Something slimy and alive crawled into his mouth and across his tongue. David pulled back from between her legs, spitting the mass onto the ground. A fat slug scrambled along the grass and away from the couple. David gagged and shuddered as he realized what was crawling across his tongue. *Probably crawled in from the grass, I suppose that's what you get for fucking out—*

"ARGH!" She sat up and reached out, her cool fingers wrapping around David's hard cock, distracting him from the slime-covered invertebrate that was recently in his mouth.

"Jewwanitchoogotit." David pushed her back down on the grass and spit into his hand. He lubed up his member and wiped the excess saliva along her cold pussy lips. He crawled up against her, running the head of his cock teasingly along the outside of her cunt.

"Aunnnnnng." She bucked her hips, pleading to be impaled on his thick shaft. David couldn't hold back anymore, the odd chill of her fuck hole was too much for him to handle. Her pale white blue eyes locked with his brown ones as he thrust hard into her.

"Shiiiiiiiiiit." David hissed as he sank into her. He kissed her stinking mouth and fucked her harder, feeling his balls tighten with every stroke in the cold, dry depths of her cunt.

As he started to cum, she bit down onto his tongue, drawing blood into their mouths. David ignored the love nip, as the sensations of his hot load shooting into her polar pussy were too much for him. He shuddered as his orgasm ended and his organ began to deflate, still tucked away in the frigid recesses of her now spunk sticky vagina.

David kissed her on the lips and rolled off of her, as he swallowed the coppery tang of blood that had pooled on his tongue. He panted, staring up at the clear sky as she crawled up beside him, resting her head on his shoulder and draping an ashen arm over his chest. He stroked her bright red hair as his eyes became heavy and sleep took him away from his drunken reality.

When David awoke, the redhead was still curled up against him. He watched her as she slept, thinking how beautiful she was. Her pale, blue veined skin glistened with morning dew against her shock of bright red hair. His eyes travelled down her lithe body past her pendulous breasts and to the cold cavern between her legs, into which he had ventured to the previous night. He willed his cock to rise, but there was nothing, no response from the once fully functioning member he used the night before.

"ARGH." David cried into the morning sunrise. He was looking to say, *what the fuck?* But the words didn't come out.

"Huunnngh." She stirred beside him and sat up, opening her white eyes to the morning, as she growled hello. She kissed him with her fetid mouth, her dry tongue sneaking past her rotting teeth and into his now saliva-less mouth. He pulled away from her and inspected the pallid flesh of his hand, running a finger along the lines of light blue veins. He remembered her bite as he felt the scab along his desiccated tongue and realized what had happened to him.

David finally got it.

This is why my cock won't work. David thought with a tearless sob as he looked from his withered hand, to his zombie lover and down to his shriveled penis.

Everyone knows that dead things don't rise.

Love's Lament

Kate Monroe

The question of how to seduce a zombie wasn't one Erica ever thought she would have to confront—hell, until a month or so ago she didn't even believe in them. These days, though, no one could deny the incontrovertible truth that had sunk its claws into the fragmented remnants of their society. Zombies were real, and they walked the Earth.

Why, Erica even kept one in her basement.

The rest of the neighborhood was abandoned. She hadn't seen anyone, alive or dead, for over a week. The television networks went down near the start, and the radios stopped working four days ago. It seemed everyone fled their towns to escape the onslaught, but as the panic swept through her little corner of town, the barricades she put up to keep them safe, once Scott had staggered home and told her what happened, had held firm.

Therein lay the problem. She was never lonely before, not in a world thriving on the hectic bustle of modern life. That life was gone now; all that remained was bitter, lonely despair. That was why she kept him.

Stiffs, they called them in movies. She'd looked things up in one of the books scavenged on a food run; nobody bothered to take the books when the malls had been raided. *Rigor mortis*, the textbook said. None of the textbooks, of course, explained what happened to the body if it kept moving once the heart stopped and decay set in. For that, Erica had turned to fiction.

Armed with her new knowledge, she set to work. There was only one question the books had not been able to answer definitively: how much of the person remained behind once the zombie had taken over? Erica intended to find out.

When they first moved in, Scott had fitted half a dozen bolts and locks to the door leading down to the basement. She laughed at him at the time, but now found herself grateful he had done so. They wouldn't be needed any more, though, so Erica did not bother to fasten them behind her as she slowly descended the stone steps, tense in feverish, debauched anticipation of what was to come.

No sooner had she begun to revel in the aching throb of lust threatening to her inflame her, than she shivered as a blast of chill, fetid air swirled around her bare feet and legs. It was the midst of winter, and the chill of the snowstorm had clearly begun to penetrate the lower levels of the house—and no wonder, for the only heating was the small fire she managed to fashion in the bedroom upstairs.

Even if the gas pipes had been working, she would have kept the heating off to slow the decay, something else she'd learned from the book. As it was, such precaution hadn't been necessary. One of the last broadcasts Erica heard reported the government had cut the utilities off across the worst-infested areas of the country; they did so for the safety of the surviving citizens, or so they said. She didn't care about their ulterior motives. All she cared about was the shuddering shape slowly emerging from the gloom of the dimly lit basement.

Time to put the next phase of her plan to action.

She glanced from side to side as the gentle clink of metal announced her return had been noted. The scented candles she lit, before going to change, blazed merrily, their tiny dancing flames a beacon in the darkness. They ticked off two key requirements for tonight; light for them to see by, and something pleasant to mask the malodor of vomit and decay entrenched in the basement.

Ignorant to the horror around her, Erica unleashed a low moan, and reached beneath her dressing gown to gently squeeze each of her breasts in turn when her wide eyes found what they sought. As her nipples stiffened against her deft and practiced fingers, she stared directly into his eyes in the hope of finding any trace of the man she knew.

"Hey, Scott," she said softly. "It's me, baby; it's Erica. Have you missed me?"

Scott did not answer, but the sickly gray pallor of his bloodless skin darkened as he lifted his head to watch her. For a moment, she thought she glimpsed a flicker of recognition in the impenetrable depths of his milky eyes, and her breath hitched as she took step closer.

The books she had devoured this past month might preach he was no more than a shell, an empty remnant of the man she loved; but to her he was still familiar. Despite the changes forcibly wreaked upon him, the sight of him was enough, as always, to stir an unquenchable burst of desire that wound its way through her heated veins, bringing a rush of blood to her skin as she gazed at him.

His legs and arms were bound to the heavy chair she had placed him on before he changed, but Erica didn't think Scott would disapprove. He'd been into bondage before. Maybe he still was. Of course, before the zombification she'd always been the one tied up, but things had changed now. She had to take charge of everything, including this.

His eyes fixed upon her as she shrugged away her dressing gown. The fabric pooled around her feet as the air wound itself around her bare body like a lover's embrace. Emboldened by the hunger on his face and his hoarse grunt echoing around the silent basement, she rolled her head to the side as she reached between her legs.

Erica could hold nothing back. She missed this; she missed *him*. Now he was here in front of her and hers for the taking, she could not tear her gaze away. Each flick of her thumb and forefinger against her swollen clit sent her soaring towards the climax she had been deprived of since fate had seen fit to turn her boyfriend into a monster.

Her legs were shaking wildly as tiny thrills of desperate,

painful arousal pulsed from her core, and she knew the very best way to sate them. Her touch was never enough, not when Scott was with her. All she could do now was hope he would be as able as he ever was to oblige her.

Erica fell to her knees and held her breath as she tugged at his belt buckle with her teeth. A putrid stench threatened to overwhelm her, but she gritted her teeth and focused on the task at hand. When she wrenched his trousers open, his cock sprang forth, stiff and hard, just as she had anticipated. With a heady rush of triumph, she straightened and gave her breasts another gentle squeeze, closing her eyes as she did, to imagine Scott's cold hands upon them instead, and Scott's fingers now trailing a line of fire down her abdomen to glide inside her with ease.

His groan in response seemed a forceful demand, one she had never been able to defy. She straddled his lap and placed the palms of her hands against his torn shirt to brace herself, then drove down to take the full length of his cock inside her.

If Erica tried hard enough, she could almost pretend life was as it had always been. They performed this dance so often, it was second nature to her, but even as she rocked against his cock and gave herself over to the thrill of fierce, pounding lust beating out a tattoo against her tight ribcage, Scott inadvertently wrenched her back to the here and now.

He threw his head back with a loud, gurgling roar as his jaw thrashed in a vain attempt to close around the vulnerable curve of her throat. She had to be careful, to stay out of reach of his teeth; she realized what they would do given half the chance. It wasn't time for that, not yet. Consumed by sharp and painful awareness, it was all she could do to concentrate on her body's frantic demand to be given the release she craved. The rush of pleasure was all she needed now.

One last fling, an ode to all they once had.

Life as they had known it was over. Hope fled when she'd realized what Scott was becoming. There was nothing left to live for; but Erica did have something to *die* for.

She was ready.

She pushed down against Scott's cock. He jerked, straining against the bonds. Her body quivered like a bow, teetering perilously on the edge of an orgasm she knew would rob the breath from her lungs and the blood from a heart that no longer wanted to beat.

Love lived in her heart, and it was destined to conclude in only one way. Erica couldn't help but think in that moment they were meant to finish this way. Together.

She closed her eyes.

As she came, he bit down—hard.

Together forever, just like they'd always wanted. Two zombies, one whole.

Hey, Girl

Erik Williams

--Hey girl. Did I mention how fine you looking tonight? No, I'm not just saying that. Why would I lie? I mean, you say you not feeling good but you looking ... damn, my dick's aching. Know what I'm sayin'? Yeah, I see you blushing. Pale to fire engine red at the speed of light. Shit, it's taking all my self-control not to kiss you right now. But that's how much I respect you. No way I'd push myself on someone who's not feeling well. That'd be fucked up, yo.

--Something must be going on cuz I'm getting texts and voicemails left and right. But I'm not going to check them. I'm all yours. More wine?

--Don't worry about it. I got stuff that'll get the stains out. Wine's easy to clean up in this day and age. Why don't you go freshen up? Sushi probably didn't agree with you is all. And stop it; you're sexy no matter how you feel. I'm telling you, I want you to get me sick. That's how bad I want you right now. Willing to risk the flu and everything. Just to pleasure you.

--Todd, what the fuck? You know I'm with Cindy. So what? Some people are getting sick. Big fucking deal. Yeah, yeah. Look, is it important enough to interrupt me right now? No, Todd, the answer is fucking no. You know how long I've been trying to close the deal on this snatch. I'm telling you, it's tonight. Dude, are you fucking listening to me? I said I'm getting past BJ land tonight. I'm going balls deep for sure. She's not feeling well and I'm buttering her up real nice. Probably go down on her. Make her come and boom, slip that shit right in—motherfucker, are you listening?

Fuck stop screaming, bitch, you sound like—I gotta go.

--Hey girl, how you feeling? You looking better. Little sleepy, but better. Hey, come here. Got a bit of drool hanging on your lip. There, that's better. Know what? I know what'll make you feel aces. Come here. There. That feel good? Yeah, that's what I thought. Rubbing that button always makes you quiet. Purr for me, baby.

--Shit, girl. I thought you were coming. Didn't know you were getting sick again. Don't worry. Go clean up and I'll take care of this. You know, I got to strip out of my clothes now. Maybe that was your plan all along.

--Frankie, what the fuck? Between you and Todd, I don't know who's calling and texting me more. So what? I'm dealing with a bit of a crisis here myself. Thought I was gonna take down Cindy but she's got the flu or something. Started finger banging her—by the way, her snatch is as cold as an ice cube for future reference—and then dived on that muff. She started fucking bucking and spasming. Coming like crazy, right? Nope, fucking heaving. Next thing I know, I got red wine and sushi puked all over my back. Figure this shit ain't happening tonight. I'll just take the BJ and let her go home and eat some soup or some shit. Frankie, did you hear a word I said? Of course, not, you're too busy worrying and repeating the news to me. Well, why the fuck did you call if you didn't want to talk. One way conversation with you ALL THE FUCKING TIME!

--Hey girl. You want me to take you home? Look like you could use a hot bath and some sleep.

--You okay? Hello? How about you come sit and chill a minute? Collect your thoughts. I'll get you some water.

--Small sips. There you go. Hard to talk, huh? Throat sore? Nod for yes. Don't feel like nodding? Achy neck, huh?

--Let me text this asshole real quick: IT'S NOT THE ZOMBIE APOCALYPSE, DOUCHE! Sorry, Frankie's just being a tool. At least Todd stopped calling.

--Hey girl, I know you're not feeling well and all and I'm gonna take you home right quick. But I got to say, and I don't think I'm trying to be an asshole, but you got all sexied up and I got all worked up rubbing the sweet clit of yours. And licking it, good god I almost came just tasting you. But you know, I didn't, as much as I wish I did.

You know that myth about blue balls? Well, that shit ain't no myth. My boys be hurting bad. And I'm just looking at you now, how your mouth is hanging open and that drool be dangling and, man, I can't help but want to stick my dick in there. I know, I know. I'm talking with my dick. But that's what you do to me, baby. Make me want to do dirty things to you.

--You sure you okay with this? I mean, we don't have to. I can take care of myself. Maybe rub one out looking at them banging titties of yours. Say no or shake your head now.

--Hey girl, your mouth feels good. Nice and wet. Cold, but wet. Yeah. Love how you just letting me do everything. Such a turn on. Feel how hard I am? Course you do. Like it when I move your head back and forth? Like me making you do stuff? Yeah, you do. Bet you don't want to go home at all. Bet you want me to take my dick and jam it in you. Say no— oh you can't, can you. Cuz you're taking it so good.

--Damn girl, I didn't think you could take it that deep. And no gagging. Man, I almost came when I felt how tight your throat was. Can I do it again?

--Yeah, baby. That's it. Keep taking it. Tell me when to stop.

--I'm almost balls deep, baby. God, I'm gonna come. I'm gonna come right down your fucking throat—

--AH, FUCK FUCK FUCK—WHAT THE FUCK—I'M BLEEDING—FUCK—WHAT'D YOU DO—FUCK— OH CHRIST OH SWEET CHRIST!

--Frankie, you there? Look man. I can barely talk. Pretty weak right now. Will you shut the fuck up and listen? I know, all right. I know. Cindy's one. She hurt me pretty bad. I'm bleeding and hiding in the bathroom. Popped a half bottle of Advil to kill the pain. Fuck you, I ain't telling you what happened. All you need to know is she's one and she hurt me bad and I need your ass to come here and get me out of here.

--On my own? Fuck you, I'm on my own. You still owe me for bailing your ass out of jail.

--I can hear her Frankie. She sniffing at the door. Come on, man. If I don't get to a hospital, I'm gonna fucking bleed to death.

--Frankie? Frankie?

--Hey girl, I can hear you sniffing. Pawing. It's okay. I get it now. I guess I got what I deserved, huh? Wasn't very gentlemanly what I did. And you being a zombie and all— shit, who could make something like that up?

--At least I'm numb now. Can't feel anything below the waist. That's not even the worse part. None of it. The pain, the numbness. The worst part is the cold. I'm so fucking cold.

--Not much longer now, girl. You can stop that sniffing and pawing. Won't be anything for you to chew on soon. Hell, I'll be like you probably. Motherfuckin' zombie. Ha!

--Hey girl. I just want you to know I'm sorry and shit. Wish this could have worked out differently. I'll see you on the other side in a few.

To Kiss the Bride

Rebecca L. Brown

"I was married once," I told her. This girl I'd never met before. We crouched amongst the ruins of some other person's life. The upturned sofa, cushions torn and tumbled loose. We rested our backs against the debris, catching our breath. No light—although only a few would have eyes enough to see it. There are monsters more dangerous than the undead. Monsters more familiar. I hear them some nights calling to each other as they find their pleasure in the blood of others. Live or undead—they shoot for both. I'd move on, if I thought things would be different somewhere else.

The girl—she wasn't one of them. No. Her clothes were old and worn and filthy—like mine—the body underneath too lean. Her eyes too wary. She watched me and I understood she recognized in me the weariness she felt. The ache of sleepless nights and long unlovely days.

"Are you alone?" She asked—and I answered.

"Yes. I am now. I was married once." I'd kept the ring long after it had fallen from my finger. I wore the memory on a strip of cloth around my neck as if to keep her with me—my Vanessa. I had learned never to wish she was with me. She was dead—or else undead. Better not to know which one. Better not to have to place the bullet in her once sweet skull ...

"I ... I never was." She said. "And now I never will be." There was a longing in her. Had there been some man or other she had waited for impatiently—or else a woman? Had she dreamed of off-white frills and bridesmaids diving for a thrown bouquet of flowers?

You may kiss the bride—

"I don't want to die without—"

Yes. She had waited—and now?

"I don't want—" to die in the hands and mouths of rotted corpses, or else as the prey of street gangs without knowing—

Once, she had been beautiful. I saw that, now I knew to look for it.

"I—"

We kissed—or else, I kissed her and she didn't pull away. Instead, she pressed herself into me. Clung to me as if my touch—my warmth—was everything she had ever needed to feel.

"Not here. This way." I took her hand—or else she gave her hand to me.

The bathroom, ruined, like everywhere else. Everything else—except for her. I locked the door behind us—that it still closed was a wonder in itself.

And then—

I kissed her again. Pulled her close so we shared each other's warmth.

"I—"

"Shh." I had to guide her hands. She let me. Let me press my lips into her throat. Her chest. And then—the way she tasted.

"Oh …" A sigh, almost. Her fingers pressed me down and held me there. Pulled me in closer. When I pulled away, she moaned again.

"Please—" We kissed again. I slipped my tongue between her lips and let her taste herself. My hands explored her body, pausing here and there to tease—and then, I slipped inside her. Made her moan again. Again. Her fingernails sinking deep into my shoulders. Deep enough to draw a little blood.

* * * *

We lay together, our bodies bare against the cold, cream

plastic of the bathtub. Neither of us moved—why would we want to? Where would we go?

"Melissa." She said—and for a moment I misheard her. Almost, but not quite. Perhaps I wanted her to be somebody else—just for a moment.

"Here. I—" I slipped the shoelace cord from round my neck and over hers. Not quite a marriage, but—

She smiled unsurely. Frowned as if not quite sure she understood what I had given her—or what I wanted in return.

"I don't expect—"

She smiled. "It's okay."

Not quite the wedding of her dreams, I thought, abruptly conscious of my ruined body. How the ribs showed through my skin. The sores which itched beneath my hair.

Perhaps she had the same thought, although I didn't see her that way. No. I beheld instead her pale blue eyes, the fading flush which bloomed across her cheeks.

Eventually, the girl—Melissa—moved away. Stood awkwardly in the small space between the fixtures and redressed herself in rags—a backwards Cinderella returning to her squalor from a short escape to—

No. I smiled. I was no handsome prince. Not anymore. Although once I was good enough, perhaps, to earn a second look from pretty girls.

It was only then I heard the noise, or else realized I had— the sound of scratching at the door. They must have heard us. Heard her. The undead, drawn over to our hiding place by the sounds of the stolen moment of pleasure we had shared.

"Oh—" She heard them too. I wondered if, like me, she had forgotten. "Oh." She caught her lower lip between her teeth.

I forced a smile. A shrug.

"They can't get in." I didn't know that—couldn't know— but the words reassured her. "If we're quiet enough, they'll go away." Perhaps they would. Some other sound or movement might steal away their attention if we waited long enough.

What other choices did we have? To open the door after all this time? To let them in?

I held her again, enjoying her warmth against my chest despite the way the scratching seemed to echo through us, filling up the tiny room despite the smallness of the sound.

"I—"

"Shh ..." I told her for a second time. No need for words. Not now. Not when instead we had our warmth. The touch of living flesh, one person to another.

Body Bag

Shaun Meeks

David stood in front of the dented steel door taking in a deep breath, knowing that the other three men watched him. No doubt they were curious as to the type of man he might be. Well-groomed and well dressed, but he gave nothing else away. Taped up at eye level was a paper sign with a sad attempt at script that read, "Candy."

"A few rules, champ," one of the men said. David turned and noticed the larger of the three, the one he had given the money to, spoke. "First, you can hit, cut, choke, or fuck her. It's all good. But if you fuck her, dong bags are on the night table along with rubber gloves and dental dams. We don't want a mess."

"How thoughtful." David smirked.

"Hey, we like repeat customers, and I know once you get a taste of Candy, you'll come back. Enjoy yourself. Clock's ticking!"

David opened the door and was immediately greeted by a scent familiar to him. He tried not to react too strongly as the odor of decayed flesh and the sweetness of baking bread filled his nostrils. He stepped into the room, shut the door and let the intoxicating aroma engulf him, closing his eyes and just breathing it in.

He felt himself throbbing, pulsating.

It was perfection.

Reminding him of work, only better.

He licked his lips, thinking of his nights in the coroner's office, alone with the cold, naked and vulnerable. How often had he caressed icy, hard flesh, slid his moist finger into a fatal knife or bullet wound while stroking himself? He had photos in his house of some of them; their beauty falling away from their faces as the muscles had given up trying to keep up the charade.

Death excited him.

The cold skin against his, the smell of blood spoiling and tissue decaying.

Yet he had always wanted more.

Now, he had the opportunity for just that.

Lying on the bed before him was an exquisitely built woman; long, smooth legs, subtle breasts, a tight stomach, and full blonde hair. Her skin was grey, her underside purplish-black where the blood had settled. The only imperfection he spotted—a patch of skin someone had flayed from her, possibly the man before him. The flaw didn't bother him in the least. It made her more beautiful, in fact.

Slowly, he reached his hand toward her bare stomach, his body electric with utter excitement. He studied her face as his fingertips neared her skin, saw her turn her head to gaze at him. She opened her mouth at the sight of him, exposing toothless gums.

How considerate. They really have thought of everything.

She moaned as his warm, soft fingers caressed her icy, grey skin. He gasped at the sensation, gliding them along to her back where the blood had pooled, the skin a little more unyielding there. He grabbed hold of her waist, his fingertips pressing deep into her back and he could feel the hardened spot crackling as the coagulated blood loosened.

This was a dream come true.

Night after night, working in the glare of fluorescent lights and looking down at whatever dead woman he found himself inside, he always wanted more—something impossible. His need for cold flesh, the scent of cells coming apart, degenerating to become no more than dust, would make some question his sanity. If word got out of how he found love in the lifeless, he was sure he'd not only lose his job, but his reputation as well.

Still, he longed and lusted for it, yet he wanted something even more.

What he wanted was impossibility.

Yet here she was. Perfection.

"You are wonderful," he whispered to her as she moaned and moved under his touch.

"You are a miracle."

There had been rumours, reports on the news from people here and there, usually in some small town. Bodies rising from the dead. Not in swarms, not like a cheesy drive-in movie, just random cases. The word zombie seemed so silly, like saying werewolves or vampires existed. And as a medical doctor, the thought seemed even more absurd.

There was no denying Candy though.

She was moving, moaning, asking to be pleased.

And she was dead.

David knelt down beside the narrow bed, close to her and she thrashed against the restraints that held her limbs.

"Shhh ..." he whispered, kissing her soft thigh, his nostrils filling with the heady scent of her. "You're alright. I'm not going to hurt you. Not like the others. You are too beautiful to ever hurt."

He slid his tongue down her thigh, tasting her, undoing his pants as shivers raced over his body. He licked the bottoms of her feet, then stood and let his slacks fall to the ground, exposing himself to her.

"Don't worry, Candy. I'll make sure this feels as good to you as it will for me."

He knelt on the bed, between her spread legs and pulled his shirt off. He wanted to be inside her so badly, to have her soft, tight, velvet-like pussy squeeze down on him until he exploded inside her, but he'd paid for an hour with her, and he wanted to make the experience last.

He let his finger slide up her thighs toward the small tuft of blonde hair between her legs. The hair was trimmed and looked like she had died shortly after a Brazilian wax, and he wondered what she had been like when alive.

God! She really is dead, isn't she? Dead, but alive.

The concept made him that much more excited and he moved his head down toward the patch of hair.

His lips gently grazed her inner thigh.

He moved his mouth toward her waiting pussy, so gently her hair tickled his lips at first. She smelled wonderful. None of the women he had taken on the cold steel beds of the hospital ever smelled this good, this real.

She smelled like a living woman, the pheromones coming from deep inside her, mixed with her dying skin, combining to drive him closer to the point of losing control.

He spread her lips, releasing more of the intoxicating aroma and slid his fingers inside.

"You're a bit dry. But that's okay, happens to everybody. Let's see what I can do about that."

David pushed two fingers into her, taking her clit into his mouth, licking and sucking as he thrust his fingers in and out of her.

She seemed to moan louder, the pitch of her voice changing.

She was enjoying it.

Loving it.

Perfect.

Fucking someone dead, cold and decaying was wonderful, but having them still able to move, moan and react was so much better. Amazing.

His saliva mixed with her own wetness, slicking his chin and fingers. He moved even faster as his cock throbbed achingly.

He couldn't wait any longer.

David hovered over her for only a second, the head of his cock just barely touching her cool skin. He gazed down at her face, her skin beautiful, despite the discolouration of her flesh, and her blood filled eyes, even though they seemed unable to focus on him. She moaned, and he realized she wanted him as much as he wanted her, and could wait no longer, pushing himself into her wet pussy.

It was tight, and cold, as though she was full of ice cubes, a slight warmth came from the friction of his movements.

He thrust hard into her, pulling out slowly, letting her feel each pulse of his cock. His hands slid up the hollow under her ribs to her nipples, toying with them. He brushed his fingers against her lips, pushing them into her mouth.

She moaned and sucked on them, her toothless mouth gnawing at them. He smiled, loving the sensation as his other hand twisted a puckered, grey nipple. As dead as she might be, he felt her respond.

She raised her ass off the bed and moaned, seeming to beg for more.

His orgasm swelled, getting ready to burst inside her. He wanted to hold back, to make the moment last, but Candy suddenly cried out, moaning and shaking and he knew she was cumming on him.

The sensation was too much.

He clenched his teeth as he came, gripping her hips hard, feeling the skin sliding loosely on the bone as the muscles were no long holding her together as they should. It was exquisite, the combination of his hot cum filling her and her cold muscles clenching in a delicious rhythm. Breathless, he pulled out to watch his cum oozing out of her.

I could love her, he told himself as he began to get dressed. As he did, he glanced at Candy's sweet face, her mouth opening and closing as though trying to speak. He had no doubt she was trying to express her love for him.

"Don't worry, Candy. I think I love you too." He walked towards the door and turned back to her one last time. "I'm going to talk to your boss and buy you a life with me. It'll be just like that movie I saw years ago. I'll make an honest—"

A pain exploded in his stomach, echoing through his body. He screamed and fell to the ground, fiery pain coursing through him. David tried to stand, but his legs had given up and he collapsed again just before the door burst open and two men charged in, guns drawn.

"What the fuck's wrong? I thought she'd gotten you?"

The big guy said, holstering his gun and leaning over him. David tried to speak, tried to tell him ...

But all he could do was moan.

"Oh shit!"

"What?"

"This idiot! Check the garbage."

"Nothing. Ah, shit. She's leaking all over the bed!"

"Fucking moron, bare backing a body bag. He's infected."

David moaned, writhing with pain.

"You tell these people a simple thing and they don't listen."

He stood up and was silent for a moment.

"Okay Sammy, run and get me the wet vac from the van. I'm going to give Candy a quick clean up before the next client comes."

"What about him?" Sammy asked when he returned. He stared down at David as the man slowly died.

"Take him in the room next door. Strip him down and cuff him to the bed. Eventually we're going to get some freak that wants to fuck a dude."

Sammy and another man began to drag David out as he screamed. The pain became worse with the movement, light flashing behind his eyes in small bursts. He wanted to plead with these men, beg them to stop, but he couldn't speak. Each breath he took burned his chest and brought tears to his eyes. What they had said was madness. He wasn't dead, or infected, just sick.

They had to help him.

"Oh, and when you get him strapped down, use these." He tossed pliers to his partner, with a sinister grin. "He'll make a great little cocksucker."

Playing a Game

Eric Stoveken

The streets of Philadelphia looked like a slaughterhouse. Blood stained lampposts and broken windows lined viscera strewn sidewalks as packs of zombies roved the streets. Chaos reigned. Society had collapsed within the city limits as quarantine had been become a death sentence for anyone still living.

Eight stories above Market Street, Michael Saunders—the man who was partially responsible for the apocalyptic hellscape—couldn't bring himself to care about the nightmare outside. He didn't speculate about the possibility the reanimated abominations would inevitably breach the fortified lobby of his apartment building, swarm the stairwells, and make their way into the apartment he and Dawn shared.

They existed in a state of denial fueled by pure carnal bliss. Perversely, their confinement had become a vacation. Their work in the lab had afforded little time together as a couple. The intellectual rigors of their project to create a rejuvenation serum had often left them too exhausted to revel in the more physical pleasures the world had to offer.

Now, confined to their apartment with rations enough for several weeks, Dawn seemed to have turned her full attention to their sex life. This newfound libidinous streak kept Michael from contemplating the horrors outside. Even when Dawn's occasional uncoordinated stagger reminded him of his possible role in the madness, his worries soon melted under her eager touch.

It could've been a coincidence. After all, the small amount

of BL-6 compound he had used to revive Dawn after a blood clot had its deadly way with her was all that had ever been created. There was no reasonable way Dawn's resurrection from death led to the grotesqueries of the last several weeks.

What was more, she was nothing like the walking cadavers in the streets outside. She remained Dawn: articulate, graceful, and sexy as hell. She had no discernible craving for human flesh.

At least, not in any carnivorous or deadly fashion. The only observable side effects had been a slight diminishment of physical coordination, periodic slurring of words and, of course, the unhinged desire to fuck Michael within an inch of his life.

As morning dawned on the fourth day of the quarantine, Michael awoke to the sight of Dawn in his favorite satin slip, her hair still tousled from the previous night's escapades. She loomed over him at the bedside with a disjointed smile on her face and a length of rope of in her hands. "Shall we play a little game, love?" she asked.

The question was rhetorical as she immediately straddled his chest. The slip rode up on her thighs. Her naked sex pressed against him. He placed his hands above his head and allowed her to tie his wrists to the headboard. She slinked down his body, running her nails across his flesh, drawing the slightest hint of blood in places. Michael inhaled sharply followed by a trembling shuddering exhalation.

Dawn straddled his hips, grinding against him, and fully arousing him from sleep. "The game goes like this. You tell me the naughtiest thing you've ever done. If I think you're lying I'll punish you." She accentuated this point with a hard slap across Michael's face that caught him off guard. "If I think you're telling the truth, I will … reward you." This second point she emphasized by sliding herself up and down the length of his hard cock.

"Um … okay. Let me think."

"Don't take too long. Hundreds of cannibalistic undead might bust in here at any moment. Would be a shame if I didn't have a chance to fuck you one last time before they tear you apart."

Michael recoiled as best he could in his bound position. "Whoa there, babe. That was a little dark."

Dawn shrugged and continued to grind against him. "You're still hard."

"True enough." Michael didn't waste too much more time thinking. "Promise you won't get mad?"

She ground against him harder, almost allowing him to slip inside of her. "You never know. Besides, you might like it if I get mad."

"A couple of years ago when you had passed out after a night of serious tequila consumption, I had my way with you while you slept." Michael eyed her, awaiting a response. Initially, there was none. "So, do you believe me? Or do you think I'm lying?"

Shifting her hips, she impaled herself on him with a satisfied growl. "Oh, I believe you. Do you know why?" He shook his head. "Because I was only pretending to be asleep." As she spoke, Dawn increased the pace and intensity of her gyrations. "I let you drag me to the edge of the bed, dangle my legs over the side, spread my thighs and use my body like the piece of meat that it is."

Her confession and dirty talk pushed Michael to the brink of orgasm, a brink from which she deftly pulled him back. She was not through with him yet.

From somewhere outside, came the sound of gunfire and a scream as another thug with delusions of survival was overwhelmed by the undead horde. The noise startled Michael who craned his neck to glance at the window.

His attention was redirected when a vicious slap came across the face, rattling his entire skull and rocking his head all the way to the other side. "Pay attention when I'm fucking you!" Dawn bellowed, her lip turned up in a violent sneer. It took her an extra moment to calm down and in that moment Michael realized the look was not just a sneer, but a baring of teeth.

As Michael tested his bonds, Dawn brought herself under control. "Back to the game. My turn. Do you want to hear the naughtiest thing I've ever done?"

"Yes?"

"Aren't you sure, Michael? Are you getting scared, Michael? I think you're going a little bit soft inside me, Michael. But you, like me, are just a piece of meat and I can make your body do what I want, can't I?"

She leaned in close to him, wrapped a hand around his throat and started nibbling on his ear, all the while milking his cock with her well-developed kegel muscles.

As his body responded she whispered in his ear, "See? Gunfire and death in the streets, you trapped in your own bed, and an increasingly irrational lover on top of you and still you are throbbing hard. I own you."

She brought herself upright again and laughed. "So I guess it's my turn then."

She made a coy little show of pretending to think about her answer before looking Michael in the eyes and coldly declaring, "I caused the zombie outbreak." She continued fucking him with a vigor his body could not deny.

"How?"

"It's amazing how much BL-6 a girl can synthesize when she's not afraid to kill for the necessary components."

"What?!"

"I soaked the ground of all the best cemeteries. I snuck into morgues and injected quarts of the stuff into every corpse I found. It's in their saliva now. Surviving death is a contagion thanks to me."

"Why?"

"For the same reason those poor bastards are killing and eating any living person they come across; because I hate you. We all hate you. You can delude yourself all you want, but I am one of them. I am a zombie. You are fucking a zombie and your body doesn't care, because your body is a slab of meat that loves what my cunt is doing.

"I don't understand. Why—"

"Imagine finding out you are an electrical impulse. Your body can't hold a charge and off you go. You are nothing and everything at the same time.

Maybe some people are prepared and melt into the cosmos and are fine, but face facts. Humans have strong egos. We define ourselves as ourselves, identity is everything, and as we go crackling through the air with no anchor with which to associate ourselves we *envy* the living with a longing that changes almost immediately to hate."

Even as she was describing her loathing for Michael and all living people, Dawn continued to ride him. She expertly manipulated his body, causing him to physically react even as his mind was recoiling in unmitigated terror.

"The dead hate the living with more force than you can imagine, because as a living person you can only conceive of the power of a hydrogen bomb or the Big Bang. Until you've been dead, you don't comprehend hate."

"But the BL-6 brings them back. Shouldn't they be happy?"

"You think this is the same as being alive? You think simply re-entering this recharged bundle of neurons is the same as life? It's like operating a machine. We know how this thing works, but it doesn't quite happen. It's not effortless anymore. Every motion requires thought and that thought is of forcing a pile of meat to move. As much as we hated being dead, being trapped in this bloody costume is a million times worse.

"What's more, you can only make this thing work as well as you understand it. I'm doing okay, because I know the body well, and you applied the BL-6 quickly. Twenty minutes of death felt like a hundred years, but I still remembered how this sack of flesh works.

"Even so, nothing is the same. I may be better off than them when it comes to the physiology, but the endocrinology is different. They sort of understand the mechanics, they can sort of walk, they can grasp and they can feed and they can look out through gelatinous eyes and recognize the world around them. However, none of us can feel in the irrational chemical way of the living."

Michael couldn't believe what he was hearing. "Dawn, you need to fight this. You'll be okay. You've been okay so far, you just need to—"

"Do you think I can ever love you again? Ridiculous. I recognize I once loved you, and I realize what that once meant, and I remember how that felt when ... I ... *could ... feel!*" Again, she drove her point home with increased sexual vigor, humiliating Michael with how easily she made his body ignore their circumstances.

"That is irrelevant now. I can't make my heart flutter at the sight of you. I can't give myself the warm glow in the pit of my stomach. All I can do is glare at the man who has trapped me in this prison of flesh, and sense the hate vibrate within me.

"I now know we are all just electrified meat. Steaks and chops and quarts of blood given the illusion of life by chance electrons coursing through this buffet. We, the dead, eat you the living because we want you to experience what we do, and because we still hate you."

Michael couldn't take any more. He began to weep. Dawn gazed down on him, her face no longer bothering to convey any semblance of emotion. She kept fucking him, urging his body towards orgasm. "Perhaps that wasn't the naughtiest thing I've done."

Michael opened his mouth to say something, but words failed. A thud sounded in the hallway, shuffling footsteps, doors being clumsily opened. "Before I woke you up, I went to the lobby and destroyed the barricade. I wasn't joking when I said hundreds of the undead might bust in here at any minute."

Dawn stared at him with both contempt and idle curiosity. "All the same, I bet I can still get you off before they get here."

I Was Legend

Jake Elliot

Robbie Neville couldn't believe his good luck. With his jeans pulled around his ankles, he sat bare-butt on the abandoned bar at the old biker clubhouse he'd frequented before the world turned to shit. Here in the sleepy town of Altus, Oklahoma, he was on the verge of rapture, receiving the best head of his life from the hottest girl to ever ride the back of his bike. Glancing over the curve of his protruding belly, the young woman in pigtails rooted all the way down on his slick pole. He didn't know her name and didn't care— was she even legal—did it matter? Again, he didn't really care, for forty-five year old Robbie, life had never been this good– –not ever.

His eyes rolled back in ecstasy, "Damn baby, you could suck start my Harley any day of the week!" Only Robbie never owned a Harley. He rode a Honda Rebel he'd bought back in '92. He was younger then, less rounded. Hell, now weighing nearly 300-pounds, he weighed almost as much as the bike he rode.

Even riding the ole' Reb, he'd still gotten his fair share of pussy. The gang he'd once ridden with used to tease him for his girly bike. Where were they all at now? Robbie didn't want to think about it. Still, his old gang's opinion of his Rebel never stopped the girls from wanting a ride. Gas, grass, or ass, baby, no one rides 'Doc' Robbie's bike for free. Even now, with the world as it is, his rules still apply.

The girl servicing him, her hip-huggers might very well have been painted on. When she walked, her ass dazzled the mind like liquid gold. Possessing a gymnast's body—lithe, sleek and built for any activity that could last all night long, Robbie knew he didn't need that much time. Hell, at this rate, if he lasted another thirty seconds ...

She looked up at him with big blue eyes watering, he wanted to grab those long blonde pig-tails and explode right there. Then, against the door ... *bang-scrape* ... an uninvited sound. She pulled up and off of him, wiping saliva from her mouth. She blinked and fear flashed in her pretty eyes.

"Oh, come on *baybee!*" He kicked off one old sneaker with his other foot while trying to free his thick legs from the black denim bunched at his ankles. "I'm ready to give you everything in the *world.*"

Her pig-tails swished from side to side. "You said we wouldn't get caught here." Her Oklahoman twang rose Rob's stub nearly half an inch more, "You said we'd be safe."

He grinned, showing brown tobacco-stained teeth. His East Texas dialect rolled out thick as he pointed to the wall where a Confederate flag hung, emblazoned with a grinning white boar wearing Ray Bans, "Look honey, I used to run with the gang who owned this bar. That door is steel-framed. The damn thing's so tough it'd take SWAT or the gawd-dang Air Force to blow that door down. Those ... those people out there ... they ain't gettin' in here. Not without a stick of dynamite."

Groaning much like the people outside, he stretched over his immense belly in a grueling effort to pull off the stubborn pants hung up around his feet. "Now come on ova' here and tend to my stick o' dynamite." He shook his stubby cock at her with a meaty hand.

"I don't know," her tone reflected doubt. A louder bump sounded against the door, and an awful moaning followed. Like a chain reaction, several more moans echoed from the first. She asked, her tone still doubtful, "Are you sure ain't no one else but you in all of Oklahoma?"

"Hey," he opened up his arms. He was losing his erection. He'd get it back once she took off those jeans. Trying not to sound desperate, he added, "Who did you see in Lawton, hmm? All those deadbeats, and that's it for Lawton. Even with the army base right there, who showed up to save you? I rode in like a knight on a black horse. I swooped you up and got you here. Things sure ain't looking any better for Altus." His charmless smile cracked through a mangy beard—his chubby cheeks forced his eyes to narrow, squinting lines.

She nodded, her blue eyes lighting with an idea, "So if I'll show you some real love over on the pool table, you'll take me on your bike anywhere I want to go?"

Trying to match her sweetness, he said, "New York or Los Angeles, I'll make it happen." He sounded a bit froggy, so he cleared his throat. He really wanted to make this sell.

"How are we going to get out of here with all those guys out front?" she began to unbutton her tight pink sweater, starting at the lowest button.

He felt the rush of blood to his head as he hopped down from the wooden bar. He stumbled with euphoric dizziness while telling, "Behind the bar there's a trapdoor in the floor. An escape hatch was built here at the clubhouse in case the law raided and VIPs needed a way out. The tunnel ends right beside where I parked the bike." He whipped the black Tap-Out t-shirt up over his head and his man-breasts jiggled. He tossed the tee over his shoulder and stood buck naked.

The girl managed to keep one button hooked, the one in the center of her chest. Her hands poised over the last button, she said, "Get on up there, cowboy."

"Ooh wee!" He squealed, looking a lot like the bleach-white pig on the banner over the door, only with a beard, and without cool sunglasses.

She sauntered back, giving a little jiggle as she pranced, asking, "What's my name?"

"Huh?" Robbie expressed, his jowls drooping from his cheeks.

"You an' me, we're gonna re-populate the world, right?" He nodded, his eagerness shining like headlamps in his eyes. She unbuttoned the last hold and the sweater popped open. She was blessed with plump, creamy breasts dotted with soft pink nipples, and she asked again, "What is my name?"

Smiling, with chew tobacco stained teeth, "Oh, not now baby, we are almost to heaven."

"You know the old sayin' about the last man on Earth?" Her country accent made it sound as if she'd said, "Arth." She inched close to the door and finished, "The one about if you was the last man on Arth, I'd *still not do you*. You know that one?"

He rolled himself off the table, "Baby, you best come over here and pay tribute to the man who's got the bike. I'll *take* what I want and leave you here as sloppy seconds for those things outside. I ain't gotta take you nowhere."

Her hand shot out, twisting the steel lever that released the dead bolt. *Clank!* It slid back into the door. "You crazy bitch! What are you doing?" He stepped forward totally naked, hoping to stop her, but knowing he'd never make it.

"Crazy bitch!" She mimicked while whipping open the door. She stood behind the door as Robbie Neville screamed a high-pitched and frightful wail. From the other side of the door flooded in the rotting undead.

The stink of decomposing meat reached Robbie as the door swung wide. Turning, he saw the girl gagging by the door. With his belly jiggling, he ran over to where his pants lay by the barstool as an army of shambling, hungry dead filed into the empty pub.

As arms reached out for his portly form, naked 'Doc' Robbie shoved his heavy body through the first wave of rotting corpses like a bowling ball rolls through ten pins. His head spun with nausea as rotting flesh broke free and smeared across his naked body.

Wiping putrid undead jelly off his bare arms, Robbie stood cornered near the once lit satellite jukebox. Ignored in the sky above, satellites hovered over the earth, waiting for an Earth-based signal to relay down to this candle-lit bar. There were no more transmitters—every electrical sender and receiver on Earth was dead. Dead permanently, the true opposite of the shambling meat with teeth, and grasping claw-like hands.

Dead like the naked man holding his pants in his hands.

"You bitch!" He insulted one last time while watching her rush to the other side of the bar. She dropped the board at the service well, blocking the two zombies reaching out for blond pig-tails. She dipped down vanishing from sight, but not before he'd stolen one last eyeful of her still unbuttoned sweater. He heard the latch of the trapdoor slide open, and then the creak of hinges as the old door opened. It should have been his exit. This was his club before the walking dead took over the world.

The undead stumbled closer to the naked fat man. How did the dream so close to true shift into this living nightmare? Not full breasts propped behind a pink sweater, but nails which were filthy from clawing up from the grave, reaching out to grab Robbie Neville. Not pretty blues, but lifeless blank eyes—some shriveled and others bloated in varying shades of decay—each staring out at nothing. Moans and gnashing teeth chittered as the fetid meat shambled ever closer to their next meal.

In a desperate attempt to cannonball through the clumsy ranks of the undead, Robbie avoided being grappled by claws, yet long streaks of red skin raked across his fat body as clawed fingers failed to keep hold. He'd knocked the first three backwards and made a daring leap to try and catapult his thick body over the bar.

He kicked off with all his might, but Robbie didn't have the momentum to clear the smooth wooden barrier. Gravity proved to be the greater force. Half over the bar, he looked down and saw the trap door open and waiting for him. Behind him, his giant hairy butt pointed to the mob of shambling horrors. An unwelcomed hand grabbed the inside of his thigh.

"Uhhhnggg," moaned the eternal hungry like a chorus without tune.

Kicking frantically, he pulled himself atop the bar as another pair of clawed hands latched onto an ankle, allowing the first zombie to bite deep into his rump. His immense belly squeaked against the polished wood as the eternally ravenous yanked him backwards and to the floor. Body after body fell upon his naked form. Buried under the exhumed bodies of the living dead, Robbie Neville's legendary night had turned foul.

As he shrieked in pain, as terror held him in its rancid embrace, he heard the electric start of his trusty Rebel firing loudly outside. Blood spilled freely from where teeth tore into his body. Robbie struggled momentarily, but as the bike sped off outside, so fled his hope and soon after his life.

* * * *

She felt the night air rushing through her hair, her pig-tails flapping streamers. Bare breasted, her open sweater flapped at her back like a superhero's cape. Riding the little Rebel like a Valkyrie shooting from the gates of Asgard, the little bike ate the road with a vengeance.

The night sped past at breakneck speeds while Angela's mind hung suspended in a vacuum of empty thoughts. I sucked off a fat man and he didn't even know my name. What a loser!

Now I'll need to stop for mouthwash. I'm done with Oklahoma; maybe I'll meet a real cowboy in Texas ...

... and her thoughts went on and on ...

Lord and Lady

Tarl Hoch

The silence of the mansion bothers Halitus far more than he is willing to admit. As his unsteady tread echoes off the rotten wood, he resists the urge to glance over his shoulder to see if he is being followed. The locals hadn't attempted to breach their treaty with him for a few months now, and their continued cooperation was starting to make Hal second-guess killing the last party they had sent up.

As he passes through slivers of silvery moonlight, sharp as knives across the rotting carpet, he stops at one of the tall windows. One hand plays with a tiny figure of Pluto on a rawhide cord around his neck. Halitus watches the moonlight play off the pendant before looking out at the land around the mansion.

The estate had been his father's and his father's-father's. This plantation, unlike anything else ever seen at the time his father had finally given up his grip on life, and he had inherited it. His mother had soon followed the path of her mate, leaving Hal to face the cold nature of the world around him.

Below, he observes the groundskeepers going about their work under the gaze of the glowing silver orb in the sky. Weeds are removed, and what few plants remain are carefully pruned and watered. One of the workers looks up at the house. The man's mandible is missing, his tongue lolling out of his neck like a shriveled slug. One eye is missing as well, and Hal makes a note to check on the worker tomorrow night. It wouldn't go well to let decay set in too far before repairing the normal wear and tear.

Pulling away from the window, Hal continues down the hallway. He passes lamps of witch-fire that glow in their sconces, their sickly green light making the shadows dance around them.

Halitus tries to whistle a tune, but the sound dies on his lips almost as soon as it starts. Motor control of that type seems to be failing him more and more as of late. He grins to himself; living forever was proving to be more work than he had anticipated. But the task kept him busy when the locals were quiet.

At the end of the hallway, his cold hands grasp the edge of the doorway as he heaves himself through the opening. His eyes come upon the library, and his heart leaps, despite its sluggish beat. The room was his treasure, not his father's. Hal had built it up from the near empty shelves until they had threatened to burst like maggot-infested flesh.

With fingers worn almost to the bone, he caresses the ancient spines as he passes, sometimes stopping to trace the fading lettering imprinted in the leather. There were treasures contained here some men would bargain with Satan himself for. Yet despite their worth, his eyes were finally pulled away to something far, far more valuable.

"Halitus, my love."

The voice sounds like a death shroud pulled across moldering wood. Halitus pauses in his stride, his eyes taking in the most valuable treasure of his entire world. The thing he had defied Heaven and Hell for, and won.

Eadwine Crouch. Daughter of an English Lord, the most beautiful woman in the country, and his wife. He had won her in a fierce courtship against another Lord, but his wit and cunning had won out in the end.

Hal's love lay upon one of the fainting couches, a small book held in the most delicate finger bones he had ever seen. She glances up at him from the brittle pages and smiles.

"You seem troubled, my love." She whispers, closing the book and setting it to rest on a side table. Eadwine's dressed in one of her better gowns, the fabric a shade of pearl with very little discoloration to the lace that edges everything. Her corset is tied its tightest and Hal's eyes roam over her body before being drawn up to her eyes. Warmth floods his own body, the closest thing to life he ever feels—but only when she is around.

"One of the gardeners needs work." He moves next to her and goes to one knee, his kneecap hitting the hardwood floor with an echoing thud. His gaze alights on the book sitting beside her. "What were you reading?"

"Nothing of much interest, my love." Eadwine twines her fingers through overripe wheat yellow hair before reaching out to run them along the side of his face. Hal closes his eyes as her hand brushes his face, leaning into it, letting the magic of her touch tingle along pale flesh.

Opening his eyes, he meets the watery blue of her gaze and smiles, mirroring her gesture with one of his own.

"How I ever ended up with you is a question I have often asked myself my beloved."

At his words, her eyes widen and the corners of her lips curve upwards. Shifting, she leans back, moving one leg to the floor while leaving the other on the couch.

"You know why." The words are more a purr than anything else and Halitus feels the warmth in his chest flare from embers to flame. He knows he should stop now, lest the help see them.

Instead, his hand moves to her stocking leg mounted on the edge of the couch as he rises up. One leg moves awkwardly to the other side of the couch before he sits, her legs on either side of his upper thigh. She makes a sound in her throat, wet and bubbling as his touch caresses along her legs. Where their skin touches, there is a tingling of something otherworldly. Hal has always referred to the sensation as proof they were meant to be, but for now he uses it to make his beloved gasp and twitch.

Eadwine's hands move along her corset, pricking herself where one of the whalebones had snapped and torn free of the fabric. Hal is quick to take her finger, eyes intent on the thick, black tar leaking from the puncture. His eyes close as he takes the digit into his mouth, parched tongue sliding along her skin, tingling as he sucks the fluid into himself. Low in his body he stirs, flesh long withered now alive as his member thickens.

"Oh Hal," his love whispers as she leans forward, her spine popping with the movement even as she lowers her hand down to grip his hips. "It's been so long."

Shifting himself forward, he presses his hips against hers, their mouths finding each other. There's a rasp as her lips brush his before he opens himself to her. Tongues meet like dried parchment as they brush against each other. He makes a low groan in his chest as her fingers brush through the sparse hair on his scalp, crawling along the places where the skull shows through.

Hal's hands slide ever upward along her inner thighs, making her shiver as his fingers reach the top of her stockings and slide under the edge of her undergarments to touch her skin. Breaking their kiss, she gasps towards the ceiling.

Her hands move down his body, fingertips claw his shirt, leaving rags in their place as she finds his pants. With a cannibalistic growl, she yanks them open, the button flying off into the witch-fire burning in the hearth. He responds in kind, tearing at her undergarments, making short work of them even as she frees him from his confines.

At her touch, he lets out a growl of his own, the crawling sensation racing along his length before she leans back to present herself to him. Despite her state, she was moist as grave mold. She guides his member to her folds, sliding him among her flower before finding the center.

Halitus pushes into her and she throws her head back to let out a scream of pleasure, causing the cobwebbed glasses on the mantle to shatter. Eadwine's legs wrap around him, pulling him deeper, his hard flesh shoving and spreading hers the deeper he moves. When his hips meet hers she pulls him down to her with a hungry moan.

His thrusts start slow but gradually gain speed, the couch

scraping the wood below as each push rocks it. The witch-fire flaring with each scratch of wood on wood, the flames curling higher and higher like serpents among the trees. Outside, the workers pause in their toil to gaze at the green flares of light from the mansion. More than one moans, hands dropping their tools to reach towards the light.

Hal's eyes open as he looks down at his lover, her gaze meeting his through half open eyes as she pulls him harder and harder against her. She snaps her teeth at him with a giggle, before throwing her head back and crying out as his hips crack against hers.

"I'm close," she croaks, biting her bottom lip, tearing the flesh with her teeth.

Halitus can feel her tightening around him and he snarls, moving faster and harder inside her, feeling something give in her hips as he drives against her again and again. Eadwine's cries are quick and sharp now, pounding against the walls, driving the rats out with squeaks of pain.

And then it hits them.

His head jerks back, mouth opening far too wide as what must surely be his entire being is poured from his loins into Eadwine.

Her mouth opens in a scream of incomprehensible words as she claws at his body with her fingers, tearing away sections of skin and viscera.

When their passion is over, Halitus falls to the floor, shoved away by Eadwine as she gathers the remains of her petticoats around her. Looking at her lover she shakes her head, her hair flowing a little closer to its original form than it had moments before.

"Halitus," she rises and prods his body with her foot. "You were always so confident in your ability as a necromancer. You forget you're not the only one who can read, my 'love'." Reaching down, she picks up the thin book. Flipping through the tome she comes to a well-worn page and starts to chant in a low voice.

The grounds keepers in the garden, the maids in the bedchambers, the chef in the kitchen, they all start to tremble as each syllable slithers from Eadwine's lips. Slowly, piece by piece, they begin to crumble, while her body starts to regain its previous splendor, like a motion picture machine in reverse.

When the last word spills from her mouth like wine, the entire mansion is as still as the grave.

Eadwine takes her first real breath in decades. Pink fingers run through sun-kissed golden hair. Moist, luscious lips open in a smile revealing teeth as white as snow. Rich ocean colored eyes gaze down at the corpse at her feet and she pouts.

"How long did you think I would let this charade go on Hal? How long did you expect me to live under your spell? I'm aware you're the one who poisoned me when I told you I was to wed Lord Bodkin. You never won me over; you kept me chained to you the only way you knew how."

She chuckles, savoring the feeling of blood in her veins again, the beat of a heart she never thought she would have again. Reaching down, she yanks the small charm from around the lord's neck, the rawhide cord snapping easily.

Stepping over his body, she twirls the tiny pendant in her fingers. With the riches hidden away in the mansion, Eadwine can go wherever she wants in the world. After all, she has eternity, and the world is her playground.

With a girlish giggle, she skips out of the room, never once looking back. The only sound the tinkling of her wedding band as the ring falls to the floor, and her laughter—fading into the night.

To Lust Beyond

Andrew Freudenberg

I think it was Groucho who said he wouldn't belong to any club that wanted him as a member. My Uncle Jed once told me never to fall in love with a stripper. Two truer pieces of advice were rarely given. I can't say I wasn't warned.

When a friend says they want to take you to a club without a name, you have every right to be suspicious. When they won't tell you where you're going, it's time to ask some hard questions. Of course you could make the fool's choice, throw caution to the wind, and hope for the best. That would be me. Grinning like an idiot.

The place was hidden in an old warehouse on the edge of town. I say hidden, but the Feds had better things to do than bust tasteless entertainment venues Out of sight, out of mind. Security was heavily armed and obnoxious. After relieving us of an obscene amount of cash they waved us in.

The inside stank of beer and over excited males. There was another smell too. An odor all too familiar in these troubled times. I glanced at my friend but he just shook his head and put a finger to his lips. I shrugged and took a look around the dimly lit space. Chairs had been set in concentric circles around a raised platform enclosed in steel bars. A caged walkway led out to an unseen back room. A dozen men sat sipping beers and murmuring amongst themselves. We grabbed ourselves a couple of drinks and got comfortable.

Before long, a single red light came on above the stage. Loud rock music assaulted our ears and we waited for the action to begin. From the shadows, a girl appeared on the catwalk, dressed in fishnets and leather. I squinted in the darkness, attempting to get a better look at her before turning to my companion.

"A strip show? All this for a strip show?"

He hushed me and told me to wait. The girl appeared confused as to where she was meant to go but it still took me by surprise when a minder stuck her with a cattle prod. Sparks flew and I expected her to go down, but it didn't faze her. Instead the prodding sent her stumbling into the main area where she grabbed the bars and screamed. The crowd went wild but I stayed silent, staring in disbelief.

You couldn't deny she had smoking curves under her outfit. You had to admire her long legs and luscious shock of blonde hair. After that, the graying pallor of her skin caught your eye just before you realized half of her face was exposed raw flesh. As she got closer, the drool running down her chin became obvious. I could see now one of her eye sockets was empty and only three fingers remained on one of her hands. She screeched again, exposing broken stumps of teeth and blackened gums. I was spellbound.

The music became more primal. The girl began to dance. It was ugly and erratic, but she definitely had something. She began to strip, tearing at her clothes. Her stockings ripped quickly but she made slow progress on her skirt and top. As I stared, entranced, other audience members began creeping up to the stage and dropping something.

"What the hell is that?"

"Meat," he snapped at me before turning his attention back to the main attraction.

I watched as she grabbed some of the dripping offerings and stuffed them into her mouth. It was admirable how she did so with one hand, while wrestling her clothes off with the other. Eventually she won the battle with her skirt and waved the garment above her head, mumbling unheard obscenities as she did so. The crowd cheered and threw more tidbits in her general direction. Encouraged, she gave her top a final tug and it flew free. The crowd were on their feet, showing their appreciation with abandon. That was when it happened.

For a split second I caught her eye and something incredible passed between us. Just for an instant, the rage and the hunger were replaced with something tender and we were connected. Time spun gearless and then reality sped up again, plunging us back into the moment. I gazed at her nakedness on the stage and swore she'd be mine.

That night my dreams revolved around her. We sipped cold champagne in a hot tub. Instead of water, we reclined in a soup of entrails and decomposing limbs. She slipped beneath the surface only to reappear between my legs with a smile on her face. I wiped some of the gore out of her hair and leaned down to kiss her. As we lost ourselves in each other, disembodied lips and teeth took tiny bites of us until we had been completely devoured. I woke up feeling like a new man.

I returned to watch her dance every weekend for the next three weeks. Here and there, I learned a little about her. Her name was Beth. She was twenty-three and came from an expensive part of town. "An uptown girl", the barman had told me. Of course, that was back before the virus hit. Now "uptown" was home to thousands of stumbling un-dead kept at bay by armed volunteers. Nobody was forthcoming with details on how they'd caught her, but the task couldn't have been easy. I saw a couple of other girls strut their stuff but they sickened me. They were dancing corpses. Only Beth had that special spark when she danced on the stage. Every time I went to that lowly place my admiration for her grew, and I cannot deny I became obsessed with her. She always noticed me and we'd exchange our split second connection again. I thought of nothing else anymore.

After my third visit, I decided I needed to make a commitment to her. I wanted to give her a gift cementing our relationship and letting her know I was serious. It came to me as I lay in bed half-asleep. What she really loved was meat. Perhaps it was fate, but at that moment my neighbor decided to make his presence known. His preferred method for dealing with the end of the world was getting stinking drunk on vodka. Understandable. Unfortunately, almost every night he also got the urge to crank his stereo just as I attempted to sleep. Of course, I'd tried asking him nicely to shut the hell up, but my requests hadn't been well received. In fact, the black eye was only just beginning to fade. I jumped out of bed, full of purpose and direction. Grabbing my bedside Beretta, I headed into the corridor and pummeled on his door. As the door opened a wave of screaming guitars and alcohol breath hit me.

"You again?" he muttered through a three day growth. He glanced at my pajamas and sneered.

"Me again." I put a bullet through his forehead and gave him a shove to ensure he fell inside his apartment. A quick search of his kitchen turned up some sharp looking knives, and I set to work like a man possessed. By the time the sun came up I was covered from head to toe in his blood, but I had a bag full of the good stuff.

That evening I waited until she stared right at me and headed up to the stage to present my gift. She snarled in gratitude as I threw the flesh at her feet. Her eye glowed as she scooped up the sacrifice and crammed the fresh offering in her mouth. I'd never seen her look so enthusiastic and neither had any of the other customers. They eyed me and my bag of meat, but I'd taken care to mutilate the body well enough it was unrecognizable as human. I was ecstatic she seemed so pleased, but I started to worry about her. A black patch on her otherwise perfect stomach seemed to be growing steadily. I noticed something wriggling about beneath the surface of her skin. Also, she had lost a couple of fingers on her other hand. I imagined one of her fellow dancers had bitten them off and cursed her keepers for not taking better care of her. If she lost any more fingers she'd never be able to get her clothes off and she would be redundant. They would kill her.

Amongst the morsels of information I'd gleaned off the bartender was the fact they kept the girls in a walled compound at the back of the warehouse. There was no doubt in my mind I needed to rescue her from her fate. If she was running on borrowed time, I wanted us to have at least a little of it together. We deserved that.

It took me another week to get up the nerve, but I found myself standing outside the brick walls of her compound at five o'clock in the morning—clad entirely in black, and carrying my neighbor's head under my arm. Piling up a couple of old beer crates got me on top of the wall. Inside the compound, the three girls stumbled around aimlessly. The bastards hadn't even bothered to dress them after the show, but the cold didn't appear to be bothering them. They hadn't noticed me.

"Beth!" I half whispered, half shouted. This got no reaction so I shouted the same thing a little louder. "Beth!" This time she spotted me, her one eye fluttering up to the wall. "It's me!" I waved the head at her, still not sure what to do next. Just as I thought I detected a hint of a smile on her face, we were interrupted.

"What the hell are you doing up there?" One of the gorillas from security shouted. He looked extremely pissed off. I thought about trying to explain but deep down I knew he would never understand. I pulled out my Beretta and shot him in the face. While that took care of one problem, it also unbalanced me. I fell off the wall and into the compound. I landed, winded, on my back. The girls wasted no time moving in. Uncle Jed also used to say three's a crowd, and I figured I should start listening to him. I emptied the clip into the other two girls and observed Beth to see what she would do. Unbothered by their executions she sat down heavily on my chest. I smiled and pointed to my neighbor's head, lying a few yards from us.

"I brought you something."

She inclined her head and wriggled. I could feel my passion growing and for a moment I thought about unbuckling my jeans. She breathed hard as she leaned towards me. Her breath stank of death and decay. I put my hands on her waist; she was soft and cold. I relaxed as she nuzzled my neck before sinking her teeth deep into my flesh. The pain, her gift to me, was electric. When she sat up, her lips were red and moist. A tear ran down her cheek and I wiped the moisture off with a finger and tasted it. Salt and anguish. It tasted good. Hunger overwhelmed me ....

Till Decay Do Them Part

J.G. Williams

The skies above Compton Street raged angry red, caused by numerous fires a few miles away in the city. Explosions rattled the windows of an old terraced house, while rumbling tank tracks tore up the road and shook its foundations.

Marcy stood at the bedroom window, arms folded, viewing the carnage. It was early morning, but smoke and debris falling from above had almost turned day to night.

Jimmy lay in bed, his shoulder length black hair tousled like a mop, engrossed in a game on his DS. Marcy turned to face him.

"So ... What are we going to do about it?"

"About what?" asked Jimmy, without looking up, frantically pressing keys on his game.

Marcy sighed, pounced on the bed and snatched the game out of Jimmy's hands.

"Hey, boy, wake up. There's a zombie apocalypse happening!" she squealed, legs astride him.

He looked up at her, his hair covering his twinkling green eyes, smiled, shrugged his shoulders and said, "What *can* we do angel? The army seems to be dealing, best we just stay put, and ..." He placed his hands on her waist and squeezed playfully. "Make love."

Marcy smiled, her long blonde hair tickling his nose. "You and your libido, totally insatiable."

Jimmy pulled her close, his hot breath tickling her neck. "Only for you, angel. Only for you."

* * * *

At midnight, the zombie horde pushed forward, breaking through the confines of the city centre. Ravaging all in their path, they left a trail of blood, bodies and severed limbs. Those that could regenerate followed the crowd, baying for blood.

The troops had failed with their quarantine procedure and the beasts were spreading towards perimeter lines. Gunshots and screams echoed to the heavy night sky. Hell had arrived on earth.

* * * *

A loud explosion woke the lovers. Jimmy leapt out of bed, stumbling in darkness to the window. "What the fuck?"

"What ... what's happening Jimmy?"

"They've got through the perimeter! The bastards are outside! Hundreds of them!"

Marcy raced to his side, staring in disbelief at the ugliness below. "Oh my God, what are we going to do?"

"You stay here. I'm going to check the barricade downstairs."

"No! Don't leave me!" she pleaded, grabbing his arm and pinching in panic.

He winced, kissed her cheek, and said, "I'll be right back."

Marcy watched him hurry from the room, then turned back to the window. The zombies below were tearing into an elderly man, blood and gore spilling from their hungry mouths. Nausea swept over her, making her fall forward, knocking against the window. The hungry horde stopped what they were doing and stared up in unison. Moaning loudly, they slewed toward the terraced house. Her house ... where Jimmy was, downstairs.

She sped to the top of the stairs and called out. "Jimmy! They've seen me! Quick, get back up here!"

Jimmy stumbled in the darkness, pushing everything he found against the door to re-enforce it. "Hide, Marcy. If they break through I'll try and lead them away from you."

"No, Jimmy. We die together!"

Suddenly the door exploded with grasping, bloodied hands through the woodwork. Jimmy picked up a piece of metal and swung frantically at the monstrosities, but couldn't stop them. Their inhuman strength forced splintered wood and debris into his trembling body. He rushed to the living room, snatching a chair; he hurled the projectile through the window and quickly followed the crashing glass.

"Over here, you bastards! I'm over here!" He waved his arms.

Their heads turned to his voice. On sight, the gathered crowd started to peel away and move toward him.

"Come on, you freaks." He bellowed, jumping in the air.

As they drew closer, Jimmy turned on his toes and ran down the street, the horde at his heels.

＊＊＊＊

Marcy squeezed herself into a small, built in cupboard. Her body doubled so tight, her knees crushed her chin. She found it hard to draw breath into her constricted lungs. Outside, she could hear Jimmy goading the blood thirsty crowd. Tears ran down her face. They should have taken the pills, like they planned, died in each other's arms. But now … they were separated. How would they ever find each other again, in this land of death?

＊＊＊＊

Marcy was awoken by a soft-spoken angel whispering her name.

"Marcy, are you okay angel … It's me, Jimmy."

Opening her eyes slowly, she recognized the face beside her. She mouthed his name as she struggled to get out of her prison. "Oh, Jimmy, thank God. How did you get away?"

"Ah, they aren't that bright." He smiled. "Slow too, I only ran into one straggler. We scuffled a bit, but I'm okay."

Marcy held Jimmy tight, then felt something wet on his shoulder. Stepping back, she peered at the wound. "Oh, no. Jimmy, you've been bit."

Marcy tried everything to stop the virus spreading through Jimmy's blood stream, to no avail. Over a matter of hours his features changed and his speech slurred. Marcy was heartbroken. She loved him so much. She would hold him close, caressing his failing body, making love to him for hours, until he fell asleep.

She only felt safe when he slept, for she knew his craving for flesh was becoming stronger. While he slept, she bathed him in cologne, in an attempt to cover the stench. His nails were coming away from their beds, and the hairs on his greying flesh crawling in tiny lice-like creatures. Any normal person would have left, or killed him, but her love flooded from every pore.

As she bathed him, lost in thought, Jimmy awoke. Through blind man's eyes, he saw a shadow before him. Raising quickly, he bared black teeth through thin lips, lunged and bit into Marcy's neck, tearing away the flesh.

Marcy pushed him off screaming, "I told you not to bite!" She covered the gash with her hand, ran from the room, to stumble awkwardly down the stairs.

* * * *

Marcy awoke next morning in a tangled heap at the foot of the stairs. Struggling to straighten her limbs, she managed to rise. Her jaw wasn't right. She limped over to the living room mirror and stared at her reflection. Her blue eyes had a milky film covering them, and her jaw seemed misaligned. Jumbled thoughts rattled through her brain. Looking again, she took her chin in her right hand and cracked her jaw back in place; a trickle of blood escaped between her lips and trickled down the side of her chin. Standing straight, she grunted, and made her way upstairs.

Jimmy lay on the bed, his face covered in blood and his

putrid body pulsing. Marcy stared at him for a while, until the little pictures in her brain became smaller and her memories faded. Then, a strange feeling washed over her. Her dead heart began to beat against her ribcage.

She howled, tore off her clothes and leapt onto the bed.

Jimmy howled too, as they held each other close, so close their bones cracked. Soon their decomposing bodies writhed with pleasure as they melded into one.

Together forever, till decay do them part.

Love Stinks

Tim Baker

When Edwin finally stood before her, taking her all in, she was even more beautiful than before the change. It did not seem possible; alive she had been a stun-gun beauty and death did not usually become a person. But her, *she's workin' it*. She always did, a drop-dead gorgeous porn star with class. And no girl—her mature bearing and sexuality held her far above the nubile ex-cheer squad starlets of BILF Studios. While they might polish a trailer hitch well enough, she got chrome. Her name was Stellar Stacee—he called her Stell— and he had loved her since her first starring role in STACEE'S HOMECUMMING, Part One of Eleven of the DADDY NEEDS YOU series. Edwin remained her biggest fan. Probably the only fan she had left, what with the zombie apocalypse and all.

Now dead and struggling to eat him, Stellar was all his.

After breaking into the secured house and a bit of a tussle, Edwin had Stell spread-eagle on a St. Andrews cross, arms directly overhead with her wrists leather cuffed to a cross-beam. Oven mitts, with a stitched SEXY on one and CHEF on the other, covered her hands and had been duct taped to stay on—getting scratched by those long ragged nails would not be good. The usually vibrant red hair had turned to rusty iron and lay on her shoulders like al dente noodles. Her porcelain white skin had turned a steel hot summer sky, giving her a jewel-like quality. Those trademark 36D breasts stood round and perfect, as natural as God's fruit, with gray tinged, tight aureoles set-placing her forever erect, inch long nipples. Edwin had found her wearing only a pink G-string and left the lingerie on for now, preserving some of her dignity. Not a mark marred her, not a cut, bite, or bruise; the empty bottle of Thorazine and Jack Daniels in the dictator-size bed testified to her way out.

Stell bucked against the constraints, her moaning and growling muted by the red ball gag. She stretched her neck out, still trying to get a mouthful of him. Unable to resist, Edwin pulled the small red satin crotch-swatch out; Brazil waxed and smooth as the satin, her bared blue vulva disappeared between her legs. The thought of those lips lubed and wrapped around his erection caused his cock to turn and stretch in its slumber.

Edwin felt surprise at the combination of disgust, and his swelling penis, at the thought of sex with the undead. He was not into necrophilia, *no way, no how.* Technically, the total submission of the dead-as-a-rock is what turns on necrophiles, and Stell was anything but that—dead, but kicking and scratching and very bitey. Who was he to demand she change for him? Edwin loved her unreservedly and his need to be intimate with her was too great. Edwin could overlook a small thing like a heartbeat.

His own hunger growled, so he left her in that elaborate, padded, sound proofed, BDSM dungeon, closed the door behind him and walked the long hall straight to the kitchen. Edwin also knew the house as if he had lived there; her home had been the setting for many of Stell's movies: the glistening pool with the inlaid turquoise tiles and Hollywood stretched out below, the mirrored workout area, the bedroom size bath/shower/hot tub room, the movie theater. Edwin ran his hand over the smooth wood of the cutting table at the end of the kitchen island and leaned over, sniffing for her scent— Stell had animal sex by man and woman and multiples thereof in every room. Her moans and shouting orgasms still echoed for him.

In the refrigerator, all the food was ruined, but he did grab a semi-cool beer and chugged it before grabbing another. Electricity had been off for a week, after having lasted five, so canned or dried food would have to do. Edwin wondered if the undead still did their job at the electrical stations. Things had stayed considerably cooler in the walk-in freezer and some of the meat still looked good, but borderline. Hiding in the back, his naked fat ass defrosting from the floor, sat Jonah "The Bilfer" Gold(berg) in all his balding glory. Founder and CEO of BILF Enterprises, "The Bilfer" was a multi-millionaire genius of all things nasty, naughty, and nice; and also Stella Stacee's former boyfriend. His penis had shriveled to a one-hole button. A revolver lay in his lap but no hole in his head; perhaps a gentle freezing death nap was better than a gruesome lights-out. Edwin did not know if the thawing dead could reanimate so he took Bilfer's gun and put a bullet through his icy brain.

In the silence of the house he heard the muted wail of his love. Locked and isolated in this place since her suicide, Stell had yet to eat zombie style. Edwin glanced at Jonah and his heart ached for her. He grabbed the corpse's arms and dragged it through the house, laying the body out on the tile of the sauna. Above the island in the kitchen all the knives and saws he needed hung like jagged teeth. Edwin's baby was starving and he felt honored to prepare her first meal.

But first, knowing the work ahead, he had a big steak (a cooker made for a chef was by the pool) and a can of beans, eating next to a six foot statue of a couple in fornication embrace. The woman looked a lot like Stell.

By afternoon Edwin was up disarticulating "The Bilfer" into manageable parts. When Bilf was stacked like a rick of wood on the sauna bench and his soft organs marinated in a bucket, he took a shower.

As Edwin entered the dungeon dragging the tarp of Bilf, Stell went wild; straining against the straps, bucking, and pounding her torso to the padded timber, making her breasts shake in a near hypnotic dance. The movement and noise had set her off, but when the scent of meat and blood hit her, she let out a gurgling howl too horrible to describe, and her struggling increased to nothing short of murderous rage.

Stella growled and spat black ichor past the gag and from her nose.

She always was feisty.

Edwin spoke to her gently as he checked the straps. The bruises on her wrists and ankles he did not like, what was pristine, now wounded forever. *She was such a delicate thing.* He cinched up the waist strap to stop the pounding. Her head turned from Edwin to the tarp of meat and when he removed the ball-gag she snapped at him, whining.

First Stell ate a thigh, tearing away baseball sized hunks, barely chewing before swallowing whole. Her neck swelled, the food backing up in her throat enough to choke a snake. Whether that was innate in zombieness, or Stell's practiced skill of taking eight inches of man hardness down her throat without gagging, well, he liked to think it was the latter. He turned the thigh like a corncob till she got to the bone (had to watch his fingers), barely slowing down. Twice Edwin thought he heard Stell make the num-num sound.

With the closest expression of ecstasy a zombie can have, Stell ate, and Edwin fed as he caressed her body. Her breasts were cool and smooth, the skin taut, his hand tracing the near-circle curve of their size, making him lift their weight and knead. When taking her nipple between thumb and forefinger, Edwin squeezed, hard, and she growled as she swallowed.

The whole right side of Bilf she ate, her stomach growing to half basketball size. Stell's chomping had grown slower, almost leisurely, and Edwin whispered sweet nothings as he ran the last right rib across her lips, letting her nibble. His free hand, lubed with warming lotion, rubbed her pussy lips, pressing and circling. A finger dived in, slipping across her hooded clit to find the depth of her pussy. Stell was tight from worked out vaginal muscles, and she squeezed as he slipped in another finger, forcing a third. Amazed, Edwin watched her head tilt back, the boned flesh momentarily forgotten. His fingers pushed and pulled inside her, palm spanking her warming outer lips, getting her ready for the tent-pole in his pants. Edwin's body felt afire and light. He had never wanted someone so badly, and having Stell finally here before him, naked and desirous, sent his mind and body reeling with lust.

Edwin tossed the rib as his fingers still moved inside her and bent to lick her nipple. Her belly made an odd gurgling sound. He felt a jerk and looked up to catch her dull eyes staring at him. Stell moaned and snapped at him. Once the gag-ball was replaced, he striped, his cock rigid and barely moving in the air. His body seemed to be throbbing and on the verge. Her dull eyes locked on him and her breath increased and hissed through the gag.

Edwin stroked and lubed his erection as he stepped between Stell's thighs, his flat abs pressing against her gorged belly. The scent of fall leaves and spoiling beef wafted up between them. The thought that he was committing one of the society's most disturbing, sick acts, never crossed his mind. Love and lust had conquered him.

With strokes front and back, he moved his mushroomed cockhead between her warm labia. Stell's head lolled and her pelvis rocked making her lips stroke his oversensitive head. They groaned in a yearning duet. Unable to hold back any longer, he plunged into her loving fold. A rumble passed across her belly and vibrated against him. Whether Stell's muted howl held agony or ecstasy or the returning ravenous hunger, he could not tell.

Edwin shouted out her name as he thrust like an over-eager teenager. The friction and lube had warmed her vagina to living temperature and it came to life, clenching at his cock, devouring him.

Stell bucked and squirmed and he sensed her thighs trying to rise to wrap her legs around him. A metallic pop and Edwin felt her mittened hand at his shoulder, clutching at his skin through the thick padding. It moved to the middle of his back and pressed, her arm pulling him in, his chest pressing her breasts up. Stell sucked air in bursts, faster and faster, as his rhythm matched her breaths.

Edwin arched his back and closed his eyes allowing the long-awaited inevitable to arrive.

Beneath the sound of their growling shout came the noise of a large deflating balloon. Stell's stomach receded from his. Then a lukewarm flow of liquid passed down their legs. The overwhelming stench of steaming, rotting, flesh feces exploded behind his eyes. The sensory overload tripped the trigger and Edwin exploded inside her in wave after wave.

When he opened his eyes, panting from the exertion, her eyes were in his, red and blood gorged.

Edwin said, "I love you," and kissed her gag spread lips.

When he pulled out and stepped back he stared at the greenish black ichor that ran from her ass, down her legs, dripping in globs and pooling beneath her. *So this is your orgasm, my love.* Stell's foreplay was gorging on human flesh, her climax, the elimination of it. It was a hell of a thing, but who was he to judge how someone came?

Once again she began to strain at the straps, her loose arm reaching for him in hungry desire.

They are lovers now, at last, the perfect relationship. Edwin knows it will not last forever, but he will keep her fresh as long as he can. Stell does not even snap at him anymore, he treats her so well. And Edwin learned one relationship lesson through those next three months: If you want to keep a woman happy, you have to keep her well-fed.

2 is for Taboo

Craig Faustus Buck

The crowd is a potpourri of races, genders and variations, castes, ages, walks of life, and walks of death. The high school gym bleachers are packed. A lonely podium stands midcourt on the floor. Behind the lectern hangs an old flat screen banner reading, "Welcome, All In Need."

Greta DeMonde, a mid-twenties livegirl dressed in a lime-green leopard-print jacket, black skirt, and chainmail boots, puts her hand over her eyes to shield them from the glaring overheads as she searches for a seat. Her sleeve slides back to reveal the intricate griffin her ex-husband inscribed on her forearm with a razor blade and a soldering iron. Good riddance to that scumbag.

A tall, balding zoman steps up to the podium and taps the microphone. The audience quiets down.

The greeting on the banner fades out and the *Twelve Steps of Sexaholics Anonymous* begins to scroll. The group recites in unison: "We admitted we were powerless over lust—that our lives had become unmanageable."

Greta spots a seat near the back next to a man. His graying temples anchor jet-black hair greased back like the biker punks from the mid-twentieth century. He's clearly a Caste One with his tailored clothes and diamond nose-studs. Greta, hailing from C-3, isn't generally attracted to C-1s but something about him warms her loins. Maybe because she hasn't had sex since she left her husband, and the drought is getting old.

"Came to believe a Power greater than ourselves could restore us to sanity."

Greta squeezes past fragile knees. She accidentally steps on an open-toed sandal, and feels her heel crush right through a woman's toes. Greta is surprised: the woman seems too healthy to be undead, but it's getting harder to tell the zomfems from the livegirls since plummeting prices have made pharmaintainers available to the lower castes.

"Sorry," Greta mumbles, wondering what it must be like to feel no pain. The zomfem stares in dismay at the crumbled remains of her toes.

"Let me pay you for some new ones," says Greta.

"Don't worry, I'm covered," says the zomfem, waving her off. "Thank god for universal health care."

"Made a decision to turn our will and our lives over to the care of God as we understood Him."

Greta reaches the empty seat to find the spot occupied by an expensive coat.

"You mind?" she asks the man.

He smiles apologetically and removes his coat. She likes his smile.

"Made a searching and fearless moral inventory of ourselves."

She notes he's not reciting the Steps. She likes that, too. She's amused by how little it takes for her to feel a connection. Is she that desperate?

"Admitted to God, to ourselves, and to another human being the exact nature of our wrongs."

Greta glances at the man and is struck by his eyes. Their ice blue tint is faint, almost colorless, practically transparent. She can't stop looking.

"Were entirely ready to have God remove all these defects of character."

The man's eyes flit to Greta and catch her staring. She glances away, embarrassed.

"It's okay," he says. "I get it all the time. My grandfather was albino. I got his eyes. I'm Zane. Zane Daniels."

She likes his easygoing and straightforward manner.

It puts her at ease.

"Greta DeMonde."

The zoman at the podium gestures to quiet the crowd.

"For all you newcomers out there," he says, "welcome to Sexaholics Anonymous. My name is Ronald and I'm a sexaholic.

The crowd responds: *"Hi, Ronald."*

"I was addicted to sex," he says. "I blew every dollar I ever had on prostitutes and wound up living on the street. But that was before SA. Now I'm sixteen years, three months clean."

The crowd applauds. Zane rolls his eyes for Greta's amusement.

"Any first-timers tonight?" asks Ronald, "Who'll take the plunge?"

He looks questioningly at an obese man in the front row. Reluctantly, the man rises from his two chairs and hobbles to the podium.

"I'm Victorio and I'm a sex addict," he says.

"Hi, Victorio."

"I've been undead six years, but I still follow sexy livegirls onto the subway during rush hour," he says. "I'll stand behind one and rub my crotch up against her ass like I'm being pushed by the crowd behind."

"Pervert!" shouts an old woman near the front.

"We're not here to be judgmental," says Ronald.

She replies, "He just rubs me the wrong way."

Greta and Zane both burst out laughing. She begins to choke.

"Let's get you some water," says Zane. He takes her hand and leads her out.

As the door closes behind them she says, "Thanks for getting me out of there."

"Thanks for the excuse," he says. "You must be here on a plea bargain, too."

"Two years, weekly. Is it that obvious?"

"It didn't take much to get you out of the meeting."

She bends over the drinking fountain, knowingly

presenting, for his appreciation, the curves of her black latoid skirt as the fabric silhouettes her ass and reveals her legs. She's proud of these assets, having spent long hours at the gym sweating to sculpt them. She wonders if zomfems work out. Can you tone up after you're dead?

She turns back to catch Zane raising his glance. He took the bait.

"I know what you're thinking," she says.

"That doesn't take a genius," he says with a nod toward her skirt.

She's pleased he doesn't pretend he wasn't looking. His eyes are driving her crazy. Without thinking, she steps up to peer closer, close enough to be called kissing distance. He doesn't flinch. He doesn't avert his eyes.

"There's something different about you," she says.

His eyes are like hot ice as he looks into hers. The warmth in her loins grows moist.

"Is that good or bad?" he asks.

"If you're lucky," she says, "bad can be very, very good."

"It seems we're backsliding on our Twelve Steps."

She smiles, then licks her upper lip. His eyes follow her tongue.

The gymnasium doors open and the crowd floods out.

"Let's get out of here," he says.

His place is downtown in the C-1 sector. The shops have doorbells and serve champagne; the apartments are large; the roofs are laden with gardens; the streets are patrolled. Greta feels nervous, like she needs a visa.

Zane leads her into a lavish former newspaper building whose Deco architectural detail has been restored to impress. It works on her. The elevator sweeps them silently up twelve flights in a heartbeat.

He opens the door to a sleek, modern apartment but Greta sees only the breathtaking view through his glass walls.

Beyond a sea of multicolored city lights, the gibbous moon paints a dazzling silver brushstroke across the onyx surface of the Pacific. Greta squeals like a happy child and twirls, grinning and tingling. She wraps her arms around Zane's neck and reels him in.

My first C-1, she thinks.

He seems tentative until their lips touch. Then he heats up. She pulls his shirt from his pants and snakes her hands beneath the silk, across his stomach, up his chest. He's solid and cool to the touch. She is on fire.

His hands roam her body too, tracing her back, cupping her ass, sifting her hair, brushing her breasts as he unties the laces of her bustier.

She rubs his fly and he swells under her palm, fueling her own passion.

Then, through the haze of her lust, she senses something fighting the flow. Gently but firmly, he's pushing her away.

"We need to talk about this," he says.

"What's there to say? I want to fuck you."

He walks away, leaving her stunned. He opens a teak cabinet to reveal a bar stocked with booze she's never heard of. A lot of singles—single-malt, single-cask, single-batch, single-barrel—most older than she. He takes his time splashing something into snifters, then finally faces her.

"A C-3 isn't good enough for you?" she asks.

"I don't care about caste," he says, "but I'm a zoman."

It takes a moment for his meaning to land, hitting her like a wrecking ball to the gut.

"Not funny," she says.

"Not joking. I'm sorry."

"You've got color, you've got substance, you've got a sense of humor."

"I'm still undead," he says. "I mean, technically."

If jaws really dropped, hers would be six floors down.

"I kissed you," she says. "If you were undead I think I'd notice."

"I'm using this next-tech bio-regenerator called Nanocell. It's revolutionary, almost like being alive."

"If you're a zoman, why bring me here? It's illegal for us to have sex. The law's for your own safety."

"Nothing to worry about. For the first time since I undied, I'm generating new cells. No more brittle flesh. No threat of breaking off inside you."

He yanks a finger back and forth to demonstrate the elasticity of his flesh.

She has a hard time absorbing this concept. She remembers a high school story about a zombie who tried to jerk off and literally jerked his dick off. She never thought the tale was funny but she knew it might be true.

"It's still illegal," she says. "It's been the law since before I was born."

"But I don't need the law to protect me anymore. And besides, they only give you a citation. Cheaper than a speeding ticket."

"I've never even *known* a livegirl who's slept with a zombie," she says, tantalized by the thought of a forbidden sexual exploit. "Are you good at sex?" Her own words embarrass her. "I mean, not you personally, but zombies in general. Can zomen do things liveboys can't?"

"I don't know. I don't know of one person who's ever had postmortem sex. At least, not that they'd talk about. But when Nanocell goes on the market, it's going to ...."

He mimes an explosion.

He continues, "That's why Big Pharma is dumping all those old-school bio-regenerators on the lower castes at half price. They've got to get rid of inventory. Once Nanocell hits the market, you think any C-1 who can afford the stuff is going to buy anything else? Look at me!"

He pinches his forearm and stretches the skin to demonstrate that, when he lets go, it snaps back to the original shape as if it were live flesh.

She falls into a black leather chair, intrigued.

"Have they done any experiments? I mean, have they put a zoman and a livegirl in some lab and let them go at it?"

"Not as far as I know. They just finished the rat trials. The unhuman trials started a few weeks ago. I lucked out and got picked."

He hands her a snifter. She chugs the whole thing.

"Why me?" she asks. "There's a billion other livegirls out there."

"I don't want just any livegirl. I want the promise of something more. I sense that in you."

This strikes her as sudden, but still flattering. There's something about him that attracts her in ways that seem deeper than her addiction to sex.

He says, "We could be the first zoman and livegirl to ever experience safe sex. We could usher in a whole new era."

She laughs. "They'd have to revoke the sex ban for that. And until you get the right to vote, Congress is never going to pass a law that lets you near living flesh, even if the only zombies who eat people anymore are fringe fundamentalists."

"Forget the law. It's just you and me. Here. Now."

"I still need to know. Why me?"

"Because you're beautiful. And because you're not afraid."

Those eyes.

"What the fuck," she says, tossing her snifter over her shoulder to smash on the floor. "Let's do this for science and make us some history."

He pulls her to her feet.

"Let's *really* make history," he says. "Let's go for love."

She smiles and pulls him close to part his cool, supple lips with her tongue.

Meat

Tim Marquitz

Amy stared at the door of the nondescript shop. Its tinted, bare windows reflected her doe-eyed stare above the glowing open sign. Her heart thundered a cannonade, beating faster every time a car drove past. She'd stood on the sidewalk for the last twenty minutes, willing herself to knock, but her arms hung limp at her side, hands trembling. Despite the chill in the air, sweat dotted her brow. She let out a wispy sigh as yet another vehicle crept past, imagining their eyes on her, shame threatening to set her feet to scurrying. Amy clenched her teeth and turned back to the shop.

A young woman stared from the open door. "Can I help you?"

Amy's hand flew to her mouth. It was a long moment before she could force sound from her throat. "I ... I—"

The woman smiled and Amy's cheeks warmed. "You're here to see *him*, aren't you?"

"No, I uh ..." her voice trailed off, and she nodded.

A soft smile broke across the woman's lips. "It's okay." She waved Amy inside, the subtle scent of anesthetic and incense leading the way. As the door closed behind them the woman looked to Amy, eyes narrowing. "I'm Carol. I think I remember you from the club before ... well, you know."

Amy nodded. The *Zombie No-pocalypse* people called it: a government experiment gone wrong, people returning from the dead to infect the living. The whole thing lasted all of a month before the CDC put a cure in motion; one they'd apparently been working on since George Romero first released *Dawn of the Dead*. The end of the world fizzled, less than 100,000 people zombified across the whole of the planet.

It was the best thing to ever happen.

The tiny storefront was dimly lit and sparse, two chairs set out on the white tile floor. A lacquered counter stood near the back, pink drapes decorating the walls. The looming darkness of a doorway hung behind their soft veil.

"You *are* here to see him, right?" Carol asked, slipping behind the counter. Her tanned face was expressionless but her blue eyes were wary.

Amy dug in her pocket and produced the card she'd been given. She walked quickly across the room and handed it to the woman. Carol smiled upon seeing the signal, the tension in her shoulders easing.

"Just had to be sure."

"I understand," Amy squeaked out, barely a whisper, though she wasn't really sure she did. All this had to be illegal, but she couldn't imagine who would care. She wasn't doing anything wrong.

"All I need is a credit card, and he's all yours," Carol grinned, "at least for an hour."

Amy handed the card over without hesitation, doing her best to hide the trembles that made it dance at the end of her fingers. Carol was professional enough not to mention it. Once she had the card, she pulled aside the drapes and motioned for Amy to follow her into the dark hallway beyond. Amy coerced her feet forward, the shadows deepening as the drapes fluttered shut at her back. Her breath clung heavy to her lungs as she followed the woman past a dozen closed, steel security doors, each with a tiny porthole set in their center, until she came to stop at the end of the hall. Carol blocked the view of the magnetic lock and keyed in a code, the beeping rhythm echoing in the corridor. She leaned back, her hand on the latch.

"He's not exactly the same as he used to be, you know?"

Amy sighed. She *didn't* know. As often as she'd gone to the club to watch him dance—to watch him strip—she'd never managed anything more than a couple of quick gropes while she plied him with dollar bills as he strutted by. He'd never shown any interest in girls like her. Amy clutched her chest, her small breasts little more than speed bumps on the way to her narrow hips. She adjusted her glasses and looked to the busty Carol, but kept quiet. None of that mattered anymore. She'd forked over her money like all the rest. He'd have to pay attention now.

"Have a good time, but whatever you do, don't remove the mask or the straps. Understand?" Carol waited for her to nod before pulling the door open.

The sharp tang of disinfectant stung her nose as Carol ushered her forward, the air noticeably cooler. Amy stumbled inside, her vision tunneling before she'd any sense of the room's size or décor. Carol shut the door behind her, but Amy hardly noticed, the quiet *thump* miles away. Her eyes were on *him*.

He laid spread eagle on the bed, leather cuffs tight about his pale ankles and wrists. Amy's pulse *whirred* in her veins. It was really him. She forced her feet forward, the vague pressure of being timed spurring her on. She'd imagined this moment so many times it blurred in her mind until she had a hard time remembering what was real and what was fantasy. He would never understand just how much she loved him, how she longed for him, but he would recognize her passion, she promised.

She drew up close and set a hesitant hand on his shin. Goose bumps sprang to life when she touched his cold skin, prickling her arm. Her gaze trailed up his naked thigh, and she felt a cloying wetness swelling between her legs at what she saw. There, in all its glory, stiffer than she'd ever seen it, his erection pointed at the ceiling, thick and towering—a skyscraper standing over the skyline of his smooth crotch.

Memories flashed as she drew closer, her trembling fingers seeking the massive member she'd dreamed of so often. Her hand wrapped about his cock, and she was surprised to find the flesh was warm and pulsing with life in defiance of all she imagined. She slipped her other hand around him, one too small to completely encompass him. A shudder ran through her, her legs shaking. She'd wanted this forever, and now here he was; hers at last.

She glanced up at his face for the first time, strangely surprised to have not noticed it wasn't there. In its place was a bulky, green gas mask that enclosed the entirety of his head. The lenses were tinted so black she couldn't see inside. Slim plastic tubes ran from either side of the mask to disappear under the pillows at the head of the bed. Amy sighed. She'd wanted to look him in the eyes, wanted to know if somewhere deep down he might recognize her, might remember, but it was a small wish amongst the whole of her desire.

She could wait no longer. Amy hurriedly undressed, tossing her clothes into a pile on the floor, and climbed onto the bed. She could hear her heart in her ears, the roaring wash of waves pummeling her as she crawled to squat overtop. Patience faded in the heat of her passion, and she lowered her sex onto his massiveness without hesitation. The tip slid in with ease, she was so wet. She was suddenly full of him. Her nails dug into his hips to hold her steady, but her legs threatened to give way as she felt herself ready to burst. Amy gave in to gravity and swallowed all of him inside. Her knees sunk onto the bed as the first wave of orgasm hit, anticipation pushing her over the edge. She shuddered and twitched, impaled upon his cock, grinding into his pelvis.

When at last she could open her eyes, she steadied herself and straightened, drawing stuttered breaths. She'd barely gotten over the shakes when she heard a quiet hiss. Her eyes snapped to the translucent hoses. A whirling mist tumbled through them, spilling into the mask. There was a sudden twitch beneath her, and Amy couldn't hold back her moan as he inched deeper inside her. She tightened her grip as he bucked again. His hands clenched and tugged against the creaking restraints, but Amy had no time to wonder at their security. The hissing continued and he responded to its serpentine call. Where he'd lay still beneath her at first, now he twitched and shook, pressing up into her with abandon.

Amy's vision blurred as he slammed his crotch against hers, the length of him piercing her deeper and faster than she'd ever been. Unable to catch her breath, her legs tangled in his, she helplessly rode him as he thrashed beneath. Despite fear—despite everything—Amy felt yet another orgasm rattle through her, and then another, and another. She gasped as he continued to fill her, his hips pounding into her with an animalistic fury. The room spun around her as she came, over and over.

A quiet *snap* wormed its way past the ringing echo of her throaty moans, but she'd no place for it in the throes of her primal ecstasy. She'd wanted him like no man before and now she had him, every inch. Amy felt his fingers tangle in her hair, pulling her closer. She gave in, her breasts pressed hard against his cold chest. An electric thrill shot through her, and she heard him grunt his pleasure.

"I love you, too," she told him as he muttered against her neck, the nip of teeth scraping skin.

* * * *

Carol heard the woman scream and ran to the door, whipping open the viewing porthole. She slammed the glass shut and swallowed hard, her stomach tangled in knots at what lay inside. Her gaze snapped to the magnetic lock, breathing a sigh at the green flutter of light. She dug in her pocket and pulled out her cell phone, dialing with quick stabs of her finger.

The other end picked up after the second ring. "It's Carol, sir," she breathed into the receiver. "Meat's killed another one."

Carnage Kandy

Teresa Hawk

They crashed on purpose. Lotta Carnage and Kandy Cakes knew how to make an entrance. Their shiny, pink, customized 1970 Dodge Dart Swinger plowed through the dead automatic doors of Smith's grocery store. The car skidded past the rotten produce section, kicking a wake of year-old weekly specials into the air. Carnage jerked the wheel hard to the left, downshifted, and stomped on the gas. The tail spun into a donut, leaving a thick rubber circle on the dusty floor. The impressive maneuver took out an endcap of stacked, mouse-eaten Captain Crunch boxes that ruptured with stale cereal and rodent turds. A cloud of tire smoke and cereal dust lingered as both women hopped out, but left the engine running.

Kandy slung her Mossberg 12 gauge shotgun across her back like a guitar—they made beautiful music together. She kicked over the broken display with her knee-high Doc Martens. Her long, natural, red hair curled around her pretty face, contrasting against her green eyes. Skipping down the aisle made her rockabilly miniskirt bounce, flashing Carnage with an intermittent peak at her ass. Kandy fiddled for something in an open yellow carton crammed into the pocket of her blue raccoon fur vest. Her saw dusted hand emerged holding a couple twisted pieces of tissue paper with bulbous ends. She threw one of the TNT Pop-Its against the concrete floor and it produced a loud, satisfying *snap* that made her grin.

"Come out, come out, where ever you are," she mocked. Kandy counted on dirt nappers following her noise.

She flicked another to the ground. *Snap!*

Blood stained the bleached ends of Carnage's brown dreadlocks. Her manic and exaggerated eyeliner looked like war paint. Always braless, she wore a tight-fitting tank under a long, olive-drab military jacket weighed down with ammo and speed loaders. The bottom of her jacket brushed against the handles of her two long barreled .357 Magnums. One holster hung on each hip from her thick gun belt. Each had a strap secured around her strong thighs. Impressive, but the pièce de résistance of her ensemble was the grossly oversized black, strap-on dildo she attached *outside* her shredded, denim shorts. Her all-leather cock and pistol rig intimidated the burliest of manly men.

They believed Armageddon was the best thing to ever happen to the shitbag world. The End meant true freedom. They took anything, went anywhere, and did whatever they wanted. Carnage found her pillaging partner stranded in Utah last summer. Since then, Kandy Cakes evolved from a prude hyper-Christian, Martha Stewart wannabe into a punk-bitch, warrior, sex kitten. They were a tribe of two. Kandy felt safer killing hordes of infected biters with Carnage than she had when living in the suburbs with her husband back before the pandemic. The old world seemed so far away, and her memories like watching black and white musicals with the volume muted.

Kandy filled a basket with canned pineapples, peaches, and pears and ditched them in the back seat. And then, she tossed a whole handful of noisemakers. *Snappy, snap, snapiddy, snap!* Two failed to pop. She picked them and threw them extra hard to the ground. *Snap!* One was a dud. She hated that. Then she sprinted a few aisles over and came back with a cartload of bottled water and loaded it into the trunk next to several cases of ammo. Carnage strutted down the next aisle and retrieved a variety of canned meats and a bottle of Clamato juice.

On her way back, she grabbed dried pasta, canned vegetables, and a bottle of olive oil so big it needed a handle.

Stinkbags moved so damn slow. Before the first walking fungus farm made it inside the store, the women had loaded their goodies into the car and were ready to jet. Carnage stomped on the gas and mowed down three shambling rotters on the way out. Thick, browned blood, the same consistency as bird shit, splattered up from the grill. Kandy laughed and leaned out her window. She blasted a crawler in the parking lot with her shotgun, then went for the double tap, blowing the creeper in half. As they sped uphill away from Vegas and towards Summerlin, Kandy looked over her shoulder and lifted up her skirt to expose two perfect, plump, milky-white cheeks, flossed by the thinnest red lace thong.

"Damn girl, I'm driving here," Carnage said, trying to split her gaze between the road and her girlfriend's ass.

Carnage nailed a walker with the right corner bumper and it spun and bounced down the passenger side of the car like a flat tennis ball. Kandy barely ducked inside in time to miss getting hit by the human road kill. She laughed and whooped like a psychotic cowgirl at the doomsday rodeo. They sped out of the valley towards the last edge of stucco McMansions carved into the mountainside. Kandy slid across the bench seat and pressed herself up against Carnage, who responded by reaching into her bra with her free hand and stroking her breast. Kandy cooed with delight and teased her silicone dildo.

"You want that?"

"Yes."

"Then, suck it."

Kandy leaned down and licked the dildo, while Carnage stroked her long red hair. She started sucking, like it mattered more than anything in the world.

"I know what you want, Kandy Cakes."

"MMMmmmm," Kandy said around a mouthful of dildo.

Carnage drove around the dead-end barricade, off the pavement, and into the desert. The sun hung low in the late afternoon sky. In less than an hour, it would duck behind the mountain and cast them in a shadow. After a half mile, she spun around and parked the car. Kandy rose from her lap and kissed her with passionate tongue. Carnage reciprocated deep and hard, then pushed her away.

"Let's do this!"

"Yes!" Kandy said, breathless.

They both slid out the driver's side, and Kandy hopped up on the trunk with her legs dangling over the gas cap. Carnage double-checked her revolvers, confirming that six brass primers filled each stainless steel hole. She slipped her guns back into their holsters and got the shotgun. Kandy kicked her thong into the dusty dirt, spread her legs wide, and touched herself. While watching the show, Carnage added two shells to the magazine before setting the long gun on the trunk. She pulled six professional-grade bottle rockets from the back seat and set them up downhill, pointing them into the valley. After lighting all the fuses with her Zippo, she hiked back to Kandy, who plunged two fingers deep into her own pussy and then licked them.

"Delicious, Kandy?"

A firework shot and whistled into the air, and Carnage grabbed the jug of olive oil and set it next to the rear tire.

"Come have a taste," Kandy said as she lay across the trunk and lifted her hips high into the air.

The first rocket exploded in the air with a loud *bang*.

Carnage slid her hands down the inside of her girlfriend's soft thighs. The next firework launched as she brushed her lips against the inside of her knee. Kandy cooed in delight. Carnage kissed, licked, and sucked her way down, then grabbed two handfuls of ass and lifted her higher. The twilight sky flashed green. *Bang!* The explosion echoed. She dove in, licking and teasing her clit, making Kandy moan.

"Louder," Carnage said before burying her tongue deep into her hole.

"Yes! More. More. Make me scream!"

Whistle. Carnage ate her out with unmatched enthusiasm, and brought Kandy to an ear piercing orgasm. Red. *Bang!* Echo. Afterwards, Kandy stretched across the trunk to recover. The rest of the fireworks whizzed and whistled and exploded. Satisfied with the show, she caught her breath and hopped down to kiss Carnage. Their tongues probed. Kandy seized the fake cock in her tight fist and gave it a yank.

"Bend over," Carnage commanded.

Kandy complied and leaned against the car trunk. Her left boot rubbed up against the rear tire and her right knee banged against the pink metal. Carnage lifted her plaid, pleated miniskirt around her waist, exposing her white ass and luscious pussy.

"Are you ready for this? You know what ammo sponges they can be."

"Yes!

Carnage spanked her ass with the dildo until it stung. Then she rubbed the red spot gently, blew on it, and kissed away the pain. Kandy squirmed as Carnage wedged the dildo in the folds of her mound and rotated her hips. She popped the top off the olive oil and poured it down her girlfriend's crack. Oil dripped on the dildo and down the side of the car. Kandy wiggled and tilted to get the oil in all the right places, and managed to guide the silicone cock into her vagina hands-free. She pushed back until the whole dick was jammed deep inside. Then Carnage started sliding in and out. She went slowly at first, but Kandy escalated the force and speed, moaning with pleasure all the way. In less than a minute, they pounded hard, fast, and violently. Carnage loved giving it to her from behind. It felt like power. Kandy moaned and screamed so loud her cries echoed off the mountain side.

"You know that if you come, I'm going to keep going until this is done?" Carnage said.

"Yes! I know. Do it!"

Carnage forced the cock deep and worked into a furious pace. As Kandy screamed with pleasure, she saw the first pus target shambling uphill towards them.

"Yes! It's working," Kandy screamed, "There's one!"

Carnage drew her pistol. She aimed. Then she took a deep

breath and pushed all the way into Kandy. They both held still. Carnage adjusted her aim, exhaled, and pulled the trigger. Her shot landed right below the ghoul's right eye. The back of its head blew off. Carnage started thrusting again as the meatbag dropped into the dirt.

"Yes. Oh my god, fuck me!"

"Yes! Yes," Carnage said as she rose towards her own climax. She thrusted, she shot, she fucked, and she killed. The intoxicating rush of adrenaline and natural ecstasy made the game more dangerous, amplifying their high. Carnage shot nine rotters. They let the last brain eater get within fifteen feet, and then Kandy delivered the final shotgun blast into its chest. That's when they came together—hard.

The dead walked the earth, but it was anything but hell. These women loved every fucking minute of it.

Love Revived

Carrie-Lea Cote

With arms raised above my head, I lifted my face to the sky. I felt the tingling of Power building around me. It danced down and around my skin, until pooling and writhing deep in my belly.

It was hot inside of me, throbbing with the pulse of my speeding heart. I stifled a moan of pleasure from the tension building between my legs, and bit my lip.

All but gasping, I said the last few words of the Incantation the old Mambo Woman had given to me.

Power and pleasure rippled through my flesh as one. Pulled from deep within me, the Power ran down my legs and poured in the grave plot where I stood alone in the darkness. Taking deep breaths, I looked down at the dirt and trembled from the Power leaving me, shaking like the aftermath of an orgasm.

The Power seemed to caress the blood on the grave dirt. My right hand tingled and itched where I had cut for the blood at the start of the ceremony.

"Blood from the Dominant Hand of the Supplicant to start the Rite. Blood from a Beating Heart to feed the Rite." The words sounded loud to me, even as my voice was quiet in the night air. I glanced down at the bloodied husk of what once had been a large, white chicken.

And finally—pulling the blade from my belt, I groaned with unnatural pleasure as I cut deep into my left hand this time—letting the blood drip down to join the rest on the ground.

"Blood from the Beckoning Hand to seal the Rite."

Another jolt of electricity shot into my body, causing pulsing hot flashes to swirl into me before peaking and again racing down my legs, using me as the conduit for tonight's work.

Groaning, I slipped to my knees. The bloodied dirt stained my jeans, soaking into the fabric. I expected the blood to be cold. Clotted.

Instead the blood was hot, hotter than when I had spilt it.

The ground pulsed beneath me, echoing my heart. I pressed my thighs together and rolled my hips, biting my lip and moaning as my swollen, sensitive folds ground against the hard seam of my jeans. My eyes never left the grave as I waited, grinding my sex in slow circles, riding the erotic sensations from the Ritual.

Suddenly, I heard the ground echo dully with the crack of wood, followed by a faint scraping. Staring like a mad woman at the grave, I rubbed both my bloodied palms against my thighs, grinding more blood into the fabric. I rocked my hips against the crotch of my jeans again, and shivered, hoping the Ritual would be successful.

Then the impossible happened. The biggest cliché of my life and a sight that sent thrills of horror and lust tingling through my body. A grey hand broke the surface of the dirt, clawing and grasping at the air above before slapping at the ground, starting to dig itself out. A second hand joined its mate in mere moments, and before I knew it, I was watching the body of my dearly departed husband pull itself from the grave.

Studying him closely, I noticed no signs of decay on his flesh. Beneath his burial suit, his body appeared just as perfect as when he was alive.

Scrambling to my feet, I found myself towering over the man who towered over me in life. The role reversal burned in my fevered imagination. Now I was the stronger one. The one in charge. I bit my lip as he lay face down on the ground, as if catching his breath. Knife gripped tightly in my hand, I stepped towards the dirtied figure.

"Al? ... Alan ... can you hear me?"

He glanced up and turned wide, white filmed eyes towards me.

This was the moment when I would find out if the Rite worked properly or not. I stood there, hoping the blood I spilt at the end of the ceremony would bind him to me as intended. That he would recognize me as his Master, and God willing, remember I was his wife. Or would he be a mindless ghoul, reduced to baser instincts? He moved to kneel in front of me and, oh so slowly, reached out and ran the tips of his fingers along my bare ankle. I closed my eyes and licked my lips.

"Guh ... Grrr .... Gigg ... les ... Gig-gles ...?"

My heart nearly flew from my chest. He knew me! Not just by my name, but by the nick-name he had given me on our first date. I threw the knife to the side and dropped to my knees in front of him. Brushing my hands all across his body, face and hair, dislodging dirt as I kissed him all over.

A low moan escaped his lips as his eyes closed. The flesh beneath my fingers was firm, whole, and slightly colder than my own. But that could have been because of how fevered I felt. My hands traveled down his shoulders as I kissed his ear and neck. I pulled and tugged at the clothing covering him. I needed to touch him. To see him. To be sure the mugger that killed him seven months ago had not taken him from me permanently.

At first, he caressed me back hesitantly, but the more I touched him, the bolder he grew.

The more like MY Alan he became. I closed my eyes and leaned into his body. His hands were strong under my shirt and his fingers brushed against my skin, caressing, stroking. Pressing my fevered lips to his chilled ones, I kissed him deeply, pressing my tongue into his mouth. He tasted of earth, magic and blessedly, Alan.

Moaning into the kiss, Alan gripped the front of my shirt hard in his hands, and pulled. The sound of my t-shirt tearing was loud in the night air. I squirmed, and my pussy gushed against my already wet panties. Impatiently, he fumbled with the front clasp of my bra for a moment before tearing it down the center too. Whether it was the incantation I said, or his passion for me coming back from the grave with him, I didn't care, just as long as he kept touching me.

With fevered actions to match his, I ripped at his shirt front. Little pearled buttons sprayed out as I tore it open. My breath caught when I saw the neatly sewn wound over his heart where the knife had gone in. Dipping my head, I licked the spot with my tongue. He groaned my name above me and shivered, his hands catching up in my hair as he pulled me to him.

Pushing the tattered suit from his shoulders, I ached to hold his bare flesh against mine.

But he had other ideas.

With a deep, growling noise, Alan pushed me back against the ground and moved to hover over me. Rich, dark earth sprinkled off his hair and his shoulders as he took off his suit jacket and shirt. My memory piqued at the sight and flashed to times in the past when he was this eager for me. This frantic to have me.

I groaned and closed my eyes as a shot of liquid heat pulsed between my legs. As he gripped the waistband of my jeans, I undid the zipper and lifted my hips, letting him pull them unhindered off my legs before tossing them to the side. My cheeks warmed with a blush as I noted the tricky bastard had gotten my panties with them. It had always been one of his favorite tricks.

As I lay naked and exposed to him, he paused for just a second to look at me. His gaze took in my tangled brown hair, my sweating, flushed face. Following the blush down to my pert, tan nipples, down past the slight weight gathered at my hips and my stomach.

His gaze stopped at the slightly curled strip of hair at the apex of my thighs. The spot of his attention clenched in need as he humped the air above me, the bulge in his pants having grown notably thicker under the thin fabric.

Reaching up to his crotch, I ran my palm over the length of him as I undid his pants. Revelling in how long, how steely hard he was, my brain barely registered he was colder than me. There was no need to worry on that. I was hot enough for the both of us.

With a deep, animalistic grunt, Alan pulled my hands away from his member, and pinned both my wrists above my head with his one hand. The other pushed at his waistband, until his pants and underwear slid down to hang at his knees. His erection jumped free of the fabric and jutted out and up in front of him, pulsing in time with my beating heart. Licking my lips, I admired how the turgid flesh was only a shade pinker than the grey of his body and moaned. I arched my back and lifted my hips, my folds swollen and dripping with desire.

He stared at my glistening pussy, his free hand stroking his thick length, teasing me with his actions. With a grin, he began pressing down onto me, guiding himself into my dripping hole. With one thrust he buried his cock deep in to me. Forcing my slick folds to spread for his swollen length, he made me whimper as he pushed deeply and bottomed out. With a deep, shuddering moan, he held himself in me, forehead pressed against mine. My body jerked under him, and he pulled out a little, just enough that the pressure against my cervix was lessened.

Whispering his name, I wiggled my hips against him, moving his cock blissfully inside of me as I wrapped my legs around his. With a groan, he lifted his head from mine and arched his back, pushing into me again. Letting go of my hands, he braced himself on either side of my shoulders. He thrust into me, pushing his swollen length as deep as I could take him. I cried out from the sensation of him moving in me. Using my freed hands, I gripped his back with one, and with the other, started to rub at my clit between our straining bodies.

Immediately I clenched around him and he moaned, a deep, primal and guttural groan. In response, I thrust my hips to meet him as he slapped into me. I could feel my orgasm building, cresting. The time-stopping spasm came from deep within, my head thrown back and eyes closed in ecstasy.

As in the past, my pleasure spiked his, and in seconds, his thrusts got harder, deeper, and more erratic. Then it hit him. He growled once and pushed deep into me. I cried out as a wet, slick rush of coolness flooded into me. I shuddered at the balm it had on my battered insides.

With a final moan, he collapsed on me, his lungs drawing breath to fill the void his cry had left. My heartbeat slowed; I hugged him tightly to me as my eyes burned with tears.

"I love you Alan. Welcome back."

Glory

Jay Wilburn

Sin became worse once everyone died.

Reverend Jimmy familiarized himself with sin before the dark resurrection overtook the Earth. The way the dead rose took him by surprise too. He read scripture and God had thrown a curveball.

"Please, don't … please don't … please …"

Reverend Jimmy hissed. "Shut up. You need to beg God … not men … never men."

Jimmy drove the knife into the kid's back again. He had run out of spots to avoid piercing organs. He needed him to live through the glory. The boy whimpered and began to shake. Jimmy suspected the Holy Spirit had not filled him.

"You're a twenty year old man. Time to put childish things behind you."

The boy's eyes slid closed. Jimmy pressed his hand harder into the boy's neck, holding his sweaty face against the wall. He kept his knee in the small of the boy's back. The rub and struggle aroused Jimmy and made him angry.

Jimmy shook his head. "Come on. Come on. I know you are hungry."

With the bloody knife, he reached up between the boy's legs. The point of the knife ponged against the sheet metal wall. He lifted the blade slowly, scraping it against the wall. His teeth gritted from the noise. The boy's soft bits rested on the flat of the knife. He slid it out the hole in the metal wall underneath the boy's glory. The boy's tight flesh grazed over Jimmy's wrist. He felt the cold. The reverend's tongue slid out of his mouth and he groaned. He bobbed the blade up and down shaking the boy's glory where the outside world might spot it.

"Come on, you soulless bastards. I know you're hungry."

He heard their groans of ecstasy as he got their attention. "There you go. Come and get it."

He pulled the knife back too quickly and gave the boy a nick in a tender spot. The boy's eyes shot open for a moment and he shuddered. He passed back out almost immediately. Reverend Jimmy held up the boy's entire weight and kept him pressed to the wall and out the hole. Sweat coated Jimmy's forehead as he strained.

The metal wall popped as the dead hands and bodies pressed and clawed from the outside. Their broken fingernails ground against the metal. Jimmy shivered at the noise.

The creature outside locked its teeth together over the boy's glory and his eyes shot open. He screamed and his face turned purple. Veins stood out on his neck. The boy pushed back, threatening to take out the entire wall with his violence.

Reverend Jimmy dropped down and jammed his shoulder against the boy's bare buttocks. Dark blood soaked into the reverend's shirt from the holes in the struggling kid's back.

The monsters outside continued to chew. A spurt of blood shot back between the meat and the hole. Jimmy turned his face to keep it out of his eyes. The blood ran down his cheek and pearled under his collar around his neck.

The boy's screams covered Jimmy's moans. The reverend watched the light through the hole to the outside. He witnessed the remains of the glory pulled away in shreds. He could not see the monsters' eyes, so their former identities remained a mystery. He glimpsed the teeth and white, speckled tongues working. He observed one grey claw of a finger dig at the stump of the boy's manhood as the creatures jostled to get their own pieces for themselves.

The boy stopped screaming and went limp. He started to fall backward.

Jimmy stood up and held the body against the wall. The monsters continued to bite, claw, and lick at the hole. They missed more than they caught. He had to keep the boy's body in place long enough to finish the process or the dead would keep attacking until they took down the thin, metal wall of the soup kitchen.

"Come on, kid, what are you waiting for?"

The boy's eyes opened again, but they remained undilated. His teeth snapped at Jimmy's arm. The only pulse he felt with his arm against the boy's neck was his own. The boy growled.

"Louder ... give them something to sink their teeth into, kid."

The undead creature tried to turn around to attack Jimmy. He struggled to keep the bloody monster in place. The heat left the body quickly.

Finally, Jimmy heard the roars outside die away. The metal stopped crinkling. He couldn't see them, but he knew they were wandering away. The boy's dead body growled at Jimmy again.

Jimmy rested the point of his knife against the boy's temple. Without his soul, the boy showed no fear or reverence for Jimmy's knife.

"You shouldn't have violated yourself for my food. You failed the test. Your soul wakes in Hell and now your body will rest."

Jimmy drove the blade through the skull until he heard the tip pong on the wall on the other side. The dead muscles relaxed and he let the body fall to the floor off his knife.

Jimmy stared down at it. The stiffness in his own glory subsided. He needed to wait for the crowd outside to disperse before he dumped the body. He also needed to clean the edges of the hole before using again.

Jimmy wiped his knife off on the boy's shirt and walked through the kitchen to the empty cafeteria. The round tables sat in rows in the dark hall.

Some of the chairs had been scattered when the boy tried to escape. The smear of blood from the first stab stood out against the waxed floor.

Jimmy sighed.

He began resetting the chairs around the tables.

Jimmy still believed he made a better front man than a manager, but God's glory trumped man's desires. He ignored the stir under his zipper and kept setting chairs.

He looked at the bloody skid mark across the floor and sighed. He walked back to the closet and picked up the mop and bucket. The mop smelled of dirty, gym socks. He used to rinse it out well enough to brush his teeth with it, but he couldn't spare the water. He filled the bucket with a mixture of blue cleaner and bleach. He added a small helping of grey water from yesterday's cooking and wash water. He needed to save what he could for working the toilet in his office. He had already drunk the water from the other toilets.

He prayed for rain again and wheeled the bucket into the cafeteria. He proceeded to mop the bloody floor with dirty water smothered with bleach.

He wished God had granted him the grace to continue the broadcast at the His Glory Broadcast Network affiliate. He built a viewership. He developed a brand. He fell from grace. He could have warned people of the punishment coming, but instead he preached to homeless opportunists and alcoholic losers in a tiny cafeteria. As an encore he mopped up vomit every other night. He fell from being a light on the hill to a jar of clay faster than the big time televangelists. The producer had not even let Jimmy come back in one last time for a tearful confession and contrition before the audience he built. They denied his swan song. They wiped him up and hid him from the public.

Jimmy left out the mop and bucket. He still needed to clean the backroom.

He leaned against the side of the candy machines and stared through the broken glass over the empty springs. Candy machines in a soup kitchen seemed an odd choice, but they made a small fortune for the center. Volunteering teenagers expelled quarters in endless supply. Homeless men seemed to shake out enough change to get a candy bar with surprising frequency. Jimmy had his own personal money changers. The late director didn't trust him with a key so, he smashed the glass and helped himself.

Hiding sin in a smaller market proved difficult. Jimmy found stalls that accommodated his temptations. Sodomites lay in wait on the other sides of holes for him to backslide again and again. Jimmy knew all the codes and all the etiquette. The reverend exposed his glory and fed it through for them to service. At those moments, he did not have to shame himself by touching it to keep it hard. He did not have to see the sin. Before the act was over, he thrust into the walls hard enough to tear the dirty places to the ground. Before his discovery, he started using more than their mouths. After he lost his show, he started reciprocating and served the glory of evil men.

Jimmy gagged once and closed his eyes.

Pounding started at the door and he nearly sliced himself on the broken glass in the frame of the machine. He waited silently. The pounding erupted again in a steady pattern.

"That is the rhythm of a soul."

Jimmy ran to the door and undid the lock over the mail slot. He swung the cover open and peered through. The man outside glistened with sweat over his dark skin and muscular frame. He wore a skullcap and had multiple weapons over his shoulders. He dropped down to his knees to peek through at Jimmy.

Jimmy smiled. "Oh, that's perfect."

"Brother, I need help. I'm not a bad person. I'll take off my weapons inside. I'll follow your rules."

"Sounds great. I have food and some water."

The man glanced back at the road. Jimmy could see the lifeless bodies wandering out from behind the houses and through the trees.

"Great, let me in, preacher. We have company."

Jimmy picked up a sawed-off shotgun from the umbrella bucket by the door and fed the remaining stumps of the barrels through the slot.

"I have to know you mean what you say."

The man turned back around and then stumbled backward onto his butt on the stoop. "Hey, be cool, preacher."

The man held out his hands and stared down the bore of the reverend's short shafts. Jimmy looked at the man's big, curled fingers and he imagined how they would feel. He shivered. Jimmy stood up still holding the gun in the slot at waist level. He unbuttoned the front of his slacks.

"What are you doing?"

"I want you to take me into your mouth."

"No, let me in. They're coming, damn it."

The fear in the man's voice did the trick without Jimmy having to touch himself. "Then, you need to work fast."

Jimmy heard the man shuffling on the stoop. He quivered as he waited to be touched or shot. Jimmy had no shells for his gun, so it was the visitor's choice. He was disappointed when he realized the man was running. Jimmy dropped down to his knees to watch.

The man ran and his muscles rippled as they clawed at him. They used their teeth and tongues as they took hold of him. Jimmy began touching himself. The man didn't fire a single shot. Jimmy couldn't tell if he had been bitten or not. As the man fled from sight, Jimmy's shame climaxed and he closed the mail slot.

He cried as he walked back through to the backroom. He stepped over the boy's body. He didn't bother wiping off before he fed his sticky shame through the bloody hole.

He struck the metal wall with the hilt of his knife. "If your hand offends you, cut it off."

He reached under himself with the blade and jiggled his shame for them to spot. As he heard the growling and shuffling, his glory returned even though he had just been spent. He left it hanging out longer than usual.

Reverend Jimmy wondered how it would feel if they touched it. He licked his lips and waited a while longer.

Subject Zero-Zero

Alex Chase

The days I remember best are the few just prior to the outbreak. Most, think about the beginning weeks—about the planes falling from the sky, the burning cities, the undead wandering the street—but not me.

My story begins on the morning of August 7th, 2013, as I left for work.

I brushed a napkin over my mouth and snatched my briefcase, leaving half-eaten eggs behind on the table. My wife, alarmed at my haste, could do little more than stare as I placed a kiss on her forehead before walking towards the front door.

"I love you, Ophelia," I called. I meant that as much as I had when I slid the gold ring onto her finger. I found her physically revolting, but in all other respects, she was beautiful. She understood I had never found people attractive. Though she seemed disappointed, she didn't fight with me over it.

"I ... love you too ... is something the matter, Max?" She looked worried.

"No, no, I just have to head in early today. I'm sorry, honey. I'll be home for dinner, ok?" I paused, hand on the doorknob.

"You're not in trouble, are you? I know you can't talk about your work, but ..." She approached me, her straw-colored hair gleaming in the pale rays of the morning sun.

I smiled. "If I were, I would tell you to take Junior as far away as possible, ok?" Junior had been conceived during the one and only time we'd made love throughout our entire marriage. Once was enough.

She bit her lip. "I wouldn't want to go without you."

I cocked my head, wondering where her concern came from. "You come first; you know that. I don't care, as long as I don't endanger you."

She smiled wearily and kissed my cheek. The secrecy took a toll on her, but I loved my work as much as I loved them, and she realized that. She wouldn't dare to suggest I take time off. Besides, with my salary, she couldn't complain.

"I'll call you if something comes up, ok? Love you, babe." I left.

I heard her whisper, "Love you too." The door swung shut behind me.

I drove off to Dextro Labs, where I'd spent fifty hours a week for the past decade solving the mysteries of the human genome. That's where the real object of my desires awaited.

My heart belonged to Ophelia, but I couldn't stand the hot, wet, sloppy nature of intercourse. At least, that's what I used to think.

Then I met Zero.

Dextro Labs' activities could be summarized in one word: transcendence. Its research divisions constantly worked to make the human species stronger, faster and smarter. For the most part, they'd been unsuccessful. The company nearly went under, but the Department of Defense approached them with a contract for the creation of a controllable contagion which might be released on an unsuspecting population, breaking it down from within.

During an experiment with cross-strain dRNA replacement, one researcher had unwittingly cut herself with a scalpel. An untested virus was introduced to her system. Within a few days, she died.

A few hours later, she stopped being dead.

The lab had several different technical names for her new state and for the virus, but no amount of jargon kept the word 'zombie' from floating around the hallways.

I had been transferred from developing a neural

enhancement drug to become the head of the Subject Zero case study shortly thereafter. That was the day I realized the undead were the only beings I could be with.

I got stuck in traffic and reached the lab later than intended; Pierce was already there when I arrived.

"We've determined her saliva does, in fact, bear infectious elements. Being bitten would result in the virus engaging the injured human and fully taking over within a few hours. Her own biotoxins are far more potent than the viral strain she was infected with." Pierce, a hook-nosed man in his late twenties, had been a late addition to the team. He'd pulled strings to get the position but proved himself worthy of it.

I complimented him, but paid little attention. The day passed in a blur of tests, read-outs, culture samples, and blood drawings. Zero was kept shackled with a metal bar clamped over her mouth; the infection increased her strength, coordination, and reflex responses. Rabbits were released into her containment cell three times per week so she might feed.

My superiors were too interested in results to kill her, my team too scared to risk any lesser confinement. I, however, thought of her differently. I put my theory to the test after ten agonizing hours of watching Zero strain against captivity.

"Are you leaving?" Melissa turned. She was in her early twenties—a graduate summa cum laude from Johns-Hopkins University with a doctorate in infectious diseases. "Soon. I have a few more tests I want to run," I said.

"Would you like help? I can stay if you'd like." She started back.

"No, I insist. Go home, rest. I'll see you tomorrow."

She appeared disappointed but turned and left anyway. I turned and made sure the security cameras were off.

I entered her cell and took in the firm, curvaceous beauty of Zero's bare form. Her shapely body had barely begun to decay. Blood rushed to my groin, though her gore-caked mouth and hungry white eyes would've made any other man run screaming.

"I know what you're really like. You're not a monster,

you're a Neanderthal. A modern woman with the mind of a scared cave dweller," I cooed. "You don't deserve to be a prisoner. You just want someone to understand you, don't you?"

Her blank eyes seemed to focus on me as her grunts became softer. Zero's heaving chest made her ample bosom sway, the pale mounds jutting off into space, their cool blue tips reaching out for human contact. I opened her shackles and released the clamp at her mouth.

Cold, smooth hands gripped the sides of my face. Zero stared, moving her hands across me, but didn't attack. I slid my hand up to her left breast and squeezed experimentally. Her hand slid lower, across my chest.

Already my cock swelled. My thumb and forefinger rolled her nipple as my other hand found her hip. Zero began breathing more heavily, her hands tracing my broad shoulders and winding down towards my waist.

Her nimble fingers sent an electric surge through me. I brought her closer, cupping her buttock. Her breath was on my neck ... but not her teeth.

I had been right. She wasn't a flesh hungry monster—her cognitive functions had just been crippled. My pants hit the floor in an instant.

Zero moved down on all fours and waited for me. I placed the quivering tip of my phallus to her lower lips, driving myself in, inch-by-inch, savoring the tight, clean sensation. Her body still lubricated itself, allowing easy entry, but not in the putrid, excessive amounts normal people produced.

Zero groaned with each thrust, her genetically enhanced body both giving and receiving pleasure far more intensely than any human could have.

I shuddered—not far from climax. Years of waiting for this moment—a moment I hadn't even thought possible until a few weeks earlier—had left me too pent up to take things slow.

I picked up speed, the violent spasms of my desperation

forcing my bulbous shaft deeper. My swollen testicles slapped against her clit; her cries grew louder and more shrill as they made contact. I wrapped my hands around Zero's hips, sinking my fingers into her. With one final gasp, I buried myself within her walls, exploding in her.

I leaned over her, a smile etched on my face. Having slaked my lust, I glanced down and realized the gravity of what I'd done. I fumbled to buckle my pants, then, as much as it killed me to do so, shoved Zero back into her restraints. Still dazed from her own orgasm, she wasn't able to resist; otherwise, it was likely she could've killed me.

I grabbed my belongings and headed home. Despite my recent exertion, a strange warmth spread through my groin. It stole across my body and, before long, I was flushed, my heart racing. My member throbbed and demanded attention once again.

I know Ophelia noticed my perturbed state, but she looked the other way.

On the other hand, I couldn't take my eyes off of her. She had become beautiful; my eyes took in every inch of her. Another throb commanded me to penetrate her. As she served dinner, I debated taking her right there on the table. If my son hadn't been present, I would have.

I couldn't think about that, though; I focused on the too-delicious food, the melodious sound of my wife's laughter, the shine of the life in Junior's eyes, and managed to pass the night without seeming too unsettled.

As I went to bed that night, Ophelia greeted me, nude. For once, I didn't mind sating my wife's desire. She wasn't an idiot; she'd been waiting for me, her husband, to gaze at her that way for years, and she wasn't going to let the moment slip away. I laid her back, spread her legs and took what she'd been dying to give me.

The next day started uneventfully. I woke up, showered, ate, and went to work. Zero's tests were normal and her behavior eerily calm, as if she no longer cared about freedom. Melissa, however, seemed more stunning than usual. Her shirt revealed far more of her small bosom than I'd noticed before; the enticing sway of her hips was almost too much for me to handle.

I didn't stay late with Zero that day; I returned home at around four, agonizingly aware of how colorful the world was.

So when I entered the house, I was too aware of the red on my living room floor. I followed the trail to Junior, lying in the center of the living room.

His head hung loosely about his shoulders. The flesh of his neck had been torn away, leaving nothing but his spine to keep the two parts of him together. I gaped with wide and wild eyes at a trail of bloody footprints leading to the back door.

Ophelia's ring lay nearby, drenched in Junior's blood. My wife stood, silhouetted in the doorway, gnawing on a lump of raw meat. She turned to me, her blank eyes taking me in, before she turned and walked away.

The scene was too bright. Too colorful. Too real. It didn't make any sense.

Then, it made perfect sense.

Zero's saliva wasn't the only infectious fluid her body produced. I realized with a sinking dread I'd been turned into a carrier—a typhoid-Mary 2.0—infecting the world with zombies, one orgasm at a time, hence why Ophelia didn't attack me.

I whipped out my phone to warn my superiors about the potential crisis. I knew that, if I did nothing, Ophelia might infect others.

Then I stopped.

Many more people would become cold, clean, beautiful creatures. It would be a world of Zero.

I smiled, and put my phone away.

I, Maxwell DeRosa, am responsible for the near-extinction of the human race.

And I regret nothing.

Die with Your Boots On

Lisa Woods

Sammy jumped out of her silver Mazda SUV intending to run for the door of the convenience store, under the blazing late afternoon sun. The store was the first one she had seen on Highway 75 that hadn't been in flames, or piles of ash. Her gut twisted when she spotted an old pickup truck in the parking lot as well. What if others were inside?

Fuck it, Sammy thought. She was in desperate need of provisions. Her supplies of food and water were getting low. She would have to take the chance and hope for the best. She tucked the 9mm she took from her father's nightstand after he succumbed to the disease—she bashed his brains in with an antique, brass lamp to keep him from turning on her—securely in the back of her denim shorts. Eleven in the clip and one in the chamber, safety engaged, like Daddy taught her.

She reached into the SUV and retrieved the machete she had found in the barn, before she left the farm. She remembered watching her home retreat in her rearview mirror through tears she hadn't realized filled her eyes. That had been weeks ago.

Lost in her reverie, Sammy didn't notice the two Dead shamble around the dumpster she parked next to. The first was a woman, one arm attached to her shoulder by a bit of muscle and sinew. If not for her blood smeared face and shirt, and the dangling arm, she would look almost normal. Newly Dead then. Still, a zombie was zombie no matter how fresh. Sammy dispatched her with the machete.

The second wasn't so fresh and the rancid stench of

decay filled Sammy's nostrils. She wrinkled her nose in disgust; she hated the ripe ones. She buried her machete in the top of his head and the blade went in all the way to his upper lip. That's why she hated the old Dead. They were ... mushy. And messy.

The zombies dealt with, Sammy returned her attention to the store. Approaching the glass doors, she shifted the machete to her left hand and grabbed the gun from her waistband. She peeked through the dusty glass door.

A face appeared on the other side, surprising Sammy so completely, she lost her balance and fell on her ass in the gravel parking lot. The door opened and, without thinking, she leveled her 9mm at the stranger's head.

"Stop right there! Don't take another step towards me or I will blow your head off, mister."

The man stopped and put both hands in the air. "I'm not armed and I don't mean you no harm. Really. You should come in. There's not a lot of Dead around here but there are some stragglers. I've been safe in here for a couple of days. There's food and water. Come on!" He stepped towards her and extended one calloused hand. Initially, Sammy regarded his proffered hand as if it were poisonous snake, but then she took it and let him help her up, leading her inside the sweltering store.

The store was dimly lit, but Sammy's eyes adjusted to the gloom. She walked through, marveling at the bounty remaining: beef jerky, candy of all kinds, chips, water, pop, even a small selection of canned goods. Plenty enough for two, so unless the stranger turned out to be a pervert rapist, she might be safe here, for a while anyway.

"So, you got a name?" Sammy asked the man as she finally turned her full attention to him. He was older than her 23 years she guessed, maybe upper twenties or even early thirties. He had the muscular look of a farmer or a cattle hand wearing jeans, a short, sleeved tee-shirt that had once been white, and cowboy boots. He had dark, brown hair under his John Deere baseball cap, but his eyes were a beautiful, piercing green that made her knees feel like jelly when he glanced at her.

Suddenly, she became self-conscience about her own, bedraggled appearance. Sammy knew she was more attractive than most, but certainly not supermodel material. She ran a hand over the long, blonde hair she had pulled back in a ponytail to keep it out of her eyes while she drove, not wanting to use the air conditioner in order to conserve her precious gasoline.

"Brody," he replied, holding out his hand. "Brody Tucker. I'm on my way to Tulsa to see if there are any survivors. Maybe pick up some provisions. Started out about 700 miles north of here in Iowa. What about you?"

She took his hand and shook it politely. "Sammy Roberts. I've just came from Tulsa. Nothing there. Everything's gone."

"You from Tulsa?" Brody questioned.

"No, my family had a farm south of Okmulgee. That's how we held out so long. We were able to be self-sufficient for quite a while. But the Dead eventually found us. They got Momma, but only managed to bite my Daddy a couple of times." Tears began to fill her eyes again. "I had to smash his head in with Momma's lamp before he could eat me." Tears overflowed and streamed down her dirty face.

Brody reached out to her and pulled her into his arms. Surprisingly, Sammy didn't feel awkward letting this stranger hold her. Their bodies seemed to fit together like two pieces of a puzzle, and she laid her head on his chest. Her body responded to his closeness in spite of the circumstances. He made comforting noises, as if she was a baby, and she didn't try to stop him when he pulled the elastic band out of her hair. He stroked it and put a rough hand on either side of her tear stained face and gazed into her eyes.

"I'm not going to tell you everything is going to be okay. There is nothing but destruction and the Dead from here to Des Moines. South doesn't sound any better. But we have food right now and a relatively safe place to hole up. How about we just hunker down here for a while and see what happens? Save some gas and keep each other company? I can't remember the last time I had myself some decent company who didn't either want to eat me, or kill me for my truck or whatever else I had."

"Sure," Sammy replied. She slid down the front counter of the store and sat with her back against it and her long, sun kissed legs in front of her.

"Why don't you have a seat?" She motioned to the spot next to her.

"I won't ever turn down a seat next to a pretty lady," Brody joked, sitting down beside her.

"How do you know I won't eat you?" she asked, feeling bold, tossing her hair back and smiling at him.

"Well, now, I guess I don't know for sure, do I? But, I suppose there would be worse ways to go." He laughed, the smile lines on his face crinkling. "I'll take my chances."

"Really?" Sammy's voice was husky now and filled with desire. A dam had broken somewhere inside her. After so much death, blood, and terror, she just wanted to feel alive one more time before she, herself, died. And who knew how long that would be. She longed to make a physical connection with someone in this new, God forsaken world.

She shifted around to face the man beside her, reached out and took one of his large hands and put it on her full breast. He gazed at her hopefully, but unsure of her intentions until he saw the lust burning in her blue eyes. He picked her up and sat her on his lap so she straddled his legs. Sammy pushed off his cap and entwined her hands in his dark hair, pulling his face to hers and covering his lips with her own. With no conscious thought, her hips began to move against the bulge in his jeans in an ancient rhythm of seduction. She moaned deeply, wanting this, needing him and the release they would bring each other to block out the horror of the previous months.

Brody grabbed her by the hair and wrenched her head back, kissing his way up her neck to her left ear. His hot breath was heavy with passion, as she continued to move against him on the floor. Having taken all the teasing he could stand, he grabbed her shoulders and flipped her off of his lap and onto the dirty floor of the store, both beyond caring at this point about anything except how quickly they might undress.

Finally unencumbered by clothes, Brody covered Sammy with his body, and began to press against her with his erection. Sammy opened her legs and wrapped them around his waist, welcoming him, and when he pushed his way into her completely, she screamed with the sheer life-affirming pleasure of it all and raised her hips up to meet him. They were both sweating from the heat and the exertion, and the sweat made their naked bodies slide erotically against one another. She shifted her legs down to encompass his legs between them and as he thrust into her she began to counter thrust so that her pussy, hot and wet, clamped down on him with each inward thrust.

"I'm going to come." She moaned and bucked underneath him, and with one final shuddering thrust, they climaxed together and went limp. Panting, they separated and rested on their backs, hands entwined.

Brody leaned over her and took one of her erect nipples into his mouth, suckling and rolling it between his teeth. He released the nipple and smiled at her. "It sure has been nice making your acquaintance, Miss Sammy."

"Likewise," she replied. "Unfortunately, I think this is our last hurrah."

"Why would you say something like that?"

Sammy pointed to the glass doors behind her head.

"Holy fuck!" Brody yelled. "Where did all those fuckers come from?"

"Tulsa, Collinsville, Ramona. No way to know for sure." Sammy answered as she began to get dressed and pull on her boots.

"No way we can take on so many."

"There's also no way these glass doors are going to hold out much longer," Sammy sighed. She took her gun and machete off the counter where she had left them. She handed Brody the machete and disengaged the safety of her gun.

"What the hell are you planning to do?"

"I'm going to kill as many of these assholes as I can. And then I'm going to die with my boots on. You coming?"

Brody looked at her with a small, melancholy smile. "I suppose so. I'm really glad I met you before ... you know. Glad the last time was with you."

"Me too."

"Can I ask you one last question? Your shirt. What the hell does that mean?"

Sammy looked down at her black shirt with four large, white letters on the front and laughed. "It says YOLO."

"YOLO? What the hell is YOLO?"

"You only live once."

Brody stared outside at the sea of Dead gathering around the store in the fading light. "Huh. Must be what they mean when they say something is ironic."

Sammy brought her gun up and put her hand on the lock of the door, the glass already beginning to crack under the pressure of the bodies pushing against it.

"Yeah, I think you're right."

Sammy flipped the lock and stood back waiting for the Dead.

LOUP

Pepper Scoville

Donnie tossed the bolt cutters aside and held the chain link fence open as the others crawled through. Piper focused her video camera on him. "As you can see, they've gotten lax with the security precautions. Budget cuts mean more money for the bigwigs but fewer rent-a-cops." Donnie said, as he grinned for the camera. Piper nodded and paused the recording.

"How did it look?" Donnie asked and held his hand out for the video camera. Piper kept it just out of his reach. It always irritated her that Donnie never trusted her with anything. He double checked everything she did and always insisted on being in charge. Hell, he didn't even like her to be on top when they messed around.

Donnie reached over and snatched the camera away. As he scrutinized the images he chastised Piper. "You know this needs to be high quality, right? If we want to be taken seriously as activists we've got to bring the goods." He shoved the camera back into her hands. Piper fumed as she tucked it back into her bag.

He wouldn't have even known about the facility if she hadn't told him what she overhead at the coffee shop. A couple of guys in khakis and polos bitched about work as she made their café mochas. Nothing unusual about that until one said, "It's the teeth you've got to watch out for."

Piper leaned closer as the second one said, "You'd think they'd slow down as the virus progresses."

The virus.

After the outbreak, when the government managed to

quickly contain the reanimated corpses that rose up, there had been rumors about what the government had done with the newly undead. There was talk of labs where inhumane experiments were conducted. Some people even said that's how the virus began in the first place. Occasionally, there were sporadic recurrences and containments but they rarely made the news anymore.

The Business Casuals, as Piper nicknamed them, came in almost every day. She knew the facility had to be within driving distance. She became friendly with them, even flirty. Bit by bit she pieced together all the information LOUP needed.

They ducked through the ragged opening and crept across the dark grounds. The hair on the back of Piper's neck stood up as the sounds of moans and shuffling reached her ears. Donnie glanced back at her.

"Scared?" he teased.

She shook her head and tried not to shiver.

As the couple reached the main testing facility, they found Erin and Xander spray painting LOUP across the wall.

"Great job, guys." Piper said.

Donnie admired the graffiti. "You do have wicked hand."

Erin shrugged with practiced cool.

"Ready to change the world?" Xander asked. The others smiled back. "Let's do this!"

Piper switched the camera back on. Donnie gave the lens a roguish smile and threw the doors open with a flourish. The group charged in but stopped abruptly in their tracks.

The stench hit them first.

Decay.

Rot.

Death.

As their eyes adjusted, their bravado failed. Shambling beings, once human, reanimated in a mockery of living filled pens throughout the room. Double doors faced them from the opposite side of the room.

Piper peered closer. Some of the dead stood statue-still, while others lurched mindlessly from one side of the pen to the other. Like a skipping record, some mimicked past movements on an endless loop. A woman "polished" the edge of the pen, wearing a dent in the metal. A man stepped forward and raised his arm, then stepped back only to repeat the gesture again and again.

The farthest pen, shrouded in shadows, appeared empty. Donnie motioned for them to follow. He nodded to Piper and she turned the camera on him. He cleared his throat. "As you can see, the poor undead persons are held here in horrid conditions. We here at LOUP, Liberators of Undead Persons, have heard ghastly rumors about medical experiments and other vile atrocities committed against these helpless individuals."

Donnie stepped back against the pen. The shadows behind him shifted. Erin noticed a blinking red light in the corner of the ceiling.

"Guys ..." Erin said.

Xander followed her gaze. "Crap. It's a camera."

Donnie shook his head. "If they'd seen us, there'd be alarms."

The electronic eye whirled and turned. "Pretty sure they've seen us." Piper argued, despite the dirty look her boyfriend gave her.

A shape rushed from the darkness behind Donnie. Without a moment to react, hands grabbed Donnie and pulled him into the pen. His screams shattered the calm. The coppery smell of blood filled the air. The rest of the undead, sensing a change in the environment, threw themselves against the pens' gates. The metal frames shook as the zombies struggled to reach the activists.

The door to the outside flew open as guards charged in. The uniformed men tackled Xander immediately. Erin screeched as a woman with half a face grabbed her hair and tried to drag her into a pen. The guards rushed over with cattle prods and shocked the half-faced woman until she released Erin. The young woman's relief was short lived as she was thrown to the floor and handcuffed.

A guard snagged Piper. She kicked and screamed. The guard lost his balance and stumbled back within reach of the zombies. The other guards rushed to help him, giving Piper just enough time to dart through the double doors at the end of the room.

The well-lit corridor was a startling contrast to the dark holding area. White, sterile-looking walls were dotted with evenly-spaced doors. Piper grabbed the doorknobs as she dashed down the hallway, desperate for a place to hide. They were all locked.

Adrenalin pounded through her veins. She raced down the hallway and slid around a corner. Footsteps slapped the clean tile as the guards neared. Piper grabbed the last door's knob.

She froze in surprise when it opened.

Voices thundered behind her. She slipped into the room. The door closed quietly behind her as the guards rounded the corner.

Crouching by the door, she tried to slow her breathing. A low growl sounded from the darkness. She wasn't alone.

A young, naked man lay pinned to an examination table by straps and restraints. Piper couldn't help but think he must have been beautiful in life. Soft, dark curls framed his face. Blood-red eyeballs surrounded icy blue irises. His slender, muscular body hinted at an active life as opposed to bodybuilding or gym worshiping. Tattoos swirled and tinted his skin like stained glass on a church. Only the bared teeth and sanguine eyes gave away his true state.

Piper stepped forward. Her fingertips brushed his bare stomach. He lurched forward, restraints straining. His skin was cool and hard. It reminded her of stone. Confidence growing, she allowed her hand to trace the curve of his abdomen down to the wiry hair at his pelvis.

She gasped as his cock grew hard. *How did that happen? Rigor mortis?* Blushing in the darkness, she glanced around.

Stupid, she thought. *I'm alone.* Her nails ran up and down his length. The growl in his throat became more of a purr.

"You like that?" She grinned. *Even if he didn't, what could he say?* Warmth spread through her as the desire for the beautiful dead man mixed with a sudden surge of power. She could do anything she wanted.

Anything.

She wrapped her fist around his girth and slowly pumped her hand up and down. Her other hand cupped his balls and gave them a gentle squeeze. The harder he became the more inflamed Piper felt. She released his shaft to shimmy out of her leggings and panties. Bracing her arms on either side of the man, she crawled onto the table.

Now it was her lip that curled. The young man lunged forward and snapped his teeth when she straddled him. Piper grabbed his hair and forced his head back. He struggled and she laughed. Cocking her hips she felt his length slide between her wet lips. She worked it back and forth, drenching it in her juices.

He purred again. She angled herself so his tip brushed her entrance. Easing down, she let his cock enter her inch by inch. One hand on his chest kept her at the right angle as her other hand snaked down to rub her clit. His cool skin made her shiver as it filled her.

She was so engrossed in the sensations as they overpowered her she didn't hear the door lock behind her.

She rocked on his hardness, faster and faster. Glancing down through heavy-lidded eyes, she realized the man was no longer trying to bite her. His head lolled on his neck, his mouth slack. He almost looked normal. Her muscles clenched as the first wave of her orgasm hit. She moaned and spasmed.

A burst of light blinded Piper as the fluorescent tubes above flashed on. She pitched forward as the last wave wracked her body. A hidden speaker crackled.

"Well, hello there. How are you feeling?" Her head whipped around as she searched for the source. Below her, the man bucked against her. Something cold and slimy burst inside her.

"Oh, God," she moaned.

Piper tumbled off of the table. The cold slime dripped down her thighs. Her hands fumbled for her clothes.

The voice chuckled. "Oh, no. Don't be like that. You've been very helpful to us."

She pulled her clothes on, gagging against the slickness, and rushed for the door. Panic flooded her as the handle twisted uselessly in her hand. Tears streamed down her face and she sunk to the floor.

"Calm down and listen. Are you listening?" Piper sniffed and nodded. The voice continued. "The video has been confiscated. Your friends have been dealt with. We don't want to hurt you so don't give us a reason to."

The lock clicked open. Piper turned as two men in hazmat suits opened the door. The voice droned on. "Come quietly. We're curious about the repercussions of your actions. We just want to observe you for a couple of days."

Her gaze fell on the naked man. He lay still, docile. The low growl, now more lazy than threatening, roiled from his throat.

"We've tried so many ways to relax the reanimated but nothing works. Tranquilizers, shocks, restraints. We never thought to appeal to more base appetites. If the virus isn't transmitted sexually, who knows? You may have a new job."

One of the Hazmat-suited men glanced down at her. She recognized the twinkle in his eyes.

"Beats slinging coffee, huh?" He chuckled. His partner tightened his grip on her arm.

The Business Casuals.

Piper let herself go limp, the way Donnie had taught her to do if they were caught.

"Dead weight is harder to move," he said. She wondered how much what was left of Donnie weighed as they dragged her from the room.

The Long Wait

Steve Lockley

Alice was already up and out of bed by the time Martin woke. Last night he wanted to hold her forever but the stress of their wedding day proved too much for both of them. They fell asleep in each other's arms not long after climbing into bed, with sex at least a heartbeat out of reach.

The wedding had been rushed, and their escape from the city more than a little stressful; the minister keen to perform the ritual and complete the formalities quickly so they could be on their way in search of safety. They had been waiting for so long, committed to each other but desperately clinging to their beliefs despite the carnage going on all around them; saving themselves for their wedding night, but not expecting the long awaited night to turn out the way it had.

The dead were at every turn, standing on street corners and shuffling along streets littered with damaged and abandoned cars. At last they managed to weave their way through stationary traffic and make their getaway. When they finally reached this small cottage in the mountains they thought they were as safe as possible. They only hoped a solution would be found before too many people fell prey to the contagion. They had seen enough death already, and didn't want to witness any more. This isolated cottage would be their safe haven until the madness was over.

"Alice?"

No reply. He called again, this time more urgently, but nothing more than silence greeted him. A mixture of fear and curiosity gnawed at the pit of his stomach. He threw the quilt to one side and shivered as the cold air hit his skin. He padded out to the landing at the top of the stair, listening for any sign of movement. A sense of relief washed over him when he heard a noise coming from the kitchen. *They were safe here*, he reminded himself. *Safe and far away from the danger.*

The stairs creaked as he made his way down, still calling her name. He thought he heard her singing but walking into the kitchen he found the room empty, with the radio playing to no-one. How long there would be a station pumping out music was hard to imagine. Maybe a day would come when they fell silent. Perhaps new music had already stopped being created.

The back door stood open and a cool breeze reminded him he wore nothing but a pair of boxer shorts. He stood in the open doorway and called her name into the wind but she didn't respond. It took a moment for him to spot her standing on the edge of the small patch of land they planned to cultivate. She wore nothing but the skimpy pajamas she had slipped into before falling in bed, exhausted, giving him only a momentary glimpse of her nakedness. As he watched her he wanted her more than ever, the urge stronger than he had ever known it, but he wanted to savor the moment of innocence.

"Come back inside. You'll catch your death of cold," he said. "Let me take you back to bed and help warm you up." The words tumbled from his mouth with a sudden urgency.

She turned slowly and he realized something was wrong about the way she moved, but he didn't understand what it might be, even though the answer stared him in the face. They had not managed to escape the madness taking place in the city; they had brought it with them. But still he wanted her as much as he had ever done.

She shuffled back to the door, her face slack and lifeless, but he was not afraid of her, or of what she had become. Even death would not part them, not now they were so close to knowing each other in the way they had longed for. She took his hand, clearly unaware of what was happening to her. He was sure some tiny spark still burned behind her eyes. He also realized there was every chance he was fooling himself.

He helped her up the stairs to the bedroom, encouraging her up every step of the way while he wiped his own tears away. There was nothing in this life for him without her, and he had to take the moment while he still could, while there was still a chance she knew what was happening.

They lay together in the bed, naked for the first time, while he ran his fingers across her dead and dying flesh, teasing her nipples in the hope of some kind of response, but there was nothing. He held her close and wept as he made love to her, trying to imagine the child they had dreamed of making together but now no longer would. He moved faster and faster inside her, wanting the sex to be over as quickly as possible.

When at last he lay on her, spent, but unwilling to release her from his embrace, her need started to rise. He felt the sudden stab of pain as she sank her teeth in his skin and began to chew on the flesh below his neck. He made no effort to stop her. His blood washed over her, soaking the bed, and he buried his face in the pillow. He fought back a cry of pain, but knew she could no more help the need driving her than he could have held back the desire that had gripped him. This was the only way for them be together for whatever time they had left.

Angel of Mercy

Wednesday Silverwood

Tracey had been gone a long time.

Fuck. Where is she? Chris thought to himself. How long could she draw this out?

He tried to twiddle his thumbs, but even that became hard to do when tied, spread-eagle and butt-naked, to his four poster bed. He had finished counting the flies on the ceiling (sure were a lot of flies up there) and started to feel painfully cramped. His wrists chaffed.

He had nearly drifted into sleep when Tracey's gorgeous silhouette appeared in the doorway. It was so dark by now he could hardly make her out.

"You sure took your sweet time," he said. "I almost thought you'd forgotten about me."

She stumbled to the bed and began nibbling the soft flesh of his neck.

"Hmmm. That's nice," he cooed. "Wait, not so hard!"

"Braiiiins!" Tracey mumbled back at him.

He was instantly awake.

She looked hideous. Her hair stuck up all over her head, and her lipstick (or something) was smeared all round her mouth. Worst of all, her skin had turned a sort of blue-grey and she had a hungry gleam in her eye.

"Ahhrg!" Chris shouted, pulling at his restraints and wishing they had used the silk scarves today. "Shit!"

Suddenly, a terrific crash sounded and a woman in a long leather trench coat burst into the room. She levelled an enormous weapon at Tracey before picking her off with a single shot, and turning her attention to Chris. The first thing he noticed about her were her beautiful eyes. The second thing was the sneer on her face.

"You sure picked a fine old time to be getting it on. Don't you know there's a level three zombie threat going on outside?"

"Well, there wasn't when we started, I can assure you."

She raised an eyebrow at him, and looked over the room.

"Any more of them?" she asked. Chris shook his head.

"Of course, that's some people's thing. Zombie sex. They don't last long though, if you catch my meaning." She gave Chris a meaningful glance, taking in his tousled hair and strong features. Then she shook her long hair over her shoulder and readjusted the weight of her weapon.

"No, zombie sex is not my thing, as you put it, and she wasn't a zombie when we met." Chris said. "So are you going to get me out of here or what?"

"I suppose I'll have to, since it's my job an' all." She smiled. "Though you do look pretty good lying there."

Chris blushed and tried to shift his position from under her gaze. His taut muscles writhed under his constraints.

"I'm Major Angel Phoenix, by the way. Zombie Eradication Force." She took a step closer to the bed. "Pleased to meet you."

Chris found himself blushing again. She really was one of the most beautiful women he'd ever seen and he admired the way her leather pants clung to her slim legs as she crossed the room.

He wasn't bad looking himself, he thought, glancing up at his reflection in the mirrored ceiling. *After all, he worked out.*

Angel pulled a set of bolt cutters from her back pack and bent towards him.

"While you're down there, love." Chris said with his best boyish grin and she smacked him hard in the face.

"Shit, I was only joking," he said, and they both looked down, surprised to see he was becoming erect. But then, he was pretty aroused. Tracey had never been able to get that part of S&M role play quite right. Poor Tracey, she'd never wanted to hurt him. Well, at least she hadn't before she became a zombie anyway. He sensed Angel would have no such compunction.

Chris shivered as Angel held up the bolt-cutters.

"So you want me to cut you loose?"

"Yes. Obviously, I do."

"You'll have to ask me nicer than that." She said, taking off her leather coat.

Chris was surprised to see how curvaceous her figure was under the heavy garment. From his narrow experience he had expected a lot of these army types had boyish figures, but Angel was all woman. She slithered out of her army issue t-shirt and undid her bra, exposing her full breasts. He felt his muscles hardening.

"So, like, what level was this zombie threat, did you say?"

"Oh, it's nothing that can't wait." She answered, unzipping her leather pants.

* * * *

She was getting back into her clothes when Chris thought of something.

"You know, Angel. You never even asked me my name." He grinned. "I never would've picked you for that sort of girl."

"Oh, I know who you are Mr. Chris Slate, Head of Slate Industries. In fact, I know Slate Pharmaceuticals is one of your companies too."

"Hey, those allegations were never proved! We had nothing to do with the ZOMBII strain. We were cleared of all wrongdoing."

"Well, I should think so too, the amount you pay your lawyers, to say nothing of the officials you bribed. But I've been doing my own research and I think we both know the truth. Do you want to know why I joined the Zombie Eradication Force?"

"Not really. But I expect you're going to tell me."

"You're a very confident man, Mr. Slate. I'm surprised you're still so arrogant in your position."

Chris sighed to himself. It was true. He never knew when to keep his mouth shut. Angel was dressed now and she sat on the edge of the bed and lit a cigarette.

"My whole family were killed by zombies. I joined the force as soon as I could and I swore my revenge. I couldn't believe my luck when there was an outbreak in this sector. I knew your reputation, so I hoped you'd be in some compromising position. Lucky for me, you were. Of course, I didn't realize you would be so hot! So I thought I might as well have some fun too. I mean, now I'll be the last person to have had Chris Slate, not that I'll be telling anyone, of course."

"What! But you can't leave me here!"

"Sugar, I can do anything 1 want." Angel smiled and extinguished her cigarette. She stood up and buttoned her trench coat.

"This area's secure, Colonel." She called into her walkie-talkie. "Moving out."

"Rodger that," said a disembodied voice at the other end.

"Angel! Please!" called Chris. His eyes were wide. He couldn't believe what was happening. But she had already turned away.

"Night, night," she called back at him. "Don't let the bed bugs bite, yeah?" She laughed and blew him a kiss, before she shouldered her gun and left.

There were lumbering shapes moving in the darkness as Angel moved out into the night. She made sure she left the front door wide open.

After all, Angel of mercy just wasn't her style.

Quiet Consummation

Katie Young

When the dead first started coming back, the streets filled with these rotting, shambling husks intent on eating us alive, we survivors were still intrinsically linked by the internet, phone networks, televisions and radios. They urged us to barricade ourselves indoors and not to venture out unless absolutely necessary. But the airwaves fell gradually silent and we became increasingly isolated. We knew we were on borrowed time, and we craved some last vestige of human contact. The compulsion to find our friends and families in different states took hold, and these strange, secular pilgrimages made. Most of them ended as you'd expect.

For me, the end times compounded the crippling loneliness and futility which always dogged me. I had no one. I would die alone, either in the maws of a stinking undead thing, doomed to become one of them, or by my own hand. Only cowardice kept me from slitting my wrists on several occasions when the constant, creeping depression tipped over into despair.

But, crazy as the concept seems, as time passed, I *wanted* more than I ever had before. Hell came to Earth, and brought with it a sense of entitlement. Didn't I deserve *something* before shuffling off into the long, cold nothing? Back then, the notion was a whisper, a tiny seed of an idea taking root in some dark recess of my mind as I padded aimlessly around my apartment. I'd been relatively safe up on the seventeenth floor. Our block hadn't been breached, food was rationed and we coexisted in relative harmony, but I knew the peace couldn't last. Everyone was friends while the going was good, but the supplies would run out someday soon.

Now *he* was the only thing which gave me joy. His green eyes, half closed in perpetual pleasure, burned holes through me from the framed posters on my walls. His hair, thick and glossy, teased carefully into a dark pile of curls which fell slightly to one side. His lips were plump and blushy, inviting as the soft flesh of a peach. Kit Etheridge. He wasn't what you'd call A-list, but he'd been in a few long-running TV shows and the odd movie, and his beauty attracted a small but fervent following of devotees. I tried to keep my desire for him on the down-low. People can be cruel, and I realized the sort of things they would say. I'd had a few boyfriends, but they never worked out. Nothing I felt for them could compare to the idea of him.

Tucked up in my bed for endless days and nights, drapes drawn against the encroaching horrors in the streets below, I watched everything he'd ever done on a loop, even though I knew every line of dialogue, every gesture, every expression by heart. I'd lie back, listening, close my eyes and slip my hand into my underwear. I'd touch myself to the sound of his voice, drawing it out until I couldn't hold back any more, and I'd come, shuddering, his name on my lips, before letting sleep pull me under. It was an odd sort of peace.

One night, I awoke to raised voices bleeding through my thin bedroom wall. I sat up and pressed my ear to the cool plaster as the argument escalated. I didn't catch the whole thing, just snatches, but Mrs. Crawshaw from the next floor up seemed to be accusing Evan next door of having skinned and eaten her beloved tabby cat. Evan denied doing so, of course, but I had my doubts. Not just because Evan was half Korean, but because months and months had passed since any of us tasted fresh meat, and if this whole zombie situation had taught me anything, it was not to underestimate the lengths to which hunger will drive a person. I made up my mind then and there, coverlet up over my head to drown out the shouting. I would leave this place before it was too late and I ended up dead in my bathtub with a belly full of pills, or with my head in Evan's cooking pot. I would find Kit.

I took my handgun, ammo, a few changes of clothes, make-up, hairbrush, some dried food, and bottled water. I snuck down the fire escape and made a break for it. The risen were slow enough to avoid most of the time. Only when they started to herd in huge numbers did they became a real problem. I was surprised to find my car still where I'd parked it all those months before, covered in a fine layer of ashes and dust, and the engine started after a couple of tries.

Once on the road, a weird sort of euphoria washed over me. I was going to find Kit. It seemed the end of civilization gave me the kick up the ass I needed to finally go after my dreams. The roads outside Wichita were littered with burnt out cars and debris from accidents—the legacy of panic and a mass exodus from the city. As I hit the highway, I found myself driving faster and faster, maybe half hoping I'd flip the car: a split second of pain, then blessed oblivion. I'd be smeared all over the asphalt, carrion for the birds and the hungry dead. But there remained a chance I wouldn't die. I'd be trapped in the wreckage and I'd never get to see Kit in the flesh.

Flat farmland became desert as I drove west. I'd stop now and then at deserted gas stations to scavenge for fuel, food, and tools. In the guttering yellow and blue lights of these long forgotten convenience stores, it was easy to mistake myself for one of the revenants. I'd lost too much weight, and my face was hard and etched with fear and sorrow.

I drove for two days, stopping every few hours to sleep for a little while. It was the sleep of the hunted, hardly restful, but necessary. Finally the busted up Hollywood sign was in my sights. I drove around the hills, mowing down the dead in my path. Most of them slow-cooked by the Cali sun, coming apart like squishy, over-ripe watermelons. Laurel Canyon crawled with them. My heart sank as I drove past houses and complexes and gated communities, only to find them all overrun. Walls had been torn down, pools stained rust-brown with old blood and the sidewalks spattered with baked-on viscera.

At last I found Kit's place, according to the old internet forums, shielded from the road by cedars. The gate was busted open, so I drove as close to the front door as I could and got out of the car, gun drawn, safety off. I tried the handle and found the huge door opened easily, the lock splintered. I stepped into the spacious hall and listened. Nothing. I called out, quietly at first, then louder when there was no response. Of course, I thought him long gone. Probably fled the country or gone to be with his family.

I made my way upstairs and scoured the rooms. I opened his wardrobes and buried my face in his clothes, the scent of cologne and freshly laundered shirts locked into the fabric.

I inhaled deeply and my pulse picked up as I realized I was taking tiny particles of him into myself. Tasting him. I rubbed my cheek against silk and suede and cashmere. I went into the en suite and put his toothbrush in my mouth. I lay on his bed and rolled around on his sheets. I put his pillow between my legs and humped my hips up as I imagined his hands on me. I was lost to the fantasy when I heard a crash outside the room. I sprung up and ran to the landing in time to see him disappearing into one of the other bedrooms. I could tell by his gait that Kit had been turned.

I scurried down the stairs and out to the car. I retrieved some rope from the trunk, tied a loop at one end to make a lasso and went back inside. He stood at the top of the stairs. I ascended slowly, watching him watching me. A large bite marred his right forearm, but other than that and his pallid skin, he looked exactly as he did in all my posters. He started towards me, so I leapt up the final few steps, barged past him, threw the rope over his head and yanked. He went down hard, snarling and grasping at his neck and I dragged him across the marble floor. I flung the end of the rope over his bedroom door and tied it off around the handle on the other side, hoisting him to his feet. Everything happened in a blur, adrenaline making me strong and fast, setting a delicious tingle off over my skin. I paused, catching my breath, unsure of what to do next. He was still so beautiful. Pale like the moon. His eyes were a little bloodshot but still so green, and he tracked me with an expression of such hunger I immediately felt a pulse of slick seep into the cotton of my underwear. I stepped closer to him and he struggled, arms outstretched, trying to touch me. I stayed just out of reach, shucking my clothes as I held his eyes, enjoying the desperation, the raw desire oozing from every decadent cell of his being.

"You want me?" I asked, voice hoarse with arousal.

He writhed and jerked on the end of the rope. I leaned in another couple of inches and took hold of his clawed hands. I put them over my breasts and gasped as his fingers scratched and spasmed, my nipples hard, his nails digging little red furrows in my flesh. His strong white teeth gnashed together as he tried to drag me closer to his mouth.

"Take it easy, my love," I cooed. "I'll give you what you need."

I dropped to my knees and unbuckled his soft leather belt. His fingertips pressed marks into my shoulders and snarled in my hair. I welcomed the sharp sting as he tore out strands in his frenzy. I pulled down his pants and underwear, revealing the soft, white length of his cock, stark against the dark thatch of pubic hair. I swallowed hard and dipped my head to brush my lips over the silken head. He made a long sort of groan then, like some sense memory took him over, and twitched against my mouth. I put my tongue out to taste it, my clit throbbing and hot like bruising. He smelled stronger here, almost gamey, a lingering taint of corruption under the soap and cologne. I nuzzled his crotch and touched myself, listening to his grunts and the soft, choked off noises he made as he strained and bucked. It was close enough to everything I'd ever wanted and I came, bearing down hard on my own sticky fingers as I gasped out my release.

Now I sit slumped with my face pressed to his cold thigh for a few moments, looking up. His perfect mouth is pulled into a grimace, lips chapped and blue. The rope has bitten into his throat and drawn blood, though it's blackened and sluggish, not red and vital. Soon he will start to bloat, his muscles and skin becoming pulpy and loose. His hands tug at my scalp, restless jaw working. I wipe a tear from the hollow under my eye and stand, let him take me in his rough embrace and tilt my head for a kiss. His breath is dry and stale, a bitter wind on my face. There is a moment of elation, the plush press of those lips, then pain blooms, exquisite and all-consuming as he bites down on my tongue. At the first warm, brackish gush, a look of sated calm settles in those green eyes, and I know I've found my purpose.

Some Like It Rot

John Palisano

Jerry Hatrick opened the door to Elizabeth Cotton's hotel room and realized something was very wrong. She lay on her back—not on her stomach with her butt up in the air as usual. He spotted the distinct rocket-shaped red pill bottle on her nightstand amongst the other bottles and knew right away what had happened. She'd taken Zethromorax, the newest designer pill making the rounds of young Hollywood. *It'll Shoot You To The Stars!* The ads were inescapable. Its users experienced a super nice and fuzzy sensation ... believing their minds were expanding. Yet, for every person who enjoyed a good experience, three suffered miserable side effects, like spontaneous diarrhea. *To the stars?* More like a run for the porcelain border. Every once in a while, there'd be a person with whom Zethromorax would not only disagree, but turned them into walking shells, barely able to speak or function. Zethro-zombies, as TMZ and Entertainment Tonight had branded them. The drug already counted a few B-listers as victims.

And now, his boss, Elizabeth Cotton, was another Zethro-zombie, which meant he'd be out of work. Who would hire an assistant that let his client get gacked away on Zethromorax? How would a zombie sign his measly paychecks? His career would be toast. He'd have to move back to Michigan and work at the Juicy Burger. Jerry feared he was a goner, as far as Hollywood was concerned, if he didn't fix Elizabeth Cotton. On top of that? He'd never sell his spec script.

He rushed over to Elizabeth and put a hand to her

forehead—cold as ice. She made a gurgling noise. Her skin had gone a pale grey. Her lips moved, but no real words came out. She smelled like rotten eggs and gasoline.

At least Elizabeth hadn't died. He put the back of his hand to her cheek and found her to be clammy. Her skin appeared gray and rotten; she only moved a little when he shook her shoulder. Usually Elizabeth woke up talking a mile a minute, but she rolled on her back and moaned. His stomach sank.

One of the two stooges Elizabeth brought home the night before slumped on the floor by the air conditioner. He wasn't moving. Jerry watched him for a moment, but saw no signs of breathing. "Tell me you're not dead," he said. "And where's the other guy?" Against his better instincts, Jerry reached out and shook the man's shoulder. "Hey? Come on, man. Wake up."

No response.

He stood up straight, sighed, and put his hands to his side. Jerry glanced down at the guy, then turned around to Elizabeth.

Taking the bottle of Zethromorax from the side table, Jerry looked it over. "Wes Zemeckis?" he addressed the dead man. "Thanks for bringing this shit with you."

* * * *

The night before, Elizabeth brought the two men inside her room. She took turns kissing them. "Give a girl some privacy, hon," she'd said to Jerry, and he scurried into the hallway and waited while she had her way with the stooges. He winced, listening to the action. What kind of job had he taken? He felt like a pimp. Showbiz wasn't all everyone made it out to be, just like that overplayed Journey song had warned. Of course, it wasn't glamorous: everyone knew that. Actually? It was downright degrading. He went home after an hour.

* * * *

Zethromorax came to the attention of the L.A. party scene accidentally. Originally intended for poor, unfortunate souls suffering from epilepsy, Zethromorax had not been intended to get people high. Somewhere along the line, an adventurous Goth popped one and discovered the pill didn't just help a serious illness; it also created a euphoric sense of suspended animation and heightened reality. Users reported their minds became crystal clear and they came to vast conclusions about the world while under its influence: finding their inner selves in ways previous armies of self-help gurus and spirit guides could not. The downside being, for every person who claimed Zethromorax expanded their minds, three others wound up brain dead. It was a roll of the dice. Didn't matter if the person was smart, or stupid, or beautiful, or, God forbid, ugly. Nope. Zethromorax just spun the wheel of fate.

He wondered why Elizabeth would take Zethromorax on top of everything else? Was she suicidal? She always had to be 'hip' and 'sly' or whatever, didn't she? He usually shook his head and looked the other way from most of her diversions. But this time, she'd lost. Damn. Jerry heard Elizabeth's excuses in his mind: *"I get stage fright when I wake up in the morning."*

Jerry would have to prep Elizabeth for the interview, despite her compromised condition.

He nudged her. Maybe there was something he could do to snap her out of it. Leaning down, his face searching for hers, he said her name, his voice higher pitched, as though talking to a toddler. Doing so was nothing new; Jerry always talked to Elizabeth like she was a baby. "Elizabeth?"

She groaned, but she didn't sound like her usual helium-voiced self—more like a 300-pound man with emphysema. Jerry bet the vocal anomaly was another side effect of the Zethromorax. *Not dead yet. But not really alive, either.*

He put a nervous hand on her shoulder. He shook her. "Come on, we have an interview in less than an hour."

He glanced over to the fellow on the floor next to

Elizabeth's bed. Elizabeth stirred and groaned. He shook her again, and she rolled away from him.

A putrid smell wafted from her, reminding Jerry of the diaper genies he used to change for his younger sister when they were growing up. A person could wrap shit in paper and plastic as tight and tidy as possible, but shit still found a way to get through, no matter how many bags you used. Smelling that same sharp stench coming from Elizabeth made him gag.

She rolled on her back and opened her mouth. Her skin looked darker than he remembered; Elizabeth normally appeared paler. Instead of red, her lips were blue. Large dark circles rimmed her eyes, which made Jerry think she sort of resembled a panda.

"Are you all right?" Jerry said.

Her lips opened, and she attempted to talk, but only gibberish came out. "Mmm—whhaa—whaa."

"Elizabeth?" he asked, trying again to reach her.

"Mmm—whhhaa—whaa."

Jerry had an idea. He couldn't call the police, of course. If he called her regular doctor, he would be toast. It was, after all, Jerry's unspoken responsibility to babysit her. So instead of calling them, he called Big Louie. Her agent.

"We've got another Indian." Big Louie said.

Jerry took his phone away from his ear and checked the LCD screen to make sure he'd dialed the right number.

"Those motherfuckers. We won. We got another Indian." Big Louie said. Some static and a slight pause, and then, Big Louie came closer to the phone. "Tell me something I want to hear."

"Elizabeth's still alive."

"Well then, wet my pistol," Big Louie said. "One less PR job I've got to deal with." He heard the sound of Big Louie drinking, and Jerry imagined the heavy man looking out his office window and shooting his wheat grass while on the phone.

"Someone gave her Zethromorax last night."

A pause.

"Why, you silly little man? Can't you even control what goes in and out of her system? If she lives through this, you're not going to." Big Louie always threatened Jerry whenever he got the chance.

"I can't be with her every second."

"Now what are you going to do? Is she speaking?" Big Louie said.

"Barely."

Big Louie sighed. "So she reacted to it poorly. One of those ones we've been hearing about. Damn. She's taken so many drugs I'm surprised she isn't immune."

"The guy that gave her the drug, Wes, is all blue and he ain't moving," Jerry said.

"Where are you?"

"Horizon Hotel."

"Shit."

"Shit what?" Jerry said.

"You're shit. I'm not the one in an upscale squat box with a dead guy and a zombified movie starlet. Maybe I can call up George Romero or Eli Roth and get her some background work on their next zombie movies. Hell, everything's all about zombies these days. Maybe she'll be good."

"I heard there's a way to reverse the condition ... make it better." Jerry offered.

Another pause. Jerry heard Big Louie put down a drink. "I'll have to make a call or seven." And just like that, Big Louie hung up on Jerry.

Jerry sat on the edge of the bed. Elizabeth had turned completely on her back. She wore a mischievous grin. "Oh, don't you look at me like that."

He knew what was coming.

She moaned. "Whhh-ubb. Whhh-ubb." She kicked her legs and feet at him. "Whhh-ubb. Whhh-ubb."

"Oh, for God's sake," Jerry said. "Fine." He put up a finger. "But, only until Big Louie calls back and tells me how to get you out of this mess."

Rubbing her feet was not easy. Her flesh had become

soft, reminding him of over-ripe fruit where the skin might easily slip right off.

She groaned and moaned, sounding as though she were being made love to. Jerry rubbed away. He peeked at her and she had shut her eyes. She cocked her head back and stuck out her tongue, flicking it toward the ceiling. She still had her chiseled features; high cheek bones, strong jaw, perfect nose. He thought of how, only a few years back, he'd been in college reading about the stars in Hollywood, and how he'd always thought she was beautiful ... almost as good looking as Grace Kelly. He never thought he'd be in charge of her day to day comings and goings, and he never thought he'd actually be able to touch her. Yet, here he sat, massaging her undead feet, waiting for her agent to call. Not a doctor, or a lawyer, but her agent. Hollywood made no sense to him.

As soon as the phone rang, he stopped rubbing.

"No." Elizabeth managed to say.

"I have to take this." he said. "We need to fix you."

He slid his phone on.

Before he could say, "Hello," Big Louie jumped right in.

"Okay. She needs to be pregnant."

"What?"

"You know I don't like repeating myself, so I won't. Do the deed, my friend. It's the only way she's going to be able to counter the crap you let her take. Something happens when the body initiates a pregnancy ... must be the girlie parts that take care of things. I don't know. You know how that asshole likes to use big words and pretend he's smarter than everyone just because he puts rubber noses on all these morons."

"You called her plastic surgeon?" Jerry said.

"He understands all about recreational drug use. Makes sense, of course. Some of his clients come in for stuff just so they can get painkillers. He can't get some of them off the crap, so they get another procedure, and boom! They've got another scrip'," Big Louie said.

"That's smart."

"That's why you called me, right?" Big Louie said.

"Umm ...,"

"Put your little dinky in her winky and call me when the deed's done," Big Louie said. "And good thing she's a girl, huh? Otherwise you'd be really screwed."

"Guess so," Jerry said.

"Bye, Candy Face." Big Louie hung up.

Candy Face? What? Big Louie seldom made much sense, and Jerry's mind raced, trying to figure out what he'd meant. Was he out of his mind? Was he really supposed to make love to an undead Elizabeth Cotton? While a dead guy lay in the room? Didn't zombies eat people? What if she tried to munch on him?

Well, he wasn't sure but as far as he remembered, the folks that suffered the undead-like after effects didn't get the flesh eating trait. That seemed to be something the movies made up. Still, Jerry didn't think he trusted hearsay. He realized the chances of getting eaten by a shark at the beach were slim, too, but after he saw 'Jaws'? Forget it. He was strictly a pool swimmer. And making love to Elizabeth? He decided then and there he would play it safe. Missionary. No crazy positions, especially where he wouldn't be able to see her mouth.

He wasn't sure how to convince her to make love to him. She did let him rub her feet. In fact, she insisted on his doing so just a few minutes earlier. He would start there.

"Your feet still achy?" he asked.

"Mmm," she moaned. Apparently Elizabeth wasn't entirely without her normal human reactions.

He rubbed her feet, and once more felt the sloshy looseness of her skin on top of her muscle. Repulsive. She was practically a corpse.

But he was also kind of turned on. This was Elizabeth, after all. He'd wanted her from the first time he gazed at her picture, the pinup of his dreams.

And here he sat, moments away from the ultimate fantasy fulfillment. She was his for the taking in such a ... compromised state.

"Do you like this?" he said, moving up and away from her feet toward her calves.

Elizabeth moaned. He glanced up and noticed her eyes were closed. Thank God.

He moved farther up her legs, near her knees. "That okay?" She didn't protest, she just moaned. Jerry eyed her face and saw she looked absolutely in another world of bliss. Even though her skin tone had changed, she remained beautiful to him. Finally, she would be his, if only for a short moment.

This, of course, would breach all sorts of ethical dilemmas, but Jerry didn't care. Everything would be worth it in the end. Even if he lost his job—even if he lost her. There was little else he could think of other than coupling with her.

Reaching to her thighs, his massage technique became harder and more aggressive. Maybe she even liked things rough, judging from her moans. Or maybe her moans meant he was hurting her? He wasn't sure, but he paced his bet she was excited and turned on like him.

Something buzzed inside Jerry's pocket—his iPhone, signaling him.

"Shit." He stopped massaging Elizabeth, and slipped the phone from his pants pocket. *The interview.* He clicked the iPhone off and shook his head. "How in hell am I going to get you downstairs?"

He stood and stepped nearer to Elizabeth's head. He slipped an arm under her neck and raised her head. She seemed to weigh nothing. "Come on, it's Showtime."

For a brief moment, Elizabeth's eyes seemed to come alive. Maybe she responded to something he said.

Jerry Slid his arm under her upper back and lifted her. She sat right up. Behind her on the sheets, a silhouetted stain marked where she'd been. She reeked of sweat. When she opened her mouth, he swore she tried to form words. Perhaps she was mentally locked inside her own body and trying to get out. *The story of her life*, he thought.

"J-j-j-y," she stammered. "Erry?"

She'd said his name.

"Hey. I'm right here. You're going to be okay. We just need to get through this interview, all right?" he said.

"K-k-kay."

Maybe all was not lost. Maybe the pills hadn't completely annihilated her. The public, and the media, were used to her slurring her way through every other interview and role. She had become a joke—a punch line.

Elizabeth sat upright on the bed and Jerry stared at her outfit. She still wore her pajamas. He wondered if it would be appropriate for the interview for her to be wearing her bed clothes. He quickly decided her outfit would be fine. They could get away with sunglasses and a quick touch up. He'd tell them she had the flu or something.

As he lifted her up, his leg moved the dead guy and Jerry jumped. "Shit."

The dead guy fell over in a slump. He wondered how he was going to take care of a dead man in his starlet's hotel room, but psyched himself out.

"One thing at a time," he told himself. "Take it easy."

When he turned around, Elizabeth smiled at him. He noticed her teeth.

She could really take a big chunk out of me with those pearly white choppers. I'd be a goner.

She sat on the edge of the bed grinning stupidly.

Jerry looked around the room and spotted Elizabeth's sunglasses.

He grabbed them. Then he went into the bathroom to fetch her hair brush. When he returned, he found her just as he left her. He brushed her hair and put the sunglasses on. She didn't react.

"Come on," Jerry said. "Can you stand up?"

He slid his hands under her armpits and lifted her. As he did, Jerry felt the heft of her breasts on his forearms. He couldn't help but be turned on, just a little bit. Even though she was zombified, he still found her sexy as all hell.

They stood, face to face, with his hands wrapped around

her. Her pungent breath assaulted his nostrils as she gazed at him with faded eyes. He almost kissed her, but stopped himself. *What was he thinking? She was his boss.*

"Do you think you can walk?"

She didn't say anything, but when he took her hand, he found he was able to lead her away from the bed and toward the front door. It was working. She was working.

* * * *

Ty Spectrum sat in an empty bar on the ground floor of the hotel. Everything smelled like Pine Sol and lavender, and he was trying to figure out why. He'd only been there five minutes when he observed Elizabeth Cotton enter. He couldn't believe she was early. There were many horror stories about how she'd keep people waiting, and how she was an impossible Diva, and that even when someone had an interview with her, she would rarely answer questions directly, and she'd often ramble on about tweety birds or oxygen bars, or whatever other random thoughts floated through her brain. He was surprised to see her show up still wearing her pajamas, though.

He rose and put out his hand. "Ty Spectrum," he said. "From *The Haven* magazine."

Jerry met his handshake. "Yes, of course," he said. "I know who you are. But listen, Elizabeth's come down with a horrible flu, so go easy on her, okay?"

"Oh," Ty said. "That's too bad." They were close to where he'd been sitting. "Is this an okay place for us to have our interview?"

Jerry scanned the room. "Sure. No problem." They each took a chair.

Ty took out a small digital recorder, started it, and put machine on the table.

"So what's it like working with a big director like Michael Bay again after such a long time doing bit parts? It's almost as if you're on the verge of a comeback."

Elizabeth smiled stupidly. Jerry was relieved. If only she would ...

"G-good," she said.

Talk.

Jerry couldn't believe it.

Ty waited for her to say more, but she didn't. He sighed a little, looked down for a moment, then glanced back up. "So you're saying you think this might be your comeback role?"

It took a moment, but Elizabeth responded. "Yes-ss."

They went on like that for several minutes, with Ty asking questions, and Elizabeth barely answering.

Ty reached for his digital recorder. "That'll about do it," he said. "I think I've got enough."

Then Elizabeth started moving her mouth up and down. Strange guttural sounds came out of her for a few seconds before she spoke. "It hurts," she said.

Jerry was mortified.

"What hurts?" Ty asked. "Hollywood? The movie business?"

"Everything hurts," Elizabeth said, her voice broken and weak.

"The world hasn't been kind to you over the past few years," Ty said. "But you're on the verge of a breakthrough. Even Oliver Stone said he wanted to work with you."

"I don't like this," she said, and turned to Jerry. "Make it go away."

Ty asked, "I think she wants me to leave."

Jerry put up his hand. "It's okay. Just wait a sec."

"Make it go away," she said again. Her smile had disappeared and she seemed deathly serious.

Jerry turned to Ty. "Did you get what you needed?"

Ty nodded.

* * * *

Jerry went to put his card key into the hotel room door just as it swung open.

"Never thought you'd be back." Big Louie stood inside their room. "How'd the interview go?"

"She's talking," Jerry said. "A little bit."

Big Louie ushered them inside and shut the door. Two other men crouched near the dead guy.

"That's good," Big Louie said. "You're still going to have to reverse the process." He studied Elizabeth, taking a step toward her. He lifted her sunglasses and stared her straight in the eye.

"Yeah. You're still going to need to take care of that," Big Louie said. "You up for it?"

* * * *

"Do you know how hard it is to get a zombie to pee on a stick?" Jerry asked.

On the other end of the line, Big Louie said, "I don't care how hard it is. It's been over a month. Any signs of her period?"

"Well, no," Jerry said. "Who knows if she'll even get a period in this state?"

"You've been living in that house for a long time all shacked up. We need her to be seen outside somewhere soon. Don't let me down. There's a lot of money on this. She's on the upswing with her career. We can't kill momentum."

"I know, I know." Before he could say anything else, his iPhone beeped and the call ended. Big Louie was not one for such niceties as saying goodbye.

Jerry turned around and saw Elizabeth sitting on the couch. Over the month since she'd turned,

she'd barely made any progress. Her skin darkened and she was covered in purple bruises. She still rarely talked, and seemed most happy sitting on her couch watching the *Teletubbies* or *Thomas The Tank Engine*. She didn't eat, but he did manage to get her to suck down protein shakes through a straw. He had her wearing diapers for the most part, as she wasn't aware of her bowels.

Jerry felt as though he were taking care of a baby.

He slept in the same bed with her at night, and they'd made love several times, and each time she seemed more responsive than the last.

Jerry was falling in love. When he touched her, she touched him back. She smiled the whole time.

They still hadn't kissed, though. He didn't want to awaken any possible dormant zombie traits in her ... he kept picturing kissing her and her biting off his tongue.

* * * *

Two weeks later? Two stripes on the EPT stick. Jerry was thrilled. Elizabeth's eyes were clearing. Her one word answers sounded clearer. Her skin looked better, with the bruises finally starting to heal. She was even warm in some places, which was a nice surprise.

He wanted to call Big Louie, and so he did. Jerry lifted Elizabeth from the couch and danced with her, and so what if the theme to Sesame Street played in the background? She was getting better, after all. He wanted so badly to kiss her, especially seeing her lips turn redder by the hour.

Jerry held her close and they wrapped their arms around one another. She gave him a squeeze, which surprised him. Her strength was returning. He knew soon, everything would be okay and as it should be. She'd made it out, and he swore to himself he'd never let anything in the world—like zombification or Zethromorax—get between them again.

He made the same promise to the little bump in her belly. And all was well.

Sympathy for the Dead

Alex & Celeste Turner

The years of shame and guilt always melted away whenever he saw a new girl. If he hit it off with her, then that shame and guilt became an aphrodisiac for Ian, those negative, destructive feelings the price he paid for love.

And it was love. Every time, with every girl. Him loving her. Kissing her. Caressing her. Making love to her. The freedom was she didn't have to love him back. She lay still, quiet, totally prone. She was his. Her silence, her long, cool, passive body offered consent, acceptance—and to Ian that meant love.

There is a magical thing that happens when one communes with the dead. Ian would breathe in their intoxicating scent, caress their smooth, cold flesh, and he imagined he heard their secrets. He felt the pain and joy they experienced in life. He touched a life the world had given up. He set them free in a wave of love only he could provide.

8:15. The janitor was almost finished, and Ian sat in his office. Waiting. Thinking.

When he was younger, the kids in school made fun of him. To them, he was always alone. To them, he was the boy in high school who got turned down by every girl. To them, he was a loser. Ian didn't mind, even back then. He knew he was destined for something greater, something more profound. Something subtler than they would ever understand.

Thinking about that time always made him think of that one night, that turning moment in his youth. For some people it's the first time they smoke. For others, the first time they drive a car. For others still, when they are finally out on their own. It's the moment when a child realizes they will grow up someday, and someday can be whatever they want it to be.

In high school Ian was a thin, tall boy with white blonde hair and small, quick brown eyes. He had a nose he'd never grow into, described as "Roman" by some, "hawk like" by others. He lacked pubescent acne, but he was constantly mocked by other boys in school, shunned by most girls, and feared by his teachers. If the media trained schools to fear any high school subculture, it was he of the combat boots and trench coat.

Ian liked to relive one particular night in high school. He had an encounter with a girl. She wasn't a member of any particular clique. She was smart. She dressed in khakis and sweaters both hiding and accentuating her already-voluptuous figure. Nobody made fun of her. She was probably going to be valedictorian. And she was the local mortician's daughter. She approached Ian because he was "different," "smarter," "soulful." They spent one night together at her father's funeral home. He learned her interest in him was purely as a witness. She wanted to share her passion with someone—someone who wouldn't judge. Someone who might get it. Ian did.

That night, watching that conservative, buttoned-up girl strip off her clothes, climb on top of the not-yet-embalmed corpse of a recently dead man, her breath shallow, cheeks rosy, Ian discovered there was more to life, to love, than the books in school and movies on TV revealed. That night, seeing that girl's excitement, the swollen lips of her sex redden and drip fluid like tears as she rubbed her body up and down the length of the corpse, set Ian free. That night, watching her lap the blood oozing from the dead man's lips as she rocked herself to a screaming orgasm, Ian found his purpose. He understood. Years later he wouldn't remember the particulars of how she asked him to go there, how she framed the invitation; in time even the memory of her ripe, young body and the cold, blue body of the dead man would fade.

So he did the only logical thing he could. He studied hard in Chemistry class. He completed an Associate's Degree in Funeral Service. He got his accreditation. By the time he turned 21 he was a fully licensed mortician. He moved to a small town in Maine, far away from his family, and far away from the Bible belt mentality of Asheville. After three years as an assistant at a family-owned funeral home the owners decided to retire. He bought the business from them. By the time he turned 30 he was a well-respected member of the community, known for his quiet, gentle nature, his respect for the families of the dead. He had money in the bank and a comfortable living space above the funeral home. The morgue in the basement, parlors, and showroom on the first floor, and a spacious apartment for Ian on the top floor. It was Ian's castle, his sanctuary, a place for him to commune with the dead. He treasured it.

Most importantly, the business provided a constant stream of possibilities. In the years since he'd trained, Ian had learned a lot. He'd become a proficient romancer. A lover of the dead. He considered each new girl a gift, as he was a gift to her. He always picked girls between the ages of 19 and 30. His tastes ran to thin, brunette women with full lips and long hair. Every now and then, if there was something exceptional about her face, he'd choose a blonde or more voluptuous girl. Variety is important, especially when you haven't found The One. Ian didn't know if Molly was The One, but he was about to find out.

Ian was brought back to the present by the sound of the clock on the wall striking nine. He didn't know how long he had been sitting there, but surely long enough. The janitor should be long gone, and Molly waited.

He liked to make love to them before he embalmed them. Riskier, of course, but he used protection and if the circumstances were right, she might still be a little pliable.

He made his way down to the morgue. He never brought

his girls into his apartment. It was dangerous, impractical … the morgue made the most sense. Most of the time, after one amazing encounter, he'd go ahead and embalm her corpse. He didn't employ a make-up artist. He did that himself. From his time with her, through her placement in her coffin, he guided her every step of the way. He was her guardian and lover, escorting her into the afterlife sated, beautiful, at peace.

He barely noticed the other bodies in the morgue. Each draped in a sheet, waiting for embalming, for makeup, or some other ministration that would prepare them for the funeral ahead.

He looked at Molly, lying on the table, brown hair splayed in a corona around her head. She was more beautiful than he'd first thought. She had Cupid's bow lips, parted slightly. Her open eyes may have been green. She had only been dead about 2 and a half hours and a film already formed over the corneas. She'd died peacefully, a car accident with a single puncture to the femoral artery. Rigor mortis hadn't set in all the way. Her slim hips and small, peach-like breasts were in perfect proportion to her thin waist, her long legs, slender arms. Ian hadn't even touched her and already he had grown uncomfortably hard.

He'd removed his suit jacket in his office, along with his tie. He started talking to her, telling her how beautiful she was, how he was here now, how she shouldn't be scared. While he told her, he unbuttoned his shirt. While he told her again, he unbuttoned his pants.

He walked to her, standing so his manhood touched the cold metal table. The shock always made him shudder, but it was the first indication of foreplay. It meant it was almost time. Without that cold shock of metal the experience couldn't begin.

He touched her cheek. Her skin was smooth. He traced her jaw, her delicate neck, and the underside of each perfect breast. He grazed the nipples with the backs of his hands, an act that would make a live woman sigh, perhaps, or arch her back. He bent to kiss her perfect lips, and slipped his tongue just inside her mouth to taste her, trace her teeth, be inside her.

His breath quickened. It was time. He slid his hand down her flat stomach, over her pubis, lightly downed with dark, sparse brown hair. He parted her cold, dry lower lips and inserted a moistened finger. He couldn't wait any longer. He slid on a lubricated condom, poured a measure of lubricant on her lower stomach, and rubbed it in. Again, another act that would have a live woman squirming with pleasure and want, demanding, aggressive, merely readied his sweet Molly for his affections.

Groaning, he entered her. The walls inside her were tight in the early throes of Rigor Mortis. He wouldn't be able to last long. He gazed into her milky, round eyes, sucked on her full lower lip. He slid his slippery hands over her breasts, squeezing, and to his surprise, her nipples hardened.

He sat up abruptly. He should have panicked. His heart beat faster than his rising ardor would have caused. The body, Molly's body, erupted in gooseflesh. His mind raced. Was it possible this girl was still alive? *No*, Ian thought, *she was pronounced dead at the scene!*

No breath moved her chest. No sound came from her throat. Her arms and legs were as stiff as they'd been, but her inside muscles clenched suddenly, holding him though he tried to pull out.

This had never happened before.

Her sex tightened on him even more, and he began to move inside her again. Was it his movements making her head tilt back, a dead mockery of a live woman's ecstasy? Was it his imagination her breasts seemed to swell, like they strained to meet his touch? He couldn't think. He couldn't stop. He quickened his pace, and the body below him, once his sweet, passive Molly, newly his, began to move beneath him.

Ian had never had sex with a live woman. The closest he'd come was watching the girl from high school ride her way to orgasm on a corpse. This was a whole new experience for him. He came hard, in long bursts, and collapsed onto this strange, responsive body starting to make noises in the back of its throat.

He raised his head and studied her, and through her milky eyes he saw no semblance of life. Yet her mouth formed a sideways little smile and she cocked her head ever so slightly.

Shocked, he jumped off the table, pants in a pool on the floor, and stared at her. Her fingers twitched. He moved back a step. Her torso started to rise off the table. She turned toward him with a crooked smile and reached for him, fingers outstretched.

He took her hand, and she awkwardly swung her legs off the table. He took her other hand and she stood before him, pale nipples and soft brown hair, with dead eyes and that Cupid's bow mouth open as she leaned into him.

The figures on the table began to rise. He heard the stirring from the metal drawers before her teeth pierced his neck. As she tore a chunk of his flesh away, he noticed the two other bodies on the table start to move. He fell to the floor, bleeding and dizzy, and her hands slipped in the blood and smeared it down the length of his body before she moved in for another bite. His last sensation was a stronger sense of arousal than he'd ever felt. His last thought was …

This is The One.

Beautiful Music

Daisy-Rae Kendrick

Toby was taking so long to answer the door. Usually I was quite patient and savored every moment at his house, even standing on the doorstep. Today, however, I felt the changes starting deep inside me. It was uncomfortable and I had no clue how long I had left. Not having seen Toby for a week, I only hoped he was at the same stage as me. What would I do if he was farther ahead? My heartbeat sped up as I anticipated seeing him. He was taking so long.

* * * *

At 28, I wondered if I was too old to start learning the piano, a long held dream of mine. Toby came highly recommended, so I decided to give it a go. I had been nervous when I turned down the street and beheld the beautiful Edwardian houses. Toby was sure to be posh and would have an impeccable accent and dress sense. As I climbed the steps to the large front door I glanced down at my dress, faded from wear and repeated washing, and wiped my hands down the front before pulling the brass handle. I heard a tinkling inside the house and wondered if Toby would answer the door himself or if he would have a butler. The door swung open and a tall slender blonde haired man in his mid-30's stood before me smiling.

"Mary-Ann, I'm guessing?" he said, and although well spoken, was far from posh. I nodded and, at his invitation stepped across the threshold.

"I'm Toby, obviously, and I will make you one promise.

We will soon be making beautiful music together—ha haha."

His laugh was deep, infectious, and I found myself smiling back and my shoulders relaxing. As we walked to the music room, a large room on the left, I took the opportunity to study Toby. He wore jeans and a mustard colored jumper, and I spotted a little chest hair poking out the V of his sweater. I glanced away before he caught me staring. I liked this man, he put me at ease. He had such a natural, easy way about him and he didn't seem to mind I said very little. He chattered on about his musical experience and qualifications, and played a sweet melody on the baby grand I would be learning on, so I could hear the sound the instrument was supposed to make once I took over as the pianist.

* * * *

Over the following weeks I looked forward to my lessons and practiced every opportunity I got. I desperately wanted to please Toby; and, once I had played my "homework," I held my breath until he flashed his brilliant smile and told me I had worked hard and my finger positioning continued to improve each week. I savored every minute of the 30 I spent at his house, and it wasn't long before I realized I had fallen completely in love with him. I shivered every time our fingers touched when he was showing me hand positions or a method of changing between chords, and I flushed when I felt my nipples stiffen. Half of me hoped he hadn't noticed; but the other half prayed he had.

At night I dreamed of his fingers slipping inside my blouse and rubbing my nipples, then tearing off each other's clothes and making mad love right there on the rug. Every morning I awoke in a sweat with wetness between my legs. I was so shy though, I would never let on about my secret desires for fear of rejection. I knew he would never mock me, but the thought he might not feel the same or tell me to find another teacher filled me with dread, and made me more determined to keep my true feelings hidden.

* * * *

I had been visiting Toby for about 7 months when it happened. The apocalypse. People died. People changed. People rotted and decayed but still lived. I saw people I loved eaten, devoured, ripped apart and yet my thoughts inevitably turned to Toby. What would happen to him? I couldn't bear the thought I would never see him again. Although I hadn't been bitten, I sensed the changes starting. I was a changer and I hoped Toby was too.

I kept myself hidden until my usual piano lesson time and hurried to the street of Edwardian houses. Some had been demolished and some abandoned. Toby's house however, still stood, although the roof was partially missing. As I stood at the front door waiting for him, the desire I had harbored since we first met became like a fever in my stomach. My mouth watered at the thought of his face. I was going to die so I would do the one thing I never thought I might. I would tell him about my love for him; and, if he rejected me, at least it wouldn't matter for long.

The door finally opened, and there he was—even though I could see he was a little farther on—I was overjoyed to see him also changing. *We still had time.* How much I didn't know. Gone was the smile I had come to love, instead his eyes were dark, deep, and full of lust. My stomach flipped and my underwear became wet. Toby reached out, grabbed me by the arm, and pulled me inside. Not bothering to close the door, he walked me to the music room and turned me to face him. My breathing became shallow and rapid; my mouth went dry. He said nothing, but his eyes roamed my face and neck and dropped to my breasts. I deliberately hadn't worn a bra, so when my nipples hardened they were visible under the thin material of my summer dress. I heard his breath catch and his eyes locked on to mine. Pulling me to his chest, he covered my lips with his and prized them open with his tongue. My knees went weak and I started to fall. He picked me up with one strong arm and sat me on the curve of the piano. We stared into each other's eyes for a moment or two and then I felt the start of the pain. The change was upon me. The fire spread from my stomach to my breasts, my nipples became so swollen I cried out when they threatened to burst out of my dress.

Sensing my fever, Toby lifted his hand as if to unfasten the straining material; instead, he ripped the front open, exposing my large bare breasts. Buttons flew across the room. Before I even caught my breath, he took my left nipple in his mouth and sucked, gently at first, then harder, until my nipple scraped along his teeth and the flesh tore. The desire was exquisite. The fire inside me spread to my neck and down to my vagina. I opened my eyes and witnessed Toby's face changing. Skin ripped, exposing the sinew of his cheeks. Lust shot through me at the sight of his blood, and I bent my head to his neck, the tuft of chest hair against my cheek. Sinking my teeth into his loosening flesh, I savored the tang of his blood—mixed with the heady scent of decay and sex—and said two words into his ear.

"Devour me."

Ripping what remained of my dress to shreds, he pushed me back on the piano and spread my legs, tearing at my underwear. I stretched out, the strings digging into my back, slowly sinking into the skin. Tiny pieces of my flesh becoming lodged in the hammers created such sweet music when the keys were caressed in just the right order. The blood leaked out, and veins twanged on the wire strings; but this only spurred me on. I needed Toby. I *had* to have him. My underwear lay in tatters at my side, and I felt him pushing my legs so far apart my hips dislocated. I screamed with the sweet exquisite pain and then ... the sweetness of his tongue lapping at my vagina. Pushing his fingers inside, opening me up to his desire. Instantly my orgasm grew and I snarled, entwining my fingers in his hair.

I pulled his face deeper into me. Hair ripped out, and I threw it away, only to grip more and thrust my hips to him.

As my orgasm ripped through me, an ear tore off in my hand as I came in his mouth. He sucked my essence deep in his throat and as he pulled away, I could see my womb was no longer a part of me but was being swallowed down with my juices. Blood, mucus, and our bodily fluids mingled together, flowing from us to the bowels of the piano.

The stench of decay and rotting flesh was overwhelming. I looked up to his face and observed he had not much visage left; his nose was gone, cheek ripped open, and he had swallowed most of his teeth along with my orgasm. His left arm hung ragged at the elbow, and he stood on a bent and broken right ankle. He was not yet sated and dragged me to the rug where I had dreamed of making love to him so many times. But this was not lovemaking. This was complete annihilation of each other, and better than anything I ever fantasized.

Toby's penis was huge, engorged, and sticking straight up. I had no idea how long it would be that way, so I guided it inside me and let him pump harder and harder, both of us screaming with each thrust as flesh tore away and slipped off our bones. With a final, earth shattering shriek, Toby reached orgasm, and as his semen flowed into me, life flowed out of him. His last shuddering breath coincided with the final throb of his penis.

Knowing I didn't have long left, I tried to slide out from under him. His dead manhood detached inside me, and as I moved, his flesh slopped off his bones on the rug already soaked with every part of our last act together.

As the fire climbed up my spine into my brain, I waited to die—eternally joined with him on our final journey, making beautiful music together just as he promised.

Being Superhuman

Angeline Trevena

Carmilla zipped up her bag and lifted it, testing its weight. She had only packed what she absolutely couldn't live without, but she still needed to make it lighter.

"Carmilla, we need to move." Jones appeared in the doorway.

Carmilla glanced at her bag, shrugged, and slung it over her shoulder. As they emerged into the open air, they both squinted in the light of the full moon above them. Carmilla stopped, staring up, her mouth open.

Jones placed an arm around her shoulder. "We've lived underground for a long time."

"Feels like forever."

* * * *

They traveled as quickly as they could without exhausting themselves, and when the horizon began to glow, announcing dawn, they searched for a safe place to rest.

Jones pulled Carmilla to a stop, pointing across the cornfield in front of them. In the gloom Carmilla could make out the shapes of a number of farm buildings.

"We need somewhere to get some sleep, maybe even find some supplies." He nodded towards the field. "Move slowly and stay close. We don't know what's hiding in there."

They moved through the corn, their ears pricked, their hands clasped in one another's. Somewhere ahead of them a creature called out—half scream, half groan.

"Hurry," whispered Jones, pushing Carmilla forward.

The creature called out again, closer this time, and another responded. They weren't the brainless, single-minded creatures the media portrayed them as; they hunted in packs, only striking when they outnumbered their prey.

As they broke from the cover of the cornfield the creatures wheeled around to face them.

Their eyes were empty of humanity; they had forgotten who they had once been. Carmilla froze. Jones pulled on her arm.

"Come on!"

She blinked and forced her legs into action. Jones released her hand as they ran, and she kept her eyes focused on the front door of the house. Behind her, Jones called out. Carmilla skidded to a stop and spun around.

"Run!" he screamed.

Two of the creatures had grabbed him, and more were on their way over. Carmilla ran back to him, wrenching him free and pulling him into the farmhouse. Jones slammed the door behind them, sliding the bolt across.

"You shouldn't have come back for me," Jones said.

"We may not have much of a future, but I do not want to spend it without you."

The house was dark; the grimy windows emitting minimal light from the outside. Carmilla wrote her name in the thick layer of dust on the sideboard.

"Looks like this place has been abandoned for ages," she said.

"Well it won't be for much longer. There'll soon be an entire army of them outside. We just need to find some supplies and have a quick sleep. Old places like this always had pantries."

They made their way to the kitchen and Jones disappeared into the storeroom beyond. Carmilla pulled open a drawer, digging through the mess of mismatched cutlery. A potato peeler was the sharpest instrument she found. She pulled open another drawer. Wooden spoons. She opened another and smiled at the array of kitchen knives.

"You'll be coming with Mama." She chose the biggest knife and slipped the blade into her bag.

Jones reappeared with his arms full of cans and packets. "Looks like they were planning on waiting it out. They've practically prepared for a ten year siege."

"So where are they?"

Jones pulled a notebook from amongst the food cans, flicked it open and handed it to Carmilla. The pages were filled with scribbled notes, transcripts of radio broadcasts and magazine clippings.

"This is some kind of reserve, a safe community." Carmilla paged through the book, unfolding a large map taped into the pages. "This isn't far. We can get there."

"I think it's our best chance. Let's get some of this food packed up. Pass me your bag." Jones pulled her bag open, peering inside.

"Didn't I tell you to only bring absolute essentials?" He pulled out a pair of leather handcuffs.

"You never know," Carmilla said. "You can't trust anyone."

Jones pulled out a small leather whip and laid it on the table. He reached in the bag again and held up a studded dog collar and lead. "And this?"

Carmilla snatched it from him. "That really is an absolute essential. It's my favorite."

Jones dug his hand back into her bag and pulled out a large, black vibrator. "And what about this?"

"With this virus only affecting men I'm going to be very bored waiting around for the end of the world. I bet a lot of women will end up wishing they'd packed one of those." Carmilla slid over to Jones, running a finger up the length of the vibrator. "Or you might be glad that I packed some of this."

"Oh really?"

Carmilla picked the handcuffs up from the table, dangling them on her forefinger. Jones smiled and dropped the vibrator, grabbing Carmilla around the waist and pulling her up against him. He kissed her hard and Carmilla took hold of his wrists, lifting his hands up to the back of her head. She slipped the handcuffs on him and clicked them shut.

"I hope you packed the keys," he said.

Carmilla shrugged. "I didn't think they were a necessity." She pressed her hands against Jones' chest, slowly unbuttoning his shirt, running her fingers over the intricate designs tattooed beneath. She leaned forward and placed her lips on his stomach, working them down over the slight curvature, pulling his trousers open.

She tugged off his shoes and socks, discarding them across the tiled floor before easing his trousers down over his hips. She moved forward, gently forcing him to step back, and again, until his buttocks rested on the edge of the table. Carmilla gave him a half smile, a smile that always meant trouble, and then she pushed him hard, forcing him onto the table. Cans and packets of food clattered to the floor as Carmilla wrenched off his underwear and climbed astride him.

Carmilla pulled her hooded jumper off, revealing a figure hugging leather corset beneath. Jones raised an eyebrow.

"What?" Carmilla asked, feigning innocence. "If I have to face the end of human existence, I want to look totally smoking when it happens. Now shut the hell up." Standing up above him, Carmilla pulled off her trainers and pushed her jeans down over the leather hot pants she wore beneath them. She knelt back down. "Now you can't say that these weren't an absolute necessity."

"Oh no," said Jones, "they were most definitely essential." He extended his handcuffed hands, reaching for the zip on the front of her shorts. She pulled away.

"Oh no you don't." Leaning over, she pulled the kitchen knife from her bag.

A look of panic flashed across Jones' face, heightening Carmilla's excitement. She placed his hands up above his head and raised the knife.

Jones screwed his eyes shut as it descended, slipping

through a link of the handcuff chain and embedding into the table, pinning him in place.

Carmilla slowly unzipped her shorts, tooth by tooth. The zip ran down between her thighs, and then up to the waistband at the back, allowing her to peel the two halves away easily. She gazed down at Jones' hardening cock, her heartbeat pulsing through her groin. She moved forward, leaning down and pressing her lips against Jones', running her hands up and down his torso, grabbing his hips. She shifted her weight and took hold of his penis, wrapping her hand around it. She moved again, placing herself right above his cock, brushing the tip of it with her groin.

Jones groaned. "I want you so bad," he said.

Carmilla smiled and pressed her hips down, forcing him up inside her. She moved back and forth, slowly at first, spreading her hands out on Jones' chest. She moved faster, driving him deeper each time, digging her fingernails into his flesh. Jones tilted his head back, his mouth open, his eyes closed. Carmilla lay against his chest, driving her hips backwards over and over. Jones arched his back as he exploded inside her, calling out her name.

****

The reserve was an old airbase, surrounded by high fences topped with razor wire. Carmilla pressed her face up against the metal gate.

"Hello!" she called out. "Hello!" She rattled the gate.

A woman stepped out from behind a building. She wore standard issue boots and an army uniform that she had modified into shorts and a camisole. Carmilla waved madly, tears of relief running down her face.

"Oh thank god this place is still inhabited. My name is Carmilla."

"What's that with you?" the woman asked.

Carmilla peered down at Jones. He was huddled at her feet, his arms gripped around her legs. His sunken eyes were rimmed with shadows, his skin grey.

He shivered up against her, blood dripping from one ear.

"This is Jones. He's not been well."

"Not been well?" said the woman, her hand tapping the gun at her hip. "He's infected."

"No he's not. It's the flu, that's all. We spent a few nights outside."

The woman raised an eyebrow. "That's not flu." She glanced behind her. "Alright, but you keep him out of sight. I'll take you to the quarantine hut, it's empty and out of the way."

* * * *

Carmilla touched Jones' ice-cold skin. He was staring at her, a desperate look in his eye. His eyes had faded to a pale grey over the last few days, his skin bleached to white, but the fever had finally broken. Carmilla had kept him as quiet as she could, but a few curious women had come by and rumors were spreading.

"I'm hungry," Jones whispered.

"I know my darling, but not now. I don't know how much longer we'll be allowed to stay here."

Jones tugged at the leather handcuffs that kept him chained to the bed frame.

"I'm hungry."

Carmilla crawled over to him and pressed her lips against his mouth. He pushed forward and took her bottom lip between his teeth, drawing blood.

"I want you," he said, licking the blood from his lips. "I want you so bad."

"Alright." She climbed astride him, running her hands over his newly toned torso. "You're so strong now."

"I feel superhuman," he said.

"You are superhuman." Carmilla pulled his jeans down over his thighs, running her hands over his cold skin and wrapping them around his hard cock. She slowly crawled up the bed, easing him inside her. The sensation was so much more intense, his penis thicker and harder than it used to be. She groaned as she moved back and forth, his teeth nibbling at her breasts.

With a jerk, Jones broke free of the handcuffs, grabbing hold of Carmilla by the shoulders. He pulled her to him and sunk his teeth deep into her shoulder, another bite scar to add to the collection. Carmilla rolled her head, digging her nails into Jones' tight skin.

In a single movement he flipped her on her back, holding her in place with one hand pressed on her stomach. Jones pulled her legs apart and smiled up at her.

"I want you so bad," he said. He ran his tongue the length of her inner thigh, pulling his lips back to reveal his teeth. Carmilla balled the bed covers in her fists as Jones pressed his face between her legs.

Stiff

Matthew Scott Baker

The stainless steel table was freezing cold to Tyler's bare ass as he sat in the partitioned area and waited for the doctor.

The eighteen year-old was naked except for the thin hospital gown that covered his front but did nothing to hide his backside. He shivered in the cool air as goose bumps played across his skin and silently prayed the doctor would hurry up.

He didn't have to wait long.

The pale white curtains parted and a bald, mustached man entered. He wore a white doctor's coat and a grin. In his hand was a vial of bright green liquid.

"And how are we feeling today, Mister Burkhart?" the doctor asked.

Tyler shrugged. "Fine, Doctor Shunt."

The older man glanced studiously over Tyler for a second before nodding.

"Good, very good," he said. "Are you ready to get started?"

Tyler gulped. "Um ... yeah. But I gotta be honest, doc ... the idea of getting a needle jabbed into my dic—er, penis, doesn't thrill me."

Doctor Shunt clapped a hand on the young man's shoulder.

"It'll only sting for a minute. But believe me ... the reward will be well worth the pain."

Tyler grimaced, but nodded. He pointed at the vial. "Is that it?"

The doctor held the vial to eye level. "Sure is ... this little concoction is called Lot 214 and will revolutionize sex as we know it."

"And I'm guaranteed a lifetime supply of the stuff for participating in this experiment, right? Along with the money?"

Doctor Shunt turned to a small tray next to Tyler's table and picked up a syringe.

"That's correct," he answered as he stuck the needle into the top of the vial and began to fill the syringe. "Your only responsibility is to report any side-effects you might notice during the testing phase."

Tyler nodded, his eyes glued to the needle. He kept talking in an attempt to appease his nervousness.

"Um ... and ... there are girls ... uh, female participants, who are, uh, willing to ... you know ..."

The doctor chuckled as he withdrew the needle from the vial.

"Don't be nervous, Tyler, this whole experiment is about sex, so it's perfectly fine to talk about intercourse. Yes, there is a female participant you will be having sex with after the drug is in your system. We have to test the product, after all."

The older man put the vial on the tray and then turned towards Tyler. The green substance in the syringe stood out in stark contrast to the front of the doctor's white coat. A wave of panic overtook Tyler and he clenched his backside.

"Uh ... wait a minute ... what about ... what about the rumors?"

The doctor took a step toward him.

"What rumors, Tyler?"

"That this is a zombie drug ... that if you take too much, it kills you but resurrects you somehow as a zombie."

Doctor Shunt shook his head as he took another step forward. He was within inches of Tyler now.

"Tyler, we've been over this before, you know better."

He took hold of Tyler's arm and pushed him back onto the table. Tyler closed his eyes as he rolled on his back; the frigid steel bit into his skin, but he was too scared to care.

"Explain this to me again, doc. Please."

Doctor Shunt pulled up Tyler's gown, revealing the young man's flaccid penis. As instructed, Tyler had shaved his pubic hair.

"Alright," the doctor answered as he picked a spot an inch or so above the base of Tyler's penis and swabbed the area down with iodine. "This particular experiment is to test a new sexual aid that will make it possible for men with erectile dysfunction to lead a healthy sex life without the need for a daily pill."

Without warning, he jabbed the needle into Tyler's groin. Tyler jumped on the table and screamed as pain lanced into him. The doctor 'shhhed' Tyler in a soft voice but forcefully held him down on the table.

"Easy, Tyler," he soothed. "As I was saying, this serum, Lot 214, is comprised of a cell-deadening agent which, in layman's terms, 'kills' the patient's sex organs without taking away any of the sensation." Tyler's body was rigid; he trembled as he began to whimper. The doctor depressed the syringe and the green liquid began to flow into Tyler's body. Doctor Shunt continued his monologue.

"This death of the penis, if you will, induces a sort of rigor mortis effect in the member, making it incredibly hard ... but the nerve endings remain intact, making sex pleasurable."

The last of the green liquid vanished into Tyler's bloodstream and the doctor removed the needle from his skin. He continued to speak as he gingerly placed the needle back on the tray.

"Because Lot 214 can damage other parts of the body, the serum is mixed with a solution of gene-encoded nanobots, microscopic robotic organisms that regulate the drug and keep it in the designated area of the body."

Tyler took several deep breaths as his fear subsided. With the needle gone, his resolve began to strengthen. He stared at the ceiling as he spoke.

"And what if the nanobots fail?"

Doctor Shunt shook his head again.

"Can't happen. They are semi-organic in nature and there are billions of nanobots in this single solution, not to mention they self-replicate." He smiled as he stripped off his rubber gloves. "You'll be fine. Trust me. Now, let's go meet your lucky lady."

* * * *

Moments later, Tyler stood in front of a beautiful blonde woman wearing a similar hospital gown. Doctor Shunt had introduced her as Maddie and escorted them to his private room. The room contained a bed and nothing else. The next phase of testing was to commence here: the practical application test. In short, Tyler and Maddie would have sex.

Tyler's groin remained sore where the needle had been, and his skin felt weird. His whole body felt weird for that matter. The serum gave him the sensation of being high one minute and having the flu the next.

But he was horny beyond belief; the front of his gown stuck out like a tent lying on its side.

He and Maddie both wore bracelets transmitting their vital signs back to Doctor Shunt; he would monitor everything from two rooms away. His only instructions to Tyler and Maddie before he left were to "have fun."

"So," Tyler said sheepishly, "how do we do this?"

Maddie snorted.

"If you don't know by now, you're in the wrong place."

Tyler frowned at the remark, but Maddie laughed and touched his arm. "I am so kidding ... sorry. Just nervous, I guess." She gave him a sultry grin and led him to the bed.

"This is how we do this," she said. She turned to face him as she sat down and slid out of her gown.

Her naked body beckoned to Tyler like a beacon. He gaped at her, noting her perfect breasts and, like him, her pubic hair had been shaved. Lust surged through his body like a starving beast. His cock, already rock hard, began to pulse.

Before he even realized what he was doing, he fell on her.

Maddie received him without a word. She fell backwards on the bed and spread her legs, wrapping them around Tyler's waist as he entered her. Tyler grunted as he shoved into her; the desire burning in his body was beyond lust. He didn't just want Maddie's sex ... he needed it.

"Slow down," Maddie whispered. She wrapped her arms around his neck and matched his rhythmic thrusts as he pounded in and out of her. Tyler ignored her and continued his pursuit of climax, his naked body slapping loudly against hers in a steady pulsing motion.

Within seconds, he felt close and gave a long, deep grunt as he released inside of her. Maddie moaned as the warm gush filled her, pushing against him even harder than before. They stayed in that position for a full minute before Tyler's body finally sagged.

He pulled back from her, his body now weak and spent. He looked into her face, an apology forming on his lips ... but then he paused. Maddie stared at him strangely. She wore a confused expression. Her eyes darted left and right, as if she was trying to solve a problem.

"What is it?" he asked. He pulled out of her, noting that his penis was still granite-hard; a thin strand of semen trailed out of her as he exited, ending on the tip of his erection.

"Are you ok—?" he began, but the question died on his lips as his eyes lingered on his groin.

His semen was bright green.

"What the—?" was all he managed to get out before Maddie screamed.

Startled by the sound, Tyler leapt off the bed. Maddie shrieked as she clutched at her stomach. She rolled to her side and fell off of the bed. She hit the floor with a sickening crunch, but the screams did not abate.

Tyler watched her, stunned.

Surely Doctor Shunt would see her elevated vitals and come to check on her.

On the floor, Maddie began to thrash. Her screams fell to a gargled choking sound that resembled a cat trying to expel a hairball. She arched her back and thrust her hips upward, but then slammed back down on the concrete floor. Her eyes rolled back in her head, revealing the whites of each orb.

The door behind him suddenly flew open and Doctor Shunt rushed in.

"What's happening?" he cried.

Tyler could not answer. He continued to stare at Maddie in dumb silence.

The doctor dropped to the floor and tried to restrain the girl. Despite his efforts, Maddie continued to gargle and thrash about.

"Help me hold her!" Shunt shouted.

Tyler finally snapped out of his reverie and rushed to help. He grabbed Maddie's legs and pushed them to the floor, while the doctor attempted to subdue her upper half. Maddie appeared not to notice. She threw her head back and released a massive, banshee-like shrill.

As she did, her vagina erupted and a thick green mucous splattered Tyler on the face and arms. Her body slumped and she lay still.

Stunned once again, Tyler's eyes were wide as he studied the substance on his arms. He looked up to Doctor Shunt; the man stared at him with an expression of awe and horror.

"Oh dear God ..." Shunt began. Temporarily forgetting Maddie, the doctor leaned over to Tyler and studied the liquid.

"Oh no, no, no, no, no," he murmured. "This can't be happening ..."

"What is it? What's going on?"

Doctor Shunt glanced from Tyler down to Maddie. The girl remained still. When he looked back to Tyler, the man's face was ashen white.

"The nanobots ... they got into your semen."

Tyler whipped his head up to look at him.

"What? How is that possible?"

Shunt shook his head.

"I have no idea, but they somehow transmitted to her.

Which means they're not working, which means—"

His reply turned to a scream as Maddie lurched forward and bit a chunk of flesh out of his side.

Tyler scrambled backwards towards the door as Maddie sat up and tore the doctor's throat out. Blood sprayed the room like a sprinkler. The zombified girl turned her attention to Tyler.

Tyler understood he had just doomed the human race. A single act of sex had created the first zombie, but he knew more would come. The realization overwhelmed him. As Maddie clawed her way towards him, Tyler slid down the wall and waited for her.

As her teeth bit into his flesh, he absently wondered if he would still have his erection as a zombie.

Sickness Inside

T. Fox Dunham

Husband and Wife crawled from the twisted frame of the car. The skirt of her dove white wedding dress burned to her flesh, exposing pale thighs. Crushed plum bruises decorated her limbs. She dragged herself from the fire, smothering her burning dress on the pavement. Husband stumbled behind her, adorned in his tux. The accident shredded the suit, and burned his hair to his scalp, showing skull. Clotted blood fell like rotten crabapples from a slash on his neck. They broke free from tethered cans hanging on the car's bumper.

The other driver, manacled by his seatbelt, clawed at the windshield of his truck. He moaned for rescue, for freedom. The married couple ignored him and stumbled forward, compelled by a hole deep in them, a hunger. She wept but no tears fell. She knew not why she wept. Old instincts still influenced, the echoes of memory now fleeting as higher functions died. A random neuron fired, as flashes of recollection burst in her moribund mind like fireworks, stunning her numb body.

The day. Their families celebrating. Dancing together alone. Finally. They saved themselves, not for religion, but to only share their bodies with true love. The longing. Tonight it would be satisfied.

Husband paused, tripping out of his shoes. Wife fell into his legs, and she reached to pull her broken body upright. She clutched his hips, wrapping her arms around his thin frame, brushing her fingers through torn fabric. Her hand slid down to his cock, down his balls. He moaned at her touch, and they paused, no longer aware of the next step, the carnal ritual.

Need clawed from their petrified hearts, and Wife screeched the rabid sickness for which she could find no remedy.

They were driving to the mountains. She couldn't wait. She unzipped him while he drove. She gripped his rod, stroked it. A taste of their honeymoon night. He'd lost control of the car.

A shotgun blast reported from barren birch woods by the road. The couple turned to the sound, shambling across an empty rural route. They tripped through brambles and brush, ripping more scraps from their tattered wedding outfits. Their white flesh glowed in the moonlight as they followed a dirt road to a cabin on the marsh. An old man with whiskers on his chin fired his shotgun into the wood. Another zombie dropped. The old man cracked open his shot gun and fed shells into the breach.

Wife saw the old man through cracked foggy eyes. The hole within her ripped wide; her mouth spilled saliva. She lurched to the old man with ballerina feet and bit into his neck before he could raise his gun. Hot blood burst from his wound, painting her pale skin and white dress in crimson stains. Her husband joined the feast, and their bodies pressed, thighs rubbing, mouths passing close as they devoured. The old man's mate stood in the doorway and shrieked. The couple moved on her and tore her fatty old flesh.

With their bellies bloated and sloshing with pulped flesh, they staggered to the cabin. So full of meat, yet hunger raked at Wife, demanding more. Her numb lips tingled. Chemical mechanisms still active in the oldest parts of her brain fired. Repressed desire boiled over. Like a sickness, surging through her, and Wife screeched and clawed at the cabin walls. Husband twisted his head and looked upon his bride's visage. He reached to touch her, running his leathery fingers down her neck, under the shoulders of her dress and along the side of her breast. Electrical impulses fired in her rotting brain. Memories sparked.

Their long awaited night together. Lost in death. Stolen from them. Forever cursed to lie in cold earth, their hunger never slaked. Divided between a dielectric of soil, trapped in two coffins and blocked from reaching, touching.

Husband's eyes sharpened. He moaned, his jaw moving as if imitating speech. His face glowed in the flickering flames of the hearth as he lumbered to her, pushing her weakened body to the floor. Wind blew in through the doorway, lifting shreds of her wedding dress, showing the round curve of her bloated stomach, the contour of her breasts. Her hoary stockings cut into her bloated legs. Her violet nipples swelled and tingled. The nerves still fired. He gazed over her and dropped to his knees. He laid his chest on hers, pushing his ribcage on her breasts.

Her body raged for the stunning touch of Husband. She raked down his chest, ripping away his jacket. She tore his shirt to find his charred skin. Husband pushed his palm down on her ribs, running it along her stomach. He plucked at the elastic strap of her white thong then snapped it free. The soiled panties slipped down her leg. He clutched her thigh, pinching hard, and pain pulsed through the dead flesh. She gasped but didn't exhale, just letting air gather in her lungs. He ran his fingers in the crimson triangle of pubic hair. She arched her legs and lifted her hips, following the motions of his hand. He pressed cool fingers to her dry pussy lips. She sensed a hint of pleasure through her frozen body but felt buried beneath the earth as Husband punched the dirt. She twisted, moaned … shrieked.

He pushed, sliding first one finger, then a second, into her cunt. As he pressed his face to her mouth, he missed her lips and snapped flesh off her cheek. She whimpered as razor sharp teeth sliced through the skin.

Husband grunted, feeling inside her. She reached by instinct for the tool that would satiate the clawing hole. She fondled his balls, grabbing his hard shaft and pulled the skin over its dark head, over the purple mushroom. His cock pulsed in her hand, and she squeezed. He moved his hips to her motion. He pressed it to her leg, and she guided him into her orifice. He jerked his hips, hammering at her tight, parched pussy. She growled and lifted her hips, bringing his cock in deeper. He tore her lips and forced himself to the hilt. Pressure punched her groin. He drove in and out. Still, she only sensed the rubbing. She screeched. He grunted in shared frustration.

Husband pressed his lips to her shoulder and bit the flesh. She sensed the pressure from his teeth, the pain ripping up through her neck and down into her chest. It triggered dormant nerves. A minute orgasm stung from her stomach, and she moaned.

She bit Husband's neck, and his body shook. His cock pulsed deep within her. Each spouse chewed on the other, ripping chunks of dead flesh to the bone, scraping skin from ribs, digging into stomachs. The pain carried pleasure, waking the nerves.

He pushed harder, faster, rocking his hips, breaking her pelvis on the floor, pulverizing his bride.

Her body melted. Clotted blood smeared down their flesh. Pleasure surged. Her enlivened pussy clenched his cock, and he lifted his head and yelled. He shot his stored cum deep into her hollowed body, filling her through her abdomen, into her chest.

Husband collapsed on Wife. They had torn through muscle and sinew, shattered bone and sliced nerve. Unable to pick themselves up or carry themselves away from the cabin, they lay, spent, on the floor.

She still clutched his cock within her.

The National Guard soldiers found the couple hours later and raised their rifles. One bullet shattered both of their heads.

Adaptive Foraging Strategies

J.D. Hibbitts

Not having anywhere to take my wife after the bite, I decided on the woods. I'd been planning us a camping trip for some time, but somewhere we'd given ourselves over to our work lives: Cindy in a non-profit, spending her weekends planning or proctoring some committee meeting or another, while I'd taken a second job loading block. The thought of sharing my two-man tent made my cock throb with want for my wife again. The loading job had toughened my back for ground sex and I felt ready. I loved the way our salty and sour animal fluids used to leak from our bodies afterwards, the husky decay of fall air ripping through mesh tent windows to dry us like a towel.

I figured Cindy had another month before the hunger swallowed up her mind like all the others the media kept showering us with—though I wasn't entirely sure. What I did know was the raw meat off the hibachi buffet wasn't satisfying her anymore. She needed something fresher. Dog. In a way, I didn't mind adopting them. It filled a hobby less void I'd fallen in, and the look of release as soon as their cage was opened made me feel like I was performing my humanitarian duty. Besides, Cindy only craved the wormy ones that seemed to have two paws in the grave already. Win-win, in my book. The hardest part for me was replaying the *Old Yeller* scene each evening behind our house. Though she'd developed the taste, Cindy hadn't been able to kill and butcher on her own.

During our retreat, I wanted to show her how to gut and skin for herself. I figured I'd be able to get some venison backstrap out of the deal eventually as well. Another win-win.

A fat, three-legged French Poodle had been my undoing. The poor thing had a bad case of kennel cough and snorted in miserable sadness the whole ride home. He couldn't even hold his head up for me to put him out of his misery. For as much as I loved my wife, I couldn't squeeze the trigger on another dog.

"Pack up some clothes," I said to Cindy that night. "It's about time I made you sufficient."

She sat naked behind her basement dinner table, save a pair of black laced panties and her purple cooking gloves. Nothing got her as hot as the thought of food. She loved nothing more than for me to massage ground sausage between her shoulder blades while I fucked her from behind. After we finished, she would ravenously devour every meat crumb she could find and suck my fingers clean. I preferred this to the crying silence I had to endure from her in the shower as the meat grease beaded her back and swirled down the drain.

I could tell she was disappointed when she saw my empty arms.

"What did you do with the dog?" she screamed.

"Find something warm," I said. "I'm bagging you a deer instead."

The dissatisfied opacity of her eyes warmed into the excitement I'd seen during so many of her dinners. She scrambled over the table, pulled my shirttail over my head, and slid her tongue along my sternum, as if she were savoring every pulse of blood rising to my skin. She drove my hand to her crotch, not letting me steer where I wanted.

"Later," she said, trying to push me away. "After dinner."

With my index finger, I traced up the soft cuts in her stomach muscles to her left nipple, just begging me to nibble it. I leaned over and began gently tweaking with my teeth and the edge of my tongue, feeling the irregular oval expand and harden from the damp friction.

Her nipple ripped off in my mouth like a scab.

I tried to pretend I had done so on purpose.

"You can spit it out if you want," Cindy said, looking down at me.

I did. Even tried to apologize.

She smiled. "It'll grow back tonight. Be good as new after we get some deer."

It isn't true what they say about the undead. About the continued decay. While her heart no longer beat, something still lit within her. I thought of my Cindy's body as a Japanese lantern, her milk paper skin stretching over a rigid bone frame. Some days the new light within her shone with a selective glow beneath, while on other days the light burned with such intensity I thought we would both be consumed.

With the exception of her delicate skin, the bite mark was the only evidence of her metamorphoses. It was a ripe cyst with a light aroma of old walnut husks. Cindy told me the fluid tasted like cinnamon, but I refused to try it. She drained the cyst weekly and never in front of me. There were some parts of her condition I refused to acknowledge.

Just under an hour, I had the car packed with our new dog and everything else needed for the weekend. To save daylight, I dropped Cindy off at the Ming Dynasty Buffet and drove to one of the new sporting goods places that had been springing up all over town recently. I found Cindy a pink handled skinning knife and I bought two boxes of shells. After we finally got on the road, Cindy settled the poodle in her lap and fed him with hunks of sliced weenie. The brown bag of shells filled the space between us. What I didn't tell Cindy—I hadn't decided who they were for yet.

Gravel roads crosshatched mountains remnant of volcanoes and glaciers. The nearest town was over an hour's drive from where I planned to take us. The clouds billowing overhead were swollen and gray. A clothesline weighed down with fresh laundry more likely to freeze than dry. *If this weekend were a success*, I thought, *how many more would we have left together?* Cindy smoothed the patch of her missing areola with the back of the knife blade.

"How's the nipple?" I asked. "Mending okay?"

Cindy undid the top buttons on her blouse. "See for yourself."

I was careful this time. Her new skin felt like a potato chip, only spongier around the edges.

"Welcome to your new body," I said.

"It's your body, too," Cindy added. "And I can't wait for you to tear more of it off me."

After a few wrong turns and detours, I found the trailhead parking. We had to hike a few miles uphill, but I knew about an old logging road that would cut time. Cindy volunteered to tote the tree stand if I packed in everything else. Near dark, we found our old spot. I leaned my pack against a tree and surveyed camp.

We passed fresh deer scat on the way in and I thought I'd be able to poach something before we lost light. Cindy agreed to put up the tent and unpack while I hung the tree stand. With all the sweating we'd done already, I knew we'd be brewing up our old scents soon enough.

My life's loneliest hours dripped by in the tree stand as I waited for any animal to pass in front of my sights. A violent wind carved through every branch, oscillating them like fan blades. The motion made any clear line-of-sight impossible. Trudging back through the dark alone, I worried I'd have to finish off the poodle if Cindy couldn't hold on through the night. It made me glad we hadn't named him yet.

Our tent door was open, Cindy's ankles hung out the front with her panties dangling from the rain fly. She was ready to have her stomach and pussy stuffed. My blood knocked at the walls of my veins for the chance to have my wife ride me with the same raw and holy passion she hit me with in our basement. But I knew it wouldn't happen. This made twice I'd failed as her provider.

"Honey," I said, toeing the mud from my boots before I slipped them off. "Just how hungry are you right now?"

"Didn't you see anything?" Her voice had the smooth delivery of a non-committal stranger. She could have been any girl standing behind the counter at a quick stop. Her tone didn't put me at ease.

She needed to be fed.

I took off my belt and stripped. I climbed into the sleeping bag to spoon my wife, and reached up to gather any warm pussy juice I might swirl my cock in as I teased her ear—taking special effort to avoid her neck cyst. Nothing. My muscles ached with the diametric shock of hiking through humid cold. At first, I barely noticed the pressure of Cindy's hand around my shriveled member, but her strokes restored enough flow to get me semi-hard. She shifted over to face me, her limp-wristed attempt at a tug job more like a handshake. I tore her hand away and pinned her arm behind her head. She wasn't wet enough for me to enter, so the delicate lips of her pussy fell away like rose petals when I thrust my first few inches inside her. Cindy didn't moan or scream. She drew in her knees until they almost covered her breasts. What little she bled was enough to lube myself the rest of the way without tearing anything else.

Cindy grunted, "More." The bristles of our pubic hair made scratchy rasps as she hammered her hips against me. Like whatever she ate, the insides of her vagina sucked and swallowed everything put in front of it without savoring the pleasure.

I came with the weak and hurried certainty of a celibate pervert. Outside, our three-legged poodle clawed at a tent wall and whimpered. Cindy kept grinding me until I went limp and oozed out of her. She patted the underside of my chin with her thumb with a few soft taps before she rolled away from me.

Much later in the night, I woke to barking and the hot slosh of something plugging my ear. A horseshoe ring of blood spilled down Cindy's mouth. I blindly reached toward a ripple of pain on the left side of my head. The top half of my ear was gone. All I found was the mangled crescent moon indentation from Cindy's teeth.

She spat what she had been chewing into my palm. The

meat looked like a melted pair of wax lips.

"I'm so very sorry," she said. "Somehow I must have latched on in my sleep."

Panic waded through the half-awake fog of my thoughts in slow steps. I counted back, thinking how long it had taken for Cindy to turn. Just under a week. Already, I could feel the dull slowing of my heart as I moved towards what I was becoming.

It was too late for me. But not for us.

We had the communion of our own bodies to feed us— an ouroboros of ripe, undead flesh. Nothing without, only within. Our new need entering the shared chain of eternal and selfless hunger. I gave Cindy the knife she'd dropped, and fed her the piece of my ear she'd taken. Then I placed my head in her lap to offer the rest. Instead of cutting on me, she flayed away a narrow strip from her breast. She chewed me while she cut. When she was satisfied there would be enough, Cindy raised me to her virgin hole, and I suckled until my mouth went dry. Even as the knife separated me from my ear, a new one grew in its place. I tore away another mouthful. Cindy chewed on in silence. Without speaking, we knew each other's thoughts: *This is the body I give unto you. Take from me. Eat.*

Bill's Birthday Gift

Lori Safranek

Bill Damson really hated his best friends right now. He glared through narrowed eyes at the four big dumbasses, standing around the table like little boys, giggling and giving each other high-fives.

Their big birthday gift to Bill stood on the table right now, dressed in a black corset, fishnet stockings, and the tiniest thong Bill had ever seen. Actually, the first thong Bill had seen on a woman in person. Until now, he'd only seen them on racy music videos and porn sites. Which he no longer looked at, not since he became engaged to Lindsey.

The girl on the table squatted in front of Bill, her knees spread wide, giving him a very generous view of her crotch. Thongs did little to cover up anything, Bill noticed. He could see ... well, everything.

He was still angry at the four men he had grown up with. They had long been disappointed in Bill's inability to share their love for strip clubs, hot chicks, and filthy sex. They still loved him like a brother, even after he became engaged to *Lethal Lindsey*, as they dubbed her.

As his birthday gift swayed on her high heels in front of him, her crotch still beaming at him like a spotlight, Bill stared up at her face. She was quite pretty. Not at all the hard-edged drug addict Bill would expect in this line of work. She had long brown hair and big sexy eyes, the color of blue denim. She winked at him and licked her lips slowly and seductively. She smelled great, too, and her large breasts spilled out of her corset.

Bill stood, overwhelmed by his reaction to the stripper.

Unfortunately, Bill had an enormous erection, a fact that became evident to everyone when he stood up. The front of his khaki pants were in full tent-pole position.

The dumbasses cracked up laughing again, slapping each other on the back and shouting.

"Go, Billy!"

Bill scowled and sat back down. He looked right back into the lovely, shaved crotch of his birthday gift. God, what was her name anyway? He hated thinking of her as "The Birthday Gift."

"What's your name?"

She blinked at him in surprise. She smiled a little. "Stacy. My name is Stacy. You're Bill, the Birthday Boy, right?"

Bill nodded and felt his cheeks redden. Stacy laughed and rose from the squat she had held for an impressive length of time. She stuck out her hand and Bill helped her step down from the table. When she stood on the floor, Stacy was barely the height of Bill's shoulder. She was so tiny. When Bill glanced down at her, he noticed her big blue eyes and then her big, creamy white breasts. He averted his eyes.

"Stacy, you can go now," he said, gritting the words out through clenched teeth. He tried to think of Lindsey, but made the mistake of glancing back down at Stacy and her boobs. White, creamy, soft ... he shook his head.

"So, I don't know if they already paid you," Bill said, pulling his wallet out. Stacy stopped him.

"Nah, they paid up front. And the birthday boy doesn't tip," she said. She jabbed a thumb toward his friends. "Those guys should give me a tip."

"Oh," Bill said. "They'll tip you, trust me."

She shrugged and smiled at Bill. His eyes started to drift to her breasts again, but he snapped them back to her face. He stepped past her and toward his friends.

The door to the private dining room crashed open. A waiter ran in and slammed it shut behind him. His eyes were huge, his face pale and sweaty.

"Zombies!" he shouted. The men gazed at him blankly.

Stacy was adjusting her thong and didn't pay attention. The waiter stared wildly around the room. "Didn't you hear me? There are zombies in the dining room!"

"What the hell? Are you high?" Bill asked.

The waiter looked affronted. "Of course not, I'm working. There are God damned freaking zombies out there. They already killed most of my customers."

Tim, the youngest of the group, moved toward the door. The waiter flung himself in front Tim.

"No. Don't open it. They'll get in," he said. He was shaking so hard now, sweat was spraying off him and some hit Tim right in the face.

"Dude! Back off with the sweat," Tim said, pushing the small waiter aside. Tim reached for the handle and carefully opened the door. He peeked out for less than a minute, then slammed the door shut and started pulling a table in front of it.

"Come on, block the door dammit, he's telling the truth," Tim yelled. "They're everywhere! Eating people! Block the door!"

The other men sprang into action and soon had the door wedged shut with chairs and tables. They heard the zombies, pounding on the door, but it stood firm.

"What do we do now?" Tim said. They all stood staring at the door, at a loss.

Then the lights went out.

"What the hell is going on?" Bill shouted. The others were grumbling too.

"Maybe the zombies cut the power lines," the waiter said.

Tim snorted. "Zombies don't think like that."

They all started groping in the dark, trying to find chairs to sit in. A number of bashed shins and stubbed toes later, they were seated around the table, waiting. Waiting for what, they had no idea.

"You think the cops know about this?" Mark said. "You know, maybe they're on their way?"

Bill took out his cell phone and dialed 911. After a great

deal of confusion, he managed to get his point across and the operator promised to send help.

They settled in to wait. Someone's cell phone rang. The ringing stopped and they heard Bill's voice.

"Hello? Yeah, Lindsey, I'm still at dinner," he said. "Listen, honey, turn on the news. Yeah, I understand you hate watching the news, but do it. Okay, are they saying anything about zombies at the restaurant? What? Of course I haven't been drinking!"

The phone beeped as Lindsey hung up. The others burst out laughing, even Stacy.

"Wow, honey," she said. "You got yourself a real ball-buster there."

"You have no idea," Bill said, his voice flat. "No idea."

The other men laughed and started swapping stories about Lethal Lindsey. Like the time she had ruined a business deal for Bill when he caught her spying on his lunch meeting with a customer. Lethal Lindsey strikes again.

What about the time ... as the stories rolled on and the laughs got louder, Bill sat at the table with his head in his hands.

Bill yipped in surprise when something touched his knee. Luckily, no one heard him, since he quickly realized it was not a zombie. Not with that small hand now caressing his thigh. Whoa. Stacy. Had to be. What was she doing? Her hand slid up Bill's thigh slowly and all he could think was, *Uh oh.* He froze in place.

When her fingers reached his crotch and brushed his erection, he came to life, jerking back in his chair while trying to keep quiet. All he needed was for his idiot friends to find him like this. Stacy moved her hand back to his crotch and slid her fingertip inside his fly.

I am a dead man, Bill thought as sweat trickled down his neck. Lindsey will kill me. This is going to happen. I cannot stop now.

Stacy slid his zipper open and one soft, gentle hand reached inside his pants. She fumbled a bit finding a way into his briefs. Bill could not help it, he moaned. His friends were laughing and carrying on, and the zombies were pounding on the door, so no one heard him.

Thank God. Oh please, Jesus, do not let those lights come back on until she is done, Bill thought.

He shifted his hips forward on the chair and heard a soft giggle from under the table.

Stacy had his hard cock in her hand now and Bill stopped thinking about Lindsey altogether. Her hands slid up and down the shaft as her tongue took quick little licks all over the tip.

As she slid her hand down on his shaft, she sucked his dick into her luscious, wet mouth, swirling her tongue around the tip as Bill whimpered.

Stacy gave another little giggle, which Bill felt vibrating all the way through his balls. She leaned forward and took his whole cock into her mouth. She moved her soft lips up and down the length of him, building a pressure in him he was sure was going to explode far too soon.

Stacy drew her head back, letting his solid member slide out of her mouth. Involuntarily, Bill moaned and shoved his hips forward, seeking the warmth of her mouth again.

Oh, man, don't tell me she's stopping. I will have a heart attack.

Stacy had her lips on him again. He gave a relieved sigh. She started moving up and down, and Bill's hips rose off the chair. With a quick move, Stacy opened her mouth wider and took his entire length down her throat. She began moving rapidly, sucking and licking, taking as much of him as possible. Bill's head rolled from side to side, and he felt his orgasm sizzling right on top, ready to explode.

Instead of pulling away so he didn't cum in her mouth, like Lethal Lindsey did the one time they had attempted a blow job, Stacy sped up her sucking and slurping until Bill lost it and came in her mouth. She kept swallowing his juices and sucking him dry.

Zombies! His eyes flew open. Good, still no light. The guys were still laughing and carrying on and zombies still pounded on the door.

He heard sirens, and they sounded close. Stacy put his dick back inside his pants and zipped him up. She gave him a kind little pat and started moving away. Before Bill could reach for her, to thank her, the lights blinked on. Stacy sat in a chair, not a hair out place, looking bored. Bill caught her eye and she winked.

The others were quiet now, listening to the sirens and sounds of cops calling into the restaurant. "This is the police. We are entering the building. Please remain calm."

The friends in the private dining room gave each other high fives and the little waiter crossed himself. Stacy stood up and started gathering her things. Bill took the opportunity to whisper to her, "Thank you. That ... that was amazing."

She smiled at him and shrugged one shoulder. "Gave you something to think about while you're sleeping with the ball-buster you're marrying."

Shots could be heard in the restaurant. Presumably, it was the cops killing the zombies. The pounding on the door to their room stopped, the zombies attracted to the confusion in the main restaurant.

Eventually the cops found them in the private room and guided them through the blood-splattered, gory scene, and into the moonlit night.

As they each were checked out by paramedics and were found healthy, the friends gathered into a group. Tim, as usual, got his humor back first.

He chuckled. "Wow, Bill, Lethal Lindsey will do anything to keep you from having fun!"

Bill scowled and the others laughed. Bill caught Stacy's eye as she walked past. She winked at him again. He smiled and waved goodbye.

"She didn't ruin my fun," he said under his breath. "*Not. At. All.*"

Headshot

Frankie Sachs

"When there is no more room in hell, the dead will walk the earth." - George A. Romero

Ash helped Jackson through the narrow window serving as their front door. All she saw of his injury was a jagged hole in the fabric of his shirt, and a slow well of blood. Red droplets fell through the metal grate of the fire escape to the ground below.

The dead milled beneath them in a frenzy, emitting eerie whistling, guttural moans, the noises they could make with whatever soft tissue hadn't liquefied inside them. The living dead decayed, but slowly. Someday they would be nothing but walking skeletons or mummified bones in shriveled, leathery skin—things that would topple and crumble to dust. But not yet.

Inside, Ash found a can of juice and a package of Oreos in the food stash. "Take off your shirt," she told Jackson, "I'll try and stop the bleeding; you need to eat something."

That he didn't argue, or try and doctor himself, told her how bad off he was. He peeled the shirt away, wincing as the fabric stuck to his back with dried blood, and tugged at the skin around the wound.

He crunched cookies and sipped the juice while Ash pressed gauze to the wound to staunch the bleeding.

"What happened?" she asked.

"Don't know," he said, his voice husky with fatigue. "They were all around; I was backing toward the alley ..."

She understood. The pack had surprised them.

"Was it a bite?" she asked. Anything else she could deal with, as long as she could stop the bleeding.

"I don't know. Maybe."

Ash lifted the gauze, careful not to pull away the newly clotting scab. *Not a bite, please not a bite.* She didn't say the words out loud, didn't want Jackson to realize how afraid she was. The wound didn't look good, a four inch tear in the flesh, a chunk of muscle missing. She dabbed cotton soaked in peroxide around the edge.

The ragged perforations around the wound might have been caused by something else, Ash told herself. A piece of jagged metal from one of the wrecks littering the street. Shards of broken window. But sickly bruising already radiated out from the even punctures.

Tooth marks.

Ash felt a sick cold in the pit of her stomach. If he had been in better shape, Jackson would've guessed something was wrong, but he was still weak and disoriented from blood loss and pain. Ash finished cleaning the wound, packed it with gauze, and wrapped an elastic bandage tight around to keep it in place.

"How bad?" he asked. Always practical.

Her heart felt as though it were wrapped in iron bands. "You'll live. Now rest."

Ash pushed Jackson toward the bedroom they shared, where they held each other against the dark and the loneliness and the memories and the dead.

They lay together under a pile of blankets. He shivered. Not fever, not yet. Just cold because he'd bled out so much. She wrapped her arms around him, careful of the wound under the bandage, pressed herself against his bare chest. Even now, under the copper tang of blood, he smelled of forest and spice and man, and Ash breathed him in.

* * * *

Ash woke to Jackson gently stroking her back. He was

warm, but not yet feverish. "Are you awake?" he whispered.

"Yeah," she whispered back.

He continued stroking her and Ash ran her own hands over the smooth skin of his back, skirting the bandage. Jackson was lean and muscular, strong. Ash pressed her head against his chest so he would not see her face in the moonlight slanting through the window. She did not want him to find the sorrow there.

"Are you hungry?" she asked. She wanted to do something for him. The big things, the things that would make it right, those she could not do, but the small ones—to make sure he was warm, fed, comfortable—those were within her means.

"No," he said, "Not right now."

She relaxed, let him hold her. Comfort, the feel of another warm body. To not be alone. That she could give him.

Ash kissed his neck softly, and felt, more than heard, his sharp intake of breath. Jackson pulled her tighter to him. There was always an urgency. They spent their days existing, every trip for food, water, fuel for the camp stove, might end badly. Every time they made love might be the last time either of them would touch another living person.

Jackson's fingers laid a trail down her spine, firm along the skin of her naked back. They reached her belt, slid over the coarse material of her trousers, and he pulled her firmly against him, her hips pressed to his. He was hard against her, and her urgency met his own.

This was, she knew, the last time she would ever kiss him, hold him against her. Be held. After tonight, she would be alone.

Ash twined her fingers in Jackson's hair and pulled his head to her. She kissed him, fierce with need, pulling him with her, on top of her, careful of the ragged hole in his back.

He kissed her back, his lips firm and hot and Ash thought, maybe the fever ...

But she didn't care. She ground against him, his hips hard

and angular against the softness of her inner thighs.

He pressed her down, sat back on his haunches and loosened her belt and jeans, then his own. Ash raised her hips. She wanted him, now, without hesitation. Wanted to forget, for a few moments. "Fuck me," she said.

* * * *

They lay together exhausted, silent. Ash never asked Jackson what he thought about after sex. She didn't want an answer. Afterward, she thought of her husband. The perfunctory routine of suburban sex. How he had turned her on, but not much. How he got her off, but only once in a while.

How he was dead. Gone. And she felt like a traitor to his memory making love—not making love—fucking, with pure animal need, a man she had only known for a few weeks. But God, those weeks, now, they seemed like a lifetime.

She should have loved him better, Phil, when she had him. She should have pranced wanton in front of him. Peeled the clothes off him, pulled him into her with urgent need. When she wrapped her legs around Jackson's gleaming, sweat slick hips and pulled him deep into her, as though she could, with him, fill up the emptiness that had been left inside her, she said a silent penance to Phil. She offered to him, via the proxy of Jackson, all she meant to give, should have given, when he was alive.

She tried not think of the two little girls she had shared with Phil. The memory came, unbidden, when she thought of him, making love to him, making those children. And she pushed the memory away, shoved back to where it came from. She would not think of those children now. Maybe not ever. To remember them, sweet smelling and soft, fresh from the bath, giggling as she tucked them into bed, gently sleeping, eyelashes fluttering on their cheeks, sapped her of everything. To think of those children was to wish for death, because living with the pain would be unbearable.

She heard the beginning of the rasp in Jackson's lungs. Where their skin touched, hips, shoulders, thighs, the hand left casually on the swell of her stomach, she felt the slow burn of his skin as his temperature climbed.

The infection was coming on fast. She knew it would. The exertion. Sometimes, kept quiet, a victim might linger for three, four days before the sickness overcame them. Running, fighting, fucking, all these things helped the infection spread faster. By morning, Jackson would be in terrible pain. Spasms would wrack and contort his body as the infection spread through his nervous system. By noon, he would be gone.

By sundown, he would be something else.

Ash slipped from beneath the blankets, careful not to disturb Jackson. Healthy Jackson would have come alert, his transition to wakefulness signaled only by a slight hitch in his breathing, a tensing of his muscles beside her. Now, though, he was too ill, and slept on fitfully in his fever sleep.

Ash went to the walk-in closet that served as their armory and stepped inside, closing the door behind her. She turned on a small, battery operated lantern for illumination. Here they kept the guns, ammunition, a bow and arrows, a large, wickedly curved machete, all the weapons they had salvaged from sporting goods stores, military surplus outlets, and big boxes.

Ash searched for the pistol, a Walther P-22. Jackson had shown her when he found it. The magazine only held ten rounds and it wasn't the best gun they had. But the pistol had a silencer, and that was what Ash wanted now. Noise attracted not only the dead, but the living.

She found the gun, checked the safety, checked it was loaded and then she returned to Jackson.

In the few moments she'd been gone his breathing had worsened. He tossed and opened his eyes and she saw they were glassy and unfocused. "Water," he said.

Ash brought him a bottle of water and two tablets. Morphine, for the pain she could see starting to take hold. "Take these," she said.

"What are they?"

"Antibiotic," she said. "You're running a fever, there's an infection."

He shook his head, winced. "Save."

She said, "You need them now."

He took the pills, too tired, too sick, to fight her. Ash sat beside him and stroked his hair, shaggy wild-man hair that hadn't been cut since they had been together. She stroked his cheek, the coarse bristles he trimmed with scissors because water was too precious to waste on shaving.

Ash sat beside Jackson until the morphine took effect and he relaxed into an opiate slumber. She did not want to remember him delirious and in agony, twisting and writhing and calling out to the names of people she did not know. She positioned the silenced barrel of the Walther a hairs-breadth from Jackson's temple. She repeated to herself the mantra Jackson had taught her:

Aim for the head.

Relax. Exhale. Squeeze.

Take the shot.

S.P.Q.R.

Rob M. Miller & Jill Behe

Standing there viewing the last of the battle, she looked the lioness, regal, brilliant and dangerous, long, black hair braided and falling down her back, the right side of her head clean-shaven, proudly displaying her eagle tattoo, her *aquila*, and *ours*, the symbol of all she's given, the woman, our *mater familia*.

The mother of the *Legio*.

She muttered something and handed over the binoculars.

"What was that, Cesarina?" Bringing up the device, the Steiner 10x50 gave a perfect view of the day-long slaughter, the ranks of bruisers and mounted furies in mop-up mode, their armor and clear, polycarbonate shields now black with caked and dripping viscera, the herd of some thousands of Zulus fallen before the Legion's disciplined meat grinder. *All praise to pipe, sword, and gun.*

"I said: *Senātus Populusque Rōmānus*. The Senate and People of Rome."

"Cesarina?"

"Nothing."

The woman smiled, her face aged, but lined with wisdom, mirth, and more than a hint of sadness.

"Just thinking of what I'd wanted." A pause. "And what I've gotten."

She held my chin.

"Men, all too easily, carry their egos—"

"'Tween their legs," I said, finishing the line.

She grinned, broad and approving.

"So beautifully true." A longer moment of silence. "But

women carry theirs, too." She patted her bosom. "Right here. Remember, young one, both can be fatal."

Worry hits for this icon I've been blessed to serve. "With Macro's victory, why the heavy heart? The herd's been wiped. Probably won't be another of significance for many days, even weeks."

Her head hung low. "My baby brother ... should've named him Brutus."

"I don't understa—"

"He seeks to supplant me." She started for the horses. "And he might succeed. Claiming you for his laurel come today's success was just the latest in a series of japes. He knew of your importance to me, and your desire to join my virginal *praetorian* guard—to don a new name."

Alecto, she of unceasing anger. "I'll do my duty, Cesarina," I whispered. "I'll make the needed sacrifice."

Cesarina continued through my interruption:

"Most of my original council's gone; the younger wolves owe more to Macro than me. They've fought with him ... see me more as part of the past, some *thing*, instead of some *one*, an idea to be honored in pageantry and song, in march and service, not unlike our beloved Bellona, Minerva, and Mars. To deify my memory is not a stretch. But in the flesh? Nay. In the flesh, they howl for a man."

We mounted our steeds. "You're the *prima mater*, you're *my* mother."

"If only." She turned her mare. "No, sweet Atia, we're all fated to be replaced; that's the bane and blessing of humanity. I'd only have it be from time, the slayer of us all, rather than envy. Should've taken care of things long ago, back when it would've been simpler ... less painful. Now it may be too late."

We started our trek down the hill, joined by some furies that kept polite distance.

"Macro may sit in the *praetorium*, but you're our queen, our high priestess ... beyond seat or title. You'll not be swept aside, not by arm or guile—certainly not by *him*. The Legion's yours, by strength, steel, and vow. No one's forgotten your gifts."

"And what's that? My dear, before the Zulus, all I did was read a bunch of books. I've given nothing more than the greatest and flimsiest of power. I've given story."

"Story?"

"Should've paid more attention to Shelley and her short-sighted doctor ... would've been better prepared, for this, the Adam of all my labors."

* * * *

Returning to our *castra* amidst sentry calls of "Strength and honor," thoughts of Macro plagued, his pompous laugh, and his beefy torso, hairy and thick with age, scars, and two large pectoral muscles, the right missing a nipple, rumor giving credit to training with live blades, *pugio* or *gladius* depending on the bard. The idea of that repulsive beast pawing my body with his hateful lust brought a strange mixture of satisfaction and disgust.

The queen was right. It was an insult, not of me, a mere girl of 15-winters, raised in Cesarina's personal household, but of the sovereign herself. Macro could have—and *did*—just about any woman in the camp, soldier, support, or servant, his violent method of love-play a draw, if not for the prurient pleasure of the Legion's many sadists and masochists, then certainly for those looking to maneuver into stronger circles.

"Atia?"

"Yes?"

"Been a long day ... and riding out, you said your bottle broke. Head to the aid station and get another. We'll stable Judith."

"Yes, Cesarina. And if I may?"

The woman raised a brow.

"With the day's victory ... and other things, I'd like to visit the pits."

Cesarina nodded and brought a finger to her lips.

Understanding the counsel, I kissed my bomb-proof mare on the head, then took off to get my insulin, the magical fluid that's kept me alive these not-so-many years.

Despite the late hour, there was no concern about rousing anyone. The *castra's* always awake, forging and foraging and fortifying, sentries atop the ramparts manning the torches and Klieg lights, the *mechanicus* working their mojo on their charge of vehicles, earth movers, and bikes, soldiers in the commo tent, listening, sending/receiving communiqués to the families and communities supporting us—or needing our help—from urban bunkers to the ever so-necessary moated and fenced farms providing our rations, to the scheduled check-ins with flying patrols always on the lookout for walkers, crawlers, or squishies, and especially any herds, mounted scouts, horsed, motorcycled, and ATVs, lightly-armed—but still able to sting.

A million tasks taken for granted, but only because they were never ignored.

And, yes, the aid station.

Going now was perfect. The bulk of our soldiers wouldn't return till the morrow. There was still too much work ... bodies to burn, and *imagines* to be rendered from the fallen, tattooed skin from chest, back, scalp, and thigh, later to be tanned and then stitched into our *vexillum*, all the banners, standards, and flags adorning our *castra*, and carried by the *aquilifers* bearing our sacred eagle, the *imaginifers* the visage of Cesarina, or borne on our vehicles, walls, tents, and armor, memorializing our dead, constant reminders that the world had turned into an anvil, not to eradicate humanity, but to purge it. Yes, the Zulus were a hammer, but they were not the enemy.

The foe was fear, would always be fear.

All praise to pipe, sword, and gun.

At the aid station, few words were exchanged. The *medicus* on duty, an older man named Poenius, with a spiked Mohawk, a tattooed eagle on the right side of his head, and an inked *caduceus* on the left, knew who I was.

"Be more careful with your bottles," the man said. "Supply's almost gone."

"Understood."

"You'd better. It's red-listed, so maybe our scouts'll get lucky. Meantime, you need to ..."

"Fight for tomorrow," we finished together, the mantra a reflex. If only he knew. But that was it, nobody knew, and *nobody* would.

One mere morrow?

Ha!

I was fighting for many tomorrows—for everyone.

* * * *

Heading to the pits, I passed a small orgy on the parade field. Yawn. People already celebrating the day's new boast. Their festivity—under guard, of course; in a world where people still died from heart attacks, accidents, and other sudden cases, privacy, even in a privy, was unheard of— would probably run less than an hour. For a moment, I was tempted to join, and laughed at the thought of Macro's response were he to find my maidenhead—even if only symbolically present, given my time a horse—snatched from his grasp. Fortunately, the temptation vanished. Old enough for Macro, I was still too young to celebrate among the masses.

Way too much work, anyway, especially with men I wasn't attracted to. Better to play with the vibrator gifted by Thuria last year, after my first trial against an unfettered Zulu.

* * * *

After beating on a Zulu for 30-minutes, I asked for a small one, some crotch-biter I could play with.

"Waste of time, 'less you want three or four, and you're not rated for that—yet. Even though you gots the moves!"

Happy for Strabo's praise, I flirted with a smile.

Quartered with furies, I'd often thought of him while kneading my breasts, pinching nipples, rubbing my center, or, on rare occasion, using the way too loud phallic-shaped device Thuria had laughingly dubbed the Thor-gasm, the other women in their racks, trying to hide their shaming snickers.

"Fine, I got one, but he's fresh."

He tossed down some Vick's, the courteous act ensuring that later I'd be having a *ménage à trois* with him in mind, and the Thor-gasm in hand. After applying a liberal amount of ointment under my nose and around my lips, I tossed the vial back and readied for the Zulu in miniature to be pitched, in this case, a boy, maybe 10-years-old.

Like with all the Zulus standing by for use, its head generously wrapped in thick tape, sealing a mouth already freed of teeth, its hands, too, were finger-encased, leaving the driven cannibal with nothing but a pad and thumb in which to attempt to grip. Against such a tamed, stinking beast, I was in little danger. What observers there were paid no attention as we wrestled, or when I pinned the pint-sized monster, stuck it, and filled a syringe with gooey black comeuppance.

* * * *

Two days come and gone, 48-hours of waiting, of girding my loins, the bulk of the *castra's* forces returned, ebullient bruisers with their *gladii*, shields, and sharpened rebar, all standing without on the parade field set inside our mobile fort of moat, wall, and vehicle, ready to watch their *praetor* receive due spoil.

And ready, I am: clean, perfumed, and dressed in a shift of white linen. I ask for a moment and it's granted, time enough to release a hidden needle from my bag, to plunge it into my flank, the viscous fluid a fire as it invades my system …

… and spreads.

Stepping out of the G.P. medium, I'm greeted by sun,

warm wind, and the blast of trumpets. The *Legio* is present, in nearly full order of rank and file, with only the infirm and those under duty excused from bearing witness.

The walk to Macro—arrogant, on his back, arms behind his head, buttressed by pillows, legs splayed—seems far, but isn't. I marvel how when uncertainty is removed, even a girl can become a lioness.

With no care for ritual, I toss the shift and mount the smirking beast, falsely secure in his hubris, impaling myself on his bloated, jutting cock, the member violating me with all the indifference of a charging Zulu.

Tainting me, but now tainted in return. And then I'm gone ...

... and I'm a girl, Atia no more, but Sally Jane Williams, five maybe six, and with my ... my mother reciting *Sleeping Beauty*, my favorite ... then cradling me, she says *You're a princess, too,* and I am ... hers and hers alone—*But someday your prince will come, and you'll have your own little princess*—and it's not a fantasy, but a memory come to comfort ...

... and then a breeze blows and I'm on a grassy hill and there's a noise in this vast expanse of field and trees and blooming lilies. I turn and there's Strabo, dressed in storybook finery, grinning, and holding a ring.

We embrace.

I blink and we're on a bed of fragrant flowers, impossibly soft, and I *feel* him against me, probing, seeking, even as his fingers caress down my back as we lay on our sides, and it's not a jutting abomination, but an extension of his love, his need matching mine, the both of us becoming one, our lips seeking and finding, entwined, our hearts beating with synchronized heat, burst-ING with *p-p-passion*—

—the consummation dreamed of by every girl, every Sleeping Beauty, Snow White, or Cinderella who's ever lived.

And I'm drifting, all but ignorant of a world filled with starving *anthropophagi*, their damning virus—

—spread via bite, spray, and for the committed, through STZs, and as I float ...

higher ... away, there's only ... the brief
satisfaction of
Macro's
Screams
Bidding
Me
Farewe—

Ménage à Trauma

Dan Larnerd

Arm in arm, the lovers walked out of the storm and into the Caputo Hotel, the sight of the rundown lobby more chilling than the rain outside. The smiles dropped from both of their faces. James pulled Marisol close and they sighed together.

They were both young and attractive. James was roguish with a five o'clock shadow and blonde hair. With bedroom eyes and a dark complexion, Marisol was sexy and sultry. Together, they resembled a couple out of a fashion catalogue. Not one for the upper crust, but one for trendy young people who wear designer scarves and skinny jeans.

James glanced around at dusty chandlers and worn out velvet chairs. The walls were covered with peeling wallpaper and faded photographs of socialites and mobsters. Curious stains covered the carpet. He took in a breath of the stale air and almost coughed.

"So this is what a two star hotel looks like," he whispered to Marisol.

Marisol answered, "Just be thankful you're on this adventure with a five star lady."

James smiled. "Let me know when she gets here."

Marisol gave him a playful jab to the shoulder. The clerk at the front desk wiped a gob of crud from her one good eye and put down her copy of the want ads.

"You folks her for the séance?" she said with a voice as gloomy as the hotel lobby. "I think they've already started."

"Not us." James pulled a copy of an email confirmation from his coat pocket. He handed it to the hotel clerk.

She grunted as she began to punch numbers into her computer. The clerk smacked her lips and said, "You two don't look like the normal trash that stay here. Figured you for the séance."

"We're just visiting the city," said Marisol.

The old clerk didn't acknowledge Marisol. With her eyes glued to her computer screen, the clerk said, "All sorts of hippy dippy types got the entire top floor rented out tonight. One of them was even wearing a turban. Bunch of screwballs … now let me get you your key."

A rickety elevator ride later and the pair stepped onto their floor. The soft murmur of chanting drifted down from the ceiling. James put his arm around Marisol.

"Adventure," he said.

She smiled and answered, "Adventure."

The door to their room creaked open. Marisol and James laughed to each other.

The room was small and filled with a queen size bed, each wall covered with mustard-colored wallpaper. A small television perched on a swiveling metal arm. Its remote control was bolted to the nightstand. A tray was set up next to the door. On top of it sat an ice bucket and a stack of plastic cups.

The pair stepped inside and threw their suitcases on the bed. The lamp on the nightstand flickered.

"Do you smell that?" asked Marisol as she wrinkled her nose.

James shut the door behind him and sniffed. He started to pull off his jacket and said, "I told you I don't care about your stinky feet."

"Jerk," grinned Marisol. She wrapped her arms around James and kissed him. "I'm glad we did this. Stinky room and all."

He returned her kiss and whispered, "Next time we won't book the cheapest room online."

With kisses and laughs, the lovers knocked their suitcases to the floor. Their lips only parted to pull their clothes off one another. In the flickering light, they moved across the bed. Together they climbed under the blankets.

Their bodies intertwined as voices from upstairs drifted through the air, the words ancient and heavy. It was soft background music to their rising passion.

Upstairs, the chanting turned to gasps and shouts. The mattress began to slightly tremble underneath James and Marisol. The entire bed began to shake.

After a kiss, James whispered, "I think this is one of those 'magic fingers' beds … maybe we jumped started it."

"And here I thought this was just a two star hotel," Marisol replied.

The lovers threw off the covers and dove into each other. Their world shrunk to each other's touch and the humidity of one another's bodies. Marisol and James were oblivious to the sound of ripping fabric.

Footsteps thundered up above them as the bed continued to sway underneath them. Little puffs of down and cotton swirled through the air. In the shuddering lamplight, it resembled snow

Marisol mounted her man and sighed. She arched her back as bits of feather stuck to her wet skin. James touched her neck and then her breasts. The sensation of hands over her body made Marisol toss her head back in rapture.

A hand followed the curves of her hips. It drifted down her backside. A finger ran down her two cheeks.

Marisol suddenly bolted forward and smacked James on the chest.

"Hey!' she scolded, "I told you before: NO BUTT STUFF!"

James held both his hands up in front of her in surprise. A look of confusion sprang across his face as he said, "I didn't—"

Marisol frowned down at him. Although she saw his two hands, she felt something grab hold of her. She peeked behind her and let out a scream, cutting off his apology.

A pair of hands stuck out of the mattress.

Each arm had pushed itself up through the downy mattress, blindly groping at the lovers. The fingernails were painted cherry red but the skin was a sickly gray with open sores. Marisol and James leaped from the bed as the hands continued to rip their way up through the mattress.

"They were touching me!" shrieked Marisol.

James swelled with caveman bravado and roared in anger. He seized hold of the mattress and flung it off of the box spring. The primal snarl on his face dropped to the floor along with the torn mattress when he saw what lay beneath.

Hidden in the box spring was a woman, her clammy skin covered in hundreds of insect bites. A gruesome gash ran across her throat. She wore only a pair of fishnet stockings and a thick coat of eye shadow. At one time, she had been a prostitute. Her visit to the Caputo Hotel had left her a murder victim.

The séance upstairs had turned her into something else.

Marisol screamed as the dead hooker began to climb out of the depths of the box spring. She reached out toward the naked pair. A deep moan rumbled up through the slice across her neck. With it, a swarm of bed bugs began to scurry out of the wound.

The lovers clutched one another as the shambling corpse groaned and lumbered toward them. She tumbled out of the bed frame and onto the dirty carpet. Another groan bubbled up from the neck wound as she began to grasp again at the Marisol and James.

As Marisol screamed again, James grabbed the ice bucket from the tray by the door. He lifted it up until it touched the ceiling and then brought the bucket down hard. His penis whirled like a fleshy helicopter blade as he made his attack.

With a heavy clank, he shoved the bucket over the corpse's head. Inside the bucket, her groans had a metallic echo. She swung her arms about blindly as she rose to her feet.

"Kill it!" screamed Marisol in a panic. "Kill it!"

James skirted past the blinded corpse and toward the end

table. He tried to grab the bedside lamp but it was bolted to the table top like the remote control.

On the other side of the room, the corpse followed the sounds of Marisol's screams. She dodged the dead hooker's wild grasps by sinking deeper into the corner of the room until her back was against the wall.

Marisol screamed, "James!"

He yanked on the lamp again but it didn't budge. The drawer of the nightstand slid open. Inside lay a large Gideon bible. With both hands, he grabbed the book and turned to face the undead woman.

"Get away from her!" he roared and hit the corpse across the back with the bible.

She howled inside her bucket and whirled toward him. Again and again he drummed the book down onto her. Each strike knocked a few bed bugs loose.

Like a boxer delivering a huge uppercut, James swung the bible underhanded. The book collided with the dead woman's jaw and sent her spiraling backward. The ice bucket shot off her head and ricocheted around the small room.

In a daze, the corpse tumbled back into the bed frame. There was a sickening crunch as her skull crashed into the headboard. She twitched for a moment and then lay still.

James starred down at the dead body. He shuddered and let the bloody bible drop from his hands. Marisol grabbed hold of him and started to sob. He held her tight against his chest.

"I hate two star hotels," whimpered Marisol.

Adam and Eve
at the End of Days

Mike D McCarty

"You fuck like you invented it." Milla said.

Kurt smiled and rolled over, lightly stroking the lateral scar running across her right shoulder. "Now that's a compliment." he said, reaching past her toned body to the rickety wooden bedside table. His last pack of reds sat on the scarred dusty wood with his father's zippo. He grabbed them both and fingered one of the last three smokes out. He offered her one but knew her answer already. She shook her head.

"Those things will kill ya."

"Yeah but they're quiet." He smiled.

As if on cue, they both heard a shuffling in the hallway and a thumping across the door, followed by a multitude of slight moans and the ominous clicking that gave him a chill. At this point, it was anyone's guess as to how many of them gathered outside the door. Had this been prior to the end times they would have smiled and thought someone else in the old hotel was up to the same activity, but those days were long gone. Now, it was survival of the fittest and live every day to its full potential.

The sun outside faded on another day.

How long had they been in here? Two days? Three?

The last few rays penetrated the dirty window and cast a pall over the room. She was backlit by the dirty light—a perfect silhouette of beauty in a world of chaos and pain—complete with flowing hair, smooth features. One of the last pretty things left he figured. He wished he had a camera. Hell he wished he had electricity. He looked across the old hotel room at the door, blood smeared down the wall next to it, parts of the carpet soaked dark brown. They were gonna want to charge him for this. He laughed.

"What?" She said.

"Good thing they don't have my credit card on file here."

Out on the balcony, where the grill stood, the propane bottle still bore dark brown splashes of blood. Empty, soot covered cans littered the balcony as well. At first he thought he'd toss them over the side, but for some reason he still felt strange about littering. She kissed his stomach; he watched as she trailed her finger along the cobra tattoo covering it.

She smiled and glanced up. "What are you thinking?"

"About how we met."

He first met Milla at the Granville Tunnel ...

* * * *

Kurt slipped along quietly, towards the darkened mouth of the train tunnel. The noise ahead told him a few of them were in there and they had something cornered. Might be something as simple as a rabbit. They went after anything made of meat and still alive. Sort of the ultimate, final "fuck you" to Peta and vegans all over the world. Once you turned into one of them, you didn't have a choice anymore. Eat meat or die trying. No one had ever managed to communicate successfully with them; they tried in the early days when scientists still cared on CNN and FOX News. But they didn't even try to communicate with us, they were brain damaged or brain dead, they only made sounds, as far he could tell. Mostly the sound they made was the awful clacking of their teeth as they bit the air once they got a whiff of something. Like a dog licking the air near a fresh steak, tasting the air with his nose. They obviously still had all their senses. Just not the sense to know what they were doing.

He wasn't even sure how you got the disease. No one

knew. Sure, they tried like hell to figure that shit out as humanity collapsed around everyone, but at one point it became faster to gun them down and burn them rather than try to reason with them or help those afflicted. Luckily, whatever the cause, the infection hadn't seen fit to cross species yet; at least *he* hadn't seen a case of it. Everything else alive on the planet just became fodder for the ultimate mindless predator: man. Maybe this was nature's way of turning mankind against itself, to reclaim the planet.

He squatted down low, his black leather pants giving a satisfying creak. He always loved the sound of leather. His hand quietly pulled his silenced pistol from his leg holster. He moved low to the ground, silent, like a predator. Being stealthy was how he managed to stay alive so long. He had finally found the one thing in the world he was good at. Survival.

When the world collapsed, he figured it was his calling. His time to shine. Be a hero again.

He moved in closer to the dark mouth of the tunnel and listened, holding his breath a moment. He thought he heard someone speaking deep inside, but this close to the mouth of the tunnel it just sounded like a muttered echo. He normally would never have considered walking into a tunnel, but he had raided an army surplus a few days earlier and found a set of night vision goggles, and an infrared flashlight. He had been wearing them for days, waiting for the right opportunity to put them to a true test, somewhere in total darkness. The goggles worked great with the light of the moon, but once you got into total darkness you couldn't see fuck all, unless you had an IR flashlight. He had used both in the Middle East, back when there was a Middle East. Both had been part of his standard equipment. He had flown Attack Gliders behind enemy lines for the Special Forces Black Flight Unit. It was like being strapped to the belly of a silent jet, but with more control than a parachute. You could base a 100 pounds of gear out of it. He had been their poster boy, a war hero. Sixty-eight confirmed kills and two purple hearts, the second a reward for a chemical burn and the reason he now sported an eye patch.

He pulled the goggles down over his one good eye, thumbed the safety off his silenced pistol and stepped into the yawning maw of the mouth of Hell. The stench of death rolling out of the tunnel smacked him in the nose. Didn't seem like a smart place for anyone living to be, but curiosity and a desire to use his new toys piqued his interest. So he pushed deep into the stygian tomb. He moved quickly from car to car, past piles of scattered dried flesh and rotting passer byes, some spilling out of their cars onto the street where they had been torn apart. Rats and wild dogs had scattered the mess, creating frenetic cave paintings in blood on the street. Life, for some, carried on in abundance it seemed.

When he first saw her in the green cast of the goggles, he could tell she knew how to handle herself; her athletic body crouched on the top of a bus, a dying flashlight scattered near the tunnel wall told a story of a hastened escape and a dropped light source. Below the bus, scratching and clambering over themselves to get at her were four skinny, greasy Deadheads.

Deadheads, was what everyone called them, and the name made perfect sense ... unless you were fan of the Grateful Dead, and he had met *one* on his post-apocalyptic travels—a guy from Wisconsin in moccasins and a dirty tie-dye shirt. He couldn't even remember his name, Johnny or JJ or something. It was a wonder the guy had made it at all in the New World. Just dumb luck, Kurt supposed. But his luck ended when he fell to a gang of scavengers he ran towards, thinking they were *"Friendly man."* They probably ate him.

Kurt slipped forward. The Deadheads hadn't turned their attention away from her yet. He had the advantage of surprise. She was lit up nicely in the failing light of the flashlight. She smiled, realizing he was not one of them. He dropped two of the Deadheads immediately, their dark, watery blood splattering the side of the bus. The other two turned, one not fast enough, as the other got to admire the pretty flash from the pistol sending it to Hell. The fourth one lunged toward him, arms outstretched, teeth gnashing in expectant joy. The gun remained silent; he pulled harder on the trigger, but the weapon had jammed, not racking another round. He backed up towards the tunnel wall and noticed the stove-piped round in the slide. The Deadhead stumbled forward like some mad Frankenstein. Kurt tripped over something and fell flat on his ass. His feet kicked away a one gallon can of propane, making the creature stumble around it. He pulled a six inch bowie knife off his belt and was about to fix things when the creature stopped in its tracks. The body started to slouch forward and the head rolled to the ground. Behind the Deadhead, in the green cast of the goggles, she stood, arms outstretched at the end of a swipe—a curved machete gleaming wetly in her hand, a smile on her lips.

When he got her out into the light he saw what he could only describe as a sexy superhero: shoulder length blonde hair, a tight fitting costume of leather and straps, a short skirt, fishnets, knee high boots, knee pads, twin Kukri machetes strapped across her back, (that he had no doubt she was very capable with), a gun holster tied to each thigh and a backpack full of miscellaneous weapons and flares. She had been surprised by the Deadheads on the bus while scavenging in the tunnel. Her search had turned up a pickup with a can of propane and a few gallons of bottled water. Someone's bug out kit. Together they made a makeshift drag out of wood and tie downs from the truck to drag the supplies along with them.

The first day was tense as they got to know each other. Each of them guarding their lives, and trying not to get too attached. You had to be that way. One day it's all smiles and laughs, and the next day you're beating hungry dead things off them like a demented piñata. He did manage to learn she had trained in Krav Maga and knife fighting for years in New York before the fall of humanity, and such skills had come in quite handy since then.

It took them a long time to find a hotel room that didn't

work on electronic key cards, one where they might easily pick the lock. They were like two high-school kids who didn't know when their parents would be home, and if it'd be okay to make the first move. They cleaned themselves up in the bathroom using a gallon of the water and the clean side of dusty hotel room towels that had been there for months. Once they were cleaned up, they went out again and scavenged at a local Wal-Mart for tins of meat and cans of soup. She found a ladies' wear department and changed her undergarments and grabbed a few other items, while he found a grill that would work with her propane tank. While they were carrying their booty up the stairs she had slipped, her boot strap giving way, rolling her ankle. She cursed not finding new boots at the store, and he had promised her he could fix them with some extra leather and needle he had in his belongings.

Once they were back in the room, Kurt got the leather and needle and Milla sat down on the bed and stretched her leg forward. Kurt dropped to his knees at her feet and fussed with the strap. His hand gently caressed her ankle as he worked a new strap into place, attaching it to a piece of the old one with a curved leather needle and some heavy duty line. Her legs parted, slowly opening more.

Did she realize it?

He glimpsed the new panties, black lace. His face flushed, and he exhaled quickly, hoping to drain the red from it. He got the strap finished and stayed on his knees a moment, exhaling again, feeling the blood rush to his groin.

"I think I like you down there," she said.

He shot her a knowing glance and replied, "I think I do too."

She slid her foot in between his legs just a little bit. His face grew hotter.

"Have you ever been nervous about meeting a girl out here?"

"Yes, I have."

"Why?"

"Because I wasn't sure if I could control myself."

Milla gazed at Kurt. "Will you?" Her foot slid in a little deeper and pushed against the bulge in his pants.

He shook his head slowly. "No."

He sprang off the ground at her, flattening her to the old spring bed, his hands on her shoulders. They grabbed at each other like ravenous animals, pulling at each other's bodies and trying to become one. Her legs spiraled around him as his pelvis ground deep into her body.

"My God, you're beautiful," he said.

Her hands ran roughly down his back. "I wanna feel you," she growled.

Their mouths met in a shocking kiss of groping tongues as he balled his fist up behind her head in her hair.

"Oh yes!" she hissed. Their tongues tasted each other with fury. He had never kissed anyone like this before. Months of pent up, post-apocalyptic sexual tension was finally being unleashed. Milla pinched his nipple hard through his shirt.

"I've wanted to fuck you since the moment I saved your ass," she said, in between kisses.

"You saved me?"

"You were almost dead meat."

Milla's hand grasped Kurt through his pants, kneading his fast growing bulge.

"Oh God, that feels good," he gasped.

"You like that?" she said. "Then I bet you're gonna love this."

Milla rolled Kurt hard to right and he landed with a squeaky thud. She jumped on him, kissing his neck and face as he reciprocated.

Her knee slid along the bulge in his crotch, pressing hard and rubbing back and forth against the smooth leather. She pulled on his shoulder length hair with a little tug as she tongued his mouth and neck. He grasped her hard by the small of the back and held her against him. Milla bit his lip and pulled back, straddling his knees.

"I wanna see your cock."

His hands slowly undid his gun-belt and leather pants.

"Show me how you jack off when you're all alone."

He started to stroke his cock for her. Her eyes lit up at the sight of him pleasuring himself. She pulled up her skirt to reveal the new black lace panties she had found in the store. Her fingers pulled them away to show how wet she was. She slipped a finger through her wet lips and applied pressure to her clit. With a moan of pleasure she watched him.

He leaned forward, grabbed her by her hips, and flipped her on her back, pulling her groin toward his mouth. She spread her legs open as he tongued her swollen clit. A sound of ecstasy escaped her.

He tasted her sweetness as he fed off her. He slid a finger inside and pulled it out glistening. He reached up to her face and slipped his finger in her mouth. "Taste yourself," he commanded.

She obeyed and sucked on his finger. She moaned and he slid his face back to her dripping mound. Kurt started to lick the lips and tease her playfully. Her hands grabbed him by the back of the head, knotting up in his hair as she held him in the right spot, demanding he be there. His hands grasped her ass firmly as he rocked her back and forth on his teasing tongue and mouth. He repeatedly darted his tongue in and out as she ground forward on him. Her breathing quickened and he heard the pulse in her inner thigh begin to race in his ear. His tongue danced across her with precision as he slipped a finger inside her again, then another. He was fucking her with two fingers and tonguing her clitoris. He could tell she was getting close the way she writhed in his grip. Her hands fiercely grabbed his head, nails digging his scalp, pushing him down deep into her. His tongue pressed hard against her clit and his fingers dove in deep as she came.

"Oh God, that's it. Oh, that's it, that's it."

Her legs twitched as she started to tense, locking him in place, squeezing him as her body shook. Kurt squeezed out from between her shaking legs and grabbed her. With one swift motion he pulled her hard to the edge of the bed. She tried to pull her legs away.

He smacked her knee down. "I'm controlling this."

He forced himself between her legs, gripped his cock in his hand and rubbed it between her hot wet lips, circling her clitoris with his swollen throbbing head.

He teased her with his cock, sliding the tip in just a little and pulling back out. He did this multiple times as she writhed like a cat beneath him. Then he pushed himself all the way in. She gasped. He paused and pulled all the way out.

She let out a yelp of pleasure as he repeated his movements. He filled her up, pushing as deep as possible. He stroked slowly at first and then started to pick up speed. He dug his cock in deep, and ground his hips in a swivel motion. She met him back with every movement. Soon they were meshing like horse and rider, slamming together in moments of heightened passion.

"Oh, baby, you feel so good." He slammed into her hard and she gasped. "You like it hard don't you?"

"Yes," she said. He slammed deep inside her again. She was rabid with desire. Her body tried to dictate the pace.

Kurt could no longer take the pressure "I'm gonna cum."

The door to the hotel burst open and two Deadheads poured into the room.

Time slowed.

Kurt watched them shamble in, his mind flashed back to coming in the door. *Had it latched closed?*

His left hand closed hard on her hips, her eyes lit up and opened wide, as he rolled to the right, bringing her with him, staying inside of her warm wetness. His right hand found the loose gun belt and shook the silenced 45 from it. She screamed out of pleasure, fear, or both. He pulled her tight to him with his left arm, and rolled over his gun arm, until his hand was free behind her. He brought it up off the bed and pointed the gun at the Deadheads. His finger tugged the trigger in quick succession and belched out three fast shots. Plaster dust and particles of wood blew out next to the females head. She had long, stringy, greasy hair and wore what was once a pink Lady Gaga shirt.

The second shot took a piece of her skull away, splattering her brains along the door jamb. She started to drop as the third shot took the dead male in the shoulder. A puff of dust kicked off his dirty gray flannel and a spray of dark gore *Pollock'd* the hallway behind them. A hot shell hit his thigh, giving him a quick, stirring moment of intense pleasure. The smell of sex mingled with gunpowder and death.

The fourth shot jammed, stove-piping the gun again. He cursed himself for not taking the time to take apart the gun and cleaning his weapon. It was going to cost them their fucking lives.

Milla rolled off of him, his stiff member slipping out of her and smacking on his belly. She dropped to the floor, and swiped up the sheathed twin Kukri blades mid roll. She continued to roll onto her shoulder, and came up in a fighting crouch. The Deadhead took after her; she swung her leg around in a sweeping kick that took him down from behind and pounced on him, sticking his head to the floor with a singing swipe of a blade. She tried to kick the door closed, but the body of the female was in the way. A third Deadhead appeared in the doorway, his arm coming through into the room.

Kurt was up, his pants still open, his stiff member bouncing with every step, his gun tossed aside in mid stride. He grabbed the arms of the fallen Lady Gaga fan and pulled her into the room. Milla kicked the door hard, slamming it on the third creature's arm, swiping at anything it could grab. So she gave him something and buried one of the blades through the small wrist bones and into the plaster wall, dropping the hand with a momentary pause and a trail of old blood that washed down next to the door jamb. She turned the deadbolt on the door and spun back around to Kurt. "That's twice I saved you."

"I reacted first."

"Only because you were on top of me."

She smiled and glanced down at his bobbing member, twitching with the beat of his heart. "I hope all of your guns don't jam."

She stared hungrily at his bobbing cock "I wanna taste you."

"So did she," he laughed.

"Yeah, but I won't bite ... much," She clicked her teeth together.

Kurt moved forward, stepping over the sprawled corpse. Milla lightly grazed her hand over him. Her nails traced the sensitive tip and stroked lovingly down the shaft as his cock twitched. She leaned in and slid it into her mouth. She expertly stroked him in and out of her mouth, rhythmically twisting her hands over the head to give him heightened pleasure. He moaned and lolled his head back, as she grabbed his balls and pulled on them, while taking him all the way into her mouth.

She worked him in and out of her mouth for a few minutes, then grabbed the base of his cock and started jerking him off hard and fierce. Her lips occasionally slipped over the head of his manhood as she stroked him. She pulled her mouth off and looked up at Kurt.

"Cum for me," she said. She backed up her demand by aggressively attacking him, taking him in fully and washing her tongue over his member.

The sensations were mind blowing, as he grabbed her by the back of the head, rocked his hips back and forth. He felt himself starting to overheat. "Oh baby I'm gonna cum."

She pulled his cock out of her mouth and jerked fast and hard with both hands, one hand constantly riding over the sensitive head. He began to explode in orgasm all over her neck and chin. She grinned happily, satisfied with a job well done. She peered around and laughed. "We better find another room; I hear the maid service in this hotel is pretty dead."

He laughed. "What's the hurry?"

* * * *

That had been days ago. Since that moment, they had enjoyed the pleasures of each other's flesh, drank the last of his whiskey, eaten heated up canned foods, and pretended they were the last two on earth.

Adam and Eve at the end of days.

They would be forced to leave soon. The canned food was down to almost nothing, the whiskey and cigarettes gone. Outside the door the audience of Deadheads gathered. The sounds of their pleasures had brought them like lemmings. The hallway sounded as though it was probably full. Leaving would be one hell of a battle. He looked at the smooth curve of her hips in the fading light and ran his hand across her responsive body.

"Tomorrow."

Perpetuation of the Species

Blaze McRob

Outright war rages between us, both sides claiming to be the dominant species. Who is right? Who is wrong? In the state of flux that exists on the planet now, there is no truth, no absolutes. We can only hope.

My side? Ah, it was forced on me, for you see, I am one of those stricken with this horrid pox decimating human-kind. We died, but we came back. And those who were spared from the disease tried to remove us from the world of the living once more, hoping to rid us from their tidy little domicile again.

Sometimes, things don't work out as planned.

My antagonists view us all as a bunch of mindless, wandering morons intent only on feeding our urges: the constant need for food, and damn well little of anything else. These fools. How wrong they are. Yes, we are undead, and our appetites might be geared to feasting on the "pure" humans, but there are many like me who can reason every bit as well as we always could. We understand the morality picture is out the window. As blood thirsty as we might seem to be to humans, it is a necessity mandated on us because of the pox. There are no vegetarian Zombies, and our meat of choice, and of need, is non-affected humans.

One part of our existence has been extremely compromised, however. No longer are we able to reproduce. The disease did something to our women, making them fertile no longer. If human-kind is able to kill enough of us off by well-placed bullets removing our brains or hearts, we are doomed to disappear from the planet.

I will not allow this to happen. Nor will my friends. This is our war to win, and while most aspects of war are rather debilitating, this is an enjoyable one. The living can become impregnated by us, and even if the pox spreads to them and they become as us, the fetus will not die. The reborn undead woman will be able to deliver a perfectly healthy Zombie baby.

The night is hot, and the air carries the scent of pheromones from everywhere. Undead though we may be, our senses surpass those of our enemies, and, in this case, our intended ladies wallowing at the height of sexual desire, wanting and needing a real man to satisfy them.

"Heh, heh," I think. "Some lovely lady will enjoy what I offer tonight."

I follow the sweet scent of a woman, stronger than the rest, talking to me, telling me she is mine for the taking, even though we have never met. Is visual contact really necessary to establish a connection between a woman needing to be loved and a man willing to give her what she is expecting and even more? I don't think so.

The closer I get to my intended, the more luxurious the sensory delights talk to me. This lady—I have no reason why—is special. Tonight will be like none I have ever experienced before.

No one else is home besides her. In times like this, with uncertainty everywhere, one would think a woman would not be left alone to be at the mercy of what lurks about. But not only is she alone, the door is unlocked.

Why?

I walk into the house and follow the stairs to her room. Not hearing any sounds coming from the other side of the door, I slowly turn the knob and walk in. She is wide awake and sitting up in the bed with a huge smile on her face.

"You came," she says. "I had no idea when you would be here, but my dreams have been answered."

"Your dreams?" I ask.

"Yes, my dreams. I am alone here. Why everyone is gone

is beyond me, but I am all that is left of a family of five. Maybe they became afflicted and left, or perhaps they became sustenance for the undead, but I suppose it doesn't really matter, does it?"

"In what way?" I ask.

"You are here to either feed on me or make love to me. I will have no choice in the matter; I will become like you either way, I suspect."

The boldness of the lady strikes me, and I don't know what to say. "You are right. Regardless of my decision, you will most likely become like me, eternally damned to walk the planet and feed on humans, people who you once loved so much."

She gets out of her bed and walks over to me, the thin nightgown she is wearing not hiding any of her charms, her rock-hard nipples protruding through the gossamer fabric, attempting, to my eyes at least, to slice the white bodice to pieces.

"Do you like what you see?" she asks.

"Very much so," I say. "You are a lovely woman."

The moistness from her vagina is pouring out from that special place and showing me the glorious gash that calls to me, the intensity of her sweet scent driving me crazy.

"I want you," she says. "It doesn't matter if I become like you. Disease or not, I am tired of being alone. I need companionship; I need love; I need you. Take me. Please."

Why my appearance doesn't disgust her is beyond me. My flesh hangs from certain parts of my body and falls from others. My entire physicality appears to resemble humans in only the most of rudimentary forms. Truth be told: I look like a leper intent on disintegration.

She reaches for my right hand and places it against her writhing moistness. Ever so gently, she removes my shirt, teasing my nipples. And then . . . and then she reaches down and massages my dick, easily at first, and with increasing ardor as I become harder and harder.

"I believe we will do just fine," she says. "You are a real

man. I need what you have. Take me. Don't hold back. Give me all you possess."

Her nightgown is reduced to a mere memory as I tear the material off her body. I can't believe the length and hardness of her nipples pulsating before my eyes and the river of love juices flowing from her pussy, drenching her downy vaginal hair with her magnificence. My fingers gravitate to her waiting vaginal opening, and I am surprised to find she is still a virgin.

"Don't worry, my love." she shouts. "You are man enough to tear my hymen apart and go deep inside. Damn, I need you. Take me to the bed. Fuck me like you have never fucked anyone before. I am completely yours."

My surprise does not last long. It is only she and I, and she is begging to be satisfied, not caring we are in a Beauty and the Beast scenario.

I carry her to the bed and lay her down. She spreads her legs out wide, knowing full well what I offer will not be easy for her to take inside. She is small and tight, and I am large and insistent. I will find it difficult to control my zeal. She offered herself to me, and I will not refuse her.

Yes, I will try to be easy on her, but my senses are going wild. She is so beautiful, so giving, and so certain this is what she wants.

Between the two of us, my clothes are removed in a hurry, and while I might not possess the body of a twenty-year old Greek Adonis anymore, what with peeling, shredding, and decay of all kinds happening now, my lady seems not to care, rubbing my dick against her super-wet pussy and leading me closer and closer to penetrating the barrier never entered before. My fingers find her clitoris, massaging that magic love bean, creating even more juices to join those already flowing down her gorgeous thighs.

Within seconds, the time is right, and I work my dick into her majestic play land. Holding back is not easy for me: I want so much to penetrate all the way and shoot my wad deep inside her, but I take my time and allow her hymen to completely become a thing of the past before I enter deeper and deeper inside the best she has to offer.

My thrusts become deeper as she opens up more to me, and she goes completely wild, having never experienced anything like this before. I am finding it difficult to wait any longer for my orgasm, her feminine wiles having worked their magic on me; but this is special, this is pure, and I don't want to ruin anything happening between us.

As much as I want everything to be perfect for her, my imperfect body creates problems. The flaking of my skin is not limited to only certain body parts. Even while I'm working my dick deeper and deeper inside her, parts of my manhood break off and remain inside. There is still plenty left to fill her vaginal cavity, but pieces of me are loose within her grand receptacle of love. And yet, it appears the decay of my body is only a prelude to regrowth, to renewal.

The decay does not last. Rejuvenation occurs even as my shaft drives deeper and deeper into her. That majestic part of her demanding my presence becomes moister by the moment.

Shaking with abandon and screaming at the top of her lungs, she reaches a place she has never been before, completely caught up in the rapture of her ecstasy, orgasm after orgasm overtaking her.

I shoot my semen deep in her, embracing the excitement of my cum exploding from my balls, through my dick, and far back into the depths of her vagina. There is no removal for me as she grabs my butt and pulls me ever deeper, refusing to allow me to remove my manhood. For how long our multiple orgasms last, I have no idea, but finally we both flop back down on the bed completely spent.

When I am able to think of anything other than the love-making we just shared, I look around and see my torn flesh scattered around everywhere.

My lady's legs are still spread far apart and a piece of discarded penis pokes out of her. I remove it and toss the dead flesh to the side, ashamed of the mess I made and knowing I must truly have sickened her now.

"I'm sorry for being such a slob," I say, "but I can't help it."

She laughs gently and purrs, "I've always heard good sex is messy, and what we just experienced went well beyond good."

I smile, knowing even if she changes, I will never leave her. She is perfect for me. Our child, or children, will be perfect.

"Now, mister," she says, "how about some sloppy seconds?"

Pretty Kitty's
Post Apocalypse Porn Palace

Jolie Chaton

Pretty Kitty sat in the office of the night club wondering what scheme she might come up with next. Skeeter, the manager, should be on his way to meet with her. She forgave his delay, knowing he was dressing his pet zombie in drag.

She didn't mind that. It meant the meeting would take up less than five minutes. He would then be on his way to *get* whatever he *got* out of today's flavor. PK, as they called her around the club, didn't understand how he kept the club afloat before the world ended. Without her ideas and fearless attitude regarding the seedy side of life, Skeeter wouldn't be capable of keeping the business afloat now.

Pre-apocalypse, this had been a strip club, simple and boring—but now, it was about to become an *'everything club,'* catering to the most disgusting fetishes for *'human'* desires. It would be the only one of its kind in the western half of what remained of the United States. Thanks to PK's vision and her desire to succeed at something, even now, her idea had become quite popular with the people who still remained in this city.

While waiting for Skeeter, she'd wandered into the lobby-like area of the club and was again stunned by the crowd of people waiting for their turn inside. Shocking, the depravity of what a man would do to touch some undead boobies. She had been the driving force behind turning the zombies into sexual toys for both the men and women. Without knowing what to do after the zombie uprising, the club remained a strip club. Some of the zombies still liked to dance and grind to the music, as if the rhythm compelled them. The show had quickly become a hit. Night after night, every sicko within a 500-mile radius practically ran to watch these rotting souls trying to hang on to a dance pole as their body parts fell off.

Every night the crowds grew. How many zombies would they be down by the end of the night? She'd mentioned to security the *talent scouts* should be sent out at earlier hours to replenish the supply of dancing zombies by day's end.

Over the last couple of weeks she'd come to notice the daily masses were no longer content to just view. They wanted more, and every day, they demanded even more. So Kitty hatched the idea of being able to take what was left of these bodies into a side room to touch, smell and do whatever their human counterpart wanted to do—for a price.

Fifteen minutes after their agreed upon time, Skeeter finally decided to show. Pock-faced and a bit overweight, Skeeter wasn't anything to look at. He wouldn't have been so bad if he at least bathed twice a week. Like most women, when Skeeter arrived, she only wanted to turn away. All the club money he threw around enabled him to feel superior to most of the survivors. Much like most of the men she had encountered in this miserable lifetime, PK planned to take all that away from him—soon.

He dragged his fetish, today's flavor, a brunette with bloated cataract eyes, harnessed upon a wooden rod with restraints holding her in place. He'd dressed her up—well as best Skeeter could manage anyways—in a white leather ensemble granting the illusion of her skin still being somewhat close to the color pink. Her face was painted up like a china doll, reminiscent of Tammy Faye's raccoon look. Apparently, this one had been named Cassandra. At least that's the name Skeeter cooed in her ear.

Whatever floats his boat, thought Pretty Kitty. She found it intriguing so many had turned to sexual fantasy with the outbreak population of zombies roaming everywhere. Skeeter's wanton lust was going to make her life so much easier by the end of day. The world collapsing into anarchy all around them made it easy for her to come up with all these nasty little things she did. Her ideas would have been impossible back when the population was entirely human.

Now she sat here, with Skeeter's fat ass and his zombie slut. *Oh well, let me finish the pitch on this idea and get the fuck out of here*, she thought, as a sick and twisted feeling sent the karma butterflies swimming in her guts.

Before this Mad-Max world they now lived in, these things would *not* be appropriate. This new world offered a freedom, a new meaning to the phrase *carnal desire*. The club needed to change according to the times and should not be just a strip club, but also a Bunny Ranch type of environment. Her vision included a brothel of undead, a play land for sickness, and a recycling of fresh zombies for tomorrow's visitor to enjoy.

This latest idea of hers would put the word *fetish* to good use. It would also be a win-win for the club. Clearly, by the number of people waiting outside every day before opening, a large percentage of people desired this.

It had to work! Secretly, she had been putting a room together for this purpose over the last couple of days. It didn't require much and the surroundings were simple, but what was going to transpire there would be on the edge of sanity.

Walking into the room, the guest would be greeted by soft lighting, candles, romantic music, a huge assortment of lingerie, and alcohol for the living half of the party to imbibe in. The colors were inviting, warm and completely washable—by someone else of course.

In this room a man or woman could choose any zombie they wanted and have their dreams come true. You see, Pretty Kitty had found out—thanks to Skeeter—many people wanted to share a romantic interlude with a zombie that ultimately ended with their own transformation. This fetish was so foreign to her, she thought it disgustingly erotic, but realized the club would make a bundle of money off the idea, and so would she. By night's end, they would have cash and extra zombies on hand.

"Yep, it's a win-win for everyone," she told Skeeter. Thanks to 'Cassandra,' Skeeter would partake as guest number one. It had been her suggestion that Skeeter pick the least worn down of the zombies to start, and perhaps even one of the same gender, just to add a little extra spice. She'd even encouraged him to choose their clothing, to make them look as vulnerable as possible, so as to help pump his own level of confidence.

Every ounce of mock-manliness and false bravado coursing through his veins was about to become hers by way of his own warped sexuality. It was inevitable, he'd get bit eventually, and then the world would be rid of one more pus vestibule. Afterward, she could reuse Skeeter as a zombie under *her* new managerial reign. She broke into a smile and started to giggle.

Ron and Lisa's Good Luck Story

Shawn Erin

"Fuck me!" Lisa cursed, as she examined the bite mark on her shoulder.

I chilled, but pulled her away from the door so I could get a clean shot at the zombie. A quick double tap from my shotgun put an end to the undead thing, and I closed the door in front of me. We were safe for now in the bedroom. Correction: I was safe for now. Lisa wept. The dirt smudged on her face and blonde hair, and the filthy, sweaty tank top she wore covered up her natural beauty. If I'd had any sense, I would have killed her then. By morning, I knew she would become an undead monster. Luckily for her, and me, and the rest of humanity, I don't have any sense.

She looked up at me, tear tracks making little dirt rivulets down her cheeks. She smiled weakly. In a soft voice, she said "Fuck me."

I didn't catch her meaning for a split second. But when she charged me and unzipped my pants, I knew exactly what she wanted. I backed away to the closet wall. "Lisa, I don't think ..."

"If you're going to shoot me, shoot me God dammit. Otherwise, fuck me."

I blinked several times, trying to assess the situation. We were holed up in our apartment bedroom, fighting the zombie apocalypse, which simply thinking about is a major mind fuck.

We were better off than most; at least we still had a place

to go to, and we were still not undead, or at least I was not. "Lisa ..."

"Dammit Ron, you often act like a horny teenager around me, and that really pissed me off about you, but now that I want to fuck my brains out, you become a celibate priest."

So what I had perceived to be playing hard to get, truly meant she didn't want sex? I wished I understood women. Perhaps someone should write a manual, or something. Zombies are a lot easier to understand, but the downside is, they just want you to become one of them: brain hungry monsters. Focus on the now, I told myself. She wanted sex now. And that was a good thing, right?

She unbuttoned my pants and shoved them down to the floor. I clumsily stepped out of them while still wearing my sneakers. My boxers followed my pants to the floor. At this point, my dick decided this was a good idea, becoming semi erect. Lisa's mouth encouraged its full hardness.

When she came up for air, she glanced at me, smiling while her left hand continued to stroke my shaft. "You like that?"

Nodding, I croaked out, "Yes, I like."

She stood, with her left hand still stroking my cock. She let go only briefly, to release her breasts from their tank top prison. Then she resumed stroking. God, Lisa can do the best fucking hand jobs. For a split second at least, my troubles evaporated. The world, our dingy apartment with lime green walls, the zombie apocalypse, or the fact that by morning I would have to blow my girlfriend's zombie-fied brains away, all disappeared at the sight of her glorious tits. Neither massive monsters, nor tiny nubs, but just right. Goldilocks boobs, I called them.

Lisa huffed. "Guys. You always stare at the boobies."

She relieved her hand of its ministrations so she could run her fingers through my messy hair. She liked playing with it, said she had never dated a curly brunette before. She pulled my head closer for a kiss. I tasted the tang of dirt around her lips as my tongue penetrated her mouth. I'm sure she tasted the same thing; I was as dirty as she. In a world where running water and electricity no longer exist, we got used to b. o. musk.

Our lips parted, and she said, "Let's get over to the bed."

We stumbled over to the bed, careful not to bump the candles and lanterns strewn about. Lisa fell on the bed, the over worn springs groaning in protest. I quickly removed her sweaty shorts and panties. It was near midnight, still hot as hell. I had once heard the zombification of humanity was due to global warming. Everyone has their fuckin' zombie apocalypse theory. I usually ignored them, as the theories did nothing to tell me how to kill them better.

I went down on her. Lisa cooed as my tongue traced her outer pussy lips, then flicked her clit. As the fleshy button became more used to my tongue, I became more daring, pulled the hood away and sucked on the actual clitoris. Lisa loved this. Her moans grew louder, and she grabbed my head to shove it deeper toward her cunt.

Lisa arched her back and yelped out her orgasm, and then settled down back on the bed, still shaking from the after shivers of coming. I stood, fearful my girlfriend might've attracted some zombies, but the fear subsided as I was too horny to think clearly.

Lisa kissed me. "You're so good at that."

I barely heard the compliment as I was so eager to fuck. She butterflied her legs and I inserted my cock, nice and slow. She moaned, rubbing her Goldilocks tits. Her hand migrated to her clit, where she vigorously rubbed.

Her moans rose and I was sure now they would attract zombies.

I heard a new moan, lower, and freaked out before I realized the sound was my own voice. I felt like a real idiot. Still, even amidst the spasms of sex, I managed to grab my shotgun, just in case.

My own orgasm quickly rose as I sensed Lisa's second one building. She yelped and arched her back, and mine became a reflection of hers. We were both way too fucking loud. We collapsed on the bed, making sure the shotgun lay close by.

I thought of fatherhood, and how I would never see it with Lisa. How crazy was that, thinking of bringing up a child in such a fucked up wasteland? Despite my nerves being on edge, I managed to fall asleep. Normally, that would have been one huge mistake.

I woke to someone shaking me. At first, I only heard a vague voice and a blurry shape. Then the shape and voice resolved themselves into Lisa. Morning light shone in our bedroom, highlighting the lime green decor. Lisa looked horrible.

Zombie! I pawed for the shotgun, but Lisa grabbed my arm and shoved it to the bed. She moaned. *Definitely a zombie.* I squirmed under her pressure, my time as a living being numbered in seconds now.

"Ron! Calm down. It's me. I'm fine." She had to repeat herself a few times before the words sunk in.

"Lisa? Seriously? That's really you?"

She nodded, tears of joy streaming down her dirty face.

"But how?"

"I have a theory."

In the days and weeks following, her theory seemed to pan out. We traveled among the scattered remnants of living humanity, spreading the word, and we quickly heard Lisa's theory indeed worked for others. Sex is the antidote for zombification.

I don't get it either. Then again, I don't get how undead monsters can exist in the first place. But there it is: fucking stops you from becoming a zombie. And it doesn't matter if you're into homosexual sex or heterosexual sex, as long as you have some kind of sex.

I've even heard the antidote works on existing zombies too, but even for the zombie apocalypse, that shit's just too weird for me.

So there you have it: the cure to stop you from becoming a zombie, in case you don't already know. And if you read this just to get off on the hot sex, I hope I've satisfied you as well.

And yes, Lisa does know about this document. In fact, she's the one who suggested I write this down, sex scene and all. She's gotten *way* kinkier. But that's a topic for another story.

Good luck, your not undead friends,
Ron and Lisa

Out With A Bang

Laura J. Hickman

Over the last few days, Daisy's confusion and loneliness had left her empty. Not because of the zombie apocalypse, but because her goal of sex at least six times a week was unfulfilled. She needed to be filled up by some jackass' juices to feel alive.

"Your behavior does not make you a real woman, it makes you a slut," Daisy's mother loved to spit at her. Unable to deal with her complaining, bitching, and hate filled insults, Daisy shoved her out the front door at a group of zombies and locked it behind her. At least her mom had been good for something.

Daisy didn't miss the people at school, but she missed being the Queen Bee, running the place and having all the stupid wannabes begging for attention. Head cheerleader, prom queen, homecoming court, and much more—girls wanted to be her and guys wanted to fuck her. Hell, even a few lesbos wanted to do her. One she even allowed in long enough to get the stupid girl naked and take humiliating photos with which to blackmail her.

As the days crept by, the batteries in her beloved vibrator died just like all the people. The loss of her B.O.B. saddened her more than the end of mankind. Well, except for the cute guys who could eat her pussy like nobody's business. Right now she'd take any old guy to lick his lips and chow down on her. Before doing anything too crazy, like killing herself, Daisy had enough sense to do some research on zombies on the 'net.

Up until a short time ago, zombies had been works of

fiction, but now, one of those crazy solar flares had hit, burning millions, creating zombies out of others. Daisy hated the sun; she liked looking pale and adding sparkles to her body to look like those sexy vampires from that movie.

After watching a few victims get bitten by the flesh-eating monsters and live, she learned something interesting—they did not become zombies. The disease or whatever the fuck it was did not transmit from the zombie to human. However, due to the sheer power of those freaks, the person bitten usually died from having their flesh ripped to shreds. Daisy enjoyed watching that. She craved the power of the zombies, the power she used to have. Now she was just another meat-sack waiting to be devoured.

Between what she learned online, watching bad horror movies with moron boys (who'd hoped to scare her so she'd snuggle up with them), and watching her mom get ripped apart by those things, she knew for certain they were dangerous. She found all kinds of other contradictory information. Daisy realized she had to learn more.

That said, the only time they became a threat was when a horde shambled by, or if you did not have a weapon. She was grateful her probably-now-dead Dad, who split when she became too old for him (right around at her 15^h birthday), had left her some guns. "Someday you'll understand," he whispered with one foot already out the door. "If you ever have daughters, come find me."

Ever since her Father left under the cover of night, Daisy longed to find the bizarre love he gave her again. Watching him slip away created an emptiness in her which she discovered could only be filled by a hard dick pumping her. Daisy wasn't stupid; she understood what her Dad did was wrong and being the queen bee slut of the school (and local college also) was probably unhealthy, but the only time she felt alive was while being nailed.

Her quest to find that feeling again led her to different men, in hopes of recreating the emotion.

About a year before the zombies showed up, Daisy

started taking a more active and dominant role in her trysts, with everyone from the star quarterback, and the college professor, to a few of her Daddy's old drinking buddies. One night with the Professor, Daisy grabbed one of his annoying ties, wrapped it around his wrists, and tied him to his headboard. She stuffed another one in his mouth to shut him up. At times the Professor reminded her of her Father. Except when he preached to her, moralizing through sex about how it was so wrong to take advantage of such a young, innocent girl. Daisy showed him as she climbed on top and rode him like a bucking bull (or at least that's what she'd wanted, but he'd never been good in bed). Her anger surged as she did not get what she needed, so she got even with his lack of enthusiasm by clawing at his chest, leaving long ribbons of cuts. With each scratch the Professor pounded her deeper, but never gave her quite the ride she craved.

She jumped off him after he spewed his juices, got dressed, and left him screaming behind the tie in his mouth. Daisy found satisfaction for the first time since her Father left, from leaving him tied up and cut up for his frigid wife to find. Her fantasy shifted to hiding in his closet and watching the bitch freak out over what her morally corrupt husband, high standing pillar in the community, had done.

Daisy started to go for the biggest, scariest guys around and got off on taking control, fucking them, and leaving them to rot. However, now that many of them had truly rotted, she almost missed them; well, she missed their dicks and tongues.

The power blinked on and off while the food supply became scarce, but Daisy only cared about the hunger stemming from her unhappy, unpleased, and unsatisfied sexual appetite. Soon the food would be gone and Daisy was too damn lazy to go hunting or even gathering. She needed to get off and die soon, because if she couldn't play pretty princess anymore, dress up, and spend someone else's money, she was done with life. She had planned on being a centerfold, marrying rich, and having lots of boys on the side, but under the new world disorder, Daisy's hopes of achieving her goals rotted to nothing. So sex was the only thing left; even in the darkest part of the apocalypse, her mind raced with fantasies of men nailing her. Now all she wanted to do was die as she had her last orgasm, the way all those disgusting older guys wanted to go when they had been with her, except for their fear of the wife and kids finding out.

Her need grew until nothing would quench her thirst for a man to slam her to the point of exhaustion, finding someone to tie up, torture, and use as a human-battery-operated boyfriend. No speaking, no touching, just driving his cock deeper and deeper into each opening on her body. She wished to die as he came one last time and let him suffer a slow and painful death, with her body draped across his as he struggled to free himself.

Even Daisy was a tad disgusted with herself on her final wish, but she figured "what the hell?" She was going to die soon anyway. Now, a week or so into the apocalypse, food rations depleted, the lights shut off, forced her to face the fact the end wasn't near, it was here. Her will to live died the same day as the batteries in her toys, but she knew she wanted to go out with a bang.

After searching for a solution, a plan formed in her mind of how to find the perfect victim to ride until her end of time.

"Zombies are pure destruction; what a way to leave this life, being nailed by the ultimate bad boy!"

She knew she was sick in the head, but dying while doing what you loved had to be better than starving to death with no outlet for fun or sense of a normal life. Daisy devised a trap to snag a zombie so she might tie him down, gag his mouth and ride him until nothing was left of either of them. The idea of being so evil gave her the strength to go on and also created a thrill in her she hadn't experienced since the first time her Father had slipped into her bedroom late one night; that feeling carried her through the next day as she smirked at her mother, knowing the bitch was no longer the "Lady of the House." Daisy was the one her Father wanted.

Daisy kept a close watch for any wandering hordes of zombies, but for the last day or so none had come by her house. She wondered if they had all started to die out or if there was food somewhere else for them.

"Food." she screamed, once she realized the problem.

There was no food for the zombies close by, which left her with two choices—one, hunt a human and leave them bleeding and dying to help bring zombies around; or two, waste what little was left of her meat to attract the zombies. To be fair, if she got another human male, Daisy would nail him, but if it was a female she would cut the bitch to ribbons and leave the dying body out to bring the zombies and the flies. Plus, Daisy worried only female zombies would show up, or even worse, male ones who had disintegrated and lost their penises. That thought scared her more than dying— being so close to an orgasm but being denied the chance to cum again before she died.

Deep down Daisy did not want to hurt a human, it was just too much drama, too much effort, and most of all, she didn't want to listen to some bitch complaining to her, "please don't kill me."

Instead, she threw out her decaying meat in hopes of luring a male zombie. She also took a gun her Father had left her to find an animal to bleed. Thoughts of her Father teaching her to shoot the rifle made Daisy's pussy ache.

With one shot she hit a deer, killing it, just as her Father taught her. She dragged the deer corpse to her house and cut it up. The blood, still warm on her hands, turned her on. Without thinking of the sickness growing inside her like an unachieved orgasm, Daisy used the deer's blood as lube and gave herself her not-last thrill. The blood created a need to feel her pussy dripping with cum as the plan played out in her mind. The first smile erupted on Daisy's face since Hell had broken out on Earth.

Her luck changed—a male zombie shambled over to her house. Daisy threw fishing net over him and before he figured out what was going on, she gagged him and dragged him to the four-poster bed to tie him up.

Her heart raced once he was secured, but the fear he might not have a dick still gripped her. Daisy sliced off his pants with the precision of a surgeon and let out a whimper of happiness—thank God it was still intact. Her pussy swelled with anticipation of being fucked by the darkest thing possible. Daisy's pulse sped up, readying her body to be filled.

The zombie stared at Daisy with a glimmer of lust. She knew even in this thing's dead mind, the memories of sex floated back through the mush of his decaying brain. Daisy rubbed his dick, coaxing it to stand straight up, so she could cowgirl his thick prick and keep herself away from his mouth (just in case he gnawed through the gag).

Her pussy pulsed as she lowered herself over the erect penis. The undead dick quivered when she tightened around his shaft. Daisy rubbed and twisted her nipples, causing her pussy to become wet. He grunted at her behind his gag. She began to grind on the shaft, willing herself to climax. As she was about to cum, hard, she grabbed the knife and cut herself, causing rivers of blood to flow over her chest and to his body. The blood covered both of them. Daisy let out a cry of pleasure, cumming so hard she thought she might die right then, but instead her heart pounded as hard as she had been slamming into the zombie's decaying pleasurable body.

Just as she prayed, the zombie broke free of his restraints and overpowered her. To help things along, Daisy pulled the gag free, allowing the monster to bite her as she came repeatedly. Daisy's vision blurred as death knocked on her door, and she passed out as she exploded one last time while being pounded hard. Bones broke, pain flared, and happiness filled Daisy as she slipped into death.

First Time

Chad P. Brown

Eight months after Amy died, the dead started rising. For all I knew, some virus or brain parasite or top secret biological weapon started the whole mess. Hell, it could've even been aliens from outer space. I didn't care.

The only thing that mattered was the possibility of Amy coming back to me.

I'd buried her in the small cemetery behind our house, situated at the bottom of a hill and bordering the woods by the creek. Most of my family had been buried there going back three generations, along with some of the neighboring Marcum and Copley families.

For three days, I watched her grave, waiting for her to return. I rationalized if she found her way home, she wouldn't be a monster like the others I had seen on TV and heard about on the radio.

I sat in the kitchen staring out the back window. I would sip occasionally from a bottle of whiskey, afraid to get too drunk, but needing something to calm my nerves.

Amy came back on a Friday.

I was sitting on the back porch finishing off a cigarette. Funny, even after two years, I couldn't bring myself to break Amy's rule of no smoking in the house. Maybe it was one of the little ways I had held on to the hope she would come back one day.

As I flipped the cigarette butt into the air, I spotted her coming up the hill towards the house.

At first, I didn't recognize her. The sun was setting behind her and she was still a good distance off. Plus, my vision had been painted in a thick coat of drunkenness.

I could tell by the lurching, shambling gait the figure was a zombie and not some neighbor stopping in to check on me.

As the zombie got closer, I hoped it would be Amy. I actually fell down on my knees and prayed to a God who I cursed just months before for taking her away. Now I begged Him to give her back.

When she was about halfway to the house, I recognized the dress I buried her in. My hands began to tremble and I broke out in a cold sweat. I hadn't been so nervous since the first time I built up enough courage to go and talk to her.

We had always joked about that day, me making her swear to never tell anyone how foolish I acted and her swearing it had been the sweetest thing she had ever seen.

Once I recognized the dress, I jumped up and jogged to the edge of the yard, squinting and shielding the sunlight with my hand to make sure my eyes didn't deceive me.

It *was* Amy.

My first instinct was to run to her with my arms outstretched, calling her name, then pick her up and spin her round and round in a circle until we collapsed to the ground—like reunited lovers do in the movies.

But I stood frozen, unable to peel my eyes off her.

To my surprise, she appeared just as she had on the day of our wedding, like a porcelain angel. I imagined kissing her tender lips, touching her smooth skin, smelling her intoxicating scent, running my hands over every curve of her body, tasting her sweetness.

I stood fantasizing about her, becoming increasingly aroused with each plodding step she took closer.

But the passion drained out of me when I saw her as she truly looked, rather than the image of her my mind conjured to protect my heart.

I screamed and ran in the house to grab my gun. By the time she reached the back yard gate, I had the barrel of my shotgun pointed right between her eyes.

Or rather, pointed between her one remaining blue eye

and the empty eye socket infested with maggots. Her skin fell away in places like cracked, yellowed wallpaper. Half of her nose had rotted off and her lips peeled away to reveal a snarling sneer of blackened, decaying teeth. Sparse clumps of hair clung desperately to her withered scalp. And the stench oozing off her reminded me of road kill stewing in the scorching sun for too long.

She moaned incessantly as her boney fingers grabbed at me, hungry to commence the feast of my flesh. But in my delirious mind, those inarticulate sounds became the distinct callings of my name.

Tears clouded my vision as I fought to force myself to pull the trigger. My hands were impotent, unable to maintain the erect shotgun as it fell limply to the ground.

In that moment, I realized I couldn't kill my beloved, nor could I live with the monstrosity who returned home.

* * * *

I lured her in the house, enticing her with my exposed flesh. Her swollen tongue darted in and out of her rotting mouth as she followed after me. I led her up to the bedroom and tied her hands to the bed with rope.

Believe me … not as kinky as it sounds.

She hissed and thrashed on the bed. A repulsive mixture of bloody phlegm and black spittle flew out of her mouth as she snapped at me like some rabid animal.

I stared at her, a combination of disgust and pity consuming me. I cried until my chest burned like a scorching ember, searing my emotions and scarring my heart.

I wiped away tears and looked at her. For a moment, I saw my Amy lurking behind those hollow, undead eyes.

And then it hit me. I knew what I had to do in order for us to be together.

I quickly untied her, avoiding her gnashing teeth, and slowly backed away until I bumped into the wall.

She slithered towards me, staring at me like some piece of

meat. When she reached me, she tore open my shirt and pinned my arms to the wall. Her tongue danced across my chest and up my neck, leaving goose bumps in its wake. I yearned for her to tear into me, but she was toying with me, building up her hunger much like a cat plays with a mouse.

Everywhere she touched, my body responded: my mouth went dry, my legs became weak, beads of sweat covered my brow, my breathing grew rapid and shallow, my heart trip-hammered in my chest. If she didn't hurry and take me, I was going to scream out in either ecstasy or horror.

I didn't know which one would give me more pleasure.

Finally, she pulled back and opened her mouth. With one swift motion, she began ravishing my body.

"Be gentle," I whispered, "it's my first time."

Love in a Laundromat

Megan Dorei

All I wanted to do was wash my clothes.

It'd been weeks since I'd worn a nice, clean shirt. You'd think as a zombie I wouldn't care. But have you ever torn someone limb from limb in dirty underwear? Not fun.

When I pulled up to the Laundromat, I realized I'd made a mistake.

There was one other zombie there, a man rushing to the front door with a clothesbasket under one arm. His eyes were locked on the dark shadows emerging from behind the small building.

They had a proper name, but we called them "haters" as a joke.

It's rumored love could have cured the zombie virus. Of course, that's bullshit. Just some hippy crap made up to shame us zombies. But nobody understands for sure why some zombies can function almost normally, and why some sink into a murderous, demented darkness. So we called them haters since, according to the hippies, hate catalyzed the virus and ate your soul.

The haters moved fast in my direction. I realized if I peeled off, they'd follow relentlessly until I ran out of gas— they liked to chase things. My only chance would be to follow the man inside. So, grabbing my laundry from the backseat, I darted for the door. The man slammed it shut behind me.

Breathing heavily, the man and I watched as the haters threw themselves at the door.

"They'll go away if we stay calm," he said after a moment.

"Yeah."

So we set off to do our laundry.

No one else was there, not even an owner. For the most part, everyone stayed hidden. Humans ventured out for food. Zombies ventured out for sex. Zombies were horny creatures. Who would have thought?

Scientists said the increased libido in zombies resulted from our higher body temperatures. Don't know if I believe that, but what do I know?

So the man and I had the Laundromat all to ourselves.

The haters drifted away, leaving us in silence. I sat at an empty table by the window, watching the sun go down. The man sat on one of the washers behind me.

"So," he said. "What's your name?"

I didn't look at him. "Sarah."

"I'm Darren."

"Mm."

I didn't like acting so rude but the whole "pretend-to-like-each-other-when-you-really-just-want-sex" thing was getting pretty tired. I mean, I was a zombie—I had ugly needs. But part of me was disgusted by the act, the heartless indifference, and the one night stands. When I had been human, I had actual relationships. Most weren't serious, but it was still nice to call someone "boyfriend".

Darren, bless his stupid heart, wouldn't be deterred. I stiffened when he came to stand by my side and stared straight ahead. I wouldn't glance at him; that's how we drew in our prey, both for food and sex.

"It's beautiful," he said.

I blinked, bewildered. I'd been expecting him to use some lame pick-up line—*Come here often? Are you an angel? Can I give you a brain?*

"Uh, what?" I replied. Genius.

He glanced at me, a little surprised. "The sunset," he explained.

"Oh," I said.

And he was right. After he drew attention to the setting sun, I realized how beautiful it was. The snow from last week had started to melt, but today was cold so everything left had frozen over. The grayish-yellow ground and the pewter-black streets interspersed with drifts of snow, tinged pink by twilight. The sun had already sunk beneath the tree line, leaving a blade of magenta across the horizon. Above, the rest of the sky turned a dark, smoky blue.

"Beautiful," I breathed.

For the first time since my transformation I'd stopped to enjoy something other than a meal.

That's when I forgot my misgivings and turned to smile at him.

He smiled back, openly and brightly, and though his teeth were sharp and yellow, and his patchwork skin gray, I didn't think I'd ever seen a more beautiful face. His eyes, like all zombies, were black, but they gleamed with vitality. His dark, curly hair had not dulled like all the others. Even his lips, though split and dry, still seemed lush; they didn't sink into his mouth like some of our brethren's did.

My heart began to pound in my chest, a sensation I wasn't used to feeling outside of hunting or scrapping with another zombie. I experienced an instant attraction to this man, but it wasn't physical. Or, I should say, it wasn't *simply* physical. And that wasn't something I had felt in a long time.

When zombies found someone they wanted to sleep with, there was never any emotion involved. Our bodies burned hot, but the sex was cold. It made leaving the next morning easier.

But this man ... I wanted to *ravage* him. I wanted to sink into those eyes and bask in their heat. The pull was feral, primal, and it wasn't just an urge. It was *desire*.

I blinked and turned away, for the first time in months heat rushed to my cheeks. These feelings *scared* me; they made me feel vulnerable. I was a *predator*. I wasn't used to being vulnerable.

Darren appeared about to say something else, but the soft ding of the washer saved me. I veered sharply away, my dirty blonde hair sweeping out to slap him across the face.

His washer dinged a few seconds later. He was about ten

washers down from me, but I was hyperaware of him. I felt his heat like he was inches from my body. I tried to keep my eyes on my laundry; I pulled the clothes out piece by piece, hoping to spend as much time there as possible. But my attempts were feeble; every few shirts or so I would glance up out of the corner of my eye. He whistled, pulling out his laundry just as slowly to match my pace.

At one point he glanced up and, nodding, cocked a smile in my direction.

I gritted my teeth, stifling a snarl. My fingers clenched around the shirt I held, nearly ripping through.

Asshole, I thought.

Unfortunately, we both had two loads. So after we were done piling our wet clothes in separate dryers, we found ourselves again returning to the washers.

Get it done, Sarah, I told myself. Just do it and leave.

Once finished, I stalked off to one of the arcade games. Even this far into the twenty-first century, Laundromats still had these old 80s monstrosities. I slipped two quarters into the Ms. Pac-Man game and sat down to play. I ignored Darren, and forcing myself to become involved in the game.

Possibly too involved.

A few minutes into it, and I jerked back and forth in my seat, muttering under my breath. Those little ghosts were some pretty tricky bastards. I only stopped when I heard half-stifled laughter behind me, and my hesitation cost me my last Pac life.

Slowly I turned around and fixed Darren with an icy, dangerous glare. He bit his lip and pretended to examine a spot on the wall.

"*What* are you laughing at?" I snapped.

He shrugged. "Dunno what you're talking about."

Clenching my jaw, I got up from my seat and stalked toward him. "Do you know what you did?" I growled. "Do you have any idea? That was my *high score!* I was on a *roll! And you killed me!*"

We stared at each other for a long time, listening to the

sound of my last shriek fade away. Then we burst out laughing.

I leaned my head on his shoulder without thinking, convulsing with giggles, and his hands touched my arms. His skin on mine sent a hot rush through my nerve endings, making me dizzy. I leaned away and his eyes seared into mine …

The washers dinged again, this time in sync, and we both jumped apart. I scurried away before he could say anything and frantically began to unload the washer.

What the hell is happening? I thought, sending clothes flying in my haste.

For a moment, just a moment, I thought of the hippies. My hands stilled and I looked up to see Darren looking at me. After a moment, he smiled and I smiled weakly back, suddenly shy.

He came toward me and I stood still, waiting. My heart flew in my chest. My blood boiled. I remembered every other affair I'd had with a zombie and knew they'd never been like this. I felt like I was flying and there hadn't even been penetration!

When we were mere inches apart he stopped. His hands cupped my face and his black eyes searched mine. I had never felt less like a predator in my life.

Then he kissed me, astounding in his gentleness, and though he tasted like death, I'd never felt more alive. Grabbing his shirt in both fists, I pulled us both to the floor.

Then we were moving, tearing off clothing with sharp ripping sounds. We tangled together, switching positions constantly, neither predator nor prey. We were some strange mix of the two, powerful and weak, rough and soft.

He cupped my breast in his mouth, trailing his tongue across my nipple, and the heat of it sent a thrill through my body. His fingers trailed up my thighs, soft and searching. I moaned, letting my head roll back. Outside, the light had finally disappeared, ushering in the night, and this was the last thing I saw before he entered me.

I screamed, something I'd never done before. It felt like flames exploding in my sex, reaching up to throttle my nerve endings. But sweet, unbearably sweet, and I reached up to dig my fingers into his spine.

Already I was seconds from coming. Sensing this, Darren pressed his forehead to mine and whispered, "Not yet."

His voice, rough and husky, turned the flames into embers, the sweetness into bearable titillation. He thrust forward and I caught hold of the rhythm, closing my eyes and leaning my head back on the floor.

I felt like I was on the ocean, riding the waves, the sun beating down. I let my hands rove senselessly over his body, drinking him in.

If I was aware of the strange, sudden smoothness of his skin, it was only dimly. We were cresting a wave, building to climax. With a gasp, my eyes flew open just in time to watch his close. Then, with a final shudder, we came with loud cries. I arched up, wrapping my arms tightly around his body and bringing him closer to me.

* * * *

"Sarah! Sarah, wake up!"

"What?"

"Our bodies."

I leaned back, blinking the bleariness from my eyes. Then I gasped and sat up, all sleepiness forgotten.

Darren, lying naked on the floor next to me, had changed. He was still Darren, but his skin was healthy and glowing, his eyes no longer black but blue. No sores, no sagging skin.

He was human.

"Darren, you're—"

"I know. So are you," he interrupted.

I looked down and gasped. The swell of my breasts, my flat stomach, my arms, my legs … all were covered in a layer of human skin.

In a flash of startling intuition, I knew what had happened.

"The hippies!" I gasped.

Darren blinked at me. "What?"

"The hippies! You know what they believe about the zombies, right?"

And I could see he understood. He gaped at me, and a blush colored his cheeks. I'd never seen anything more beautiful.

"Love, you mean," he said.

I stared at him in awe. "Love," I agreed, thinking, *Most beautiful plague.*

We sat there for a long time. Outside, the sky began to glow with the first hint of dawn.

Prize of a Fighter

Dale Mitchell

Four rings.

A clash of metal against metal, with a dull ringing echoing through the hushed crowd moments before the massive uproar.

Seven seconds.

The rush of adrenaline drowns the crowd. All focus is centered in the cage.

Two people.

One a prisoner, the other a junkie.

One creature.

Once a man, now an abomination that feasts on flesh and death.

The locks are pulled away and she risks a quick glance at her unwilling partner. Like a gladiator of old, he is a prisoner for entertainment purposes. His torso is lean with sinewy muscles bunched in anticipation, his lower body molded into a pair of aged, grime caked jeans.

Her own body is small and lethal, but she is no prisoner, except to adrenaline and the power it wields to her. Her long braid of hair is wrapped tightly around the crown of her head for safety. This is not fighting for her life.

This, this is pleasure.

As the last chain is snapped free, the final lock engages on the door and she looks back at the monster. The hanging lights sputter for a moment from the generators, plunging the crowd into uneasy darkness a few moments before gasping back to life.

It lunges, a guttural bellow of rage passing its lips. This one is not as fresh as the cage owners prefer, but still a hulk of a beast, with arms larger than her head. Additionally, the creature is fast, a surprise considering the fetid stench it produces.

The rules are simple. The biter dies. If the biter attacks one of the fighters and kills them, the fight becomes evenly matched. If the biter attacks one of the fighters and infects them, the match then becomes two biters against one fighter.

There are no weapons.

Bets are placed—usually biter versus fighters. If the match has a new fighter, the stakes are placed on how long the fighter will last, one way or another. If there are reputable fighters in the cage, the bet changes to how quickly the match will end. Depending on the fighters' reputations, the wager may become fighter versus fighter.

This is the new entertainment in a fallen world where currency is no longer money.

She moves slowly while her partner dashes forward, his hands reaching for the biter's head. It's a risky move.

Both she and her partner are veteran fighters, with reputations preceding them.

He is rough, she is vicious.

His thumbs sink into the biter's eyes, the decayed flesh yielding, giving him a hand hold while the biter attempts to drag him closer to its mouth.

She looks at his hands shoved on each side of its head, strong and large, as she debates on whether to allow the biter to infect him. Sometimes, such a fight is fantastically violent, something she craves.

Then again, he has a reputation, and she has placed a bet.

It rakes rotten fingers down his bare back, his muscles convulsing in an attempt to keep it at bay.

A foolish thought on his part to not clothe properly.

Of course, she also has a reputation.

Perhaps he was showing off when he rushed the biter.

No one likes to lose.

Stepping around them as they embrace in a deadly grasp, she kicks out at the biter's knee, dropping them both in a heap. The biter does not notice its shattered knee, and continues to batter him.

The crowd is screaming, the floor shaking beneath her boots, but she only sees his face, locked in a grimace with determination etched into the corners of his eyes.

They are a beautiful blue-gray, the color of the ocean in the burning morning light. A tipping point, for her.

She locks her fingers inside the wet sockets, sliding across his thumbs, and pulls the head cleanly from the body. At the last moment he understands and releases the head, collapsing on its torso. A dribble of black fluid oozes from the neck.

The biter's body stops raining blows, but the jaws still snap. She drops the head to the ground, crushing the skull with her boot. Wiping her hand on the rough fabric of her jeans, she helps him to his feet and entwines her fingers in his, evidence of battle around them.

She is the victor.

He is the prize.

In a world where there is no monetary currency, people pay with their bodies.

A cursory nod to her right, and they are both whisked from the arena in an upheaval of approval from the crowd. A warm shower; a luxury, awaits them in the changing rooms.

They meet beyond the rooms, still within listening distance to the arena. Groping for one another in the semi-darkness, they each want the same thing.

He is rough.

She is vicious.

Capturing his ear with her mouth, she wraps her tongue around the small silver hoop and pulls as his belt is yanked free. She rubs her body against him, the adrenaline fueling her frenzy. With a groan he pulls her by her loose braid to the wall, pushing a knee between her legs.

Her shirt is quickly discarded, her breasts small enough to be unbidden by a bra. Tugging her nipples elicits a low moan from her.

There is no other foreplay, the fight has sensitized each of them as they ride the adrenaline as high as it will take them, breathing ragged in their rush. They are stripped bare before the next fight barely begins, and he plunges deep inside her as another fighter entertains for his or her life. The orgasm takes her completely and wrapping her legs around his waist she grasps him tighter, milking him until he is pulled along with her, a final grunt issuing from his lips as they collapse to the floor.

His reputation is true.

Pulling the shirt over her head, she speaks to him with a calmness that almost always surrounds her. "Get your clothes on, and come with me."

His smile is smug as he dresses. Her reputation has warned him of what is to come, she is certain. But his smugness is not something she desires.

"Do you wish to return to the fights?"

The smile vanishes and is replaced with a drop of fear. "No."

"Then do not be so arrogant."

He grabs her then, and forces her to kiss him with a ferocity only matched against his cage fighting. Her teeth clamp down on his tongue bringing tears to his eyes, but he still holds her tight against him. Eventually she releases him, the taste of blood coating her throat.

"You might want to be careful with that," she tells him. "I plan on you using it more, and soon."

Dying Days: Chris Gray

Armand Rosamilia

Chris Gray smiled at his good fortune. The woman had been barely alive when he found her washed up on the shore, but she had no bite marks on her. She was naked, with full breasts and such a sweet ass he almost cried. He copped a quick feel before tossing her over his shoulder and taking the long way around the beach to his stilt house, the last in line overlooking the Atlantic Ocean and Matanzas Inlet.

No sense in alerting the rest of the community. They would keep her from him, and he didn't want that. *Finders keepers*, he thought. *I did all the hard work and I should be the one who gets to reap the rewards.*

Chris washed her and she mumbled once, her eyes rolling in her pretty little head, but she passed back out. He found a sexy negligee in the closet, too small for her, but he made it work by ripping the material here and there. He was getting excited now, and placed her gently in his bed.

The woman was in her early twenties, a few years younger than Chris. Thick lips, thick hips and a vagina he couldn't wait to taste. But he didn't want to rape her. *What if she dies?* He pushed the thought from his mind. He wanted to keep her here, with him, forever. Without Griff and Murph and that bitch Darlene interfering.

She'd need to eat and get well. He dragged in the mini-refrigerator from the kitchenette and placed it near the bed, filling it with bottled water and piling snacks on top. The electricity had never gone out in this grid, and they were all thankful. Of course, finding food and water kept getting harder, so they had to conserve. But she seemed worth it.

The room was dark save a single lamp in the corner because the windows had been boarded up. No use in letting the outside world know survivors were here. And the secrecy could be used in his favor …

He slipped out, making sure to close and lock the door behind him. He didn't want her wandering around the huge house or leaving. And he didn't want one of his nosy neighbors to notice he had company.

Chris acted casual as he went down the steep stairs to the stilt house, watching for zombies. He cursed himself when he saw he'd once again left the gate open at the base of the stairs. *One of these days, a fucking zombie is going to walk up and bite me on the ass*, he thought. Chris thought of the woman's ass and smiled.

"How's it going, Chris?" Darlene Bobich asked. She carried her damn machete with a Desert Eagle holstered at her side. She was a pretty girl, about his age, but she'd lost some weight lately. Chris liked her a bit thicker, in a pinch … but not anymore. He had a sweet one waiting upstairs for him, and he needed to gather the cans of vegetables he had secreted in the trunk of the Kia Spectra underneath the house. Only, Darlene was butting in her pretty head once again.

"It's going well." Chris squinted at her in the harsh Florida light. He was used to Seattle and rain. "What are you doing, wandering around? Zombies are everywhere."

"That's the reason I'm out here." She smiled, but stared at him intently. "Been on the beach today?"

Chris glanced to the ocean, just over the dunes. "I walked it this morning."

"They still walking out of the surf?"

"Here and there. I killed one, but the rest seem to be getting carried north of us and dumping into the inlet before heading away. I guess they like St. Augustine."

"I hope you're planning to join us later. John has been following a swarm of them coming right up A1A from Flagler Beach again.

We're going to wipe out as many of them as we can before they get here."

"I'll meet you." Chris crossed his arms and leaned against the car, waiting for her to leave.

When Darlene walked away, but only to the next stilt house, he sighed and stomped back upstairs. He'd have time again to get the food upstairs, and no way would he be leaving his new houseguest alone today.

* * * *

She stirred as he dropped the last three cans of beans on the dresser. He had most of the remaining food in the room now. The bedroom door remained locked, and he'd hidden the key in the top drawer of his dresser. He'd discarded all the women's clothing in another room.

Chris went to her, sitting down on the bed. "How are you feeling?"

"Where am I?"

"You are safe. For now." Chris dramatically turned his head and glanced at the door, putting a finger to his lips. "But we need to keep it down. The house is overrun by *them*."

She sat up and stared at the outfit she wore. Her nipples were hard and she covered them with her hands. "Why am I dressed like this?"

"I found you, um, nude, on the beach. This was the only clothing I could find in this house."

"This isn't your place?"

"No. I got trapped here."

She squinted. "Then how did you find me on the beach?"

Chris smiled. "You've been out for two days. The zombies grew in number. I saved you. Another few minutes and they would have had you."

"Well, thank you. I'm Amanda." She pulled the blanket around her. "It's cold. Is the air actually on? The electricity works?"

"Yes, we are very lucky."

Amanda sat up. "We need to fight our way out! There might be more survivors."

Chris shook his head and tried to look sad. "I'm sorry, but everyone else is dead. The zombies emerged from the ocean and dragged them in. You were the only one alive, and just barely." He put a comforting hand on her arm, marveling at how smooth her skin was. "Where were you?"

"We were on a cruise." Amanda put her head back down on the pillow and stared at the ceiling. "We survived for months, until we ran out of fuel and food. We ran aground outside of the Bahamas."

"That's a long way from here."

"I don't remember much after that. There was a man with me …" her eyes welled up. "I knew a couple of men and they took care of me. Who will take care of me now?"

Chris pulled her into his chest, her nipples against him. He wanted to be her protector, to take care of her, and she would be his woman. His life.

Amanda pushed away from him and stared into his eyes. "Will you save me?"

Chris kissed her as he reached around and cupped her ass cheeks. She responded by reaching down and squeezing his erect cock. They were frantically kissing now, hands all over one another.

Amanda pushed him down on the bed and began pulling his tattered jeans off with a smile. She buried his cock in her mouth and Chris nearly exploded. *Was this really happening?*

She stopped and looked up at him. "We're going to die, aren't we?"

Chris tried not to giggle like a little school girl and solemnly nodded his head. "This will be our last night on earth, I'm afraid."

"I don't want to die alone."

"You won't." Chris felt sad. Not for deceiving Amanda, but because he was starting to like her. Was this how love felt? He wanted to fuck her tenderly.

"Then make love to me," she said and slipped the

negligee off as she went down on her back and spread her legs. "I want to die happy."

Chris nearly exploded when he saw her creamy inner thighs and her pubic mound. She glided a finger into her wetness and moaned, closing her eyes.

He slipped between her legs, thinking of a hundred different ways to play this cool, but as soon as his shaft entered her, all he could think about was cumming inside her and spilling his seed. "Can you get pregnant?" he whispered in her ear.

Amanda ground her hips against him. "Doesn't matter now, baby. Make love to me. I want you inside me."

Chris began a fast pace, their flesh slapping against one another in a quick rhythm. She moaned in his ear and he was screaming in ecstasy when she pushed at his chest.

"What?" Chris said, pissed off. She'd broken his concentration. He wanted to shoot into her, and she'd ruined it. "I was right there …"

Amanda looked over his shoulder. "I heard something outside. They might have heard you yelling so loud."

"I wasn't that loud," he said. He stared down at his limp member. Now he wanted to scream. "It's probably nothing."

A sudden loud thump sounded against the bedroom door. "How'd they get upstairs?"

Amanda stood up at the side of the bed. "Upstairs? I thought we were in a house."

"We are. A stilt house."

"Then why are they up here with us?" she asked, hands on hips.

"I think I left the gate open downstairs. My bad."

"You lied to me. You kept me like a prisoner?"

Chris was annoyed now. "You're the one that fucked me, remember? Don't give me any shit." He glanced around. "We need to find a weapon."

"You have nothing to defend with?"

Chris stared at the bedroom door as another blow shook it on its hinges.

"I left the guns and the machete in the living room."

"We really are going to die," Amanda said. She went to him and put her arms around his shoulders. "Ripped apart."

Chris was about to burst into tears when Amanda reached down and cupped his manhood. "I want to die in bed."

* * * *

Darlene sliced through a zombie's neck and kicked the falling body from her path. The bedroom door had been ripped off its hinges and she nearly gagged at the orgy of bodies writhing on the bed.

Chris Gray slid off the bed, his erection obscene, and started moving to Darlene.

Darlene Bobich, zombie killer, pulled out her trusty Desert Eagle, and shot Chris in the face. The other undead stopped and turned to face her.

She smiled and began shooting.

Love and the Apocalypse

Thomas Alan Sandrage

The world can be thrown into complete chaos and disarray on any random day and people will continue on as though nothing had changed. Until the disorder affects them personally, they are apathetic. Humans search for flimsy answers in the darkness, seek out linear patterns in the arbitrary, and keep business going as usual. Julia and Roman were no different—normal people in an abnormal world, going about their lives and trying to ignore the devastation around them. Until she was bitten.

Roman was already home from work, waiting for Julia and trying to be cool. Anytime she had to leave, anytime she wasn't here behind locked doors, Roman's heart beat a bit harder. He had to work and understood the risk, but he wished she would just stay inside (even though he knew this to be unreasonable).

Business had slowed since the plague broke out, but not stopped. People still needed supplies, even if the dead wouldn't stay dead. Business as usual. Roman was a checkout clerk at the local grocery store—a position that had once earned him teasing and outright scorn from friends and family; now his job had become one of the most important in this new hierarchy. Every morning, the remaining employee's cleared the stinking, rotting things from the front doors and parking lot so the customers would have a relatively safe entrance. The things were pretty easy to rally. They only posed a real threat if a person got caught alone and surrounded. Mostly, people just walked around them.

Roman flipped through the limited channels still on the

TV. A lot of shaky news reports all said the same things over and over. That's the way it would stay until the people in charge learned something new; Roman had his doubts they ever would. Every day there were fewer channels and more static. He tried not to think about things much, but it was hard to imagine this wasn't the end of times.

He heard the front door unlocking and felt the usual drop in his stomach (her, or them?) and then Julia's footsteps clicking through the door. On his way to greet her he heard her crying. He first thought she was breaking down; who would blame her? The things they witnessed could drive anyone to madness. Roman was surprised people managed as well as they did.

"You okay, baby?" Roman asked as he put his arm around Julia's shoulder. She tucked her head under his chin and began to sob. He held her tight and rocked her. There was a sound, one Roman barely heard, like a faucet dripping.

She pulled herself away after a moment, looking at Roman with wet, puffy eyes. She rolled her left jacket sleeve up to her elbow. Roman's eyes widened. She had a large semicircle carved jaggedly into her skin, angry red infection already spreading in all directions. A bite.

"Oh ... oh, no ..." Roman said.

"I'm so sorry," Julia said through fresh tears.

Blood dripped steadily to the floor.

They both understood exactly what this meant. They had done their best to avoid it, but in the end they couldn't. They even had a plan worked out, although neither had ever hoped to enact it. But what else could be done?

Nothing.

There was no cure.

Life was being quite the bitch just lately.

* * * *

They dressed in their absolute best and went out into an unsafe evening to find a restaurant still open. All they found was a barbeque joint set up like a bunker, called The CUT-RITE House of Meat. They rapped loudly on the front door and waited to be let in by the owner, a crazy looking old man in a filthy white apron. He carried a high-powered rifle as he unlocked the door. His unblinking eyes darted about the front of his restaurant as he ushered them in quickly.

The inside of the restaurant was surreal. The thick aroma of cooking meat hung in the air. Music played in the background, some gentle string and piano piece (even the song insisted business was as usual). They each ordered the most expensive dish on the menu (most of which had been blacked out with marker—supplies were limited, after all) and neither could eat more than a bite or two. Roman kept thinking the years together had not been enough. So much they didn't get to do. It wasn't fair.

They poked at their food until it felt like a sufficient amount of time had passed, then signaled for their check. When the owner (who seemed to be doubling as the entire wait-staff and cook) asked if they needed a box, they both said in unison, "No." There were two other couples in sight, neither of which looked particularly happy, and Roman wondered how their evenings would turn out. Hopefully better than he and Julia's.

The drive home was silent. Things shambled along the sides of the street, tripping over their own feet or freshly fallen meat. Roman tried not to look. One walked out in front of him and he had to swerve hard to avoid it. Julia seemed to not even notice—lost in her own thoughts.

Once back home behind locked doors, Roman put two bullets into his father's nickel-plated .44 and set the gun on the nightstand next to their bed. After making love for the last time, he would take care of them both. This part of the plan had gone unspoken, but both knew of it.

* * * *

It may have seemed unnatural they should want to engage in sex under such strange conditions, but people must be people even in the face of death. They had been having more sex than they had when they first met lately; a result of more time indoors, but also a natural rebellion against the nightmarish world growing outside. Defiant to the end, life must at least try to go on.

Julia stepped out of the bathroom, draped in a see-through blue robe. One long, creamy leg split the shimmering cloth. Her eyes were puffy and her cheeks red from crying, but she still looked as beautiful as she ever had. Roman sat on the edge of the bed and held his arms out to her. She sat next to him and tucked her head under his chin.

"You okay, baby?" Roman's voice cracked on this last word. He struggled to control his tears. Julia nodded into his chest; then she began to kiss him. She worked her way up to his lips, first brushing against them lightly, then pressing harder and opening up to him.

They lay down together, lips locked and arms pulling each other closer. Julia felt hot, perhaps feverish under his embrace—the infection already hitting her hard. Tears mixed with their saliva as they kissed.

Roman worked his hands down the satiny fabric of her robe, finding the knot in the tie and releasing it. With delicate fingers, he spread her robe open, her poetic skin golden beneath and shining with a slight glimmer of sweat. Julia began to moan into his kisses as his hands explored the constant mysteries of her body.

Soon, she pushed him on his back as she straddled him; they became one. She was unbelievably hot inside; Roman had felt nothing like it. Gasping, he thrust upwards even as Julia threw her head back in ecstasy. He could feel her hair brushing against his thighs.

Julia's stomach was swelling. Roman tried not to look (*no, it's too soon*), but the unthinkable was happening, and fast. His body contracted as his climax was building to an irreversible roar. Julia screamed: *in pleasure,* Roman was sure. He tried to say something, but he was overwhelmed. All he could manage was, "Oh ... oh, no ..."

"I'm so sorry," Julia said, her voice gurgling.

Suddenly, her swollen belly burst. The stench of rotten, gas-blown inner organs assaulted Roman. Then the guts themselves fell out on his midriff, piling up on the mattress around him. He tried to scream; at the same time his orgasm could not be stopped. He stared into the ruin of her stomach and saw himself there, pulsing with pleasure and spouting milky white fluid into her soupy insides like a fleshy geyser in a terrain of decay.

The sight wrenched all the pleasure straight out of him and Roman felt his own guts loosening. Without knowing it was going to happen, he vomited into Julia's open guts and on his own penis. She fell forward on him, pushing him to his back again and snapping her teeth at his throat. She snarled, drooling down onto his naked flesh.

Roman tried to push her back as he reached for the gun on the nightstand, gasping for breath. He was still inside Julia, locked there as he struggled for the pistol, a mere inch out of reach. He leaned further, sacrificing his grip on Julia's gnashing jaws for one fatal second. She bit into his Adam's apple, a pain unlike anything Roman had ever known. It felt like his gag-reflex was getting crushed, ripped to pieces. But he got the gun.

He brought the pistol up to Julia's head and pulled the trigger as he screamed in primal rage. The trigger clicked, the hammer struck home, and nothing happened. The bullet was a dud, or the chamber wasn't loaded right, something messed up. Julia bit into the side of his face. He pulled the trigger again and the gun fired, but he didn't have the weapon seated right and the bullet went into the ceiling above them. Julia knocked the gun out of his hand with her flailing arms, and he realized it was over.

* * * *

Days later, the owner of The CUT-RITE House of Meat would see them in the parking lot on a cold dark morning.

The remains of Roman and Julia leaned on each other, naked and rotten. *There's a certain tenderness to it,* the owner thought, as he sighted the man with his rifle. Two quick shots later, Roman and Julia were just another couple for the stinking fire out back.

People can plan for the worst all they want, but the worst can always get worse. The light at the end of the tunnel may just be the spark down the barrel of a gun. Love may be a guiding light to help us through, but can it really save anybody?

Does it even help?

In the end, maybe love is what bites us all in the ass.

The Zombie and the Cheerleader

Laura Snapp

"Doesn't she realize he's *dead?*" a girl with black-rimmed glasses said. "So gross."

Her dark-haired friend nodded as they stood by their lockers watching me, their arms wrapped around their spiral notepads and books.

When they caught me eyeing them, they looked away, and I smiled. Social order had been restored. I tossed my blonde ponytail over my shoulder and turned my attention back to the guy lounging against my locker. Who the hell cared if he was dead? He was the quarterback. The star of the football team. "So, what do you think? Will you go with me?"

Billy's face stretched into a grin, exposing decaying teeth and grayish black gums. "I don't know Daphne. I mean, what's it worth to you? Homecoming's kind of a big deal."

The smile on my face slipped. Homecoming *was* a big deal. If I went with him, I would definitely be crowned Homecoming Queen instead of that bitch Teena. My ex-BFF. I trailed a pink, polished nail down his letter jacketed chest. "You name it, Billy. I'll do anything."

"Well, there *is* something you could do," he said. He moved closer, and I got a whiff of his rank breath. I reached into my locker to withdraw a tin of Altoids. I fished out three and popped them into my mouth.

"Do you mean something like this?" I stood on tiptoe as I pulled his head toward mine. Our lips touched. When his tongue delved into my mouth, I pushed the mints against it, then curled mine away. He raised his head, and I dropped down on my heels. "There's more where that came from," I said.

He nodded. "Yeah, I saw the tin."

I frowned. "That's not what I meant. I—"

He sucked on the mints, his bloodshot eyes dropping to my low neckline. "Show me your tits and I'll think about it."

My lips curled. I totally had him. My tits were to die for. "Sure thing," I said. I slid my fingers beneath the lace cups of my bra and tugged, exposing my breasts to his view.

His hand snaked up and he tweaked a nipple. "Nice," he said. His other hand flipped up my short, pleated skirt to caress my bare ass cheek. "Meet me beneath the bleachers after school and we'll talk."

"Talk?" I kept my voice soft, but inside I could barely contain myself. A little sex play, and he'd be goo in my hands.

He pushed off from the locker. "Later, babe."

I rearranged my neckline, slammed the door closed, and bounced off to class.

The crown was mine.

* * * *

"You're really going through with this?" Katie asked, walking with me toward the field. "You don't think it's like creepy or anything?"

"Like I haven't fucked creepy guys before. And it's not like he's *that* dead. It's only been a couple of weeks."

"But Daphne, nobody understands how he got *undead*. I mean, he was in the car accident and died, and the next thing we know, he's back in school and breaking up with Teena."

"That's her problem. If she can't handle a little thing like being dead ..." I shrugged. "Obviously the whole Team Edward thing was bullshit."

"Yeah." Katie nodded, smacking her gum. "I totally see that now."

I pushed my pompoms between my knees then released

my hair from its regulation ponytail. "Now scram. I have work to do."

"K. See you at the dance, Miss Homecoming Queen." She winked as she veered off toward the parking lot.

Smiling, I mussed up my hair to give it the *just fucked* look I knew guys liked, swiped on my signature pink bubblegum lip gloss, and ducked beneath the bleachers in search of Billy.

He wasn't hard to find. My nose wrinkled at his stench. Maybe hooking up during the heat of the day wasn't the best idea, but at least we were in the shade.

"Hi, Handsome," I lied.

He gave me a slow once-over. "Show me what you got."

I dropped my pompoms and grasped the bottom of my shirt to lift it up and over my head. I knew my plum colored bra flattered my creamy skin and the soft curves of my breasts plumped appealing over the demi-lace barely covering my nipples. "Like what you see?" I asked, letting my shirt fall to the ground.

He gestured at my skirt.

My hand immediately slid to my backside to tug on the zipper. Soon the skirt too was lying on the ground.

"Nice," he said, eyeing my matching thong. "Now that."

"Wouldn't you like a little cheer?" I pouted. I had practiced a provocative dance with my pompoms in the bathroom mirror in between classes.

"No," he said. He stepped forward until he was pressed up against me. "Show me a good time, and I'll show you one."

I inhaled sharply. "You mean …?"

"Yep."

I slipped off my white sneakers and ankle socks, then wriggled out of my thong. I pushed it into his pocket. "So you won't forget."

"Oh, I won't," he said, shrugging out of his purple and gold letter jacket.

This time, it was my turn to stop him. I slipped the jacket back on his shoulders. "You look so sexy in it." In truth, I didn't want to see any more of his gray colored skin than I absolutely had to. And rumor had it, he'd suffered major damage to his rib cage and chest. It was bad enough I had to see the gaping wound on the back of his head whenever he turned around.

He nodded. His battered hands moved to unclasp my bra. He slung it over the bleacher then bent down to blow a cold breath against my nipple. It reacted instantly, rising up to meet his lips that then licked and suckled until I felt an answering ache in the pit of my stomach.

"Oh god," I cried, unable to believe I was actually turned on. Unthinking, my hands grabbed his head and I pulled his mouth to my other breast.

He complied immediately. As he sucked and nibbled, my fingers dug deeper and deeper into his scalp. When I couldn't stand it any longer, I jerked his head away from my chest.

"Why'd you stop me?" he said. Blood leaked down his neck. I turned his head quickly to the side. Patches of his hair and scalp were missing.

I let go of his head, and in horror, stared at my fingers. Bits of hair and flesh were wedged beneath my nails. "Ew …" I wiped them on his jacket. "Maybe we should—"

"So the dance isn't that important, huh?" he said, pushing a hand through his hair. He patted several loose patches of flesh and hair back into place. "I thought you said 'anything'."

"I did." My hands spasmed on his jacket. So my hands were sticky? They'd been sticky before with cum. I pressed the flat of my hand against his crotch and his cock jerked in response. "Who said anything about stopping?"

I knelt down to unzip his jeans. His cock sprang free, and I twirled the tip with my tongue before taking him fully into my mouth. My head bobbed back and forth in rhythm to his groans as I sucked and licked and sucked some more. It was like slurping a cold Popsicle. Not even the moist wetness of my mouth could warm his cold cock. But it was hard. Bone hard.

"Enough," he said finally, pulling free of my mouth.

I lay down on the grass next to my pile of clothes and pompoms and closed my eyes. Fucking a corpse was a small price to pay to be Homecoming Queen.

"Not yet," he said with a raspy chuckle. My eyes flew open as he loomed over me. Excitement had lightened his skin to an eerie glow, while his lips had darkened to a blackish purple. "You need to be hot and wet. Ready to come. Touch yourself."

Tentatively, my hands reached between my thighs and I fingered my clit.

"Harder," he demanded.

I pressed my fingers against my pussy and stroked, feeling the nub get harder and bigger.

"That's it," he said. "Now put your fingers inside your pussy."

My fingers glided further between my legs then slid inside my wetness. I closed my eyes at the sensation of my hands against my flesh, rubbing back and forth, in and out, bringing me to the brink of orgasm.

"Open your eyes and look at me." He was stroking his cock as he watched me. "Put your fingers in your mouth."

I hesitated. Taste my own juices?

"Do it."

I slipped my fingers into my mouth and sucked. My eyes widened in surprise. I tasted good. Really good.

"Are you ready for me to fuck you?" he asked, and I nodded. "Let me see." He dropped to his knees and pressed his face against my pussy. He blew across my hot wetness and I shivered. "Not hot enough," he said. His tongue flicked inside me. "Or wet enough." He pulled my hand back down to my pussy. "More," he said.

I stroked myself, harder and faster, my fingers slipping inside my pussy. Excitement coiled inside me as I stared at Billy and watched his eyes darken with hunger until they glowed like black jewels in his gray, sunken face. His hands were on his cock, pulling and stroking in time with mine. Flakes of skin flew off his dick, from his hands, as our tempo increased. I closed my eyes as the tension built up inside me until I was squirming on the ground, on the precipice of coming. Then I felt his hardness slam into me.

He pounded into me again and again, and the cold sensation of his cock gliding in and out of my hot, wet moistness drove me over the edge. My muscles clenched around him as I lost control, sensations ripping through me like wildfire. With a final thrust, he shuddered and fell against my chest.

"What time are you picking me up?" I said when our breathing had slowed.

"Picking you up?" he said, lifting his head to gaze at me. Strands of my hair clung to the side of his face where his torn flesh seeped green-colored pus. "I wouldn't be caught dead at the dance with you."

Shock had me pushing him off of me. "You mean I fucked you for nothing?"

"No." His face peeled back into a grin. "You fucked yourself for nothing. I fucked you for fun."

"There you are," Coach said with a great deal of exasperation. His glance skittered off to the side when he noticed me lying naked next to Billy. "Good God, son. Do you know how many favors I had to call in to get the great, great, great granddaughter of Marie Leveau to bring you back to life? And for what? So you could fuck some damn cheerleader? I brought you back to win dammit. This game sets the tone for the entire goddamned season. So get your ass out on the field. Now!"

Billy scrambled to his feet and started to zip up his jeans. "Oh, shit," he said, looking down at the gooey nub where once a penis had been. His horrified gaze drifted to me. With a trembling hand, I reached between my legs and withdrew a cold, limp cock, dripping from both ends. As I screamed, Coach said, "Humph. Maybe now you'll think with your head instead of your dick, son. As for you," he kicked my clothes toward me, "get a fucking life and stop screwing with the dead. That's just plain gross."

Something Borrowed

Nicky Peacock

The creeping red stain overpowered her white satin dress. Four months wages poured into that dress, and now its sparkly silk was tie-dyed with gore. She shook her head, but her brain simply banged against her skull. She could feel it floating up there, itchy and heavy. The pain in her arm was gone and her long white gloves hid the bite mark well—the bullet holes in her chest, however, remained quite obvious and still burned a little.

With effort, she pulled herself up and shuffled around her upturned fairy tale style carriage. Half of her horse lay on the ground, writhing in his own innards. As he couldn't move, she pulled the unconscious body of the still breathing driver from beneath the wheel, and threw him within the horse's reach. Seconds later its teeth submerged in the warm flesh of the driver. She smiled, and two of her own teeth fell out.

Bells in the distance drew her attention. She was going to do something, she was meant to be somewhere ...

Walking was painful, but she managed to lope toward the sound with one hand outstretched, the other delicately holding the train of her dress.

When she reached the cemetery surrounding the church, she frowned. *Others* stood in her way. Some dressed in suits slit up the back, others naked; some even dressed in handsome uniforms, reminding her of him. She was supposed to be with *him*. She closed her eyes and tried to remember his name; a name which before so effortlessly slipped from her tongue.

Screams dissected her thoughts. People were still in the church. Were they *her* people? Did they wait for her?

She pushed forward, knocking the gathered out of her way. The church's door was closed and she heard shouting from inside. She moved to a nearby window. Its colors hurt her eyes so she thrust her gloved fist through it. The window shattered. More screams. The ones around her swarmed forward and fumbled through the window into the church.

She followed, scanning the painfully distorted faces as they were grabbed and pulled apart. She found no one she could remember. But the church was familiar. She pulled her dress up and sat on a pew, trying to block out the cries around her, the sound of teeth on bone and dripping bodily fluids.

She'd been here before, to practice for this day. She remembered the smell of frankincense, dusty leather books and the young, forlorn looking priest with his Irish lilt, with her family waiting patiently for them to get their vows right. She thought of his smile, his laugh ...

Her brain ached so she got up and pushed past the feeding frenzy. Dead eyes watched as she struggled up the aisle, holding her dress from stains. A hand grabbed at her. She looked down to see the priest on the floor; one of his arms had been ripped away and was slowly being devoured by another. He groaned at her, and flopped over like a dying a fish. He pulled up his cassock to expose a large, shiny erect penis. She staggered backward and quickly turned away.

She'd led a sheltered life, had been a good girl, she saved herself for him—wherever he was.

At the altar she found a huddle of eaters, cramming their mouths with warm flesh and wet innards. She was hungry, but another, more urgent need tickled her chest and loins. She shoved them out of her way, and saw *him*, spread across the floor like red butter. He had been their feast. She smacked at the others who grumbled and limped away.

She knelt by his side and scanned his carcass. His stomach had been broken open and his bottom half mashed into the wooden floorboards. *She was too late.*

She bent and placed a soft kiss on his half chewed lips,

enjoying the memory of him. She felt his arms about her neck and when she opened her eyes, his dead eyes staring up at her. He glanced down his ruined body, his intestines flopping like tails on a pack of dogs.

She got up and made her way back through the others. The priest was still on the floor struggling to get up with one arm. She approached him. Again, he pulled his cassock back to reveal his heavy undead member to her.

She grabbed his hipbone, pulled and yanked till the ball joint came free. She did the same with the other. He tried to bat her away with his good arm, but her focus was far too steady and soon she'd ripped out both joints and dragged the priest's naked bottom half back up the aisle and toward the altar.

He smiled and giggled as she wedded his entrails with those of the priest. She watched as they knitted together. He put his hand down to his new penis, grabbed it and smiled, his broken lips disappearing behind his teeth.

Their bodies crushed against each other, tongues locking, teeth clattering. He pulled her down to him. Straddling him, her dress obscured their tryst.

Her senses sparked alive. She imagined his heartbeat, quickening beneath her. His teeth, hard and sharp, lingered on the nape of her neck before tenderly trailing to the top of her bodice. His tongue plunged into the gaping bullet holes littering her dress like bloody pearls.

Her hand found his new, hard penis, thick and meaty. Her fingers covered its length and it eagerly nudged against her palm. She cupped it with one hand, then, with the other, pulled aside her stained satin panties.

Moving so he edged inside her, she caught his mouth in a deeper kiss. He grasped her hip as she held his penis high. A small, roll-like movement and he was inside. Their kiss deepened as she rocked on his shaft. Teeth dribbled from their gums and they each swallowed a handful, rather than ruin the moment by spitting them out.

His hard member filled and stretched her insides as she

rolled her groin on top of his. The sensation of her delicate, rotten insides splitting made her yell in his mouth. He felt it too; the warm liquid innards the bullets had created in her torso drowned his penis as he bucked upward, pushing and heaving to make her moan again.

Pushing harder, she ground their hip bones together and quickened her rhythm.

He grabbed her shoulder blades and pulled down her bodice to reveal her blood speckled breasts. Holding her hips in place, he pulled himself to a sitting position and began to devour her nipples. With tiny gummy bites he sucked and licked them clean till her grinding became so urgent he felt a warm pressure pull at his borrowed balls.

She arched her back as an explosion of cold fluid filled her insides.

Keeping her in place, he lunged forward and gripped her shoulder blades, her flesh coming away in his hands.

She cried out and flung her head back to allow her shout full escape through the church.

All the dead eyes swung to them. Some dropped bones they were chewing and others pulled themselves upright from the bloody pits of their previous victims.

She squinted at their audience and he wriggled out from under her, pulling her up alongside him as he did. He was unsteady on his new legs, so she put her arm about his waist and he put his around her shoulders. Silence.

A tall woman with no flesh to make up her face clapped. All then joined in; a chorus of sloppy wet applause and joyous grunts filled the church.

They grinned and shuffled their way down the aisle together, toward the door.

Ravenous

Lisa McCourt Hollar

Maggie stood outside the door, heart heavy. In hand, the gun she was going to use to end her husband's life weighed even more. But what was the choice? Better her than someone else.

Behind, Samuel cleared his throat.

"Maggie, no one would blame you if you couldn't …"

"I said I would do it and I will." Straightening her shoulders, she opened the door and stepped inside.

Jake looked confused when she entered the room. He knew someone would be coming, but he didn't expect this. "Maggie, what are you doing?" Then, seeing the gun, he fell silent. His eyes, at first confused, turned to anger. "They can't honestly expect it to be you?"

Setting the gun on the table beside the bed, Maggie wrapped her arms around her husband. "I volunteered," she choked, fighting back tears.

"Why?"

"Because I love you." She kissed his forehead. "It needs to be me."

Jake laughed. "Babe, you're strong, but this is a bit much—even for you."

Pushing him back, she lifted his shirt. Thick, blood-soaked bandages wrapped his abdomen. "I want to look at your wound."

"Maggie?"

"If you're going to die, I want to see the reason."

Sighing, Jake carefully unwrapped the wound in his side, revealing a large portion of flesh torn away by one of the monsters stalking their world. A similar wound was higher on his shoulder blade, and Maggie knew from the way his coat hung, slightly skewed, that his shoulder and arm were gone.

She tried to remove the jacket but he wouldn't let her.

"Billy should've let 'em finish the job."

"How can you say that?" Maggie snapped. "How could you expect him to leave you there and let them eat you?"

"I don't want this ... to be your last memory of me."

"It won't," she whispered. Kissing his neck, she let her hand graze across his belly before curling her fingers into the thick hair trailing down his chest.

"Maggie, what're you doing?"

"We only have a little time before you change ..." Groping at his jeans, she worked to unfasten the button.

"Maggie!" Jake pushed her away with the arm he had left. "What the hell—?"

"If I'm going to shoot my husband before he turns into a zombie, the least I can do is make his last moments ... pleasurable."

"You're insane."

Chuckling, Maggie leaned her head against her husband's good shoulder and breathed in his scent. He smelled good, despite the blood seeping through the bandages. Stifling a sob, she kissed his neck, working her fingers into his hair as she pulled him closer.

"What if I turn?"

"You won't."

"I might."

"Then I'll shoot you." Maggie guided Jake to bed and pushed him on the mattress before helping him struggle out of the jacket.

Jake resisted at first, but Maggie always persuaded him to see things her way. Pressing her lips firmly against his, she tugged off the jacket, revealing the damaged stub.

"I'm surprised they even bandaged it," he said. "A waste of needed medical equipment."

"Maybe you're immune."

"Right. You get bit, you turn into a biter."

"Well, you haven't yet." Pulling her shirt off, Maggie reached for her husband's hand, placing it against her right breast.

"Maggie, I don't think—"

"*Shhh* ... don't think. Right now I need you."

Despite his protests, she felt the swell bulging against his zipper and grinned. He never could refuse. She tugged his jeans off, then settled back down as she took his cock into her hand. Stroking him, she felt his erection grow and guided him inside of her.

Closing her eyes, she tried to pretend the world hadn't gone to hell around them. They were newlyweds again, living in a small cramped apartment where the water was never warm enough for bathing and the neighbors argued until three in the morning ... but they were happy. The dead didn't come back to life and try to eat you.

Jake wrapped his arm around her waist, pulling her against him, thrusting hard. Maggie moaned with pleasure, his breath teasing her neck.

"I love you," she panted, tears mingling with sweat and blood oozing from the bandage. He moaned his pleasure in tune with her own, continuing to thrust up and into her.

Pain shot through him as Maggie's knee dug in his side.

"I'm sorry," Maggie cried, moving to let him up.

Jake stopped her, pulling her back down. "Don't be. I never want this moment to end." Groping at her breast, he squeezed her nipple.

Maggie thrilled at his touch, gasping as she moved against him, this time trying to be more careful. Flicking his tongue across the taut nub, Jake pulled her nipple in his mouth. He cupped his hand around her breast and let go, taking hold of her ass and guiding her movements.

Maggie stiffened as the orgasm seized her. She felt Jake stiffen, too, releasing his seed. His nose was pressed against her neck, his breathing labored. Then it changed, his pants coming more ragged. He sniffed her ear, his fingers grasping her hair as a new hunger took hold. Suppressing the scream building inside, Maggie lifted the gun off the table and placed the barrel against his head.

"I love you," she whispered, and pulled the trigger.

* * * *

She stayed with him for an hour, holding him. Sensing her need for privacy, no one came in to check. Finally, she dressed and opened the door.

Samuel was waiting, along with three of the others. They would burn the body. There would be no chance of him coming back.

"Are you alright?"

Maggie looked at Samuel. "I'll be okay. I just need some time."

"Take what you need. We'll be moving on tomorrow. Chris says there's a large horde heading this way. We should be okay until morning; they aren't moving very fast. Unless the wind changes, they won't pick up our scent."

"I'll be ready." Maggie took one last look at Jake's body, and headed to the room she shared with two other women. It was empty ... they sensed she needed to be alone.

Curling up on the bed, she slept, dreaming about happier times and a baby. When she woke up she felt her stomach. She didn't know how, but she knew.

She was pregnant.

* * * *

It had been a week since the farmhouse. Everyone was used to picking up and leaving on a moment's notice. She wasn't used to the strange swell in her belly. The baby grew fast. She wore baggie clothes, but she worried she might not be able to hide her condition much longer. She sat next to the camp fire, fighting nausea.

"You okay?"

"I'm fine," Maggie said, smiling. Barbara had been henpecking ever since Jake, and she wished the woman would leave her alone.

"You look a little under the weather. I can talk to Sam … see if there's any medicine."

"I just need some quiet," Maggie snapped, and regretted her tone when she saw the hurt in the older woman's eyes. "I'm sorry … it's just been … difficult."

"That's okay, honey. I do tend to mother a person to death … I mean—"

Maggie stood and glanced around. "I think I'm going to go for a walk." Seeing Barbara about to protest, she held up a hand. "Don't worry, I won't go far."

Stepping in the woods, Maggie moved behind a tree and watched the others, making sure no one was going to come and check on her. Barbara surveyed the tree line, worried, but didn't move.

Samuel was talking to Billy about something and hadn't noticed she'd left … some observant leader. She blamed Samuel for Jake's death. He'd sent him scouting with only a boy for backup. That Billy had managed to kill the zombies attacking Jake, without getting bit himself, was a miracle.

A breeze blew her way, carrying a scent that made her stomach rumble. She'd stopped eating the rations two days ago. Her baby craved something else. This worried her, but she wasn't about to tell Samuel. If he knew, he would force her to terminate.

This child was all she had left of Jake. She would do what she had to.

She followed the scent to a rabbit hiding in the brush. It leaped into the open when she approached, but Maggie was quick, tackling the animal before it could escape. She ripped its throat open with her teeth, swallowing whole chunks of meat. When done, she followed a narrow path to a stream, and washed off the blood. Removing her shirt, she soaked it in the water, scrubbing at the stains, hoping in the dark, no one would notice the wetness.

"Well, what have we here?"

Maggie froze at Samuel's voice. "Ummm ... washing up."

"I can see that. But you shouldn't be out here alone."

"It's safe. Chris and Bradley secured the area before they let us set up camp."

"Rules are rules. Wouldn't want what happened to Jake to happen to you, too."

"No, we wouldn't want that," she said, fighting back anger. She suspected he'd been hoping something would happen to Jake. He never made it a secret he wanted Maggie. Now she didn't have a husband standing in his way. Looking over her shoulder at Samuel, her stomach growled. Baby was hungry. And she felt another desire building too. She'd never been with any man besides her husband but as her appetite for raw meat increased, so did her craving for sex. She wondered if the two were related. Turning to him she smiled, dropping her arms and leaving her breasts exposed. "Of course with you here, nothing is going to happen."

"Well, well ..." Samuel's hand strayed towards his zipper.

Maggie made quick work of his jeans, dropping them around his ankles as she fell to her knees. Inspecting his manhood, she was impressed. She pulled him into her mouth, sucking on his cock while she dug her fingers into his ass. Bobbing her head back and forth, she took him in deeper, fighting the hunger. Best to take him at the height of his orgasm.

When he let loose his seed, she closed her teeth, biting off his cock in one swift chomp.

Samuel tried to scream but nothing came. Maggie spit the severed member from her mouth and leaped on him, ripping his throat open before a scream found its way out of his lungs. She ate until full. This time, she didn't bother washing herself off. The blood could be explained.

She ran back to camp screaming zombies attacked her and Samuel.

Barbara held her while the men searched the woods. There were a few undead not far from the stream; the dead were always around. They killed them, and in the morning moved on. Barbara refused to let Maggie out of her sight. Maggie was okay with that. The baby was growing rapidly and she wouldn't be able to hide her pregnancy much longer.

That was okay, too. The little tyke liked Barbara's smell … and he'd be needing some food.

Death and Love in Manhattan

Clint Collins

Zombies need love, too.

I found that out when Kira, the most requested Russian girl on my escort service, finally had enough of stale crackers and hiding in her hotel room and decided to make a break for it on the streets of Manhattan. She didn't get far and was soon encircled by a ragged and shuffling group of men. All of us watching from our seventeenth floor window were ready to turn away once they fell upon her, repeating a scene we'd observed so many times since the virus swept out of a poorly controlled research lab in Mumbai.

But this time they had their cocks out and were tearing off her clothes rather than her limbs. With an almost gentlemanly solicitousness they laid her down in the middle of the street. One clambered between those praised and pampered gym-toned thighs, the red silky thong thrown to the gutter, and began to thrust inside her as others held her arms and legs. Once done, another took his place. One of them even stood guard with a crowbar and beat back those with a different kind of hunger.

My girls and I had never seen this happen before, but then we had never seen a normal and very hot woman running in the midst of infected New Yorkers. We counted, and when the last one stumbled away she had lain with eighteen zombies. Krista, my blonde accountant specializing in Saudi princes on the side, shook her head. "They just got fifty-four thousand dollars of free pussy."

Busaya, a petite and lovely girl from Thailand, shrieked and we all turned in time to see three zombie women pounce on an exhausted Kira lying on the street curled on her side.

These bitches didn't want to fuck her, they wanted to eat her, and they went for the good stuff. Two chewed into the soft, full D-cups, swallowing whole the candy-pink nipples and tearing into the white and perfect flesh with red mouths, as another bit deep into the velvety vulva, rich and foaming with zombie semen, and gobbled down the delicacy of her tender labia.

Later, when the zombies in the most advanced stages of the disease shambled in for the scraps and with palsied hands chewed on Kira's good bones, one licking the eye sockets of the brain-robbed skull with a spotted tongue, I began thinking about Maslow's hierarchy of needs.

I got an "A" in psychology, but not because I studied. On the first day of class at NYU I told my gray-bearded and potbellied professor I'd suck his dick once a week during the semester, and I never had to show up again. But I did flip through the textbook in the student bookstore and saw we all needed food, shelter, and sex, pretty much in that order. I didn't want to work with restaurants or in real estate, but I was good at sex. Really good. Right then I began recruiting college girls and in my early twenties operated out of one of the best hotels in Manhattan, completely taking over the seventeenth floor.

Sex was reliably the answer here, too. We had noticed the zombie disease was progressive. They started out confused Cro-Magnons and slowly dissolved to brain-eating Neanderthals. The first-stage disease men who had enough to eat and somewhere safe to sleep, next wanted sex. Long as their bellies were full their cocks told them what to do.

I noticed the guys who had gangbanged Kira back hanging around in the street, hoping for more. We were down to potato chips and wheels of cheddar cheese in the hotel kitchens and things were getting desperate. I grabbed a magazine and took the elevator down to the lobby. I had to hope Kira didn't die in vain.

My body still looked pretty good for a woman of forty-three and I walked out naked except for some high heels into the fading light of a summer evening. They quickly got my scent and turned. Behind me with an AR-15 semi-automatic rifle stood Dante, a former Marine gunny sergeant who served as both personal trainer and bodyguard for me and the girls.

We let them get within about five feet and then Dante shot one right between the eyes to establish a boundary. They stopped and listened as I pointed to pictures in my last copy of "Food and Wine," slowly speaking words I hoped they still remembered. I showed them glossy photos of steak, ham, chicken, quiche, and whatever else was featured. And wine. Lots of wine.

Incredibly, we never lost electricity as troops gave up most of the streets to defend the utilities, so I knew freezers and refrigerators in many abandoned apartments, houses, restaurants, delis, and burger joints were still crammed with edible food. It had only been less than a week since the virus really took hold in Manhattan.

Every time I pointed to a picture of food and said the corresponding word I also caressed myself, hoping they would get the connection. Food for sex. It was the social contract women had been making for years.

Something clicked in what remained of their male brains and the next day they came bearing gifts like earnest suitors. Those with frozen food, canned goods, and unspoiled fruit and vegetables went to the front of the line as a lesson to others, turning away those with candy bars and soft drinks. We laid out mattresses in the lobby with five girls prepping and ten girls servicing. We practiced safe sex to the extreme and we followed our "zombie love" protocol: condoms always, no blowjobs, no kissing (like that was going to happen anyway), no missionary (avoiding any drool), and be on top or go doggy style.

None of them had gotten sex in a while so they didn't last long and once they came, the prep girl in latex gloves removed the condom, pitched it into a garbage can, and slid a new one on the next guy in line. My girls moved in rotation, prepping ten, fucking ten, then helping to receive and store the offerings. Red velvet ropes and gleaming stanchions marked the way for entrances and exits and the girls on break showed the zombies the way in and out, so to speak.

I was passing out condoms to Ingrid, a Norwegian beauty who studied art at Columbia and wrapped those long legs around my customers on weekends, when I saw a face that had been poised above mine many times.

"Sanders? Is that you?"

His head turned and his lips trembled as he tried to say my name. The blue eyes that always got me moist were still clear and bright, but the gray I found so distinguished at his temples had gone white with the rest of his hair. Dashing to the end, he had a good bottle of cabernet in one hand and, if I knew him, a pack of two-inch thick filet mignons cradled in his arm.

"I'll take care of this one," I said, putting a condom in my jeans pocket and leading him to the elevator. I wasn't going to fuck the judge who protected my business and had been a favorite lover for years on an old mattress in front of a bunch of zombies. He deserved better.

I realized I was taking a chance bringing him up to my room, that he might get hungry at any moment, but from the way he squeezed my hand I could tell he wanted me, but not as food. Once in my apartment I put the steaks in the freezer and the wine in a rack and began unbuttoning my blouse. He always liked my full breasts and fingers that had not forgotten, deftly undid the front clasp of my bra. They fell into his hands with the familiar warmth of old friends and he simply held them for a long time.

I wanted to think he remembered all those weekends at his place in the Hamptons where he had us make love in every room, saying that would make him smile wherever he went in the beachfront house.

I cried when he married an old-money socialite, and on his wedding day took myself off to Rome where, among other adventures, a cute young tour guide slipped me into the

Coliseum after hours and we fucked in the moonlight where emperors watched the bloody games. I felt a lot better after, but really good when he called me three months later and scheduled an appointment. He paid full price, of course, and we met once a month until the virus arrived.

Later, when I took him down to the lobby I told Dante to take him out back behind the loading dock, shoot him, and burn the corpse. I knew Sanders would return and each day be a little worse, a little less human. I couldn't bear to watch him slowly become a monstrosity.

After kissing Sanders goodbye on the cheek I returned to supervising the zombie love fest in the lobby. Hearing some of my girls shout, I glanced up from my cataloguing of goods received to see five members of a local vigilante group pushing aside the patiently waiting zombies, trying to get to the head of the line.

"What the hell do you think you're doing? These are my customers." Hands on hips I glared at the one closest to me. We'd seen these guys before, riding around in a Humvee drinking beer and getting out to execute a few zombies before a crowd blocked the street.

"And just what the hell do you have going on here, woman? You makin' pets out of these creatures?" The leader of the gang laughed and put the muzzle of his AK-47 between my legs and slid it back and forth where not long ago I was joined with a zombie. When Sanders climaxed he said my name as clearly as he ever did.

"We're out here saving your life, bitch. Don't you think you should show some gratitude?"

I had to smile. "Sure, have your boys drop their pants and choose a girl."

The muzzle of his gun tapped my belt buckle. "You, too. I bet you're the best of them all."

I began to undo my belt and then stopped to scream as loudly as I could. The stunned look on his face as three zombies bit deep into his neck and shoulders showed me he'd never heard about Maslow's hierarchy. Right after physiological needs come safety and security, like protecting your woman.

My girls followed suit, filling the lobby with primal shrieks, and before they could get off a single shot the joyriding killers were well on their way to becoming stinking piles of zombie shit in Central Park.

Dante had come running back from the loading dock after hearing the chorus of screams, but by then we'd dragged the corpses out to the street as road kill for the most diseased and had started satisfying customers once again.

We shut the doors at five pm as the girls were exhausted and we were all tired of carrying stuff to the hotel kitchen. I told everyone to take long hot showers and meet in the kitchen at seven and fix ourselves a feast, even light the candles in the upscale hotel restaurant with the white tablecloths and celebrate the power of love, or whatever it was that would keep them standing in lines around the block throughout the night.

Once the zombies were only finding spoiled food, we would get in the five black SUVs in the basement and find a refuge. No matter where we went, I knew we, literally, had what it took to survive.

Raving Diseased

Brett Williams

Thumbs danced across the screen:
NATE: I need 2 see u.
Her reply came moments later:
JINX: 2 late
NATE: It's important
JINX: Yeah right
NATE: Srsly
JINX: Fine. Where?
NATE: Coffee?
JINX: Ur dime. 12:30

Nate arrived early, ordered a cappuccino for himself, skinny latte for her. He didn't need the caffeine. His mind swam, body fidgeted. The clock on his cell phone displayed 12:31.

12:33

Someone had brought her baby. It cried.

12:35

A bus sped by, leaving a scent of diesel exhaust in its wake. Rays of sun warmed Nate's face.

12:38

He noticed pink hair first. Nose ring. Monroe piercing over frowning face.

Jinx said, "I can't believe I agreed to meet you."

"I'm glad you did." Nate pushed the latte to her as she sat. She took a sip. He also drank.

"Well?"

"You look great."

The corners of Jinx's mouth curled up for a millisecond.

"I always do."

"True."

"You look like hell."

"I'm aware."

"You been hitting raves I don't know about? You on something?"

"No. No other raves. Not *on* anything."

"Then what? I haven't seen you around. You stopped calling *and* texting me, you shit. Why the fuck now?"

Nate's hand shook.

"Just spit it out."

"I think I got it."

"Got what?"

"You know. *It.*"

"You got the Rot?"

"I think."

"You think?" A look of sheer panic clouded Jinx's expression. "Is that so? When do you *think* you got it?"

"Unless you gave it to me—"

"I never gave you the fucking Rot."

"Well, that's kind of why it was so important I see you today."

Her voice cracked. "What makes you think you got the Rot?"

"I just do."

Jinx's beautiful brown eyes grew shiny.

"You ... I could ... I could be infected?"

Nate reached across the wrought-iron table to take her hand.

"Why do you think I stopped calling and texting you?"

"My god ... that disease rots flesh. Starting ... Starting at ..."

Nate glanced around the crowded coffeehouse patio area. His voice lowered. "It starts at the genitals. Yes, I know."

"Are you ... rotting?" Jinx pulled her hand away from him.

Nate glanced away, embarrassed. "You can't get it from simple contact, you know."

"We didn't use protection."

"You were on the pill."

Nate turned to listen to her curse. A tear rolled down her lovely freckled cheek.

"Tell it to me straight," Jinx said. "Are you rotting?"

"Yes, I am."

"Oh shit. Oh hell. Oh—"

"Shh ... It's going to be okay. You haven't noticed any ... areas, have you?"

"I haven't exactly been looking. I ... I need to check. How bad have you got it?"

Nate surveyed the area again. Everyone else seemed preoccupied with their own business. Light traffic noise helped drown out exterior conversation. He stretched open the neck hole of his T-shirt.

"Shit." Jinxed leaned across the table for a closer look.

"Not here," Nate said. "We need to get you checked."

Jinx shot up out of her chair. "Your place is closer."

They walked the block to Nate's apartment in silence. They moved briskly, weaving between pedestrians, holding hands the entire way. At the door to 3B Nate recalled the first time he had taken Jinx back to his place. Around five in the morning, after raving hard all night. They had met weeks before; however, sparks flew between them that night—and all throughout the morning—until they finally crashed, exhausted and sexually sated.

When they entered the apartment, Jinx raced through the confining space to the bathroom, where she immediately began to shed clothing. Nate paced the small living area. The last thing he wanted was to infect Jinx with the Rot. News had recently surfaced about this new sexually transmitted disease. Its origins, according to the CDC, traced back to college kids—the partying crowd. People such as Jinx and himself: weekly ravers. Once infected, the decay spread across the body. Nobody could predict how bad the infection would spread. The CDC had no cure.

"Nate, come here." An alarmed edge rang in her voice.

Although they had been intimate on several occasions, it surprised Nate she would summon him to the bathroom to, he knew, inspect her body for symptoms.

"Is that a spot," Jinx asked, obviously unable to gain clear perspective. "How did I not notice it before?"

She stood, skirt lifted, pink panties balled on the linoleum floor, awaiting his unofficial medical opinion. Despite the tense situation, Nate couldn't help admiring the long creamy legs before him. A thick patch of strawberry blonde pubic hair curled enticingly before him. The media claimed the Rot heightened sexual urges, although Nate had lusted for this beautiful young woman since they first met.

"Well? Is it?" Jinx asked.

Nate knelt down for a closer look. With fingers, she opened herself to him. Her inner labia appeared dark while her cleft appeared bruised. Purple tissue reached into the skin hidden by the lightly trimmed pubic hair. Nate combed fingers through the tight curls to see the necrotic tissue spreading away from her genitals.

"Lift your leg," Nate said.

Jinx accommodated him, thus allowing him to spot the unhealthy tissue had reached the crease at her thighs.

"Turn around."

The Rot had spread between her buttocks. Black "freckles" now danced along with the cute orange-brown freckles that had always spotted her tight rump.

"Well? Is it the Rot?"

Nate stood to embrace Jinx as he conceded the inevitable with a simple "I'm so sorry."

Jinx collapsed in his arms. He carried her out to the living room, set her on the sofa. He returned from the kitchen with two bottles of beer and two pills.

"Here," Nate said, "take this?"

"What is it?" Tears streaked down her face.

"Ecstasy. It will help take the edge off."

Jinx accepted the drug. They both washed pills down with beer. Nate held Jinx close, comforting as she sobbed hard on his shoulder. He cooed to her with simple phrases as she let her emotions pour out and the drug take effect. "The last thing I wanted to do was hurt you, Jinx ..." "I never wanted to stop calling you." "I was so ashamed ..." "I wish I had met you before I got infected ..." "Let it all out."

She cried long and hard. Nate held her silently. It felt so good to hold her close again. She smelled so sweet. It pained him to know he had hurt her so much. If the CDC developed a cure he would surely be scarred for life. But he didn't care about himself. He didn't want that happening to his pink-haired raver girl Jinx. The way she curled into him as her crying subsided elated his emotion. Of course that could also be due to the Ecstasy, however, he didn't want to give it all the credit.

He switched on music with a remote control. He selected one of Jinx's favorite play-lists. They listened, entwined, for a long time. As Nate did, a warm euphoria washed over him, and his hand began to not only comfortingly caress his damaged raver girl, but to enjoy her delicate womanly curves. Her soft shoulders, round hips, lithe thighs.

Jinx sniffled. "What are you doing?"

"I love you, Jinx."

"Do you?"

"I wish I could make it all better again."

"I was falling for you too, asshole."

"I deserve that. But I was afraid. Had this never happened, I never would have left you."

"Really?"

"Promise."

His lips found hers. They tasted sweeter than he remembered.

"I want to see," Jinx said.

"See what?"

"Your rot."

Fear of rejection clutched him tight.

"That's not a good idea."

"I must see. You owe me that much."

"Okay."

Nate removed his shirt to reveal bruised, flaking skin covering nearly his entire chest.

"Does it hurt?"

"Not much."

"It spread from ...?"

"Yes."

"Let me see."

Before he could reply, Jinx unfastened his faded jeans, slipped them off his hips.

"It's so black and swollen and big."

"I finally got that extra length and width I always wanted," Nate joked.

Tentatively, Jinx touched his manhood. The gentle sensation caused an immediate stirring in his loins. After all, this was Jinx. He loved her, lusted for her. And besides, the drug (and perhaps this condition) accelerated the libido.

"I can't go through this alone," Jinx said.

"You don't have to," Nate promised.

"Never leave me again." Her breath tickled his lips.

Nate slid a hand down between her thighs. "I won't."

They kissed. Touched and embraced each other with surging lust. A different song began to play, its thumping beat a little louder than the previous one. They left a trail of clothing on their way to the bedroom. Her sex glistened newly-rotting flesh in readiness for him. When he eased his swollen member into her, her expression changed to that of complete abandon and shocked excitement. He could tell she enjoyed what he now had to offer. Whether drug or rampant virus, the sex proved amazing. Nate took her first in a missionary position but soon graduated to many others. Jinx rode him like the raving industrial partier he knew her to be. She appeared to ride wave after wave of her own ecstasy until his orgasm released corrupt seed into her dying flesh.

Jinx laid her head on his erupting chest and said: "I don't know how all this will end."

"Neither do I, but it won't end without me."

Her Perfect Lover

C.W. LaSart

Shellia spread the blob of shaving cream evenly across the stubble on his cheeks, taking care to keep the foam neat and uniform in its thickness. A disposable razor, fresh from the packaging, lay on the table at her side.

"Did you shave every day, Beck? Did you like to keep things tidy like I do?"

Beck didn't respond. She retrieved the razor and started at his neck, enjoying the subtle scraping sound across his flesh in the otherwise silent room. With each swipe, she rinsed the foam and hair off the blade in a small steel dish of water beside her. She greatly relished this part of her job, and told Beck so as she worked.

"I enjoy the grooming. Making people look clean and presentable. After your shave I will give you a sponge bath. You'll enjoy that, won't you?" Shellia let her free hand run across his chest, fingers gently tracing the ridges of muscle, marveling at the soft scatter of hair nestled between them.

"Shellia?"

She jumped at the intrusion, spilling some of the shaving water on her smock.

"Damn it, Jeff! You scared me."

"Sorry." Her assistant stood in the doorway, fidgeting as usual. He should be used to the way she spoke to them when she worked, but he wasn't. It was strange and made him uncomfortable, but the job paid well and she wasn't a harsh boss. He would do well to try to ignore her eccentricities.

"It's nearly nine. Maybe we should finish this one up tomorrow."

She glanced up at the clock and scowled. Jeff was right, it was getting late. "No, you go on home. I'll stay and get him done."

"Are you sure? We could get him finished tomorrow morning if we work together."

"I'm sure. I haven't been sleeping well lately. I'll stay and finish. Lock the door when you leave." She smiled at him, a strained expression, never quite reaching her eyes.

"Okay. If you insist—"

"I do."

"Have you given him the injection?"

"Yes." She followed his gaze to the syringe on the tray beside her, the clear barrel full of murky fluid. "I mean I will. Goodnight, Jeff."

"Don't wait too long. We don't need him coming back on us."

"Goodnight, Jeff. Lock the door behind you."

Jeff nodded and turned to leave, pausing in the doorway for a moment.

"You know, I could've sworn this one was slated for cremation."

Shellia glared at him above her glasses, her brows drawn together and mouth set in a hard line. She sighed and rolled her eyes.

"He is. They want a viewing first. *Goodnight*, Jeff."

Waiting for the sound of the front door closing, Shellia went up front and checked to make sure Jeff had locked it as instructed. He had. Wandering into the small kitchenette hidden behind the stairs, she made a pot of coffee, whistling as it brewed. Retrieving a plate of meat and cheese from the fridge, she unwrapped the plastic covering and shook a few crackers out of a box onto the plate. Snack in one hand and a large mug of steaming coffee in the other, she returned to the back room and set both on the table next to the shaving tools.

"Well now Beck, where were we before we were so rudely interrupted?"

* * * *

People often asked Shellia how she could stand to work with the dead. Didn't it creep or gross her out? She always responded with the standard replies: someone had to do it, she felt a calling to help families in their grief, and she took pride in making sure the deceased were prepared for their final rest with dignity and decorum. But the truth was, she *preferred* the dead over the living. She always had, from the time she was a young teen and attended her first funeral. It was a boy she went to school with and he'd drowned at the lake while visiting his grandparents. Though boisterous and mean in life, she found him to be much easier to take in death. Dignified. Silent. Something about corpses appealed to her. The lack of animation, the inability to speak. They were never consciously rude, and those biological functions one might consider inappropriate never bothered her. The eruptions of gases and leaking fluids were unintentional and didn't seem grotesque. They were just a fact of life, and as it were, death. The dead lacked the capacity to be cruel, or to hold a conversation. For someone who preferred silence, would not even allow a radio to be played while she and Jeff worked, they amounted to the perfect companions.

Once Beck had been bathed, disinfected, and had his nails trimmed, the proper procedure would've involved suturing his jaw, putting in eye caps to hold his lids closed, and makeup. Shellia hadn't even done the most crucial steps, draining him of blood and filling his body with embalming fluid. There was no need to go that far, because he *was* being cremated in the morning. There was no requested viewing. Once enough time had passed to ensure Jeff would not be returning for any forgotten items, she instead set about her own secret preparations, ones that if discovered by her assistant or anyone else, would land her in jail.

Prying open the jaw with a heavy metal instrument, Shellia retrieved a pair of pliers and set about removing the teeth from Beck's mouth. It was hard work and she began to sweat, prying at each tooth and twisting until it gave way with a crack. His mouth took on the mushy appearance of an old man without his dentures. Stepping on the lever, she dropped the teeth into a waste can by the table and went about cleaning up the small amount of blood leaking from the sockets. Finished with the task, she ran a hand across his smooth cheek before giving it an affectionate pinch.

"No biting, mister." As an afterthought, Shellia picked up the syringe full of antivirus and tossed it into the can, as well.

When the dead began to walk, there had been considerable panic, and what the military referred to as *acceptable casualties*. The government contained the outbreak quickly, though, through quarantine, armed response, and development of an antivirus (in what was considered by many to be within a suspiciously short time), that didn't cure for the infected, but prevented corpse reanimation. Now, ten years after what everyone referred to as Patient Zero, the walking dead were scarce, the outbreaks isolated and quickly dealt with. They continued to use the drugs in mortuaries as a precaution, but zombies were a thing left to memory, and the laboratories where they still studied them. Because of all this, people had become less attached to their dead, less likely to want funerals and viewings out of a lingering fear. Cremations were now the norm.

Shellia unlocked a small chest in the corner, one to which only she had the key. She kept her private stuff in there, and though she trusted Jeff to do a competent job as her assistant, she didn't wish to explain to him the contents of the container, or how she had acquired some of them. Inside lay various bottles of sexual lubes, flavored condoms, and bits of costumes used in role play. These were not the sort of things one wanted to be caught with in a mortuary setting. Hidden in a false bottom beneath her sexual gear, lay two syringes. One large, filled with clear fluid, the needle wide and long. The second tiny in comparison, with only a few milliliters of amber liquid in the vial.

She set the syringes on the table and turned to admire Beck once more.

Shellia had maintained few friendships during her life and even fewer sexual relationships. Late in her high school years, there had been a boy she cared about, maybe even loved in her way, but he'd left her eventually, telling her peers she was cold in bed. The truth was he just didn't do anything for her. She tried to enjoy sex with him, but didn't get what everyone raved about. She found more pleasure in fantasy and masturbation than she could with a lover, and her fantasies bordered on the increasingly morbid as she grew older. It wasn't until her third year as a mortuary assistant when she realized her preference for corpses ran much deeper than their quiet company. Once the realization hit, it seemed like the most natural thing in the world to her. She loved the dead. Loved their quiet, their repose, the firm coldness of their flesh, even the odors of the ones not long deceased. It seemed only logical she might *love* the dead, as well.

Nibbling a cracker and drinking from a mug of coffee, Shellia let her eyes travel the length of Beck's form.

Young and fit, his body was superb; no incisions from an autopsy marred his smooth expanse of skin. She was very glad the family had refused organ donation, because the sutures would be rough and uncomfortable. Having fallen from a building during construction, the injury to the back of his head killed him, and the caved in part of his skull didn't show. If her experiment worked, she would give Jeff a few days off and keep Beck around the mortuary, sending him for cremation when he became too gamy to be palatable. She would probably have to buy him a hat, as well.

"I have to admit I'm a bit nervous, Beck. It's not my first time, but if this works, you could be my perfect lover." She touched the arch of his foot, tickled it and smiled. "No time like the present. Back to work for us!"

* * * *

The next stage of the process was the trickiest, involving

the isolation of the main arteries in the penis. Holding his limp organ in her left hand, Shellia prodded the underside with her right index finger until she felt comfortable she had located the necessary blood vessels. Once sure, she inserted the needle of the large syringe inside an artery, massaging his penis as she slowly injected medical grade silicone, kneading it with tender fingertips to ensure the fill was even, the tissue sufficiently plumped and uniform. It took half an hour to get the procedure right, and she was aroused by the end, stepping back to admire her handiwork.

"I doubt you ever sported that impressive of an erection in life, Beck. You're welcome. No, thank *you*." She considered shaving his genitals, preferring them to be smooth, but was anxious to get on with it, desperate to see if the last part of the experiment would work. She'd made it this far before, enough times that the last of the silicon she'd purchased (from a plastic surgeon acquaintance who didn't ask questions) was now jauntily saluting her from the center of the gurney. But the contents of the final syringe were something she'd never tried before and much harder to come by. It had taken three months savings and the right connections, but she'd finally gotten her hands on it. She'd often wondered what it might be like if her corpse lovers could move some. Now she need only make the injection and wait.

The room was cold, but she liked it that way, and set the thermostat another ten degrees cooler before she slipped out of her smock and folded it upon the counter. The rest of her clothes followed the smock until she stood naked in the frigid room, gooseflesh rising on her exposed skin, nipples almost painfully taut. She placed the remaining syringe on the gurney next to Beck's head and pulled over a footstool to climb up with him. Shellia spent many long moments tracing the hard planes of his body, letting no part of him go untouched. Straddling his leg, she lowered herself onto him, her most private part grazing the coarse hair of his dense thigh.

"Oh, lover." She sighed, rocking and rubbing herself

against his unyielding flesh. She looked at the syringe, then the clock. There was time yet. Plenty of time. She wanted this part of the act in case things went wrong. The night wouldn't be a total loss then. She shifted her weight and slung her leg over his hips, guiding the tip of the erection against and into her body. She'd over-filled him and it hurt a bit, but she pressed down anyway, gritting her teeth against the intrusion. His penis was also very cold, but she preferred that and soon lost herself in the rhythm of her body against his, leaning her weight forward and staring into his cloudy eyes, eyes that would never look away. Something gurgled in his gut and blood bubbled out of his mouth, carrying with it the sickly sweet scent of putrefaction. Shellia breathed it in and moaned, her hips frantic, seeking the end. Completion.

Sated, she grabbed the syringe, and without further thought, jabbed the needle into his chest, through the sternum and into his heart. She depressed the plunger, injecting the zombie virus into dormant muscle. She waited. Watched the clock for five minutes. Ten. Nothing happened.

"Too bad." She said, sighing and disentangling her body from his. "Maybe if you'd been fresher."

She curled up by Beck's side, reaching her arm across his chest and placing her hand within his. She'd wait awhile longer for him to wake. Maybe it would still work. Her eyelids heavy, she was just dozing off when she felt something. *Was that movement? Did his fingers twitch against mine?* Shellia smiled contentedly and drifted back to sleep.

The Z Spot

Benjamin Kane Ethridge

After the outbreak, the stage lights still worked. Red, blues, blinding yellows. I could not feel their heat on my skin anymore though. They brought no sweat and no gasps of hot Barcelona night air. Still, I danced here, working the pole, waiting for new eyes. Since I'd eaten all the other customers down to their bones and most stubborn of tendons, I could do nothing else.

My routine was simple. A climb to the top, an upside-down bend, a spiral down to the base and splay of the legs. Freestyle dance, make love to the pole. Repeat. Collect money and phone numbers. Hadn't taken much to work a room of men to a baited froth. I was the one they came to see. Bianca Sterling, the American slut from next door. They dreamed they would make me happy with their bodies, just because I would make them happy with mine.

They had no idea. I tasted it while I ate their brains—their cluelessness tasted tart where better men might have tasted sugary. I recognized the flavor. I'd come to Spain to be with my boyfriend, my old world dream, Jose Arias. We were going to get married. He was going to put me through art school. I'd teach. We'd set foot on every continent, hand in hand.

Instead of all that, I caught him with a blonde barmaid.

I got the job at Villa Lolita to make him jealous, angry—insane. It did all of the above. For a week and half, Jose was routinely thrown out of the club before he stopped coming back. I missed hurting him though, and decided to continue the practice on strangers. So infatuated was I with breaking hearts, all remaining thoughts of art school burned away in those spotlights on the stage.

After everybody began Turning, I waited it out with a group of customers, the other girls and our manager, Ricardo. Despite the miserable excuses for men I'd been trapped with, I lived on, but the night I saw Jose outside the club, his dead face wild and his fists pounding on the ivy riddled brick building, I couldn't bear going on. A few of the better hearted dancers sensed my moroseness and tried to cheer me, but early the next day I slashed my wrists out with a beer bottle from the kitchen trash.

I guess one of the infected customers had been drinking from that bottle and I Turned. It's not true what others say about the rotting. It's much slower than a normal corpse. Those who rotted away quickly already had significant injuries. I only sported two jagged cuts up my arms. My California tan was forever gone but I still looked like the Bianca Sterling that made men want to empty their wallets and loins.

That detail made attacking the other girls and the manager easier. Then it was their time to Turn. We fed on the customers, much how we had in life. Once the others wandered off into the city, I arranged their husks in the seats and turned on the lights. Now with an audience again, I got caught up in the endless dancing.

Dancing.

Waiting.

Crying.

Hungry.

The whole time the oddest feeling had to be how familiar this was. Something I never understood until now, in undeath: *I'd always been empty.* I hadn't killed myself for Jose. He had never really made me feel what I expected love should be. I'd been fooling myself, and hurting others had been a surprise passion that now made sense.

Why live in a world where only I suffered?

For weeks I thought I'd only be dancing alone.

Then it happened one afternoon. My audience grew by one.

* * * *

His name was Intestino Rojo and from his appearance he might have been any young Spanish peasant with the misfortune of being Turned. He wasn't rotting. He was gorgeous. And when he sat in the front row and brought his pants down to his knees, a tear duct fluttered in my dead eyes. I danced on.

Tino, as I would come to call him, appeared stunned and excited all at the same time. He ripped his black briefs away with a hungry white claw and out sprang his beautiful cock.

Another fable is how the blood dies in the body of the Turned. Much of it does, but there is a fluid, thicker than blood that slowly works through our vessels, and when the heart pounds harder, that sludge thins and we become disoriented.

Tino must have known this as he stroked, because fear caught inside his sunken eyes. But he wouldn't dare stop. His hand went quicker, sometimes going the length of the ivory shaft and other times trying to cripple the mushroom cap. Veins popped around its length and it became even taller—I wanted nothing more than to leap off the stage and sit on top of his cock, fuck away these past weeks of loneliness and hunger.

But I was too captivated with what I was doing to him. I hadn't even taken off my top yet, had only worked my hand back to the clip and Tino's head threw back and his blood stained mouth moaned like only one of the Turned might. Almost there, he gazed up at me, askance, horrified at his weakness, in awe of my power. I pressed my breasts together and my blue sequined top fell to the floor. Bending forward I hefted my right breast and licked the lightly oozing nipple.

Tino gasped and came. A crumbly white powder puffed from his hole. Dust.

Magic dust, from the looks of it, because Tino slid sideways in the torn chair, resting his head on the cadaver next to him. His nostrils flared a moment, making certain there was no meat to be had. Looking a trifle embarrassed, he tucked himself away and buttoned his pants.

The orgasm had paralyzed him. I too, felt weary from the displacement of blood in my body, but I clung to the pole and watched him intently.

"I shouldn't have done that," he said. "You're just so—I couldn't resist."

His Spanish was a little harder to understand than the normal city dwellers I'd come to know.

"I'm glad you're here," I said. "Will you stay?"

"I promised my mother we would meet at the Café Robles. That's where we used to meet after the farmer's market."

"When did you see her last?"

"Just before … everything." Tino tried to lift his head but he was still mush. "This is the most foolish thing I might have done. She could be out there right now, waiting for me."

"It's okay."

"No it's not. It's been difficult getting this far."

"Can I go with you? I can help."

His face pinched. "I should say no."

I descended the stage and went to him. I pulled him up to stand. He wobbled a bit, but I wrapped my arms around him, my breasts crushed against his chest. Dead as we were, his heart beat hot under his t-shirt.

"I should say no," he repeated.

"But you won't," I said and kissed his scabbed lips.

* * * *

Café Robles was only three blocks away. Nobody was inside, so Tino and I searched for lunch while we waited. A teenager unwittingly let out a drunken snore from his hiding place under some cardboard in an alley. I recognized him as a patron from the club, and not the nicest of nineteen year old lads as memory served. Hard on the nipples and brutish while stuffing bills in your panties.

Tino was still weary from his fit of pleasure at the club, so I used the laces from my boots to bind the teen's hands and feet. He was so stinking drunk it wasn't difficult. Once bound, we took off his clothing. Out of habit, or possibly out of wickedness, I massaged an erection out of the sleeping young man.

Leaning over his bare neck, Tino gasped. "You're not eating that, are you?"

I gave him a wicked smile and drew out another boot string. Quickly, I made a tourniquet around the base of the cock, which brought the teenager awake.

"Wh—?"

Slamming his face down, Tino tore out the teen's throat and began eating his full.

No screams, just glugs and gurgles.

I went for the stomach and innards. Enjoying the warmth of it all. Occasionally I'd glance down to see if the erection had been lost.

It hadn't.

With a deft grip, I ripped the member away from the scrotum, keeping tight hold of the base, forcing more blood pressure into the staff.

Waterfalls of blood issuing from his mouth, Tino glowered. "Put that down."

I shook my head and smirked devilishly.

"Put that down and eat!"

I stood up and slid my panties off.

Tino swallowed. "What ... are you doing?"

I took the head of the maimed cock and slid it down the sides of my thighs, coming closer to my cunt.

"Don't!" cried Tino, standing up.

I worked the head part way inside me. From this angle it wouldn't penetrate. As it was, blood was seeping through the bottom of my fist and the member going flaccid, but it felt so good rubbing against my soaking wet lips.

Tino groaned miserably and stormed off down the street. I watched him, knowing he couldn't really be leaving.

And I was right.

From around the corner, Tino watched me, filling his dead lungs with useless air. Chest huffing, rage building on his face. I worked the organ between my legs until it became pulp, but still I lathered myself with it.

Tino approached, looking me up and down. He wanted to pull me to him, but he waited. I couldn't wait any longer. I let go of the abused thing in my hands and reached for him. He took my hands in his, powerfully.

"This is how I Turned, you know," he said, looking me hard in the eyes, out of breath, out of time. "My fiancée was infected. She knew though. She knew."

"I'm sorry."

"No!" he shouted and spun me around. I put my hands on the alley wall. *"You aren't sorry!"*

Tino drove a hand between my legs and spread them wider. He opened his pants and entered me in a rush. I squealed for all the pressure giving way. He thrust again and again, spanking my ass and screaming in delight. He reached around and grabbed my tits in his fists and threatened to rip them away. They bled and festered, the fluids coursing down my belly, into my crotch where everything became sinfully wet. I'd never experienced in a man the need to fuck me like this. He wasn't just fucking my cunt, he was—

Then he went deeper and touched something inside me I'd never felt before. I stared back at him in silent wonder. I loved this man. God, how he throttled me. How could this be?

Deeper.

I climaxed with a sob and a moment later, Tino did as well.

And at that blessed, perfect moment, we heard the first bullets ring out in the street.

* * * *

I couldn't pull him up in time.

I keep thinking back to it.

How the two hunters came through, shooting everything as though ammo was now abundant. Tino got struck three times in the chest and five times in the head, leaving little of his remarkable face.

I cowered nearby, completely frozen from our love. My blood hadn't thickened again; I was heavy as a planet, but I wasn't afraid. Anything I desired to keep had erupted in bloody bits and gristle just a moment prior.

Things blurred. A man made a rude comment about my exposed cunt. A woman pushed him out of the way. She had a handgun. Big, blue steel looking thing. I stared at the weapon that would take me away from this place forever.

"You were together," she said in a familiar Spanish dialect. Sadness and exasperation were in her voice. "Weren't you? You and my boy?"

I nodded.

The woman's face broke and she turned to her bearded companion. "I want to go."

"As you wish." The bearded man aimed his rifle at me and pulled the trigger. It clicked. "Ah fuck. Do you have another box?"

The woman reached into her coat pocket and with a shaking hand, proffered him a box of shells. I closed my eyes and waited as he reloaded.

"What's wrong Maria?" he asked her.

"Nothing."

"Yeah right. Remember, we said *all* of the Turned."

"I know."

The man sighed. He looked beyond exhaustion. "Want to call it a day? You want to let this one go?"

I opened my eyes and stared at Senora Rojo.

"I should say no," she said, tearfully beholding the body of her dead son.

And though I said nothing, I agreed. She should have.

But she didn't ...

To this day I cannot understand why. Maybe because she saw in my eyes something familiar?

The loss of this man.

Nothing that dramatic; I suspect the Senora had my own proclivities for sharing her pain.

Regardless, I returned to the club to start up my daily routine. Waiting. Again.

It's been a year and I haven't been taken down by hunters yet. I'm beginning to think it's payment for my wickedness. Though I knew him for just a day, I still want Tino, more than a perfect world or a place in heaven. Some days I probe myself with my ulcerating fingers, searching for that place he found.

Maggots have long since eaten the spot away I think. Perhaps this is just as well and I should stop probing. I might envy those maggots though. Funny, but true. I would burn with unparalleled jealousy if they could still taste him there. Because I must say, once I really came to understand, there was no way I could have shared him. Not the miracle I found sitting outside the brutal lights of my lonesome stage.

Not ever.

~fini~

About The Authors

Guy Anthony De Marco: Guy Anthony De Marco is a nocturnal award-winning author living in the geographic center of the middle of nowhere. Between writing speculative fiction, brewing more coffee, and wishing the bills and the horrific mortgage would forget how to find him, he ponders how long it would take for a zombie apocalypse to reach his front door. His practical wife, Tonya, trains all of the small pets to trip the incoming hordes and wonders where all the coffee went by the time she wakes up. Guy is a member of the following organizations: SFWA, IAMTW, SFPA, ASCAP, RMFW, NCW, HWA, and hopes to collect the rest of the letters of the alphabet one day.

Visit www.GuyAnthonyDeMarco.com for more info.

Mandy DeGeit: Mandy DeGeit, hailing from Ottawa, Ontario, Canada is awesome, outspoken and spends most of her money on tattoos and traveling. When she's not writing, she's either thinking about what to write next or working on the plan for her empire. Her current publication credits include: "She Makes Me Smile": Short Story, Self-Published - May 2012, "Summer Break": Flash Story, LampLight Magazine, Issue One - Sept 2012 "This Only Happens In The Movies": Novelette, Self-Published Sept— 2012 The Only Way" - A Quick Bite Of Flesh Anthology - Hazardous Press - Sept 2012 "Humanification" - Zombie! Zombie! Brain Bang! - Strangehouse Books – Nov 2012 "Dead Things Don't Rise" - 50 Shades Of Decay - Angelic Knight Press - February 2013.

Her forthcoming publications are as follows: "Morning Sickness"—Mistresses of the Macabre Anthology—Dark Moon Books - March 2013 You can find out what she's up to by following her blog: http://mandydegeit.com. Follow her on twitter @MandyDeGeit.

Kate Monroe: Kate Monroe is an author and editor who lives in a quiet and inspirational corner of southern England. She has penchants for the color black, horror and loud guitars, and a fatal weakness for red wine. Her interests in writing range from horror to erotica, taking in historical romance, steampunk and tales of the paranormal on the way; whatever she dreamed about the night before is liable to find its way onto the page in some form or another. With stories featured in anthologies by Sirens Call Publications, Cruentus Libri Press, Angelic Knight Press, Rainstorm Press, Smart Rhino Publications and Pink Pepper Press, her published works are as eclectic as her tastes.

Erik Williams: Erik Williams is a Defense Contractor, former Naval Officer, Iraq War Veteran, and former Kenpo Karate instructor. He is the author of *Bigfoot Crank Stomp*, *Progeny*, *Demon*, and numerous short stories. He has three daughters and is undergoing testosterone treatments to continue to feel like a man.

Learn more about him atwww.erikwilliams.blogspot.com or follow him on Twitter @TheErikWilliams.

Rebecca L. Brown: Rebecca L. Brown is a British writer based in Cardiff - for more news and updates on her work, visit rebeccalbrownupdates.wordpress.com

Shaun Meeks: Shaun Meeks lives in Toronto. His recent work has appeared in *Dark Eclipse*, *Zombies Gone Wild*, The Horror Zine, *50 Shades of Decay*, *Zippered Flesh 2* and his own collections *At the Gates of Madness* & *Brother's Ilk*. His novel, *Shutdown* is due out this year. Visit him at www.shaunmeeks.com.

Eric Stoveken: Eric is a writer of strange and peculiar tales. He is the author of The Devil Yearns for the Perfect Denver Omelet and Other Revelations.

Jake Elliot: Jake Elliot lives in the Pacific Northwest, where zombie infestations have so far been minimal. Lucky for him, his wife knows Karate and can kick the ass of any zombie, thus giving Jake a chance to run away and continue telling weird stories. Jake writes fantasy fiction geared for an adult audience and you can find out more about him at www.jakeelliotfiction.com.

Tarl Hoch: Tarl Hoch is a horror and erotica writer hailing from Calgary, Alberta, Canada. His works can be found in FurPlanet's "Will of the Alpha", Sirens Call's "Bellows of the Bone Box", and Knightwatch Press' "New Tales of the Old Ones". He is also head editor for a horror anthology involving abandoned places for FurPlanet.

When not writing or editing, Tarl spends his time reading, watching horror movies, debating about superheroes and desperately avoiding the cowboy plague that is the Calgary Stampede. His Twitter is @tarl_writer and his Good Reads is under Tarl Hoch.

Andrew Freudenberg: Andrew Freudenberg is a creator of dark fiction. He has recently returned to writing seriously after a long period of musical distraction. As well as running his own label, making records and playing live he also promoted club nights including London's notorious 'Club Alien'. Although his DJ appearances were few, he did once play for Russian gangsters in Moscow. He'd never admit it though. His short stories can currently be found haunting the pages of numerous anthologies. He is also busy creating 'longer stuff'. He lives in the South-West of England and is working on a variety of projects including raising three young sons.

J.G. Williams: Jackie is a wife, mother to three grown children and nan to six grandchildren with a new addition on the way. She lives in Wales. UK. She loves writing horror, though her writing began with poetry. She has a few short stories and poetry published in various anthologies, her recent being 'Edward' in *Terrifying Teddies*. Jackie also has numerous short stories on Smashwords, and Amazon. At the moment Jackie is working on her first horror novel, *Emelia*, as well as her children's books. Her story 'Till Decay Do Them Part' is about that love word. She wondered if the passion would last after being bitten and turned, so to speak. In her story it does, until they fade away.

She is proud to be included in this great anthology.

Tim Baker. Tim Baker is a Mad Storitist experimenting with forbidden combinations of words and sentences in an attempt to create living, breathing, story beings intent on taking over the world—or at least, the small village in which he abides. Secluded in a basement with his alien born felines, he occasionally emerges to teach children Judo at a local gym. He loves long walks on the moors and candlelit butchering (of stories and movies). Previously published in *Fading Light: An Anthology of the Monstrous.* You can find his odd meanderings on his blog at: skeletonroad.wordpress.com

Craig Faustus Buck. Craig Faustus Buck is a writer of many faces having been a journalist, a nonfiction book author, an episodic television and MOW writer-producer, a miniseries writer (*V: The Final Battle*), a feature film screenwriter, and now a novelist. He is currently shopping his first novel, *Go Down Hard*, which won First Runner Up for the Claymore Award at Killer Nashville 2011 for best unpublished novel. He is a member of Mystery Writers of America, Sisters in Crime, Writers Guild of America and International Thriller Writers.

Tim Marquitz. Raised on a diet of Heavy Metal and bad intentions, Tim Marquitz writes a mix of the dark perverse, the horrific, and the tragic, tinged with sarcasm and biting humor. He looks to leave a gaping wound in the minds of his readers like his inspirations: Clive Barker, Jim Butcher, and Stephen King. A former grave digger, bouncer, and dedicated metal head, Tim is a huge fan of Mixed Martial Arts, and fighting in general. He lives in Texas with his beautiful wife and daughter.

Teresa Hawk. Teresa Hawk lives in Las Vegas where she weaves an endless parade of colorful characters into macabre tales that keep readers up all night. Her earliest influences include; Stephen King, Clive Barker, and Edgar Allan Poe. At age twelve, she wrote her first supernatural horror story on wide-ruled notebook paper with a No. 2 pencil. As it circulated, she found the horrified reactions of teachers combined with the squealing delight of her peers to be powerfully addicting. Over the course of her career, she has been a technical writer, published academic, and copy editor. Now, building on those literary skills, she injects her twisted imagination of the weird, surreal, and grotesque into gritty, character-driven horror. Prepare to have your perception altered, and hold on, because it's going to be a chilling ride into the darkness!

Carrie-Lea Cote: Carrie-Lea is a writer from Calgary, Alberta, Canada. She has stories in Innsmouth Free Press 'Dead North' and FurPlanet's 'Roar: Volume 5'. '50 Shades of Decay' is her first foray into horror-erotica and she sometimes admits that it was more fun to write than she initially thought.

When not writing, she spends her time sculpting, reading, and wishing cheetahs were native to the plains of Alberta. Her twitter is @Cattpaws and her Goodreads account is 'Carrie Cote'.

Jay Wilburn: Jay Wilburn lives with his wife and two sons in beautiful Conway, South Carolina. He has written many horror and speculative fiction stories including the novels *Loose Ends: A Zombie Novel* with Hazardous Press and *Time Eaters* with Perpetual Motion Machine Publishing. Follow his many dark thoughts at JayWilburn.com or @AmongTheZombies on Twitter.

Alex Chase: Alex Chase is an American university student who has dreamed of being a writer since he first broke the spine of a Stephen King novel at the age of eight. His short fiction has been accepted for publication with Siren's Call Publications, Pink Pepper Press and Angelic Knight Press and includes titles such as "The Curse of the Devil's Tree", "Keeping Distance" and "Whispers". Writing everything from horror to romance and what falls in between, he spends his waking hours exploring the human condition. Aside from writing, he loves learning, coffee and his family.

He can be found at www.facebook.com/alex.c.the.author, on twitter @AlexC_TheAuthor, or on his blog at theendlesschase.wordpress.com.

Lisa Woods: Lisa Woods is the mother of seven children and lives in Iowa with her family and her, pit bull, Jazzy. When she's not busy wrangling kids, or watching Supernatural and The Walking Dead, she spends her time writing horror stories. This is her first published piece.

Pepper Scoville: Pepper Scoville has been writing stories since she could hold a pencil. Horror is her first love and erotica a close second so it was a treat to combine the two. She lives in the subconscious of another, more timid writer and emerges only when duty calls. She enjoys moonlit walks and things that go bump in the night.

Steven Lockley: Steve Lockley has written around a hundred short stories in the horror, science fiction and fantasy genres along with the novels *The Ragchild,The Quarry*, (both in collaboration with Paul Lewis) *Solomon's Seal* and the forthcoming *The Sign of Glaaki* (with Steven Savile). Steve's work as both writer and editor has been nominated for British Fantasy Awards on a number of occasions and he was awarded The British Fantasy Society Special Award in 1995 for his work on the horror convention 'Welcome to My Nightmare'.

He has also served as a judge for the prestigious World Fantasy Awards.

Steve is currently working on *The Journey of the Chronic Argonauts*, a novel which brings together Sherlock Holmes, H G Wells and a time travelling Moriarty, or two.

Wednesday Silverwood: Wednesday Silverwood is a horror writer from North London, England. She has had recent work published in *Carnage: After the End Volume 2*, from Sirens Call Publications and in *Gothic Blue Book: The Revenge Edition*, from Burial Day Books. When she is not writing, you are most likely to find her hanging around in cemeteries. For more information, please see her website at www.wednesdaysilverwood.co.uk.

Katie Young: Katie Young is a freelance writer and occasional zombie movie "supporting artiste." She also works in kid's TV. She has various shorts available from Ether Books, a direct to mobile publisher.

Her story, "Not Death, But Dying," is featured in *So Long, and Thanks for All the Brains*, a zombie anthology from Collaboration of the Dead Press and her tale of wine, old gods and lost love, "I Could Drink a Case of You", was published in *Mytherium* by Indigo Mosaic. Katie also has work featured in upcoming releases from Static Movement (*Wolf Craft*) and Song Stories Press (*Song Stories: Dark Side of the Moon*).

Her story, "Atelic", was shortlisted for the 2010 Writers' & Artists' Year Book short fiction prize, and she has recently completed her first dark fantasy novel.

She lives in South East London with her partner and a couple of second-hand cats. Twitter@Pinkwood, www.etherbooks.com
http://www.facebook.com/pages/KatieYoung/1601794241 24913

John Palisano: John Palisano is a writer of weird fiction. His work has appeared in the Lovecraft eZine, Evil Jester Press, Dark Discoveries, Terror Tales, Horror Library, Dog Horn, and many others. His novel, *Nerves*, was recently released from Bad Moon books. Please visit: www.johnpalisano.us for updates, interviews with fellow writers, and essays on writing.

Celeste & Alex Turner: Alex and Celeste Turner are horror fans, collectors of bizarre objects and appreciators of the macabre. Their respective families tend to shake their heads and mutter "weirdos" under their collective breath. Alex is a geneticist by day and Celeste spends her not-writing time buying and selling antiques. They got married in a midnight service over 15 years ago and have written together every day since.

They dream of someday buying Pitcairn Island, paying all the residents to relocate, and turning off the telephone.

Daisy-Rae Kendrick: Julie R Kendrick (Daisy-Rae) is an English author living in Northamptonshire. She is a mother of 4 boys and works part time in a national Bookstore which she says is the best job in the world, other than writing of course. At the present time Julie has had 13 short stories published in the UK and the US and she is currently working on her first novel, a paranormal romance.

Angeline Trevena: Angeline Trevena is a horror and fantasy writer living above a milkshake shop in Devon, England. She has been making up stories since early childhood and in 2003 she gained a BA Hons Degree in Drama and Writing. Angeline has several short stories published in various anthologies, and is also a published journalist and poet; all the while she is (supposedly) working on her first novel. A keen blogger and social networking addict, Angeline can be found all over the internet, whether reviewing music, handing out writing advice, or chatting about the constant juggling of her writing career with being a Mum.www.angelinetrevena.co.uk

Matthew Scott Baker: Matthew Scott Baker is a trophy husband and stay-at-home dad who turned to writing when the rigors of real life began to take their toll on his body and mind. He lives in Prairie Grove, Arkansas with his wife and three kids. Prior to his current stations, he has worked in a wide variety of jobs, including video store manager, hospital housekeeper (or 'bacterial assassin', as he was known), bartender, and professional sales for a major transportation company. When he is not looking good on his wife's arm, writing, or herding the children, Matthew likes to relax with a good book or watch horror movies. Matthew's fiction has appeared in Aphelion: The Webzine of Science Fiction and Fantasy. He also runs Shattered Ravings, a blog devoted to reviewing movies, books, and comics in the Science Fiction, Horror, and Fantasy genres. He loves to converse with his readers, so visit his website at www.matthewscottbaker.com and drop him a line.

T. Fox Dunham: T. Fox Dunham resides outside of

Philadelphia PA—author and historian. He's published in nearly 200 international journals and anthologies, and his first novella, New World, was published by May December Publishing. Martyr, his second, will be published later this year. He's a cancer survivor.

His friends call him fox, being his totem animal, and his motto is: Wrecking civilization one story at a time. Blog: http://tfoxdunham.blogspot.com/.http://www.facebook.co m/tfoxdunham & Twitter: @TFoxDunham

J.D. Hibbitts: J.D. Hibbitts grew up in Southwest Virginia, but roamed the globe for a few years as an enlisted member of the U.S. Air Force. His poetry and fiction appear in the following journals: Thuglit, San Pedro River Review, Sugar House Review, Prime Mincer, Blue Collar Review, Poydras Review, Forge, and The Sierra Nevada Review, among others. He tries to keep himself away from any semblance of a web presence at the moment, so you'll just have to e-mail him at jdhibbitts@gmail.com.

Lori Safranek: Writing has been Lori Safranek's life since she became a newspaper reporter many years ago. After deciding to take a break from news writing, she chose to follow her dreams and write horror fiction. Her horror short story, "Marie", is available on Amazon. "Marie" is a devious tale of what happens when The Fat Lady in the sideshow starts losing weight. Lori also had a story in the *Dear Santa* charity anthology produced by May December Publications in December 2012.

Lori enjoys twisting reality into macabre short stories and making something horrible out of something ordinary, often with a dash of humor. Born and raised in Omaha, Nebraska, Lori has found much inspiration for her writing among the seemingly quiet, Midwestern people who continually surprise her with their strange and wonderful antics. Lori has filled her house with research for her writing—in other words, boxes and boxes of books—but she leaves enough room for her husband, Chuck, and their dogs, Arthur and Scout, neither of whom are big horror fans.

Frankie Sachs: Frankie Sachs lives and writes in the north of Sweden. Her first novel, *Chupacabra Blues*, is scheduled for April of 2013.

Rob M. Miller: Born and raised in the "micro-hood" of Portland, Oregon, he grew up as the oldest of three children, the son of a book-lover and a book-hater.

Over the years, he has been victimized by violent attackers, has victimized violent attackers, has enlisted and mustered out honorably from the U.S. Army, has taught martial arts, worked security, video store clerked, done window washing, tire retreading, and store stocking. With writing, it was after two years of free-lance stringer work, and a number of publishing credits, that he tired of non-fiction and decided to use his love of the dark, personal terrors, and talent with words to do something more beneficial for his fellow man—SCARE THE HELL OUT OF HIM.

Jill S. Behe: Jill's the eldest of four children born to Christian parents in East Central Pennsylvania. It took a while, but the rebel within finally broke free. After shocking family and friends by enlisting in the U.S. Army, then marrying—not much of a shock—birthing three sons, and getting a "family re-alignment"—again not much of a shock—she's now settling in, back in the great state of PA ... until the next adventure.

Jill began writing nonsense stories for her siblings and friends while in grade school, probably from the time she learned cursive. The writing has improved. (A good thing.) With time, maturation, and persistence, she continues to hone her craft in a variety of genres.

The Rebel has one published novel, *Mossy Creek* (Triskaideka Books, 2011) and a soon-to-be-released short in an anthology from May-December Publications. Currently, she's working on *Freezer Burn*, a "Mossy Creek" sequel, and is busily penning away short forms to splash into multiple genres.

Dan Larnerd: Dan Larnerd is a graduate of Marshall University and has worked in radio and for a few newspapers.

He lives in the Portland, Oregon area.

Mike D. McCarty: For the past fifteen years Mike has worked as an artist and show supervisor at one of the top make-up effects companies in the film industry. His list of makeup effects credits include Grindhouse, Kill Bill 1 and 2, Sin City1 and 2, The Mist, Piranha 3D and many more.

Besides having a cool day job, Mike is also a writer. Anything from short stories to movie scripts. He has a few short stories published. His first novel *Wereworld Book one: Gemini Rising* is due to be published in late 2013. He doesn't normally write stories this hot ... but he figured it would be a real fun project. If he did his job right you'll either blush or stalk him. He lives on a ranch outside of LA with his lovely wife Grace, three dogs, three horses, and three birds. When he's not writing, or killing people in movies you'll find him on his Harley in the hills of Southern California.

Blaze McRob: Blaze McRob, writer of over seventy legacy published horror novels. I was a ghostwriter long before anyone had an idea we were lurking about. Through my adventures in the craft, I-or my author alter egos-have won virtually every award to be won. But awards mean little, don't they? It is the reader we wish to enthrall, and our souls to purge. So now it is time for Blaze to write as Blaze, and time for previous recipients of my tales to write more of their own material. In addition to my dark novels, I write horror shorts, flash fiction, and poetry. Ah, the sweet rhymes of iambic pentameter intermixed with glorious free-style. I am single and have eight children, my youngest only three years old. They are my life and the reason I fight the demons and the pain. You can find out more about Blaze at www.blazemcrob.com or visit his author page at Amazon.

Jolie Chaton: Jolie Chaton is a blogger/hobby writer with a fun sense of humor. A single mother of three amazing boys, she's also has a cat, a pug, a frog, 2 hamsters and a couple fish that depend on her. Jolie hopes to find homes for more short stories in her future.

Shawn Erin: Shawn Erin lives in Denver, Colorado with

his family and two cats. When not writing, he likes hanging out with friends, breaking bones (not really a like, just something that happens), and generally being a public menace. A graduate of Taos Toolbox 2011, his first published erotic story was on circlet.com when he dared himself to submit. After that, his Muse couldn't stop feeding him naughty stories of horny people getting it on. His website is shawn-erin.com and he can be reached at shawnerin1@gmailcom.

Laura J. Hickman: Laura J. Hickman spends her life writing and creating new worlds. She has recently moved to the New England area, but spent the majority of her life in both New Orleans and Las Vegas. She has had stories published in numerous places, including Necon E-books, Pill Hill Press and 6 Sentences. Her time spent in numerous places has helped her writing grow and has found inspiration in everything from the Florida Beaches, to the haunted streets of the French Quarter to the sin filled casinos of Las Vegas.

Laura wants to thank her friends, her family and all the people who have supported her emotionally, in her writing and stood by her. She wishes to send a special thanks to her parents and her sister.

Chad P. Brown: Chad P. Brown was born in Huntington, WV. Once he outgrew his childhood fears of haunted houses, clowns, and toy monkeys with cymbals (although the monkeys still creep him out a little bit), he discovered a dark love for writing and an affinity for macabre and eldritch matters. He holds a Master's in Latin from Marshall University and is an Affiliate member of the Horror Writers Association. He released his first horror novel, The Jack-in-the-box, in October 2011 and a zombie novella, Messiah of the Zombie Apocalypse, in August 2012. He has appeared in the anthologies SPIDERS and Gothic Blue Book Vol. 2 - Revenge Edition. He is planning to release a dark fiction novella, The Pumpkin House, in March 2013. You can visit him online at www.chadpbrown.com.

Megan Dorei: Megan Dorei is a recent high school

graduate. She has just recently delved into the publishing world and in October her first short story- "Wings"- was published in Elektrik Milk Bath Press' *Zombies for a Cure* anthology. She will also have her story- "Haunt Me"- published in Less Than Three Press' *Kiss Me at Midnight* collection, "Chasing Rabbits" published in Siren's Call Publications' *Bellows of the Bone Box* anthology, "Visiting Hours" published in Siren's Call Publications' *Mental Ward: Stories From the Asylum* anthology, and "Half Jack" in Song Story Press' *Come to My Window* anthology. She lives in McLouth, Kansas, where she can most likely be found obsessively listening to music and fighting off her short attention span to finish a plethora of unwritten stories.

Dale Mitchell: A writer of romance, paranormal and sometimes a mix of the two, Dale is a down to Earth, Southern Belle that has found a voice through steamy romances. A Tennessean to her core, she lives in a colonial style farmhouse predating the Civil War. The wraparound porch is her favorite place to write, sipping sweet iced tea from a rocking chair. She claims a couple of ghosts live in the home with her who rarely cause trouble and always make for wonderful listeners. Please visit her website at http://dalemitchell.weebly.com.

Armand Rosamilia: Armand Rosamilia is a New Jersey boy currently living in sunny Florida, where he writes when he's not watching zombie movies, the Boston Red Sox and listening to Heavy Metal music ...

Besides the "Miami Spy Games" zombie spy thriller series, he has the "Keyport Cthulhu" horror series, several horror novellas and shorts to date, as well as the "Dying Days" series:

Highway To Hell ... Darlene Bobich: Zombie Killer ... Dying Days ... Dying Days 2 ... Still Dying: Select Scenes From Dying Days ... Dying Days: The Siege of European Village... and many more coming in 2013. He is also an editor for Rymfire Books, helping with several horror anthologies, including "Vermin" and the "State of Horror" series, as well as the creator and energy behind Carnifex Metal Books, putting out the "Metal Queens Monthly" series of non-fiction books about females into Metal ...

You can find him at http://armandrosamilia.comand e-mail him to talk about zombies, baseball and Metal: armandrosamilia@gmail.com

Thomas Alan Sandrage: Thomas Sandrage has worked as a professional musician, sideshow magician and warehouse technician. A lifelong horror fan, current student of Psychology and avid film fanatic, Thomas writes from his home in Colorado.

Laura Snapp: Laura Snapp is an emerging writer living in Albuquerque, New Mexico with her husband and three children. Born and raised in Minnesota, she had mastered the art of procrastination by acquiring three very different degrees to postpone entering the workforce and facing the reality of the zombie apocalypse. Then financial necessity dictated that she be forced to toil at the mines with countless other zombies until she discovered the glorious challenge of writing—and had gained sufficient experience to write on the subject of zombies knowledgeably (for example, while many so-called experts report that the zombie apocalypse has been largely contained to highly populated areas, Ms. Snapp can personally attest to their existence in the sparsely populated desert Southwest). Now, with her couch potato Chihuahua as her muse (or possibly the first canine zombie in existence), she is involved in several book projects that draw upon her harrowing experiences working and interacting with the shuffling, undead masses.

Nicky Peacock: Nicky is an English author living in the UK where she writes both adult and YA horror and paranormal romance. She runs a local writers' group called Creative Minds and belongs to a number of horror author groups online. Nicky loves reading as much as writing, and also can't get enough of horror movies and TV Series. She loves: Dexter, Game of Thrones, American Horror, True Blood and Walking Dead.

For further information on her work please see her blog http://nickypeacockauthor.wordpress.com or follow her on Twitter @NickyP_author.

Lisa McCourt Hollar. Lisa McCourt Hollar is the mother of 4 children that range in age from 21 to 3 years. If that isn't insane enough, she is taunted by a muse that whips her daily if she doesn't do as she is told and that is to write tales that will make you think twice before turning off the lights. Published in several anthologies, including the first two editions of Satan's Toybox, she has published several E-Shorts and collections and is frantically working on finishing her first novel.

Clint Collins: Currently living in northern Virginia, Clint has had short stories in *Under the Fang*, a Horror Writers Association anthology published by Pocket Books (paperback) and Borderlands Press (hardcover); *Cthulurotica* published by Dagan Books; *Lilith Unbound* by Popcorn Press; and poetry in *Vampyr Verse* published by Popcorn Press.

Brett Williams: Brett Williams is a multi-genre writer who lives in Kansas with a miniature schnauzer named Fritz. A member of both the Romance Writers of America and the Horror Writers Association, his fiction, though varied, often contains dark or twisted themes, but always proves thrilling and fun as hell to read. To find out more, visit BrettWilliamsFiction.com.

C.W. LaSart. A lifelong fan of all things horror and member of the Horror Writer's Association, C.W. LaSart has been published by Cemetery Dance Publications, Dark Moon Digest, Eirelander Press, Evil Jester Press, Angelic Knight Press and many more. Her debut fiction collection, *Ad Nauseam: 13 Tales of Extreme Horror*, was released by Dark Moon Books in March of 2012. Learn more at CWLaSart.com

Benjamin Kane Ethridge: Benjamin Kane Ethridge is the Bram Stoker Award winning author of the novel *Black & Orange*, *Bottled Abyss*, and *Dungeon Brain*. Benjamin lives in Southern California with his wife and two creatures who possess stunning resemblances to human children. When he isn't writing, Benjamin's defending California's waterways from pollution.